T0253135

"[A] gripping novel of suspense from Elliot . . . Elliot skillfully unravels layers of intersecting stories, each one integral to the overall story of the Mills family and their small-town secrets. Readers will want to see more from this author."

—*Publishers Weekly*

"Elliot succeeds in creating both a thrilling mystery and a fascinating character study of the people inhabiting these pages."

—*Bookreporter*

"With her riveting, narrative-driven, deftly crafted storytelling style as a novelist, Kendra Elliot's *The Last Sister* will prove to be a welcome and enduringly popular addition to community library Mystery/Suspense/Thriller collections."

—*Midwest Book Review*

"Suspense on top of suspense. This one will keep you guessing until the final page and shows Elliot at her very best."

—*The Real Book Spy*

"Every family has skeletons. Kendra Elliot's tale of the Mills family's dark secrets is first-rate suspense. Dark and gripping, *The Last Sister* crescendos to knock-out, edge-of-your seat tension."

—Robert Dugoni, bestselling author of *My Sister's Grave*

"*The Last Sister* is exciting and suspenseful! Engaging characters and a complex plot kept me on the edge of my seat until the very last page."

—T.R. Ragan, bestselling author of the Jessie Cole series

"Thriller Award finalist Elliot's well-paced sequel to *The Last Sister* opens at the home of fifty-two-year-old Reuben Braswell, a devotee of conspiracy theories, who's lying dead in his bathtub . . . The twist ending will catch most readers by surprise . . . [and] fans will look forward to seeing characters from the author's other series take the lead in future installments."

—*Publishers Weekly*

"Elliot skillfully interweaves the various plot threads, and credible, mostly sympathetic characters match the lovingly described locale. Fans of contemporary regional mysteries will be rewarded."

—*Publishers Weekly*

THE NEXT
GRAVE

ALSO BY KENDRA ELLIOT

Echo Road

COLUMBIA RIVER NOVELS

The Last Sister
The Silence
In the Pines
The First Death
At the River

MERCY KILPATRICK NOVELS

A Merciful Death
A Merciful Truth
A Merciful Secret
A Merciful Silence
A Merciful Fate
A Merciful Promise

BONE SECRETS NOVELS

Hidden
Chilled
Buried
Alone
Known

BONE SECRETS NOVELLAS

Veiled

CALLAHAN & MCLANE NOVELS

PART OF THE BONE SECRETS WORLD
Vanished
Bridged
Spiraled
Targeted

ROGUE RIVER NOVELLAS

On Her Father's Grave (Rogue River)
Her Grave Secrets (Rogue River)
Dead in Her Tracks (Rogue Winter)
Death and Her Devotion (Rogue Vows)
Truth Be Told (Rogue Justice)

WIDOW'S ISLAND NOVELLAS

Close to the Bone
Bred in the Bone
Below the Bones
The Lost Bones
Bone Deep

THE NEXT GRAVE

KENDRA ELLIOT

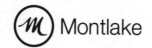

Text copyright © 2024 by Oceanfront Press LLC
All rights reserved.

Published by Montlake, Seattle

www.apub.com

Amazon, the Amazon logo, and Montlake are trademarks of Amazon.com, Inc., or its affiliates.

ISBN-13: 9781662511868 (hardcover)
ISBN-13: 9781662511875 (paperback)
ISBN-13: 9781662511882 (digital)

Cover design by Caroline Teagle Johnson
Cover images: © Silas Manhood / ArcAngel; © Aaron Foster / Getty Images

Printed in the United States of America

First edition

For my girls

1

The breeze carried the scent to Detective Evan Bolton's nose, and he instantly knew his day was going to suck.

A Deschutes County deputy next to him wheezed and jerked his head as if he could avoid the smell. *"What the hell is that?"*

Evan assumed it was a rhetorical question.

The rail-thin man in overalls leading them through the junkyard maze glanced over his shoulder solemnly. "Told ya." Silas Moon had owned the junkyard for forty years, and decades' worth of cars, trucks, buses, and campers had found their final resting place on his property. And decades' worth of teenagers had sneaked in at night to drink and smoke among the rusting metal. In his youth, Evan had done it several times, and he figured the deputy with him had too.

A rite of passage.

Silas Moon had been a fixture of Deschutes County for as long as Evan could remember. He'd always worn faded overalls. Only what was under them ever changed: a heavy sweater in the winter and often just skin in the summer. Rumors about the man had ebbed and flowed for years. Evan had heard that he'd abandoned a wife in California, heard that he'd fathered six kids with six different women, heard that he'd murdered three of those women and then created the junkyard to cover up their bodies.

Silas Moon was a man of mystery.

But Evan believed he was simply a man who liked to break down junk and challenge himself to find the little treasures that people had left behind. Moon made money selling the odds and ends he discovered in the abandoned vehicles. But after today's discovery, he'd called the sheriff's department.

Evan was thankful it was April. If it had been July in Central Oregon's high desert, the stink would be ten times stronger. It'd been a mellow spring. Nearly all traces of winter snow had vanished except for some crusted patches in shaded areas. To the west, the tall Cascade mountains still had a thick white blanket and stood out sharply against the intense blue sky.

The three men worked their way between two ancient Dodge Darts, the vehicles in the junkyard packed together like *Tetris* blocks. They'd passed a few stacks of crushed cars and a forklift with peeling paint. Fresh tracks near the forklift and a newer pair of gloves on the seat indicated the forklift was Moon's for moving cars, not an abandoned piece of machinery. They continued past a school bus with no windows, two decrepit motor homes, and a small white Ford pickup that made Evan pause and take a closer look, wondering whether it could possibly be the truck he had driven in high school. When he'd owned one, it still had a hood, along with both bumpers—unlike this vehicle.

Silas stopped at a gold Toyota Camry. The paint on the hood had faded to a pale yellow, and patches of gray Bondo dotted the passenger side. Both doors on the driver's side were bashed in, creating a huge concavity, crumpled far beyond repair. Evan could picture the accident: someone had T-boned the Camry. He fought an urge to check the driver's seat for blood, wondering whether the driver had survived. Judging by the damage, the chances were fifty-fifty.

The smell of death was unavoidable and was most powerful at the trunk, where flies crawled and hovered at the seams. A muted, buzzing chorus indicated there were far more flies in the trunk.

The deputy pulled out a mask and covered his nose and mouth. "Can't remember the last time I wore one of these things."

"Does it help with the smell?" asked Evan, who'd switched to breathing shallowly through his mouth, trying not to think about the composition of organic compounds floating in the air that carried the scent.

"Takes the edge off."

"I've smelled this once before in my life," said Silas, rubbing the few days' growth of stubble on his cheeks. "You don't forget it."

Evan agreed. But he'd encountered it several times. "You didn't open the trunk?"

"I did three months ago when I got this vehicle. I thoroughly go through each one—I would have noticed if there had been something that would cause this smell." He scowled. "Someone must have recently dumped something inside."

"Do you know where the car came from?" asked Evan.

"I can figure it out. Most of these vehicles were abandoned and then impounded. Impound sells them to me after clearing their paperwork."

"Got cameras back here?" Evan couldn't see the tall wood fence that surrounded the yard. Too many stacked vehicles blocked his view.

Silas snorted. "Only on the front gate. I can see everyone who comes and goes *legally*. Don't bother keeping track of people who hop the fence." He eyed Evan, which made him feel as if Silas was fully aware he'd trespassed as a teen. "I tried cameras back here. They were constantly messed with, and replacing them got expensive. I figured whatever little trinket or car part someone could get by climbing over the fence wasn't worth my trouble." He shrugged. "They also enjoy bashing in the windows. I don't give a shit about that. I like to do it too."

"Let's open it up," said Evan, slipping on vinyl gloves. "You got exterior shots?" he asked the deputy, who had been shooting with his phone.

"Yeah." He looked a little green around the gills. "Maybe there's an animal in there."

"Maybe," said Evan, positive it wasn't. Dead animals smelled different. He couldn't explain the difference; he just knew.

Silas stepped to the driver's door and leaned in through the missing window to pull the trunk release.

Evan stepped back as the trunk lid creaked and only opened an inch.

Damn. I have to do it.

He held his breath, grabbed the lid with both hands, and hauled it up the rest of the way, creating a nails-on-chalkboard sound. A cloud of startled flies flew out and then immediately resettled.

"Oh fuck." The deputy turned away.

Evan forced his gaze to stay on the naked body facing him as it lay on its side in the trunk. The body had been dead for a while.

Short, gray hair. Clearly male.

The victim's arms were tied behind his back, and under the crawling flies, Evan could make out a hole in the victim's forehead that didn't belong there.

Headshot. Executed?

He glanced at the deputy, who had composed himself and was taking more photos from several angles—but at a distance. "Call the medical examiner and get a forensics team out here." The deputy nodded and used the task as an excuse to move farther away.

"Found some change under the driver's seat that I missed," said Silas, showing a palm with three coins. "People ignore change, but I collect it all. It adds up," he stated. He peered in the trunk. "Well, shit. Can't say I'm surprised. Glad I called you."

Evan held out a gloved hand. "Sorry, but those coins are now part of a crime scene."

Silas reluctantly gave him the money, and Evan sealed it in an evidence bag.

"Any idea who this is?" Evan asked.

The thin man shoved his hands behind the bib of his overalls and took a long look. "Hard to say." With a scowl on his face, he leaned in close to the body, and Evan heard a choked sound from the deputy's direction. Silas straightened. "Something shiny and silver is sticking out under his leg. Usually shiny metal can be something good when I'm going through cars." He shook his head. "But I ain't touching *that*."

Evan took out his phone, snapped a picture of the metal, and then gently slid it out from under the gray leg. His heart fell as he turned it over.

It was a Deschutes County Sheriff's Department badge.

A high-pitched ringing filled his head, and his fingers froze on the metal.

I know that number.

He looked at the gray hair.

That's Rod.

Evan's friend and mentor, Detective Rod McLeod, had retired five years ago.

Memories flooded Evan's brain, and a sharp pain bloomed in his chest.

I've got to call Sophia.

Guilt swamped him, and he set the badge back in the trunk. Rod's daughter, Sophia, had left Evan a voicemail two days ago, asking him to return her call. He had been running to a meeting when he listened to the message and had forgotten to call her back.

His hands shook as he scrolled on his phone, looking for Sophia under his recent calls. He touched the entry and lifted the phone to his ear. It immediately went to voicemail. He struggled to speak. "Sophia, it's Evan. Call me. Soon. It's important." He hung up and sent her a text stating the same thing.

His gaze went to Rod's badge.

Was Sophia's call about Rod?

2

Evan paced as the medical examiner looked over the body in the trunk. He'd tried calling Sophia at Blossom Bounty, her florist shop downtown, but the employee who answered said Sophia had the day off and hadn't heard from her. Worried, Evan had called and asked Detective Noelle Marshall to go to the woman's home. He felt as if he'd had too much caffeine. Every nerve twanged in his limbs, wanting him to hunt down Sophia.

Rod's daughter had been like a sister to Evan for a long time. At one point they'd tried to date but discovered they made better friends. He was close to her twelve-year-old son, Zack, whose asshole father, Charlie Graham, currently sat in prison, partly thanks to Evan.

Evan had still been a county deputy when he arrested Charlie.

He crossed his fingers that Detective Marshall would locate Sophia. He would hate to have someone else inform her of her father's death, but at the moment he couldn't leave the scene. He knew Detective Marshall would handle it with compassion.

"I *hate* flies." Dr. Natasha Lockhart shuddered as she leaned into the trunk, conducting her exam of Rod McLeod. "*Hate them.* I prefer maggots over flies any day. At least you can see where they're going. Damned flies are all over the place." She waved an arm at the dozen near her head. "Get off me!"

Evan held back his surprise as he watched. He'd seen the medical examiner stoically assess horrendous situations and never shudder or speak so vehemently. Occasionally he had wondered what type of scene would push a medical examiner's buttons. Like him, they had to compartmentalize when faced with horrors, and the examiners he'd worked with had always presented a calm front no matter what was before them.

Today I discovered that flies push Natasha's buttons.

Once Dr. Lockhart had arrived on scene, she'd taken one look at the fly-covered trunk and put on every piece of personal protective equipment in her kit, including a papery head covering that resembled a shower cap. At previous crime scenes, Evan had only seen her in gloves and booties.

Today is different in several ways.

Over the past hour, Moon's Junkyard had become a magnet for police. It seemed as if every member of law enforcement in the county had made an appearance. Even if it was their day off.

One of their own had been taken down.

Evan had given orders for everyone to stay behind the front gate if they hadn't been assigned to the case. Twice he'd gone out to the gravel parking lot to get something out of his SUV. The lot was packed with vehicles from multiple divisions, and law enforcement milled around, their restless energy and frustration clouding the air like a heavy smog.

The deadly crime had stoked a need to be around their fellow officers and swap stories about Rod. To talk and to see each other. To come together to mourn in their own way. Faces were grim; tears were present. For some, venting was a coping mechanism. Evan had heard a few low mutters about making sure that Rod's killer never made it to prison.

He hated to hear the talk, but he understood they were letting off steam so they didn't explode. But the steam came out as ugly words.

"Find the asshole," Evan had been ordered several times as he passed the crowd. He'd nodded and made eye contact with several people but hadn't stopped to talk.

He had a job to do.

Evan waved a group of flies off Dr. Lockhart's back. "What do you think, Natasha?"

She didn't answer, continuing to gently poke and prod the body. The petite doctor moved to the side of the car and stretched over the fender to push Rod's shoulder forward to get a look at his back. Evan stepped up, placed one hand behind Rod's shoulder and his other on the victim's middle back, and rolled him forward slightly. It was more difficult than he'd expected. The trunk was cramped; Rod had been a tall man. His knees were pulled up almost to his stomach, his feet pressing against one side of the trunk and his head against the other.

The flesh was soft; rigor mortis had come and gone. Evan locked his emotions behind a door in his brain and held Rod in place for the medical examiner. He studied the body and swallowed hard as he scanned for indicators to help determine the time of death. Decomposition had clearly started. It appeared the body had suffered numerous cuts, which the flies crawled in and out of. It was bloated, and the skin had a greenish-gray marbling, but he didn't see the leakage of bodily fluids that could indicate a later stage of decay.

"Fucking flies!" Natasha angrily waved her arm again, and Evan froze as he got a glimpse of her red eyes and tears. He'd never seen her cry over a victim.

It's not the flies upsetting her. It's Rod.

Her anger at the flies was a cover. She wasn't cursing at them; she was cursing about Rod's murder.

"You were close to him," Evan stated.

Natasha sniffed behind her mask and face shield but didn't look up from palpating Rod's back. "Yes."

Evan waited to see if she'd say more. She remained quiet, her gaze never leaving the victim.

"I'm sorry," he said. "He was special to me too."

"I know," she said. "He told me you were the best detective he'd ever trained."

Her words pierced his heart, and he blinked rapidly. Evan knew his hard work had earned Rod's respect and approval, but Natasha's statement took it to another level. He blew out a breath. "Thank you for telling me."

A bit of guilt touched him because he couldn't reciprocate. He'd never seen an indication or even heard that Natasha and Rod were tight. He thought for a moment and estimated the age difference to be twenty years—maybe twenty-five.

"It wasn't like that," she said, apparently reading his mind. "I'll fill you in later. It's not relevant at the moment." She cleared her throat. "He's been moved," she said in a tone that belonged in a lecture hall. "The lividity pattern on his back does not match his current position. I estimate he was put in the trunk sometime overnight—probably early this morning." She stepped back, and Evan allowed the body to return to its original position.

"So maybe a day or two since his death?"

"Depends on the type of environment he was kept in." She removed her gloves and laid them on the body. "If that bullet hole wasn't the cause of death, it certainly made sure he was dead. I'll know more after his autopsy. In an ideal world, I'd have you move the car with the body still inside to a controlled environment to start my full exam." She glared at the dozens of broken-down cars blocking in the Camry. "That doesn't seem possible here, so I'll stick around to supervise the removal of the body. I trust them, but an extra pair of eyes won't hurt." She moved a few steps away, pulled the protective equipment off her head, and gave a nod to the evidence team, which had been impatiently waiting for her to finish. "I'm always thorough, but I'll be doubly thorough with this one." She frowned. "That sounded like I don't give my best to every case."

"I knew what you meant," said Evan. "I'd had a similar thought about my investigation." He studied the small woman. Sweat soaked her hairline and her posture was stiff. "Maybe someone else should handle his autopsy?"

"No," she snapped, her eyes instantly angry. But then she stilled, emotions flickering across her face. "I see your point, but it won't make a difference in my job."

Am I too close to Rod to lead the investigation?

Like Natasha, Evan didn't think so. Besides, all the detectives had known Rod.

"Natasha, do you have any idea of who would do this? When did you last talk to Rod?"

Sad amusement touched her eyes. "Starting already, Detective?"

Evan noted she didn't use his first name as she usually did. "I started the moment I got the call. Your insight could be helpful."

She sighed. "Sorry about that. I'm a little punchy. My brain has been in overdrive analyzing everything he's ever said to me, but honestly nothing has jumped out. I know of nothing helpful now."

"I'll need an interview."

"Just tell me when."

"Soon. I'll probably talk to his daughter, Sophia, first."

"She's been notified?"

"I sent Detective Marshall to do it in person." Evan looked back at the body, his guilt surging again. But he couldn't be everywhere at once. Rod had said those exact words to him numerous times before Evan had become better at delegating. Rod's guidance had made him a good detective. He sent a mental thank-you toward the remains.

That's not Rod. He's with Ellen now.

He pictured Rod and his wife in their usual spot on the porch of their home, welcoming Evan for dinner. He'd had dozens of meals—maybe hundreds—with them and Sophia over the last decade. Ellen had passed two years ago after a long battle with cancer, her health one of the reasons Rod had retired. Her big heart and sense of humor had made her a treasure.

"Say hello to Ellen for me," Evan murmured. "Tell her I promise to find who did this."

Time to get to work.

His phone rang with a call from Detective Noelle Marshall. "Bolton," he answered.

"Evan, I'm at Sophia McLeod's home." Noelle's voice was tight. "I don't know what happened here, but it doesn't look good. Sophia's gone, and there're signs of a struggle. Forced entry. Broken glass. Lotta blood."

Evan froze. "Cordon off the scene."

"Already done. I called for some assistance and—"

"Is the blood fresh?"

Could it possibly be Rod's murder scene?

He'd already sent two officers to check Rod's home and secure it until he could arrive. They'd reported that all appeared normal at the house except that Rod's truck wasn't in the garage. Evan had immediately sent out a BOLO for the vehicle.

"It's dried," said Noelle. "But I've got a gut feeling it didn't happen that long ago."

It has to be related.

"Any sign of her son, Zack?"

"No. But there's no vehicle here. Maybe they're out somewhere."

"I'll be there as soon as I can," Evan said. "I'm wrapping it up here." He ended the call, his mind racing.

"What happened?" asked Natasha.

"Not sure. Sounds like someone broke into Sophia McLeod's home. There're signs of a struggle and a lot of blood, but she and her son aren't there." He glanced at the forensics tech who was taking more photos. Processing the scene would take them hours. There was no point in him watching over their shoulders. Everyone would be extra-thorough today.

Before Natasha had arrived, Evan had conducted a more extensive interview with the junkyard owner, and he currently had a copy of four days' worth of gate camera footage in his pocket. "I don't think there's much more for me to do here at the moment," he told Natasha. "I want to get over there."

"Go. I'm staying for a while." Natasha waved him off. "Hopefully I won't see you later today." She winced at her words. It was a typical parting joke that both MEs and law enforcement used, meaning they didn't want to need the other person's services any more that day. Evan knew Natasha had said it without thinking, but then she had recalled he was headed to a scene where she might be needed again.

"Crossing my fingers," said Evan, and he left to work his way out of the automotive jungle.

Sophia and Zack have to be okay.

3

Rowan Wolff watched Thor jump down into the center of the two giant stacked tires and immediately spring out again—a black blur. He shot her a quick glance as he trotted to a pile of rotting boards and twisted rebar.

/not here not here not here/

He circled the pile, his mouth slightly open to catch more scent, and then turned his attention to a rickety shed, his ears forward and his nose leading the way.

She kept her gaze locked on her dog, reading his gait, his posture, and his ears. All informed her that Thor hadn't found what he wanted to find.

Rowan and her dog were in the last hours of an intensive canine search and rescue training. For five years they had worked together across the country, finding dozens of missing persons—some alive, some dead—and the two of them never stopped training. There were always new situations to experience, and Thor loved to keep working. He was easily bored; Rowan was, too, and they both craved to be challenged.

This weekend's training was on private property in southeastern Oregon. Ten acres were scattered with a variety of elements and obstacles to offer the dogs diverse experiences and to help them work on their focus. Thor had done fantastically on every practice except for struggling with the barn exercise, for which small, controlled fires had been set and extinguished. It had been smoky inside, and Thor *hated* working in smoke or near fire, which Rowan had learned in the past, when he'd needed to enter an old burned building on a search. He'd whined and stalled before entering. Every step had been a struggle for him, and it had taken a lot of effort for Rowan to calm him and keep him focused.

He'd done better this weekend with the burned practice barn, but Rowan knew he still needed more training.

She watched him exit the rickety shed and go under a fence. He looked back at her and paused, checking her location. Most dogs would stay on the move, trusting their handlers to catch up. But due to an old leg injury, Rowan wasn't as quick as other handlers. Thor knew this, and no matter how much she'd trained him to keep going, he always checked on her.

"Find it!" she ordered.

Satisfied, Thor continued his search.

"He's never going to get past checking on you, is he?" commented the trainer next to her.

"I don't think so," said Rowan. "He never loses focus when he does it, so I can live with that quirk."

The trainer made a mild sound of disagreement but didn't say more.

Rowan didn't care. For years she'd been told to train away the habit, but since it had never interfered with Thor's performance, she let it go. Deep down she was pleased her dog cared and watched out for her. Her leg slowed her down and wasn't as strong as she would like, but it didn't stop the pair of them from being damned good. They had worked with more than fifty law enforcement agencies across the country. Federal, state, county, and city. Several times they'd been hired privately when the media's or the public's knowledge of a missing person could cause more harm than good.

A few years ago, during a private search, they had found the missing and severely injured daughter of a huge retail chain owner. The very grateful parents had paid her a reward that—as long as she was very careful with money—essentially set her up for life. She hadn't done it to get paid; she'd done it because someone needed her help. Search and rescue was most often volunteer work, and people did it because they had a unique skill and valued helping others. It was never done for the money—because the money usually didn't exist. Rowan loved the job. The long hours, rotten weather, and rugged terrain only challenged them, making the two of them try harder.

At a nod from the head trainer, two other SAR handlers walked their leashed dogs through Thor's search area. A few of the waiting dogs whined and pulled on their leashes, wanting to join the fun. Pull toys appeared as the handlers distracted their dogs from Thor's work. The purpose was to keep Thor on task when he was surrounded by diversions. Setting two dozen squirrels loose in the area would have been the perfect test, but they settled for dogs.

One of Thor's ears swiveled toward a whining dog, but he never broke stride and continued his sweep across the field, his nose up, searching for the scent.

Good boy.

"Nice," said the trainer beside her.

"Takes a lot to distract him."

Far in the distance Rowan could see the "quarry" in a yellow jacket, crouched in some tall grass. The dogs primarily searched with their noses. Vision was secondary and added when they picked up the scent. Rowan opened the gate and entered the field, watching her dog work.

Thor did a little jerk of his head, pivoted, and sped up.

He found the scent.

His tail enthusiastically wagging, he spent another minute making narrower sweeps. Abruptly he bolted, finding a visual lock on his quarry. He circled the man once and then raced back to Rowan. His gaze on hers, his hindquarters quivering with excitement, he paced before her, uttering a string of chattering doggy speak.

/found him I take you to him found him/

"Good job, Thor! Good boy!" Rowan slapped his side a few times and then waved her arm. Thor bolted back in the man's direction with Rowan jogging behind. This time the man offered Thor a short game of tug-of-war, a reward for locating him and then bringing Rowan. She joined a moment later and helped celebrate with Thor's favorite ball and some fetch. Positive reinforcement was key in training. If no quarry had been present, and Thor had indicated the field was empty, they would have celebrated because he'd done his job.

She snapped on his leash and was headed toward the gate when her phone vibrated. Casting a quick look around and seeing attention had turned to the next dog's search, she pulled out the phone and smiled at the photo of Evan.

"I can only talk for minute," she said as a greeting.

"I know you're not to be on the phone," said Evan. "But I had to call." The background noise told her he was in his vehicle; his tone told her something was very wrong.

"What happened?" she asked.

"Rod McLeod was murdered. I have the case."

Rowan briefly closed her eyes, her heart sinking. "No." She'd met Rod a few times since she'd started dating Evan and knew how much Evan admired him. "I'm so sorry, Evan. I know what he means to you."

Meant to you.

"I'll head home," Rowan said. "I can skip the final exercise. Thor has proven to be a master at nearly everything they've put us through."

"You don't need to do that."

"I know, but I want to."

"I probably won't have time to see you, let alone eat or sleep for the next several days," said Evan.

"Then you need someone to bring you food. Decent food." She'd seen Evan live on fast food when he was wrapped up in an investigation. She wasn't much of a cook, but she could do better than processed breakfast sandwiches. "I won't be there until this afternoon. It's a long drive."

A sigh came through the phone. "I've missed you. I wish this wasn't the reason you're coming home early." His tone changed. "Did I ever introduce you to Sophia McLeod?"

"Rod's daughter? No. You told me about her several times. I know she has a son and that you two are close."

"I just pulled up at her house. Someone broke in. It sounds like there was some sort of struggle there. We haven't located her or Zack yet."

Rowan sucked in a breath. "I hope she's okay."

"Me too."

"I love you, Evan," she said.

"Love you too." He ended the call.

Rowan stared at her phone screen, feeling very far away from home. Who would have guessed that Evan Bolton would become the most important man in her life?

Everyone who saw the two of us together.

Her sisters and parents had known she and Evan were meant to be a couple before Rowan had. Early on, they'd seen something rare between them. Rowan had been single so long, she'd believed Thor would be the only man in her life. But Evan had quickly found an important place in her heart.

Just like Thor.

She rubbed the dog's head and gave a gentle tug on his ears. He looked up and met her gaze, his mouth open and his tongue out with three inches of dangling drool, panting happily. True love.

Two men to love. She was a lucky woman.

4

Speaking with Rowan had calmed Evan's nerves before he arrived at Sophia's home. He no longer felt as if he needed to sprint a mile to work off his excess energy.

Their relationship had been the best thing in his life recently. After they had dated for several months, he'd rented out his house and moved into hers. They'd lived together since February, and now it felt like they'd always been together. He often wondered how he'd lived alone for so long.

He'd known Rowan professionally for a few years. They would briefly cross paths when his department used her and Thor to locate lost children or adults. He'd found the tall, blonde woman attractive, but the right moment had never happened—until last summer, when her friend had been murdered and the case landed in Evan's hands. During that time, he grew close to her parents, her younger twin sisters, and her older brother, Malcolm. But he fell in love with Rowan. Hard.

"Fucking head over heels," he muttered as he shut his SUV door in front of Sophia McLeod's house.

I'm a fortunate man.

He shifted his brain into work mode and examined his surroundings. Detective Noelle Marshall's vehicle blocked the driveway of the small ranch-style house, and three Deschutes County sheriff's cruisers were across the street along with a forensics team's minivan. The home was in an older neighborhood on the outskirts of Bend, but there was evidence that young families lived in many of the houses. Bikes, scooters, and several DRIVE AS IF YOUR KIDS LIVE HERE signs dotted the yards.

He knew Sophia had moved into the home recently. Rod had mentioned it around Christmas. He'd received a Christmas email with pictures of her and Zack but hadn't touched base with her in quite a while. *Probably since I started seeing Rowan.*

He hadn't consciously avoided Sophia; he'd simply not thought of her. Rowan had filled all his available thoughts. He suspected a small part of him was uncomfortable staying in regular contact with a woman he had dated now that Rowan was part of his life. Maybe he'd felt it was disrespectful? But Sophia was like a sister to him, their dating time long in the past. He'd told her all about Rowan when they first got together, and Sophia had shared her disastrous online dating stories with him. It was a long-term, close friendship.

And now there was broken glass and blood in her home.

Concern and regret raced through him again.

I should have returned her call on Thursday.

He tried her cell phone again. Voicemail.

Sophia's house didn't have any toys in the yard, but Evan suspected the garage had several bikes belonging to Zack. The twelve-year-old loved anything on two wheels. Years ago Evan had predicted there would be motorcycle arguments in Sophia's future. As he strode up the driveway, studying the outside of the home and yard, Evan thought about the few weeks when he and Sophia had tried to date. They'd had a nice time, and she was attractive, but he'd never felt that *zing* in her presence.

Sophia had admitted the same thing.

But that zing hit his chest every time he looked at Rowan. Didn't matter if she was reading a book or scooping dog poop. When he saw her, he ached to be next to her, touch her. Something about the feel of her skin against his soothed his soul.

Evan greeted the deputy waiting outside the front door and signed the log. As he slipped on booties and gloves, the deputy said he'd find Detective Marshall and the forensics tech in the bathroom. Evan glanced at the doorframe, looking for the forced entry that Noelle had mentioned.

"They broke the glass in the back door," the deputy said, noticing his gaze.

"Thanks." Evan stepped inside.

The interior of the home was cool. From the driveway, he'd noticed that tall trees lined the south side of the home, blocking the sun's most intense heat. Evan appreciated that, but the trees also blocked some natural light, making the house a little dim indoors, even though it appeared every light in the home was on. Voices came from down a hallway to his right, but he headed toward the back of the home, wanting to see the point of entry. He gave a wide berth to several evidence markers on the floor. Each one was positioned by dried drops and smears of blood. He spotted partial shoe prints in the blood and held his foot near one. Either a male or a woman with large feet had made it.

Intruder's blood? It could be Rod's or Sophia's. Or Zack's.

Bile rose in his throat.

What happened to this family?

He focused on the back door. It was old; its upper half featured a large piece of glass, which had been broken above the doorknob and bolt. The hole was surrounded by jagged points of glass and was plenty big enough for a hand to slip through. Evan shined his flashlight on the glass and leaned close, hoping to see small drops or smears that might be related to the blood on the floor. The shards looked clean. Black fingerprint powder covered the door's hardware and frame; forensics had already done their job.

He turned to the adjacent kitchen. It was dated. All the appliances except the fridge looked original to the home, which he estimated had been built in the 1980s. The only thing from the current decade was the high-tech espresso machine. Next to that was a fresh bouquet of flowers. Sophia had always had flowers in her home, even before she became a florist. A large, framed photo was on the counter, and Evan stepped closer.

Rod, Ellen, and Sophia smiled at him. It was a candid shot from Sophia's high school graduation. She stood between her parents, looking up at Rod and laughing. He had been known for his lame dad jokes, and Evan suspected he'd just told one.

How many bad jokes did I hear over the years? A hundred? Two hundred?

Everyone told Rod his jokes were weak, but Rod didn't care. He'd laugh, slap the person on the back, and tell another.

I'd like to hear one now.

Ellen had a healthy glow in the photo. Her face was still rounded and her eyes full of light. Rod's hair was salt and pepper instead of the solid gray Evan had seen this morning. The picture was about ten years old, and tucked in one corner of the frame was a recent school photo of Zack, the resemblance between him and eighteen-year-old Sophia readily apparent. More than Evan had ever noticed.

"Her espresso machine is nicer than mine."

He turned to find Noelle Marshall standing a few feet away. She wore paper foot coverings over her heeled boots and blue vinyl gloves with her navy pantsuit. He was glad the detective was on the case. She was smart and driven, and they made a good team.

"What have you found?" Evan asked, not bothering with small talk. This case needed to be solved.

"First of all, there are no cameras—"

"What?" Surprise filled him. "Her dad was on the force for more than thirty years. He'd insist she have cameras."

"I have two deputies knocking on neighbors' doors," said Noelle. "Hopefully one of the homes has a camera that catches the street or part of this property. I'd guess she hadn't gotten around to installing cameras yet because she just bought the house a few months ago."

Evan nodded. "I know."

"I checked the sales history of the home. It was first purchased in 1982, and Sophia was the next buyer. I guess the original owners never saw any point in remodeling." She tipped her head at the back door. "No prints on the knob or locks. Must have worn gloves."

"Premeditated." Evan's gut twisted.

"Obviously there is a lot of blood out here—and what looks to be some good shoe prints, but the tech is still working in the bathroom. You'll want to see this." She strode toward the hallway and Evan followed, stepping carefully around more evidence markers and blood that led down the hall.

The bathroom door hung awkwardly, only one of its hinges keeping it in place. The hollow door had splintered where a handle should be. Evan spotted the round knob on the floor down the hall.

Someone was determined to get in.

On the floor in the bathroom, a woman was taking blood samples.

Evan sucked in a breath at the numerous smears and dried puddles of blood on the linoleum. More partial shoe prints. Someone had fought for their life. There were red-brown streaks on the side of the tub and the cabinet doors below the counter. Blood flecks dotted the lower part of the wall near an overturned scale.

"It had to be Sophia inside the bathroom," said Noelle. "I can't see Rod hiding from an intruder behind a locked door."

"Most likely," agreed Evan. "Rod would have confronted them. Probably with a weapon in hand." The retired detective had feared nothing. It hadn't always been a good thing. "You knew him?" Evan asked Noelle. He was pretty certain that she had joined Deschutes County after Rod left.

"I met him a few times. He'd already retired, but someone introduced us when he stopped by the department one time. Then I'd bump into him socially with others."

"At the diner or Ed's Tavern?" Rod had continued to frequent the law enforcement hangouts after retirement.

"Both. Knew him enough to say hello. I'd heard his wife died but didn't know he had a daughter and grandson until today." She watched the tech for a long moment.

"Could Sophia have walked out?" Evan said softly.

"As far as I can tell, there are no smaller bloody shoe or footprints—everything seems too large. Maybe she was carried," said Noelle. "We need to get a blood spatter expert in here. They can shine a light on what happened."

"The blood is completely dry," said the tech, not looking up from her work. "Hard to say when it happened. And the detective is right. You need a spatter specialist. I think there are three different shoe types in the blood, but an expert can read a lot more."

"Three?" asked Evan. He recognized the tech. Cynthia had worked many of his cases.

Cynthia glanced up, meeting his gaze. "Blood isn't my area. I know how to accurately document and do some basic reads. I can tell you multiple people were in here . . . there might be more than three."

Evan stared at the floor, not seeing footprints. "Show me one."

The tech pointed at a large swipe. "See how that swipe ends? I can tell the shoe had small square shapes on the sole, which makes me think of an athletic shoe."

Now Evan could make out the imprint, which was only three inches long and an inch wide.

Definitely need an expert.

"Did you find anything else of interest in the home?" Evan asked Noelle.

"I've only had time to do a quick check," she said. "But an outside door to the garage on the side of the house was open. Not a lot, just a few inches."

"Is there a door from the garage into the house?"

"Yes. It was closed when I arrived. I looked around the outside garage door and didn't see forced entry or signs of bloody footprints. I don't think anyone got out of here without blood on their shoes or feet, so I'd guess the attackers didn't go out that way . . . although one of them could have come in if it'd been unlocked. Someone's entry was obviously made through the back door, and the blood on the floor indicates that was an exit.

"I checked the bedrooms," continued Noelle. "Sophia's bedroom is the first one. Her cell phone is turned off, but it's on the nightstand, and the bed is unmade. Her driver's license is in her purse on a little table near the front door."

"I assume the cell phone was locked?"

"Yep. I powered it on but couldn't get any further without a password. There's a laptop on the desk in her bedroom. Also locked. When I first looked in Zack's bedroom, I thought there'd been a struggle. But now I think it's just a typical kid mess."

"Find the boy's cell phone in there?"

"I didn't see one."

"Could have been Zack in the bathroom," said Evan in a tight voice. "Maybe both of them." He shut down his mental image of the two of them fighting off an attacker. "But you said the car is gone . . . I'm hoping they got away somehow. Maybe that's why the side garage door was left open—they could have gotten away on foot."

"Like you said, she's a cop's daughter. She would have gone straight to the police if they got out."

"True." His hopes for a positive outcome were shrinking by the second. "I put out a BOLO on her car. The attacker could have taken it. Maybe with Sophia and Zack in it. But that doesn't explain the blood going out the back door."

"Maybe the attacker stepped outside for some reason." Noelle eyed the blood on the floor. "Her knife block on the counter is full. Either he brought his own weapon or found another in a drawer. I saw a couple of small dull-looking ones in a kitchen drawer when I skimmed through."

"You think it was a knife?" Evan asked, looking at the blood covering the floor.

"No bullet hole in any of the walls or the floor. No shells left behind. With this much blood, something sharp was used if it wasn't a gunshot."

Evan gestured for Noelle to follow him out of the bathroom. He didn't want the tech hearing his next words. Gossip traveled fast. He stopped in the kitchen and turned to Noelle.

"Rod had an entry wound centered on his forehead," he said in a low voice.

Noelle stared at him for a long second, alarm filling her gaze. "That's a strong message. Someone had a point to make."

"I agree. The ME hasn't confirmed it was the cause of death, but either way, it must have been done deliberately."

"Any stab wounds?"

Evan grimaced. "I think so. It looked like there could have been a lot of cuts on the body . . . but maybe it looked that way because some time had passed. Dr. Lockhart will let us know."

"Shit. Sophia and Zack could turn up dumped somewhere like her dad," Noelle said.

The same sickening thought had occurred to Evan. "Did you follow the blood trail beyond the back door?"

"I haven't had time for a close look," said Noelle. "I stopped looking for blood at the edge of the small patio; it was hard to see in the bark dust and grass, but I think the general direction was toward the gully that runs behind all these homes. Take a look." She went to the back door and opened it, carefully stepping around the glass on the floor. From the patio Evan could see several neighbors' backyards to his left and right.

"There aren't any fences," Noelle said with a small shake of her head.

Evan didn't like it either. Fences offered a small measure of security.

"Her yard flows into the brush that lines the gully." Noelle pointed to the rear of the property, where he saw a lot of bushes. "I walked to the gully edge. On the far side is a grade school. A chain-link fence surrounds its grounds—probably to keep kids from exploring the gully. Our attacker would have had to go pretty far to the left or right to get around the school's fence to access the road in front of the school."

"Or he could have continued down the gully in either direction. He could have come in that way too."

"It's a big area." Noelle sighed. "More units are coming. I'll start them walking a grid back there. Maybe we'll find something."

"Since the intruder came prepared, I suspect he also had a getaway plan," said Evan. "Maybe a car on the school road. The school is another place to check for cameras. But since it's Saturday, it might be a little difficult to get a hold of someone from the school district." He checked the time. "I want to go through Rod's house. After what we've seen here, I want a close look. I had a unit check the property, but it was locked up. I'll probably have to break some glass like someone did here."

"Hang on." Noelle went inside the home and returned thirty seconds later. She dangled a Mickey Mouse key chain on one finger. "I noticed a small bowl of keys in a drawer when I checked the kitchen for knives. Look what it says."

A printed white label had been placed over Mickey's face. It read "Dad's house." A single key hung on the ring.

Evan closed his fingers around Mickey, memories rising. "Rod used a label maker for *everything*. There wasn't a thing in his office that didn't have one of these damned little white labels on it. Everything had to be neatly in its place and easy to find." His voice cracked on the last word, his throat tight.

Sympathy flashed in Noelle's eyes.

Evan thrust the memories away, pulling himself together. "I need to get going. You good here?"

"Yes, the patrol sergeant is on the way. He can supervise the deputies doing the grid, so I can start a more thorough search of the house. I've got another forensics tech coming too."

"I'll let you know what I find at Rod's," said Evan, and headed toward the front door. His stomach churned. The labeled key chain had affected him more than the photo on the counter. He'd been caught off guard by the little embodiment of a big piece of Rod's personality.

I've got to find who did this.

5

Evan made a half dozen phone calls on his way to Rod's home. He'd silenced his phone while he went through Sophia's house, and as he left, he discovered he'd missed several calls, texts, and emails.

Everyone wanted to say something about Rod.

Evan ignored the social communications. He had no time for polite replies; he had a case to get off the ground. There had been no results yet on the BOLO for Rod's truck, and Rod's cell phone was turned off or destroyed. At the junkyard, Evan had called the phone and then lost his breath at the sound of Rod speaking on his voicemail. The recorded voice of his dead friend had been a gut punch.

He'd filled out a warrant online to get Rod's cell phone records and requested the phone's last known location. He'd also requested the phone's locations over the last two weeks. At least they had Sophia's phone, and he requested the records of her calls, too, knowing some of them could have been erased on her phone.

Results didn't happen instantly, as they did on TV. In the past, he'd had to wait weeks for cell phone records. To speed up today's process, whenever he spoke with an actual person, he told them his request for information was for a murdered law enforcement victim. The person's tone would immediately change. Everyone wanted to help.

His final call was to Rowan. She was on the road but still an hour from Bend, and he asked her to go directly to Sophia's home instead of theirs. By the time she arrived, the property would be crisscrossed with the scents of many deputies, but he trusted Thor's ability to sift through all of them. Evan wanted to know if Sophia or Zack had been taken through the backyard.

He ended their call as he turned onto Rod's street. A lone sheriff's deputy's SUV was at the curb in front of Rod's town house.

Evan parked and strode to the deputy's open window, recognizing the officer as Steve Hartley. The officer had a McDonald's shake in one hand.

He left for lunch?

"All quiet, Detective." Hartley lifted the shake. "I had my lunch delivered," he explained. A crinkled McDonald's bag was on the passenger seat.

"Good idea. I want you to come inside and clear the house with me. I've got a key."

The deputy took a long pull on his shake and got out of the vehicle.

Evan's stomach rumbled as he went up the wooden stairs to the front door. He'd worked through lunch, and the smell of the deputy's fries made him want to order his own meal.

No time to eat.

The men stood to each side of the door as Evan rang the doorbell, and then Deputy Hartley pounded on the door and shouted, "Deschutes County sheriff! Open up!" They repeated the warning twice. Evan took out the Mickey Mouse key chain and slid the key in the lock. To his relief, it turned. Evan pocketed the key, removed his weapon, shoved the door open, and stepped inside the home, covering the space to the left as the deputy covered the right.

Evan suspected there wasn't a threat inside. But procedure had been created for very good reasons, and entering the home of a murder victim for the first time required precautions.

Because shit happened. Unexpected shit.

Their job was to be prepared for anything.

"Deschutes County sheriff's office!" yelled the deputy. "Make yourself known!"

Silence.

Working together, the two men made quick work of clearing each room, checking closets and every possible location a person could hide. The home was quiet and neat and showed no indication that a crime had taken place inside.

Evan's younger sister had vanished when he was in college, and although he hadn't seen Sophia for a while before her disappearance, the feeling of dread and worry had come rushing back, very similar to how he'd felt for nearly fifteen years, wondering what had happened to his sister.

As if his guts had been hollowed out and nothing else would fill the space.

He hadn't missed that feeling.

He'd had a small irrational hope that he'd find Sophia and Zack inside. But instead of people in the house, he found more of Rod's familiar obsession with labels and organization. A home office upstairs was the last room the men cleared, and then they holstered their weapons. Evan turned his attention to the office desk. It was set up *exactly* like Rod's desk at work had been. A blotter with a huge calendar. Several stackable letter trays, neatly labeled but empty. A spinning organizer with a variety of pens, pencils, paper clips, and other home office needs.

Evan turned away, the déjà vu painful, and found himself facing two large paintings. He immediately recognized Ellen's work. It had been a hobby, but Evan had believed she had loads of talent. One painting was a rugged, rocky ocean landscape, and the other was of rolling country hills. He peered closer, looking for the tiny person he knew Ellen had integrated into each work. It was always Sophia, painted from the back. He found her near a big rock on the beach in one and under a tree in the country hills in the other. The detail had always charmed him.

Now he was angry.

"Two big gun safes," said Hartley, looking in the office closet.

The doorbell rang. Evan and the deputy glanced at each other, and then Evan moved to the window, angling to get a view of the front patio. A blonde woman stood there, holding something covered with tinfoil. No new vehicles were in front of the townhome. "Let it go," said Evan, stepping back from the window. "Probably a neighbor."

The doorbell rang again. But this time the sound was drawn out, the woman making a point that she wouldn't be ignored.

"Maybe she saw something," said Hartley.

"Maybe. I'll talk to her. Can you look for Rod's wallet and cell phone?" He left the room and jogged down the stairs. He studied the woman through the peephole in the door. She appeared to be in her sixties and held some sort of casserole or dessert in a rectangular glass dish. She looked pleasant and harmless, dressed in yoga clothing. With perfect hair and makeup. He opened the door, and she instantly scrutinized him from head to toe.

"Can I speak to Rod?" she asked. Frown lines appeared around her mouth, and she eyed Evan with a heavy dose of skepticism.

She doesn't know.

"Sorry. He's not here." It wasn't time to share the truth.

She lifted her chin and glared. "Who are *you*? I don't recognize you."

"I'm a friend. We worked together."

"If you worked for the sheriff's office, then you'll understand why I want to see some identification," she stated. "Because right now you're a stranger in his home."

There was a juxtaposition between the neighborly tinfoil-covered dish—which had apparently been made for Rod—and her demand. She meant business.

Amused, Evan pulled out his identification. She studied it closely and took a long look at his face, comparing it to the picture. "How do

I know that's not a fake? Anyone with a printer can make that, and I know they sell fake badges online."

She had a point, and Evan was momentarily stumped.

Her gaze went beyond him, and her suspicion vanished.

"What's the problem?" asked Deputy Hartley.

Evan stepped back, relieved that the deputy's uniform and presence were enough proof for the woman.

"Oh! I assumed that sheriff's vehicle was for the Struetts across the street," said the woman. "They're always causing some sort of ruckus and getting visits from the police."

"That's true," admitted Hartley. "I've been there a few times."

"Rod's not here," Evan said, ready for the woman to leave. "I can put that dish in the fridge."

"When will he be back?"

Never.

Evan couldn't speak.

"Not sure," answered Hartley. He put out his hands for the dish.

She seemed to grip it tighter. "Tell him it's from Celia. And it needs an hour in the oven at three seventy-five. You probably should write that down."

"Yes, ma'am." Hartley's hands were still extended.

Celia looked down at the tinfoil for a long second and finally passed it to him.

A budding romance?

A relationship that would never grow.

Fuck. No one deserved that more than Rod.

Rod had always said he'd never marry again, but Evan had hoped he'd find someone special to keep him company. Rod had had too much to give and deserved someone to share it with. Ellen would have understood. Evan mumbled some sort of thanks to Celia and closed the door.

Numb, he stood motionless in the hall as Hartley took the dish to the kitchen. The day had delivered blow after blow to his heart, and he wondered how much more he could take. As he trudged up the stairs to the home office, he prayed that Sophia and Zack were okay.

In the room, he gloved up before he slid the closet door open a little farther for a better view of the two giant gun safes. He knew Rod had at least a dozen weapons. Both safes were locked, and Evan suspected they'd need an expert to get into them.

"Computer tower is gone," said Hartley, who'd silently entered the room.

Evan whirled around. "Shit." He hadn't noticed at first because a large monitor sat prominently on the desk, but on the carpet underneath he saw a faint rectangular outline.

"Maybe he took it in for a repair." The deputy gestured at the neat desk. He'd gloved up too. "It doesn't look like someone came rooting through here, searching for something."

Evan said nothing. It was possible. But considering what he had observed that day, he strongly suspected it'd been taken.

He turned to the tall filing cabinet. A key sat in the lock.

Rod would never leave a key in the lock.

Someone has *been here.*

He opened a drawer and instantly recognized Rod's filing system. Rod had arranged the hanging files so that the tabs created angled lines from one side of the drawer to the other. No tab would ever be blocked by the tab in front of it. And each one had a perfectly centered label printed in an identical font and size. Evan scanned the tabs. This drawer was for Rod's home. Utilities, insurance, maintenance, and so on.

"He was organized," commented Hartley, eyeing the drawer.

"You have no idea," said Evan. He closed the drawer and opened another.

The same perfect angled rows of tabs. On the tabs were people's names and dates. Evan pulled out one and leafed through the papers. "Shit."

"Is that from a case?" said Hartley, looking over his shoulder. "He shouldn't have that."

"Exactly." No original documents were in the file on the fifteen-year-old robbery case. Evan noted they were photocopies, and that the case had been closed. He checked two more files and found similar contents. Photocopies of closed cases. "I guess they're some sort of souvenirs of his cases." He shut the drawer and opened the last one. More of the same. But his gaze stumbled as he skimmed the neat rows. There were gaps.

Evan had seen Rod relabel more than thirty files to avoid gaps. The man had claimed his brain couldn't stand an interrupted pattern.

Three files are missing.

Evan whirled around to the desk and yanked open every drawer. No files. He briefly closed his eyes, dismay flooding him.

"Get a forensics team here. Now."

6

"Good boy." Rowan crouched next to Thor and ran her hands over his soft black ears.

His gaze was locked on the dozen deputies congregating on the east side of Sophia McLeod's backyard. His chest vibrated with a low whine. He was eager to get to work.

"In a minute, Thor. Noelle's getting something for you." Detective Marshall was inside the house seeking scent articles for Thor so he could track Sophia and Zack. The back door opened, and Noelle stepped onto the patio, two plastic bags in her hands. Thor rotated one of his ears her way without removing his gaze from the deputies.

"Do you want him to smell both now?" Noelle asked.

"No. One at a time. Sophia first."

"Are all the deputies out of the gully?"

"Looks that way," said Rowan. "I haven't seen anyone else come out in the last few minutes." She'd asked for all the law enforcement walking a grid to come out. Thor didn't need them in his way. Now there were more than a dozen fresh human scents he'd have to sort through—not that she had any worry about his abilities.

Noelle handed her a bag. "That's a T-shirt and shorts from Sophia's laundry basket."

Rowan held the bag open for Thor to examine. He nosed in it for a few seconds, and Rowan unhooked his leash. "Find it!" He sprang off the patio and did only two sweeps before his head jerked and he ran straight toward the gully. Rowan and Noelle jogged after him.

"That was fast," said Noelle.

"Yep." It was fast. It was rare he found a scent that quickly.

"He didn't even sniff the dried blood on the patio," said Noelle.

"I didn't direct him to look for that."

"Amazing."

Some calls of encouragement sounded from the deputies as Thor passed by.

"Please be quiet!" Rowan said as she went past the group. She glanced at Noelle. "Have two of them follow a ways behind us and tell the rest to stay here." Rowan sped up to keep Thor in sight.

"Garcia and Jenkins," she heard Noelle say. "You're with us, but stay back fifty feet. The rest of you, stick around. Don't wander."

There were a few sounds of disappointment. People always wanted to watch Thor in action.

It is pretty awesome.

Rowan crested the gully and saw Thor waiting for her at the bottom. "Find it!" He ran twenty feet along the gully, then circled back and ran in the opposite direction. Rowan stepped carefully down the bank. The slope wasn't too steep, but there were numerous tree roots and loose rocks. There were dozens of shoe prints in the dirt. When she'd arrived, Noelle had told her the searchers hadn't found any prints in the gully yet, but clearly the searchers had left plenty of their own.

Noelle had speculated the gully search was a waste of their time, that the vanishing blood trail was a ruse. Thor had destroyed that theory within a minute of starting his search.

Rowan reached the bottom and headed east after her dog. She suspected whoever had taken Sophia had kept to the grass and short ground cover, planning not to leave footprints.

Is Zack with her?

Abruptly Rowan wondered if Thor could be following an old trail. Maybe Sophia had taken a walk in the area recently. She shook her head. Thor would follow the most recent scent, which would be the strongest. He wouldn't have left the yard if Sophia's last steps had been to return to the house.

"Noelle," said Rowan. "Sophia's car is missing, so it could mean that the attacker took it since it appears she went this way."

"I was wondering about that too," said Noelle.

After a few minutes she spotted a some colored plastic ribbons tied to brush. The searchers had marked where they'd left off when they were ordered out of the gully. Without their scents, it should be a bit easier for Thor to follow Sophia's. But Thor kept a steady pace past the markers, sweeping back and forth along the gully.

It makes no difference to him.

Pride filled her.

A hundred yards past the markers, Thor circled and backtracked a bit, darting back and forth.

He lost it.

"What's he doing?" Noelle asked in a low voice, jogging a yard behind her.

Thor tossed his head and scrambled up the bank.

"Never mind," said Noelle.

The trail went up the path of least resistance. Understandable, if someone was carrying or pulling Sophia. Rowan followed her dog, and her knee protested at the gentle climb. She ignored it as she scanned the ground for footprints. Thor stopped at the top, watching her progress. Panting, she reached her dog, and he was off again. Behind her, Noelle and the two deputies went up the bank with ease.

They'd emerged at the rear perimeter of a housing construction area several blocks from the school. The starts of a few home foundations circled a cul-de-sac. It was quiet; work had stopped for the weekend. Thor circled a bulldozer near the curb and then moved onto the blacktop of the cul-de-sac. He ran another ten yards on the new street and then reversed direction. He made several wide sweeps, running across the dirt of the construction and zipping across the blacktop to the budding foundations on the other side. His pace slowed and he circled again.

Rowan directed him farther up the street to search. He trotted, his nose up as he zigzagged, but he eventually worked his way back to the center of the cul-de-sac. The last place he'd moved with confidence. She directed him to check the five home foundations. He obeyed, but his earlier enthusiasm had waned. Rowan saw it in his carriage and the lift of his paws.

It's gone.

"I think they got into a vehicle here," said Rowan.

"But he's still searching. He'll pick up the trail."

Rowan shook her head. "He's only looking because I asked. His body language tells me it's gone."

"Makes sense to have a car waiting here," said Noelle. "No cameras in this area. And that bulldozer would provide some cover if a car parked beside it." She strode over to the bulldozer and scanned the dirt. "Looks like ten different vehicles have been here. One might be ours, but it's going to be hard to find among all these construction tracks."

A crackly voice sounded from one of the deputies' radios. The woman thumbed her shoulder mic and told the voice to go ahead.

"Is Detective Marshall with you?"

"Affirmative."

"She needs to return to the house," said the voice. "Zack McLeod was just dropped off. He spent a few nights at a friend's."

Noelle met Rowan's gaze, both speechless.

Thank goodness Zack is okay.

◆ ◆ ◆

Zack sat on the edge of the back seat of Noelle's SUV, his feet on the street and Thor planted between his legs. Thor loved kids and had given Rowan several subtle leash pulls in the boy's direction before she'd relented. Now Zack stroked Thor's fur with one hand. The boy was all long, gangly limbs and had shaggy hair that he kept pushing out of his eyes. His red, tear-filled eyes.

Pain squeezed in Rowan's chest as she watched the twelve-year-old. He was understandably distraught at the news about his mother. Noelle had refused to let him into the house, not wanting him seeing the blood and destruction.

"We can get whatever you need out of the house," Noelle had told him.

The detective had spoken with the mom who'd dropped off Zack. The woman said the two-night stay had gone smoothly. There had been no school on Thursday or Friday, and the boys had played video games most of the time, eaten a lot of pizza, and slept in until 11:00 a.m. After lunch today she'd had Zack text his mom to tell him he would be home in a while. There'd been no reply.

Before the friend's mother left, Noelle advised her to keep her house locked during the day and to call the police if she noticed any strangers near her home.

The warning had startled Rowan.

Zack could be a target.

"Zack, is there an aunt or uncle's house you could stay at for a few days?" Noelle asked. She leaned against her vehicle next to the boy.

He shook his head, still petting Thor. "No. I could stay at my grandpa's, though."

Noelle's face went blank, and Rowan swallowed hard. Zack hadn't been told about Rod McLeod's death. He'd been crushed by the news of his mother, and the detective hadn't been ready to pile on more sorrow.

Noelle pushed off the vehicle and strode past Rowan, shock in her wide eyes. Rowan followed and grabbed her arm, turning the detective to face her.

"You have to tell him. He needs to know what happened to his grandfather. Stalling will only make it worse."

"How do I break it to that distraught kid that his grandfather was murdered?" Noelle's voice cracked. "I can't. Not right now. Give me a few minutes."

Rowan studied her gaze. Clearly the situation had struck a deep chord with Noelle. The levelheaded detective's lips were quivering.

Something personal has rattled her.

"I can do it," Rowan offered. "Do you mind?"

Noelle shook her head, tears in her eyes. Rowan immediately returned to Zack before the detective could change her decision.

Rowan slowly lowered herself to a crouch beside the boy and took one of his hands, her gaze meeting his. "Zack, I'm really sorry. I know it's been a shock to learn your mother is missing, and I hate to tell you this, but you need to know that your grandfather has died. He was found this morning."

The boy stared at her, confusion in his gaze.

Thor pressed against Zack's legs, just as he did against Rowan's when she was upset. The boy pulled his hand out of hers and slid out of the vehicle to sit on the ground, wrapping both arms around Thor and hiding his face in his fur.

How many times have I done that when I'm upset?

Her dog was a great source of comfort.

"What happened?" he asked in a muffled voice.

Rowan paused, wondering how much to tell him. "We don't know yet. But the police are trying to find out."

Zack lifted his head, and Rowan brushed away two dog hairs that had stuck in a tear track. "Police? Why the police? Wouldn't it be a doctor?" Understanding filled his eyes and his face fell. "Someone hurt him."

Rowan nodded.

"He used to be a police officer," Zack said slowly. "I always worried someone would get mad and shoot him."

Rowan had had the same fear since she'd started seeing Evan.

"Did the same person take my mom?" Fear raised his voice, his eyes wide. "Are they going to kill her too?"

Rowan put her hand on his arm. "We don't know, Zack. It could be someone completely different."

He emphatically shook his head. "No. It's not a coincidence. Grandpa said to never believe in coincidences."

"I don't either," said Noelle, her voice under control. She'd moved to stand behind Rowan. "We'll figure out what happened."

"Where am I supposed to go?" He looked from one woman to the other, his arms still around Thor. "My stupid dad is in prison—not that I'd ever agree to stay with him anyway. I don't have any other family here."

"Let me talk to Detective Marshall and see if we can figure something out." Rowan pushed the hair out of his eyes, giving him a warm smile before she stood. "Thor, stay." She followed Noelle to the other side of the SUV. "Have you called child services?"

"I did while you were breaking the news to him. They don't have anyone to pick him up and asked if we can transport him to a group home."

Rowan's mouth fell open. "Transport him? That sounds like he's a felon! Drop him off at some unfamiliar place where he knows no one? We can't do that. The boy doesn't know what happened to his mother, and his grandfather is dead. Could he go back to his friend's house? The one who just dropped him off?"

"I asked the mom when she was here. I didn't tell her what happened, but I said Zack might need a place to stay for a few days. She can't take him because they're leaving town this afternoon. They have a flight to San Diego."

"I'd cancel the damn trip. This is more important!"

"She didn't know that. And I wasn't about to catch her up on the day's events."

"Shit." Rowan took a couple of steps and kicked at the dirt, her heart aching for the boy, who seemed to be alone. "Maybe Evan will have an idea."

"Evan?"

Both women turned. Zack stood near the back of the SUV, Thor at his side. Guilt swamped Rowan as she wondered how much he'd heard. "Evan Bolton," said Rowan. "He's a detective working on your grandfather's—and your mother's—case."

"I know Evan," Zack said. "He's one of my mom's friends. He worked with Grandpa."

"Yes, that's him."

"Does he still have Oreo?"

"The little dog? Oreo lives with his sister's family now. Her three kids love him very much."

"Charlotte, Theodore, and Molly."

Rowan gaped at the boy in surprise.

Zack looked down at Thor. "I've met them a few times at the sheriff's department picnics and family days. They'd come with Evan. My grandpa always took us, and it was a lot of fun," he said softly. "Theodore is cool."

Rowan wasn't positive of Evan's nephew's age, but she estimated he was a year or two older than Zack. An idea blossomed, and she glanced at Noelle. The detective shook her head and motioned for Rowan to follow, moving out of the boy's hearing distance.

"Zack could still be a target," said Noelle. "That's not fair to Evan's sister and her family. It could put them in danger."

"He could be a target at a social services group home, which would endanger a lot of people—and kids," Rowan argued. "Have you met Bridget and Victor? They live on a farm in the middle of nowhere, completely off the grid. No one would think of looking for Zack there."

Noelle was silent, indecision flickering in her eyes, and Rowan knew she'd made a strong argument. "And Zack knows the kids. He won't be with strangers."

"I'll check with Evan," Noelle relented. "It depends how his sister feels. They need to know what they could be getting into."

"It'd be best for Zack," said Rowan firmly. "They're good people, and the kids will help distract him."

"We'll see." Noelle was still uncertain.

"What's the next step to finding Sophia?"

Noelle glanced at Zack, checking that he was still far enough away. "I've got deputies knocking on neighbors' doors and asking about cameras and anything the residents might have noticed. I'll send some to the construction site road. There were a few finished homes far down that street. Could get lucky with camera views there. We'll also talk to Sophia's coworkers and friends. Try to find the connection between this case and her father's death."

"They're probably related," said Rowan.

"They're *absolutely* related," said Noelle. "I have no doubts. Coincidences like this don't exist. Zack's a smart kid to see that."

Rowan studied the boy. He was testing Thor, giving sit and lie-down commands, a small smile growing on his face as her dog eagerly performed. While Thor was on his stomach, Rowan said, "Roll over."

Zack's face lit up as the dog promptly obeyed.

The boy needs to be with friends. And a dog.

7

Evan put trust in his team and continued to delegate.

Rod would be proud.

The two cases had too many moving pieces. No matter how much he wanted to be the person who implemented every aspect of the investigation, it was impossible. His lieutenant had assigned him two other detectives besides Noelle Marshall. Evan was the lead on Rod's case, and Noelle officially had Sophia's, but they worked together, sharing all information, knowing solving one case could lead to the other's solution. Every resource available was being thrown at the cases.

Rod and Sophia were part of the Deschutes County family.

Evan had sent Detective Lori Shults and more patrol officers to Rod's neighborhood to knock on doors, do interviews, and get camera views. He sent Detective Maxine Nelson to help in Sophia's neighborhood and the area of new home construction behind it. The forensics team had finished at Sophia's home and moved on to Rod's. A blood spatter specialist was currently reviewing the scene at Sophia's. Evan hoped his analysis would shine some light on what had happened.

We don't even know if it's Sophia's blood. Or Rod's.

Evan had taken over the largest conference room at the sheriff's office. The lieutenant had also assigned two deputies currently on light duty to assist with the investigation. One had broken his leg in a motorcycle accident and was in a walking cast. The other was recovering from back surgery and moved slowly and stiffly. Investigations involved a lot of busy office work. Phone calls, interviews, background checks, affidavits, following up on tips from the public. Evan was glad to have extra hands and eyes working behind the scenes in addition to the law enforcement out gathering information. The two officers would be occupied.

Currently Evan was digging through the case copies from Rod's file cabinet. Evan had snapped photos of the file drawer tabs, hoping he could figure out which files had been removed since Rod had arranged the cases by date. Evan's goal was to figure out *why* Rod had decided to keep copies of all these solved cases, and then he'd look for cases that met the same criteria and occurred between certain dates.

Starting with the most recent, Evan began skimming Rod's cases from the filing cabinet, going through the official physical records, which were more complete than the photocopies. The officer with the back injury was still collecting more of the files. Evan still had no idea why Rod had saved records of these particular cases. Nothing jumped out at him. Swearing under his breath, he closed the first case he'd looked at, opened another, and found an inconsistency. "Shit." He rapidly checked the other cases.

He'd been operating under an assumption. An incorrect assumption.

"What is it?" asked Noelle, who was reviewing camera evidence from the junkyard. She didn't look up from her screen, her chin propped on one hand as she fast-forwarded and occasionally stopped to record license plates to look up.

"This photocopied case of Rod's—well, it's *not* Rod's. He didn't have anything to do with it. It appears several of these cases weren't his. I'd assumed they all were."

Noelle looked up. "But he kept copies?" she asked sharply. "Why?"

"That's the big question." Evan flipped through the pages. The case in his hands was a robbery at a motel. Two men had entered a room, held a woman at gunpoint, and taken her laptop, wallet, and cell phone. They'd been caught five days later.

"Whose case is that?" asked Noelle.

"Maxine's." The detective knocking on doors in Sophia's neighborhood.

"Ask her. Maybe she remembers something that could have interested Rod."

"It's from two years ago."

"I remember every case," said Noelle. "I can't list them, but if prompted, the details immediately come back."

"Yeah, I remember too," he admitted.

Some more than others.

The next two cases he looked at had been Rod's, and then Evan decided to switch to the oldest cases in Rod's files. The original paperwork on those hadn't been pulled yet, so he looked up the case briefs in the department database. Even the oldest case hadn't been assigned to Rod.

What is going on?

"The oldest case is a hit-and-run. Not Rod's."

Noelle tipped her head in thought. "I have no idea what to make of that. Maybe they're just solved cases that made impressions on him. No rhyme or reason."

"That's not helpful," Evan said in a sour tone. He noted the detective on the hit-and-run he was looking at had been Sam Durette. Sam had retired before Evan joined Deschutes County. He'd met the detective the previous year at the crack of dawn in the department parking lot when the retired detective approached with questions about one of Evan's cases. Turned out Sam had known Rowan since she was a child.

Maybe Sam will have some insight.

He made a note to talk to both Maxine and Sam.

His phone pinged with a text from Rowan asking how it was going. He decided to call instead of reply. She answered immediately, clearly driving.

"I'm going to be late tonight," he said.

"I had no doubts about that," said Rowan. "I just wanted to let you know I got Zack settled in at your sister's. I'm thankful you managed to okay that with child services."

"They were hesitant when I made the suggestion, but they're over-worked and short on space. They classified it as some sort of emergency situation to make it work."

"I asked Bridget again if she was comfortable with it. She proceeded to show me how secure their home is and assure me that someone will always be with Zack. He was excited about their rescue animals. They've really expanded their facilities and added more animals since I was here last. Now there's a blind donkey and a dog whose back legs don't work. They made him a little cart and he zooms around."

"That's Speed. Charlotte named him," said Evan. His sister's family had recently come into a financial windfall and used it to create a haven for animals no one else wanted. "Zack probably won't be there more than a day or two." Evan mentally crossed his fingers. It'd been a hell of a day, and he'd suffered one shitty surprise after another. He rubbed his forehead, suddenly very tired.

"Nothing on Sophia?" asked Rowan.

"Not yet. Where are you going?"

"Iris's house. It's baking show night."

"That's right. Say hello to everyone. Love you." They ended the call, and Evan closed his eyes for a long moment, wishing he were on the way to Rowan's sister's house too and that none of the past twelve hours had ever happened.

"Did you ever eat lunch?" Noelle's question broke his concentration.

"No." He checked the clock on the wall. It was 5:30 p.m. "I grabbed a bag of chips when I got gas. That counts."

"You think? I'm ordering Chinese because I'm starving. Requests?"

"Sesame beef."

She nodded and picked up her cell phone. "Oh, shit. Fuck!"

"What?"

"I just got a response about Sophia's ex. Charlie Graham got out of prison two months ago." She stared at Evan. "Do you think . . ."

"He has five more years on his sentence!" Evan knew because he'd helped send the man to prison.

"We both know that doesn't mean anything. Crap." She set down her phone and tapped on her keyboard. "I've got his parole officer's information. I'll call and find out where Graham is living. I'd like to pay him a visit."

"You and me both," muttered Evan. Charlie Graham was an asshole. The man was a human rap sheet with dozens of arrests from theft to robbery one. He'd been several years older than Sophia when they briefly dated, and when she got pregnant with Zack, he'd informed her that the pregnancy was "her problem" and left. Walking away from Sophia was probably the smartest thing Charlie Graham ever did, because Evan had believed that Rod would eventually murder him and hide the body.

Would Graham seek revenge on Rod? And then Sophia?

Ice shot up Evan's spine; he could picture it.

He listened carefully as Noelle talked to the parole officer. Graham had appeared at all his parole appointments and found a job at an auto body shop. Evan snorted. In the past Graham had been arrested a number of times for stealing cars and car parts. He wondered if the shop had suffered any thefts in the last two months.

Noelle ended her call. "The parole officer says Graham should be working until six o'clock. I'm headed over there." She stood and pushed in her chair.

Evan got out of his seat. "I'll go with you. I haven't seen Graham in a long time."

Noelle stepped in front of him and pointed a finger at his chest. "Do *not* antagonize him."

"I won't. He probably won't remember me."

"Bullshit. You arrested him. I read the report. Graham had a black eye and split lip. He knows exactly who you are."

"He resisted, ran, and then hit the curb with his face when I tased him. He's lucky he didn't crack his skull open."

Noelle glared at him.

"That's what happened! I swear." Evan had been tempted to continue to shock Graham with the Taser after the cuffs were on as a little payback for hurting Sophia, but he'd had some self-control.

"You testified against him. I doubt your presence will be helpful."

Evan took stock of how he felt. Rage simmered under his skin because of Rod's murder and what they believed to be Sophia's abduction. But it was manageable. It was a useful level of rage; it kept him pushing forward and focused.

"I'd like to see him. I want to judge his reaction when he hears about Sophia."

Noelle studied him for several seconds and finally nodded. She grabbed her bag and headed for the door. "You're driving. Let's pick up some deli sandwiches on the way. Chinese will have to happen another time."

Evan followed. "I'm sure we have plenty of late work nights ahead."

"True."

I also want to judge Graham's reaction to me.

He was looking forward to it.

8

Evan followed Noelle into the auto body shop.

He had expected a run-down building with bad lighting and a faded sign. A place that people would avoid at night. Instead, it was fresh and clean on the outside. Its red-white-and-blue sign looked brand new, and the parking lot had crisp yellow lines. It wasn't Evan's mental stereotype of a place that gave second chances to felons.

"Hi, guys! What can I do for you today?" The young woman behind the counter was as perky as a coffee shop barista. She seemed overly caffeinated too. The name tag on her royal-blue polo shirt read JUNIPER.

"We'd like to talk to Charlie Graham," said Noelle, matching the woman's tone and adding her own wide smile. "It'll just take a minute."

"He's working right now. How about you come back when his shift is over at six?" Juniper continued with her upbeat tone, but the light in her eyes dimmed as she looked from Noelle to Evan and back.

"How about we talk to him right now?" Noelle showed her badge and smiled.

"Ohhh." Juniper's face fell. "Let me get the owner."

"We're not interested in talking to the owner. Yet." Noelle pointed at the door that led to the shop floor. "We'll follow you."

Detective Marshall was hard to turn down. She would make requests with a smile and simultaneously project a don't-fuck-with-me attitude that caught people off guard and surprised them into submission. She was imposing and stunning at the same time, standing a little taller than Evan in her always-present heels.

Juniper became the next surprised victim and led them through the door.

They followed her past a dozen auto bays. Every bay was full, and the detectives caught several odd glances from workers as they passed by, but it appeared business was thriving. Juniper stopped at the second-to-last bay, where two men worked on a black BMW X5. They both straightened as they noticed they had an audience, and the shorter man took off his protective eyewear, his gaze locked on Evan.

Evan lifted a hand. "Hey, Charlie. How's it going? Staying out of trouble?"

Noelle flashed Evan a death glare. "Mr. Graham," she said in a friendly tone. "Could we talk to you for a few minutes outside?"

Charlie Graham blinked at Noelle, clearly trying to figure out who she was. She showed her ID. "Outside," she repeated, this time with a not-fucking-around tone.

Graham set his eyewear on the hood of the X5 and took a couple of steps in their direction. "Juniper," he said without looking at the woman, "would you ask Mr. Lawson to meet us outside?" He stopped five feet away from Evan.

Not a tall man, Graham had bulked up during his prison time. Evan estimated he'd put on thirty pounds, most of it muscle. His hairline had receded, and his nose was thicker. Probably had been broken. Maybe a few times. Evan figured his hair-trigger anger hadn't served him well in prison. Even now the muscle in his jaw tightened as he clenched his teeth, and his pulse was visible at his neck. He was struggling to keep his temper, and his gaze told Evan he was pissed as hell.

"After you," Evan said, pointing at an exit.

As Graham strode toward the exit, Noelle jabbed Evan in the ribs. "Be nice," she hissed.

Evan shrugged. They might be following Rod's killer. He didn't give a shit about playing nice.

Once outside, Graham spun around and folded his arms across his chest. "What do you want?" The question was directed at Noelle.

"I hadn't heard you were out, Graham," Evan said before Noelle could speak. "How'd an asshole like you get that lucky?" He had every intention of pushing Graham's buttons. The more off-balance the man was, the more honest the reaction they'd see in him.

"We'd like to know your whereabouts for the last few days," said Noelle. "Times, locations, and witnesses."

Surprise crossed Graham's face. Whatever he'd expected them to say, that wasn't it. "Why?"

"Because I'd like to know." Noelle pulled out a notebook and pen and looked at him expectantly. "You can start with what time you got to work today."

"What am I being accused of?" The scowl was back. "I'm not obligated to answer your questions."

"That is correct," said Noelle. "But—"

"What's going on?" A small bald man in a polo that matched Juniper's joined them and took a position next to Graham. "I'm the shop owner. Why are you interrupting my crew?"

Mr. Lawson.

Noelle turned on the charm and introduced herself and Evan. "We have some questions about Mr. Graham's whereabouts the last few days."

"Well, I can tell you he's been here from nine to six every day since Thursday. I've got time clockings if you need them." Lawson glanced at Graham and back to Noelle. "I'm fully aware of his record, and he's been a damn good worker since he started."

"I'm glad to hear it," said Evan. "Maybe he's been reformed."

The pulse at Graham's neck sped up, and he became motionless, every muscle turning to stone.

He looks ready to explode.

"How about last night, Graham? Were you at home?" asked Noelle.

"Yes," he said with a stiff jaw. "I'm living in a group halfway house for six months as part of my parole. All my comings and goings are recorded." He took a deep breath. "Just in case cops appear with trumped-up charges trying to pin shit on me that *I didn't do.*"

"What's this about?" asked the owner. "Does he need a lawyer?"

Evan was impressed that the man was ready to go to bat for Graham.

Maybe I should tell him about the son he abandoned.

And about the ex-girlfriend with cigarette burn scars on her shoulders.

Anger prickled along Evan's skin. "Sophia went missing overnight," he said, holding Graham's gaze. "Someone broke in. There are signs of a struggle and a lot of blood on the floor."

Graham's mouth opened slightly, and his eyes widened. Then a red flush swamped his face. "*I had nothing to do with that!* I haven't seen her in years!"

Evan and Noelle said nothing for a long moment, waiting to see if Graham would fill the awkward silence.

He did.

"I'm long past whatever went on between me and Sophia years ago. *It's over.* Never even think about the woman." Sweat beaded at his temples.

Do you think about your son?

"Hey, I'm sorry something happened to her," Graham continued in a calmer voice, as tendons bulged in his neck. "She was a decent kid. But I know nothing about it. You can talk to the manager where I live. He'll tell you I was home."

"What about her father?" asked Noelle.

Confusion crossed Graham's face as he straightened. "What about her father? I don't keep track of assholes."

Is he lying?

Evan had met incredible liars in his job. People who believed they could get away with anything as long as they kept repeating the same false story over and over in an effort to change what really happened. And others who Evan thought had been telling the truth but turned out to be lying nonstop. The world was full of them. Graham might have taken a how-to-lie-to-a-cop's-face course in prison.

"We just told you Sophia is missing," said Noelle. "Is there anything you'd like to ask us?"

Her voice may have sounded normal to Graham, but Evan picked up on the controlled fury.

She's also pissed that he didn't ask about Zack.

Graham's face went blank. "I don't know . . . Obviously you don't know where she is since you're harassing me. What is there for me to ask?"

Evan swore he could feel the waves of disgust rolling off Noelle. "Let it go," he said in a low aside to the detective. "He's not worth our time. He's not going to ever change."

Bafflement shone in Graham's eyes. "What the fuck are you talking about?"

"You didn't ask about your *son*!" Noelle snapped, leaning in a few inches.

Graham took a fast step back. Lawson's brows shot up, and he looked at Graham. "You never mentioned kids."

"I don't have kids! Well, not officially."

"Zack carries your DNA," said Evan. "But he's definitely *not* your son. He's a great kid. Smart, caring, gives a shit about people. He's Sophia through and through." He looked at Lawson. "I don't think he's ever seen the boy in person. He abandoned Sophia and was in prison by the time Zack was born." He turned to Graham. "I always thought Sophia was lucky you left. You gave her nothing except pain, humiliation, and scars."

"Evan," Noelle said in a low voice.

Graham took two aggressive strides toward Evan, his eyes bulging. Evan lurched out of the way.

Shock filled Graham's face and his shoulder jerked. He lost his balance and fell to one knee, his mouth wide open in shock.

The crack of the gunshot filled the air.

Graham's shot!

Evan dived to knock Lawson to the ground, and Noelle dropped. She reached out and yanked Graham to his stomach and then drew her weapon. Lawson curled into a ball with his hands protecting his head. Lying next to the man, Evan drew his gun, scanning the area for a shooter, seeing no one. They were ten yards from the shop and had no cover.

"*You Goddamned motherfucker!*" roared Graham. "*You fucking shot me!*" A painful moan came out of him.

"Who shot you?" shouted Evan, looking in every direction. "*Where is he?*"

"*You! You fucking police shot me!*"

Evan glanced at Graham. He gripped his upper arm, blood welling between his fingers as he writhed on the ground.

"Why the *fuck* did you do that?" yelled Graham.

"*We* didn't shoot you, you idiot!" Noelle shouted back.

A breath of air tickled Evan's hair above his ear, and a gunshot cracked again.

That shot almost got me.

He's in the trees.

Fifty yards away, a line of trees ran along the property to the west. No buildings were behind them, only fields. Evan fired several times, aiming a little high into the trees to make the shooter take cover.

"Noelle, can you get them to the door?" he asked. The shop was their best cover.

"Yes."

"Go. I'll cover." He fired again at the trees as Noelle hauled Graham to his feet. Lawson pulled on Graham's other arm, and they darted to the shop door, staying as low as possible.

A moment later, Noelle fired at the trees from the doorway. "Go!"

Evan lunged to his feet and ran.

It was chaos inside the shop.

Half the workers were running toward the office, yelling their heads off, and the other half—including Juniper—had taken cover behind cars and now had weapons trained on Evan's group.

Everybody carries.

"Where's the shooter?"

"Graham! You shot?"

"Who's shooting?"

The yells echoed off the metal walls.

"Put away your weapons," hollered Noelle. "And get the fuck down!" She pointed at Juniper. "You got a first aid kit here?"

The woman nodded, her pistol still in hand but no longer aimed at their group.

"Get it!" Noelle pointed at another employee. "Call 911! Shots fired. Tell them two county detectives are on the scene." She moved into position to cover the door they'd just dashed through.

"Everyone take cover and stay put!" yelled Evan. "Do *not* go outside!" He pulled Graham to a seated position on the floor and leaned him against a pickup's wheel. Blood soaked the man's coveralls and left arm. Evan unzipped the coveralls to Graham's stomach and pushed the sleeve down to get a look at his arm.

No spurting of blood. Just a small but steady flow from the wound in his bicep. The bullet had gone right through.

"Put pressure on that," he told Lawson. The owner ripped off his polo to press against the wound. Graham shrieked.

"He needs a tourniquet!" said Lawson.

"Just a lot of pressure," said Evan. "It's not arterial." His heart pounding, he joined Noelle to cover the door. She was on her phone, requesting backup and a perimeter.

"Did you see the shooter?" he asked as she ended her conversation.

"No." Her face was grim. She nodded toward Graham. "He okay?"

"Yeah. Upper arm. Through and through. Not arterial." Sirens sounded in the distance. "Anyone else hurt?"

"Doesn't appear so." She gave a shake of her head, disbelief in her eyes. "What the fuck just happened, Evan?"

"Don't know," he forced out between deep breaths, trying to slow his heart.

"If you hadn't moved when Graham lunged at you, you would have caught that bullet."

He'd thought the same, but his brain struggled to accept it.

"I felt the second shot breeze by my head," he said in a low voice. "But Graham was right there. I'm not sure who was the target."

"Rowan would have skinned me alive if I'd had to tell her you'd been shot," said Noelle. She leaned heavily against the wall. "Don't do that to me."

"Doing my best." He bent over, hands on his knees, as adrenaline dumped into his system and he fought back the nausea at the thought of a bullet hole in his head.

Were those shots meant for me?

9

Rowan took a sip of her soda as she studied her older brother.

"I want to make that." Malcolm's gaze was glued to the TV baking show, where stressed-out contestants were each attempting to assemble a complicated apricot couronne in the allotted time. "That looks awesome," he said as he stroked his dog, Zeke, on the sofa beside him.

Rowan agreed. Topped with icing and sliced almonds, the fancy, twisted sweet bread was packed with dried apricots and cranberries. "Let's plan it for our next baking day," she suggested, feeling simultaneously delighted and sad. Delighted that Malcolm was interested in tackling complicated recipes, and sad that he'd never cooked a meal or even baked a cookie until recently.

After seeing his fascination with baking shows, Rowan and her twin sisters had decided to have sibling baking days twice a month. The four of them would agree on a recipe and then have a baking contest to see who could make it the best. At first Malcolm had been paired with one of the sisters, but he'd studied and practiced all sorts of recipes and was now skilled enough to hold his own against the three women.

Rowan exchanged a grin with Iris. Having Malcolm back in their lives was a blessing and a true pleasure. Kidnapped when he was seven, Malcolm had lived twenty-five years under the cruel thumb of his abductor. No schooling, no friends, no belongings. Books had been his only friends, read on the sly when the kidnapper borrowed library books for himself. Last summer he'd escaped and made his way back to his family, deeply uncertain of his welcome because of lies told by his tormentor.

Malcolm had been skin and bones and could barely look a person in the eye when he returned. But with love, nutrition, and emotional support, he'd improved by leaps and bounds. He had put on weight and muscle and now was the spitting image of their father when he was younger. Rowan gave a lot of credit to his dog, Zeke, for helping him gain confidence and manage his anxiety. It had been her idea to get him a dog after seeing how often he sought Thor when he was stressed. Together they'd found the golden retriever mix at a rescue. The easygoing dog had immediately bonded with Malcolm, and Rowan suspected Zeke had felt how deeply her brother needed a pet of his own to love and care for.

Once a week the four siblings met up to watch reality TV and order takeout. Before Malcolm returned to their family, the sisters had usually watched trashy dating shows and emptied a few bottles of wine. Now they'd switched to food-oriented TV shows and cut way back on the alcohol because Malcolm hated the taste. Everyone was happy with the change. Rowan looked forward to the mental and emotional escape the evening always provided. She'd been thinking nonstop about Sophia McLeod and her father since hearing the news. The horrible situation made her appreciate her family even more tonight.

What would I do if my father was murdered like that?

She couldn't fathom it.

Rowan took a bite of chicken curry as she watched the bakers on TV scramble. Malcolm had chosen an Indian restaurant for that night's meal. The siblings rotated whose home they watched TV at and who got to choose the food. Malcolm's favorite food was cheeseburgers, but after he'd chosen McDonald's several times, the sisters rebelled and made a rule that if he wanted a burger, he had to pick a restaurant that wasn't fast food. He had slowly expanded his palate and now confidently selected restaurants with food he'd never tried.

Tonight they were at Iris's home. She shared the little house with her boyfriend, Matt, who didn't mind vanishing on the family's special night. Matt hung out with them plenty of other times and knew these nights were sacred to the siblings.

Iris's identical twin, Ivy, was sprawled in an easy chair, her feet up on an ottoman, her dark hair styled in a perfect flip and slicked back from her face with a black velvet headband. The twins were hairdressers and owned a successful Bend salon. While Ivy leaned more toward the elegant hairstyles and fashions of the mid–twentieth century, Iris liked to style her hair and dress with a theme. She'd been on a Barbie kick lately, and Rowan wondered how much she had spent on the numerous pink outfits.

"That is gorgeous," said Ivy as a baker took a couronne out of the oven. She took a long sip of wine, leaving red lipstick on her glass's rim. Ivy still enjoyed a glass of wine on their nights with Malcolm. "This is my night with no kid," she'd pointed out. "I can no longer enjoy a glass at home because I feel as if I must always stay on guard." Her son, West, was eight. Last summer he'd been kidnapped by one of the same men who'd taken Malcolm decades before. Rowan didn't know if Ivy would fully recover from the ordeal, no matter how much therapy she had. West had bounced back from the traumatic event much faster.

Thor nosed Rowan's hand, interested in her curry, and she scratched his chest instead. Realizing she wasn't going to share, he joined Zeke on the sofa, curling up so their backs were pressed together. The dogs had quickly become best buddies.

"Traitor," Rowan said softly, drawing a grin from Malcolm.

Ivy abruptly sat up straight in the easy chair. *"What the hell?"*

Malcolm jumped at her shout, and the dogs' heads shot up. Thor leaped off the sofa, looking to Rowan for instruction.

Ivy dashed across the family room to the tall stool where Iris sat at the kitchen bar, a glass of orange soda in her hand. Ivy snatched the glass away and lifted Iris's hand. "Why didn't you say anything?" she yelled at her twin, but then hugged her and started to cry.

Rowan exchanged a confused look with Malcolm and paused the TV show. Then she saw a diamond ring glitter on Iris's left hand during the hug.

She's engaged!

Her throat tight and tears starting, Rowan set down her chicken and came around the sofa. "Ivy has a point," she said as she hugged Iris. "Why didn't you tell us? When did this happen?"

Ivy continued to tearily berate her twin as she gripped Iris's hand and studied the ring.

"It happened this afternoon," Iris said, wiping her own tears. "I thought it'd be funny to see who noticed it first."

"It wasn't funny!" Ivy glared at her sister.

"Ivy almost gave me a heart attack," said Rowan. "And she terrified the dogs."

"Congratulations, Iris," Malcolm said with a wide smile, stretching past his sisters to give her a one-armed hug. "I really like Matt. I didn't know you were planning to get married."

"Me neither," admitted Iris. "We'd talked about it a few times but never said anything for certain. I knew I wanted to, but I wasn't certain he was on board yet." She lifted her hand to look at the ring. "I guess he was."

"How did he do it?" asked Ivy. "Where did he do it? Were you surprised? Oh my God . . . *did anyone record it?* I'll be furious if I can't see how it happened."

"Slow down," said Iris. "He had a friend record it, so relax. He knew you'd have his head if he didn't. We went for a walk along the Deschutes. You know where the newer footbridge is? He asked me there. Went down on one knee and everything." She smiled, a dreamy look in her eyes. "We had our first kiss there last year."

"I'm still going to kill him," muttered Ivy. "He should have first talked to me about this."

Rowan snorted, amused by Ivy's annoyance. "You're not Iris's keeper."

"Well, I know marriage isn't to be taken lightly. *Do not* go to Vegas," she ordered her twin.

Ivy's marriage had lasted two months. She'd been young, and he'd been a jerk. Rowan had done something similar. A short-lived marriage a decade ago had been a very wrong decision, and she'd learned the same lesson as Ivy.

"Do Mom and Dad know?" asked Rowan.

"No. We'll tell them together tomorrow."

"At least I'm not the *last* person to know," Ivy grumbled. "Now. I think this calls for ice cream. Lots and lots of ice cream."

Malcolm's face lit up. "On it." He strode to the fridge and took three cartons out of the freezer. "You were prepared," he said to Iris.

She grinned back. "I knew we'd be celebrating tonight. And ice cream would be everyone's first choice. You're all rather predictable."

Rowan laughed and grabbed large bowls out of a cupboard. She set them on the counter and looked up to catch Ivy speculatively studying her.

She's wondering about me and Evan.

"No," Rowan told her firmly, glaring hard. "You're jumping way ahead. One engagement at a time. Evan and I aren't at that point anyway." They hadn't discussed marriage. Early on she'd told Evan about her previous one, and it hadn't come up again.

Her phone rang, and she crossed the kitchen to get it out of her bag. "Speak of the devil." A smile crossed her lips. Her usual reaction when he called.

"Hi," she answered. "We were just talking about you."

"I'm okay," Evan said, his voice sounding strained. "I wanted to call you before you heard something through the grapevine. I wasn't hurt."

Rowan's stomach dropped to her feet. "What?" she asked hoarsely. "What happened?" Her siblings turned to her, alarm on their faces.

"There was a shooting at an auto body shop outside of town. Noelle and I were there questioning a subject. Everyone is fine."

Relief swamped her. "Good."

"Well . . . our subject got shot, but it's a clean wound through his arm."

"He was shot? Who shot him?"

"Don't know. It happened outside the shop, and no one saw anything. It'll be a late night. Don't wait up." Someone spoke to him in the background. "I'll be right there," replied Evan. "I gotta go," he told Rowan. "I love you."

"Stay as long as you need. Love you too."

He was gone.

She slowly lowered the phone. "There was a shooting. Evan was there, but he and Noelle are fine."

"Did someone die?" asked Malcolm, his face white. He'd seen too much death in his past.

"No. Someone got shot in the arm. Not law enforcement." Her spike of adrenaline drained away, and she tried to relax. "Let's eat ice cream." She had to force the words, wanting to distract herself and her siblings from Evan's call.

The other three exchanged glances. "Are you okay?" asked Ivy, her forehead wrinkled with concern.

"Yeah. It was an abrupt shock at first, but since he's okay, I'm good." No one looked convinced. "Just waiting for my heart to slow."

"You're staying here tonight," announced Iris. "No excuses."

Rowan eyed her sister's determined face. The stubborn twins dug in their heels when they made decisions. It was easiest to go along with what they wanted. Rowan had suddenly felt very vulnerable, and not sleeping in an empty house sounded comforting.

Evan's job put him in dangerous situations. Not as often as when he had been a deputy, but often enough to make Rowan worry she'd get that phone call that all law enforcement families dread.

"That sounds great," she told Iris. "I'll let Evan know I won't be at home." She tapped a text on her phone. "Now can we have ice cream? I really need it."

Really, really need it.

Malcolm dug into the cookies and cream.

She'd see Evan tomorrow.

10

Evan was on his third cup of morning office coffee. A clear sign it'd been a long night.

He'd slept four restless hours and woken very disoriented when his alarm went off and he noticed that Rowan's side of the bed was empty. It'd taken at least five seconds before he remembered that she'd stayed overnight at her sister's home. The realization left him feeling incomplete; something important was missing.

How quickly I adjusted to her presence.

Last night she'd texted him that Iris was engaged and sent a picture of the twins. Iris gleefully held her hand toward the camera, a diamond on her finger, while Ivy pressed a kiss into her twin's cheek, her arms wrapped around her in a big hug. Evan had smiled at the photo. The twins weren't like Rowan. They were loud and emotional—in a good way—and friends to everyone. The twins took after their dad in looks and personality, while Rowan had been made in her mother's image. He'd texted back, telling her to pass on his congratulations, and then had stared at the photo for a few long moments.

A sharp and very clear image had grown in his mind. One of him and Rowan marrying. He could see it clear as day. He'd closed his phone and stood silent in the dark outside the auto body shop. They'd never had that discussion.

We haven't been together long enough.

But he knew she was the one for him. Knew deep down in his soul. He'd known that day the previous summer when he'd gone to her house to update her on a case and seen her in the backyard, working with Thor.

I don't know what she thinks.

She had a bad marriage in the past.

He put the thought out of his mind and returned to the shooting investigation. He and Noelle had stayed late at the auto body shop, interviewing employees and searching in the dark for the location where the shooter had hidden. At about 1:00 a.m. a deputy had found a thin broken branch on a tree in the general direction from which the detectives thought the shots had originated. The short branch had been twisted and shoved downward, leaving it hanging parallel to the tree's trunk. The leaves and inside flesh of the branch looked fresh and healthy, not dried out. It'd been broken recently.

Evan had stood near the tree trunk and looked toward the shop. The branch would have blocked his view of where they had spoken to Charlie Graham. No footprints had been discernible under the tree, and when Evan stepped away, he noticed his shoes had also left no sign, the leaves and rocks disguising all prints. No shells were found either. Using the tree as a starting point, law enforcement had fanned out in the early-morning hours, searching for any sign that someone had recently been in the area. The trees filled five acres, and they found nothing besides faded beer cans and old garbage.

The shooter had vanished, slipping through the wide perimeter that law enforcement had created around the shop. Evan was disappointed but not too surprised. Perimeters were tough to implement and monitor when they contained large undeveloped areas with no roads. Especially in the dark. Thankfully, there weren't homes in the immediate area. The shooter could have entered one and created a hostage situation.

Today a team of teenage explorers would search in the morning light, and a forensics team would look for the bullets. One of the bullets had gone through the wall of the shop and then disappeared in the automotive debris, while the one that had passed near Evan's head had vanished. Evan suspected it had gone into the ground but hadn't been able to find it last night.

Interviews with the body shop employees did not turn up leads to a possible shooter. Even Charlie Graham stated he hadn't made any enemies since getting out of prison. He claimed he'd kept his head down and focused on work, wanting a peaceful life. Not returning to the reckless way he had lived before.

Evan wondered if it could have been an old enemy taking a shot at Graham.

Or at me.

As he sat in the conference room, he couldn't stop thinking about that possibility while reviewing a list of people who had received prison sentences as a result of Rod McLeod's efforts *and* were no longer locked up.

Was I the target?

He shook his head, trying to focus. Finding Rod's killer was his priority at the moment.

One of his team members had already winnowed down the list of Rod's cases, eliminating people who had moved to different states and then finding the current locations of the others through phone calls and internet searches. Evan was amused at how many were easy to find on social media, their accounts public for the world to see.

Evan had further narrowed the prospects to people who lived in Deschutes County and ended up with a list of eleven local names. Nine men and two women. He hated the feeling that he'd just filtered out the person he sought, but it made sense to start geographically close to the crime. If they could eliminate these eleven, then he'd expand. None of the eleven cases had been in Rod's file cabinet. Evan didn't know if that meant Rod hadn't copied them or if one—or more—had been removed.

He still hadn't figured out the files' common denominator.

Time is slipping away.

Across the table, Noelle had a giant to-go cup of coffee next to her computer. She'd taken a detour on her way to work and picked up her coffee and a dozen croissants from the French bakery on the other side of town. Evan had no doubts that her coffee tasted much better than his cup of office brew. He'd eaten one croissant; it was like eating buttery air. Delicious but not filling. His stomach grumbled.

I'll get something of substance later.

"I've got a lead on a vehicle in the right time frame for Sophia," said Noelle. "A doorbell camera picked up a minivan that drove by around three p.m. and then again in the opposite direction just after midnight."

"On her street?"

"No. On the cross street of that new development's road on the other side of the gully."

Evan pulled up a map. "That's a busy street."

"Not at midnight. That time of night gave me fewer vehicles to check. I like that this driver could have gone to the site early, parked, and then chosen a time in the dark to break in. He probably watched the house for quite a while."

"True. License plate?"

"Yes. Nice and sharp. I pulled up the registration. It belongs to a couple who live in the Awbrey Butte part of town—I suspect they're married since the last names are the same."

"A couple seems odd for a possibility," said Evan. "And a minivan is typically the wife's vehicle. I'm not feeling a woman for Rod's murder, even though I've got two women on my list. Physically they'd need help getting him into that junkyard trunk. He wasn't small."

Noelle nodded. "Maybe the husband is doing something the wife is completely unaware of . . . maybe he uses her vehicle sometimes. Or they are in it together."

Evan checked his list. "I've got two people to check out in the same part of town. Want to hit them all together? Since it's Sunday morning, I bet we'll have good luck."

"It's early."

"Even better to catch people at home."

Noelle stood. "Let's go."

Twenty minutes later, they parked down the street from a newer gray house with a silver minivan in the driveway. "Looks like someone's home," said Evan. "What're their names again?"

"Brandon and Courtney Strudwick. He's twenty-eight, and she's twenty-five. No priors."

"Young."

"Yes." Noelle's voice lacked conviction.

It doesn't feel right to her either.

They went up the steps to the porch after confirming the minivan's license plate matched Noelle's record. Each moved to one side of the front door, and Noelle rang the bell. After a long moment she rang it again. "Maybe no one is—wait, someone's coming," she said.

Evan sensed that someone used the peephole, and then the door opened. A young woman in pajama pants with a crease running down her cheek stared at them through the screen door.

We woke her up.

"Can I help you?" She clearly wasn't happy but kept her tone polite.

Evan and Noelle showed their IDs and introduced themselves. The woman's eyes widened at the sight of the badges, and she straightened. "Is Brandon okay? What happened?"

"We aren't here about Brandon," said Noelle. "Are you Courtney Strudwick?"

"Yes." Her expression relaxed a fraction. "Why?"

"We have some questions about your minivan."

Her gaze went to the vehicle and her brows came together. "Did someone hit it?"

"No. Can you confirm that it was driven on Northwest Stevens Street the day before yesterday around three p.m.?"

"Of course. I was on my way to work. Was there an accident on that street? I don't recall one."

"Where do you work?" asked Noelle.

"St. Charles. In the ICU."

A justification of Evan's earlier doubts swept over him. "You must get off work around midnight."

"That's right."

Which explains the return trip and why we just woke her.

"Was anyone else riding with you? Did you make a stop on the way to work?" asked Noelle.

Her tone told Evan she had mentally crossed the Strudwicks off her suspect list. Now she was just winding up any possible loose ends.

"No and no," said Courtney. She frowned. "What's this about?"

"There *was* an accident nearby," Noelle lied. "Your plate was picked up on a camera. We'd hoped you'd seen something."

"Not that I remember," said Courtney.

Noelle held out a business card, and Courtney unlocked the screen door to take it. "Call us if you think of anything," Noelle told the woman with a perfect white smile.

She and Evan headed back to their car. "Waste of my time," Noelle muttered. "I should have sent the deputy that I have checking out other leads."

"When my gut instructs me to take a look, I go," said Evan.

"Same," said Noelle. "My gut was fifty-fifty on this lead. From now on I'll only go in person when it's stronger."

"On to the next."

The next was an old pink house a dozen streets away from the Strudwick home. Evan was looking to interview Archie Crook, who had served eleven years in prison—thanks to Rod McLeod—and been out for six. He'd stayed out of trouble since then and had only picked up a warning for loitering downtown.

"I'd change my last name," said Noelle as they approached the pink house. "He must get harassed with a name like that. I imagine in prison he really caught a lot of shit about it."

When they knocked on the door, an older woman with a suspicious gaze directed them to walk around her home to a small guesthouse on her property. She said Archie had lived there since he got out of prison.

Evan had been a deputy when Archie Crook was sentenced. He didn't recall hearing of the case, and he'd never crossed paths with the man—that he was aware of. Archie's driver's license showed he was six feet three, 210 pounds, and forty-two years old. In Evan's opinion, the size made him big enough to lift Rod's body or to wrestle Sophia into submission. The case file mentioned a lot of animosity toward Rod and the officers during his arrest.

But that's not unusual.

They rounded the house and spotted a tiny pink building set back about fifty yards. As they moved toward the home, a man yanked open the door and dashed toward the back of the property. He hadn't looked their way.

"There he goes!" shouted Noelle, and she tore after him. "Deschutes County sheriff! Stop!"

Evan was a split second behind Noelle. He turned up his speed, drew even with her, and then realized it wouldn't be a difficult chase. Either Archie Crook had lied on his driver's license or he'd drastically gained weight since it was issued. The heavy man struggled to run.

By the time Evan and Noelle caught up to him, Archie was in a slow, awkward jog. Noelle reached out and gave his shoulder a hard shove. "Sheriff's department! I told you to stop!"

Archie stopped and rested his hands on his thighs, panting for air.

"Hands behind your back!" ordered Evan. The man complied, and Evan grabbed one arm and snapped on a cuff. The cuffs wouldn't reach the other wrist.

"Here." Noelle handed Evan her set.

He linked their cuffs and placed Noelle's on Archie's other wrist. Archie continued to pant heavily, his wide face a fiery red, and Evan worried he was about to deal with a heart attack. While reviewing CPR steps in his head, he did a quick search of Archie for weapons and then tugged up Archie's sweatpants, which had slipped several inches during the run. Archie Crook needed a shower. He smelled as if he'd been sleeping in his clothes for several days, and his hair was long and stringy with some strands dangling in his eyes. The man blew at them, an unsuccessful attempt to get them out of the way.

"Why'd you run, Archie?" asked Noelle. With one finger she moved the hair out of his line of sight.

He looked her up and down, seeming confused. And then his gaze locked on her shoes. "You ran after me in heels?" he asked in a shocked tone.

Noelle shrugged. "And? They're boots."

She wasn't wearing the highest heels Evan had seen on her, and the boots had a decent heel width, unlike some of her shoes. He didn't understand how women's fragile-looking spiked heels didn't break.

"Looks like you didn't ruin your shoes this time," Evan told her, referring to a story about a time when she'd sprinted after her suspect, caught him, but ruined her expensive high-heeled pumps.

Noelle snorted. "That's a rumor. Never happened. Don't know who spread that one around."

Evan was 95 percent certain she was lying.

Hysterical, loud laughter sounded behind them, and they looked toward the house. On the rickety back deck, the woman who'd answered the door watched them. "Gotcha, Archie!" She whooped and laughed again, pointing at Archie. "You shoulda seen you run! I haven't seen your fat ass move like that in years!"

"What a bitch," Noelle muttered as they marched Archie toward the home, each gripping an arm.

"That's my mom," Archie said, staring at the ground. "She doesn't mean it."

Evan felt a twinge of sympathy at Archie's hangdog expression. "Did she warn you that we were here?"

"Yeah. She called and said there was a whole bunch of angry cops looking for me, and that I better get out of the house. She claimed she'd told them I was down the street to give me a chance to get away."

"Now I *really* think she's a bitch." Fury filled Noelle's voice. "That's why you ran?"

"Wouldn't you?"

"Not if I didn't have reason for the police to be looking for me— even then I wouldn't run. What's your reason?"

"I didn't do nothing," Archie stated emphatically. "But they pin stuff on people, you know? Always looking for an easy mark to take the fall."

Noelle and Evan exchanged a glance, and she rolled her eyes.

"Well, I'm sure you two aren't like that," Archie amended a few seconds later. "You seem honest."

Evan bit his tongue to avoid a laugh. "Where did you plan to go?"

Archie shrugged. "Dunno. Didn't think about it. Just reacted."

"Can you come do that every day so he gets some exercise?" Archie's mom shouted, and then slapped her thigh as she chortled gleefully.

"I'm not taking back my bitch remarks," said Noelle.

"Oh, I don't mind," Archie said earnestly. "It's accurate." He paused for a moment. "But don't let her hear you say it," he whispered.

Evan felt bad for the guy, and he stopped their walk to the house. His gut told him that Archie wasn't their man. "Archie, where were you Friday night?"

Archie looked at the sky as he thought. "I went bowling. Got home around eleven."

"And then what?"

His eyebrows rose. "Went to bed, of course."

Not the best alibi.

His presence at the bowling alley could be checked, but time sleeping could not. "Who did you bowl with?"

"My buddy Jake."

"What kind of car do you drive?"

"Don't have one. I Ubered."

That can be verified too.

Noelle frowned. "You don't have a vehicle?"

"Don't have the money right now. If I need to go somewhere, I Uber."

"Does your mom take you sometimes?" Evan glanced at the house, where Mrs. Crook still watched them from the deck, a frown on her face. She seemed annoyed that he and Noelle hadn't joined in her harassment of Archie.

"She's always busy."

"She won't lend you her car?"

Archie's face fell. "No one drives it but her."

Evan met Noelle's gaze as he considered. "What kind of car does she have?"

"A Corolla."

Noelle gave a small shake of her head.

Too tiny a trunk and back seat to move a body as big as Rod's.

Archie's mother wasn't much smaller than he was. She leaned heavily on the railing to support herself, giving the impression that she didn't have much strength. Between the two of them, they couldn't have maneuvered Rod's body without a lot of help.

The chance that Archie was their man was evaporating.

"I'd like to take a quick look at it." Evan would be remiss if he didn't at least check the Corolla.

Discomfort flickered in Archie's eyes. "*You'll* have to ask her. Not me."

"On it," said Noelle. She headed toward his mother and engaged her in conversation.

Evan couldn't hear what Noelle said, but Mrs. Crook's expression went from annoyed to curious. He knew Noelle would get access to the car. She had an enviable skill of telling people what she wanted them to do and making them think it had been their own idea.

Noelle looked back at Evan. "We'll meet you out front." She took the stairs to the deck and followed Mrs. Crook into the home.

"I didn't think Mom would let her look," said Archie in a stunned tone as he and Evan walked to the side of the home.

As they came around to the driveway, the garage door rolled up. The old silver Corolla's back driver's side door was open, and Noelle had her head in the car, using her flashlight to look around. Mrs. Crook stood near the door into the house, reciting a recipe for beef stew, and Noelle made polite noises in response, carrying out her search. "I'm going to pop the trunk," Noelle said. Mrs. Crook didn't pause. She prattled on, describing the "proper way" to brown the stew meat.

The trunk opened, and Evan stepped forward to look, confirming that it was too small. The trunk was packed with overflowing black garbage bags. Clothes and books and old dishes had spilled out and cluttered the space.

"I keep forgetting to drop off that stuff at Goodwill," said Mrs. Crook in the middle of her monologue about potatoes.

Noelle pushed aside a few things to get a look at the carpet of the trunk. She met Evan's gaze and shook her head.

Nothing.

Evan removed Archie's cuffs. The man rubbed at his wrists and frowned. "What was this all about?"

"Just needed to know where you were Friday night. If you hadn't run, we would have asked and left."

Archie nodded, giving a cautious side-eye to his mother, who was accepting a business card from Noelle.

"I'll email the recipe right away," Mrs. Crook said enthusiastically, waving the card, as Noelle turned away and strode to Evan.

"Let's go. Now," she whispered. Evan said a rapid goodbye, and the two of them headed to his vehicle.

"What did you say to the mother inside the house?" he asked as they pulled shut the SUV's doors. "It was like she went through a magic portal and came out a different person."

"She had stew on the stove. I said it smelled delicious, and then suddenly I'm her best friend, and she wouldn't stop talking after that."

"And now she has your email. And phone number."

Noelle moaned.

"I take it her car's back seat was clean?"

"Clean? No. But it was clear a body hadn't been in there. It had as many bags as the trunk, and they were covered in just as much dust."

"Two strikes this morning," Evan said. "I've got one more stop, and then we can head back."

Noelle checked her phone. "The blood spatter specialist is finished at Sophia's. He'll have a report for me tomorrow."

"Anything on the BOLO for her car?"

"No."

Rod's vehicle was also still missing.

"Ah, jeez. I just got an email from Mrs. Crook."

Evan grinned.

"Crap. And she sent *another one.*"

"Are they recipes?"

"Yes." Noelle sighed. "I won't respond." She snorted. "And there's number three. This time she forwarded a link to what she says is a cat video. Oh, Lord. And here's two more emails with cat video links."

"Don't click."

"No shit. I'll have to block her." She set down her phone. "Now I feel bad."

"Don't. She may be lonely, but she stepped over a line with those emails."

Noelle's phone rang. "That better not be Mrs. Crook," she muttered.

Evan grinned. "She wants to know why you're not responding to her emails."

"Detective Marshall," she answered. After a second she caught Evan's gaze and shook her head.

Not Mrs. Crook.

"You said it's from Friday?" Noelle asked into the phone, her voice tight. "Can you send me the footage? How did you hear about her?" She ended the call a few seconds later. "I need to go back to the office. You'll have to check your next suspect without me."

"What happened?"

"That was Sophia's bank. She withdrew ten thousand dollars in cash on Friday."

Evan turned the vehicle around.

11

Evan's second suspect visit would have to wait.

Back in the conference room, he, Noelle, and Detective Maxine Nelson watched as Sophia entered the bank at 11:03 a.m. on Friday. Noelle had pulled up the video on a large monitor, and the image was crystal clear.

"Why isn't all the footage we get this sharp?" muttered Maxine. She'd been a detective for nearly a decade. She was tall and thin with deep-set eyes. Evan knew her to be a good investigator. Her task that morning was going through the files from Rod's home with a fine-tooth comb, searching for the elusive reason that Rod had decided to keep copies. Evan had taken a quick look through all of them with no success and then asked Maxine to dig deeper.

"It's a big bank," said Evan with a shrug. "They want to see absolutely everything and will pay for the best technology." He leaned forward as Noelle froze the video. On-screen Sophia was stiff shouldered, and her mouth was tight. She wasn't the easygoing woman he knew. "She looks stressed."

Both women nodded in agreement, and Noelle started the video again. Three people were ahead of Sophia in line, and two tellers worked behind the counter. Sophia moved from foot to foot as she waited, constantly turning her head to look around the bank.

She's scared.

Sophia finally reached a teller window, giving the camera a view of her back.

"Are there other angles?" asked Evan. He wanted to see her face.

"Yes. Hang on." Noelle made a few clicks, and the video abruptly shifted to a view from above and behind a teller, which showed every movement of her hands. Noelle fast-forwarded until Sophia approached the teller. Her countenance had changed; now she was smiling and cheerful.

"She's faking it," said Evan. He knew what she looked like when she was happy; this wasn't it. "Something is up."

"Do you think the money is for her or for someone else?" asked Maxine.

"Not sure," said Evan. "Either way, I suspect it's related to her dad."

"Blackmail?" suggested Noelle. "Maybe they asked for money to let him go?"

"It's possible he was already dead when this was filmed," said Evan.

"She probably wasn't aware of that," said Noelle.

Sophia continued to chat with the teller as she got her money. When she walked away, Evan asked for a different video angle, and Noelle found one that showed Sophia's face as she walked to the door.

"She's crying," said Noelle. "This definitely has to be related to her dad."

An outside angle showed Sophia getting into her missing car. Her car didn't leave for a full three minutes, and no other outdoor cameras could show what she was doing inside.

"This tells us that the attack in her home happened after eleven a.m. on Friday," said Evan. "Clearly she is physically okay in this video."

"Or maybe they forced her to go to the bank to withdraw the money?" suggested Noelle.

"And had her drive her own vehicle? The bloody mess could have happened after she returned with the money."

"Is she the type of woman who'd return?" asked Maxine. "Or would she just keep driving? If they forced her, why didn't she slip a note to the teller or something?"

"Because they're holding something over her head," speculated Evan. "Most likely they're threatening to kill her father. It doesn't look like anyone else is in the vehicle." He leaned closer to the screen. "But they could be hiding below the windows."

"I bet she's on her phone," said Noelle with a frown. She turned from the big monitor to her laptop. "I still don't have her cell phone records. I'll call and light a fire under someone."

"You got her credit cards and banking information already, right?" asked Evan.

"Yes. There were no big purchases on her credit cards in the last few months. The last charge was five days ago at Chevron. The bank account records I received didn't show this big withdrawal," said Noelle, "because she made it from the florist shop's business account, which was under her partner's name. Sophia is just an authorized signer on the account, but one of the bank employees who knows Sophia made the connection after I requested her records. Evan, you said Sophia was the shop's owner, but it looks like everything is under her partner, Tara Tilson."

"I thought Sophia owned it." Evan frowned. "I swear she told me that. I've met Tara before."

"She's on my list to contact," said Noelle. "Tara is the only name I have as far as Sophia's friends, and there doesn't appear to be any other family to question."

"At least I know who a lot of Rod's friends are." He grimaced. "Or I used to. I haven't contacted any of them yet."

"Want me to contact Rod's friends?" asked Maxine.

"I'll get you a list."

"I've got a phone number for Tara Tilson," said Noelle. "Since you've met her, Evan, why don't you call while I find out what the holdup is on the cell phone records?"

He punched the number into his phone, and Noelle stepped out of the room for her call, which he assumed would be rather loud and a bit heated if she didn't get the answers she wanted. He put Tara's call on speaker so Maxine could listen.

"Hello?"

"Tara? It's Evan Bolton. I'm a friend of Sophia and Rod McLeod. We met at—"

"I remember you, Detective. We met a few times at Rod's house when he barbecued. I think one time was for Zack's tenth birthday. What can I do for you?"

"Tara, are you at home?" Evan hated to break bad news if she was out somewhere.

"I am." Her tone grew cautious. "What's wrong?"

"You're on speaker with Detective Maxine Nelson and myself. I'm calling from the sheriff's department. I'm sorry to tell you this, but Sophia is missing, and we're in the middle of an investigation. Have you talked to her recently?"

I'll tell her about Rod in a minute. One piece of horrible news at a time.

"What do you mean *missing*? Rod doesn't know where she is either?"

Evan avoided her second question. "Someone broke into her house Friday or Saturday. Her purse and cell phone are there, but her car is missing."

"Oh my God." She sucked in a breath. "What about Zack?"

"Zack is fine. He had spent a few nights at a friend's."

"Okay . . . let me think . . . she texted me on Thursday evening to say she was sick and asked if I could cover Friday on my own. Usually just one of us is in the store every day, but Friday and Saturday are too busy and we're both needed." Her words came fast, worry in her voice. "Where do you think she went? That's not like her to leave her phone behind."

"Tara, what time was that Thursday text?" asked Evan.

"Hang on . . . 10:14 that evening."

"When did you last speak to her in person?"

"I worked with her last Saturday. I'm checking my phone log, and I don't have any calls from her since then. We texted a few times about work-related things last week. That's it. Who do you think broke into her house?"

"That's what we're trying to figure out. Say, I could have sworn Sophia told me she was the owner of Blossom Bounty, but on paper it looks like you are. Do you have some sort of partnership?"

"We were both on all documents for a long time, but about six months ago Sophia asked if everything could be put in my name. She was worried about Zack's father, I think. She didn't want him getting out of prison and going after custody of Zack and some of her money."

Sounds like she knew he was getting out early.

"She really trusted you."

"We trust each other," she said simply. "Her ex is out now; did you know that? He'd be the first person I'd contact about her."

"We've already gone to see him," said Evan.

"Good. He sounds like a real son of a bitch. Did you know she has cigarette burn scars from him?"

"I do know that." An image of the burns clear in his head.

"Was it Rod who discovered the break-in at Sophia's?" asked Tara. "He must be out of his mind with worry."

Evan gripped his phone. He preferred to give this kind of news in person. "I'm sorry, Tara, but Rod was killed. His body was found Saturday morning. So you can understand why we're searching hard for Sophia."

The line was silent.

"Rod is dead?" she asked hesitantly. "Was he found at Sophia's?"

"He wasn't. Her break-in was discovered when we went to notify her."

"This isn't happening." She was crying, her voice garbled and wet sounding.

"If you could give me the names, addresses, and phone numbers of your employees, I'd like to talk to them," said Evan. "Can you think of any reason why Sophia would vanish? Or someone who'd want to hurt her? Or hurt Rod?"

"I'm sorry, Evan, I really don't know. She isn't the type of person that makes enemies."

"Very true. Has there been any trouble at the store? Problem customers . . . or employees?"

"No. It's been going great. We had our best first quarter ever."

The money.

"Tara, did you know that Sophia took ten thousand dollars in cash out of the business account on Friday?"

Her silence answered him.

"I don't understand why she would do that," Tara said slowly. "Especially without talking to me about it. We need that to make payroll." Tara wasn't angry. She was confused. "It must be related to her disappearance. Maybe someone forced her."

"We're looking into everything we can," Evan said, staying vague.

Noelle came back in the room. "Evan, guess—oh! Sorry." Maxine had indicated they were on a call.

"Tara, I need to go. Please let me know if you think of something."

"I don't want to tell my employees," said Tara, her voice cracking. "We're a tight family. I don't want to upset them in case Sophia comes back."

"You'll find a way to tell them," said Evan. "You should before we talk to them." He glanced at Noelle, who was clearly struggling to stay quiet.

She has something.

Evan quickly ended the call. "What is it?" he asked Noelle.

"They're emailing the cell records and location tracking in a minute, but I asked if he could tell me her last activity. He said she sent a few texts Thursday evening and made one phone call."

"One of the texts will be to Tara," said Evan. "She just told me. Let's figure out who else she texted and then called." He turned to his laptop.

"That's not all."

The suppressed excitement in her voice made him look back at her.

"This isn't much help," said Noelle, "but it definitely stands out. Besides her phone activity, I requested her location tracking too. He mentioned after she made the last call on Thursday, she turned off her phone. They don't have any location tracking from Thursday evening until yesterday at her house. It was at the time I turned on her phone."

Evan let that news digest. "She didn't want to be tracked after Thursday evening?"

"Or she was told to turn it off," said Maxine.

"How could she go so long with her phone off?" asked Evan. "What if Zack needed her? I can't imagine that she would go to bed Thursday night with it off."

"Are you suggesting she wasn't alone at the house?" asked Noelle.

"It's a good possibility. Why don't we have the forensics report on her home yet?" He checked his email again but still hadn't received it. "They should have at least run the fingerprints. We usually get that information pretty quickly."

"It'll come soon, I'm sure," said Noelle. "Check these phone numbers he gave me."

Evan typed in the phone numbers. "As I expected, one text is to Tara Tilson. There are a few to Zack . . . and one to someone else." He pulled up a record for the number. "Oh. This one is the friend's mother where Zack spent the night. She must have been checking on him." He typed in the number for the last phone call made Thursday night. "The call went to a burner phone."

"Who would she call?" asked Noelle. "With what we saw on the cameras and now this news, I think it's a very strong possibility that Sophia was being manipulated."

Evan picked up the department phone and punched in the number of the prepaid phone. "A call is the easiest way to figure out whose number it is," he said as he listened to it ring, mentally crossing his fingers. It went to a generic recording saying the person wasn't available. "Good morning," Evan said after the voicemail's beep. "This is Detective Bolton with the Deschutes County sheriff. I'd appreciate a call back." He left his work cell number.

Noelle didn't look optimistic.

Evan shrugged. "Can't hurt to try. Could be the person who manipulated Sophia."

"And now knows the police are involved in her case," said Maxine.

"It's a burner. They used it because they knew we'd investigate."

"Or it's simply a friend who uses that type of phone," said Noelle.

"Touché." Noelle was right. "But unless someone calls back, I think we've taken that phone call lead as far as we can for the moment, so what's next?" It was a rhetorical question. They all had a hundred things to do *next*.

"Any word from the explorers searching the grounds at the body shop?" asked Noelle.

"Nothing. It's a little early, though." Evan recalled the near-silent whiz past his ear yesterday. It still made the hair on his arms stand up. "I'm still not sure who was being shot at," he said slowly. The question had haunted him since it happened.

"You can't think they were shooting at you, Evan," said Maxine, surprise on her face.

"I can't ignore it," said Evan.

Noelle leaned back in her chair. "Let's hash it out a bit. There are three possibilities. They were shooting at Charlie Graham, you, or were just shooting for the hell of it."

"Can't rule out you or the shop owner," Evan said.

"I'd say the odds are much lower. The shots weren't anywhere near me or Lawson." She gave him an appraising look. "Both came closest to you."

My thoughts exactly.

He'd repeatedly told himself he wasn't the target, but he knew he was lying. Noelle had stated it out loud and his gut agreed. The expression on Noelle's face said she was simply waiting for him to realize it. "I don't have time for this," he told her. "Rod and Sophia are the priority."

"Yes, but we were working on their case when it happened. It's most likely connected to the whole mess."

"It is a mess, isn't it?" Evan had struggled to keep the threads of the investigations neat and orderly, but they kept crossing and tying themselves in knots.

"That's only temporary," said Noelle. "We'll have everything lined up in neat rows soon."

Evan snorted. "Have you ever had a case do that?"

"No. But I can dream." She checked the time. "Didn't you tell Bridget you'd be there this morning to interview Zack? I'll dig into Sophia's cell records. I'd like to know if she called that burner more than once."

"Yep." He stood and packed up his laptop. The second suspect he'd wanted to visit that morning would have to be pushed out again. "I'll be back in an hour or two."

12

Rowan and Thor rode with Evan to interview Zack at the Kerr ranch.

She listened as Evan talked about a dozen investigation elements that still needed to be addressed. The combined investigations involving Rod and Sophia McLeod—and the shooting at the auto body shop—had dozens of moving parts. Rowan could tell Evan was struggling to keep all the balls in the air. He looked very tired, and his eyes were bloodshot.

He gives it his all.

She loved that about him. He had a big heart and a strong sense of duty, and he cared deeply about victims—all victims. He took his job seriously and sometimes believed he was the only person who could find justice for a victim. He didn't like to let people down.

And this case was personal. Doubly personal since he was searching for answers about both Rod and Sophia. Two people close to his heart.

Then there was Zack. Evan had told her he didn't want Zack to wait years to find out what had happened to his mother, as Evan had had to wait when his sister vanished. He was determined to not put the boy through that suffering. Rowan studied his profile. The stubborn set to Evan's mouth stated his mission: bring the boy's mother home.

That was priority number one. Find Sophia before she ended up like Rod.

Yesterday Rowan had been at Evan's sister's ranch to get Zack settled, and Bridget had asked a question about a rescue dog's odd skin condition. After looking the dog over, Rowan had suggested a different food and promised to bring a bag the next day. The dog food bag sat on the back seat next to Thor, who had sniffed it several times and then turned pleading eyes to Rowan.

/snacks/

"Not now."

/snacks/

"That's not for you."

Thor lay down on the seat and blew out his breath in a huff, accepting her statement but making it clear he wasn't happy about it.

"I haven't been out here in a while," said Evan as they finally came in sight of the Kerr ranch. The property was hidden away, several miles from any main roads. Bridget and Victor Kerr had been preppers for a long time and valued their privacy away from the world.

It was a peaceful place, and Rowan always relaxed when she visited. She hoped Evan would feel the rural farm's effects. He needed a few moments of serenity before he attended Rod's autopsy today. She'd weakly suggested one of the other detectives go instead. Evan hadn't said anything; he'd just looked at her.

I knew better.

They parked near the house. Rowan grabbed the sack of dog food out of the back seat, and Thor leaped out. Bridget came out of the house holding the hand of Molly, her two-year-old. She hugged Evan and gave him a kiss on the cheek. Evan hoisted Molly into the air, making her squeal with joy, and Bridget took the dog food from Rowan. "Thank you so much. I hope this makes Rex feel better."

"Me too," said Rowan. "Where is everyone?" she asked as she scanned the outbuildings. The Kerrs had added heated dog kennels, a cat and kitten house, and another barn since they decided to start an animal rescue the previous summer. It went against a tenet of prepping to have so many animals that didn't earn their keep, but the Kerrs had decided animal rescue was their new passion. An inheritance from Victor Kerr's grandfather had made it possible. The growing number of animals required many vet visits since twelve-year-old Charlotte was determined to take in the injured and handicapped animals that other people were reluctant to help.

"Zack is with Charlotte in the new barn, and Theodore and his dad went into town."

"Has the rescue's name debate been settled yet?" asked Evan as they moved toward the barn.

Bridget grinned. "Charlotte's choice won. We had to resort to flipping a coin because the kids had argued nonstop about it. I thought they'd come to a compromise, but they proved me wrong. Theodore sulked for three days after the coin flip. He still won't say the new name."

"Furry Friends Rescue," Rowan told Evan. Yesterday Charlotte had eagerly shared the name with her when she dropped off Zack. Charlotte was a girly girl who enthusiastically loved all animals and had been the driving force behind creating the rescue. Her cutesy name selection hadn't surprised Rowan at all.

"What name did Theodore want?" asked Evan. He carried Molly. Her arms were wrapped around his neck, and her blonde pigtails bounced with every step.

Rowan's heart skipped a beat as the girl nuzzled her head against Evan's cheek.

"Kerr Family Rescue," said Bridget.

"Practical and solid," said Evan. "Sounds right for him."

"He says he's embarrassed by Charlotte's choice," Bridget said with a laugh.

Rowan wouldn't be surprised if embarrassing her brother had factored into Charlotte's suggestion.

"But he's designing a logo," said Bridget. "And he's created some great options. At least this way he'll feel he had a part of the identity." She opened a fence gate, let everyone pass through, firmly latched it behind them, and then looped an additional thick chain around the post. "Mr. Beans may be blind, but we discovered he can open any gate. Luckily he hasn't figured out the chain. He's tried his best to gnaw through it, though."

"Mr. Beans?" asked Evan. Loud braying abruptly came from inside the barn. Thor's ears turned in that direction.

"He heard you. He's our newest rescue. A blind donkey," said Bridget. "Now he'll expect treats."

"Treats," repeated Molly. She squirmed until Evan set her down, and she sprinted to the barn.

"She knows where to find his treats. I swear all the animals would double their weight if Molly had her way with feeding them."

Evan nodded, and Rowan could tell he was distracted. His brain was overloaded with work, and he was worried about interviewing Zack. He'd told her he was concerned about upsetting him more.

"How is Zack doing?" he asked Bridget.

Her forehead wrinkled. "I heard him crying in bed last night and went to check on him, but he acted as if he hadn't been. I've told him several times he can talk to me about anything, and he says okay, but his gaze is very apprehensive. He ate a good dinner last night and played video games with Theodore. I heard my son tell him how his father had gone missing for several weeks last summer, and that it'd worked out okay."

If "okay" includes his dad being severely beaten and nearly dying.

Bridget smiled at her brother. "Theodore told Zack you were the best detective in the state and would find his mother."

Evan's eyes glistened, and he wiped one. "Shit, that's a lot of pressure."

Rowan took his hand and squeezed it. Every time she'd worked with him in the past—before they got together—Evan had always had the gaze of a man with a great burden. When they'd reconnected last summer, she'd immediately noticed the weight was gone. Finding his sister alive after she'd been missing for fifteen years had wiped it away.

But it'd reappeared the day before at the news of Rod's death.

Rowan wanted it gone.

The group moved into the new barn. It smelled of freshly cut wood, manure, and hay. The barn had fifteen large stalls. Several had back doors that also opened to individual outdoor paddocks. Thor wandered, sticking his nose everywhere, enjoying the myriad smells. Rowan peeked into a stall where a half dozen pygmy goats were delighted to see her. They lifted their front legs against the stall door, nearly climbing on top of each other to get closer. Mr. Beans was in the next stall, gently taking the treats Molly held for him on her flat palm. He lifted his head, ears turning and nostrils flaring in their direction, curious about the visitors. Rowan stopped to scratch and stroke the soft ears.

At the far end of the barn, Zack stood holding a wheelbarrow in front of a stall, and Charlotte threw a scoop of manure into it.

"Zack's cleaning stalls?" Evan asked his sister in a low voice.

"Why not? We need all the help we can get, and it keeps him busy and his mind off things," said Bridget. "Although he did look rather surprised when I told him he'd be helping Charlotte with her chores today. I figured she'd be the best of us to keep him distracted."

Rowan couldn't argue with her logic. She'd heard Charlotte talking nonstop to Zack since they entered the barn. It was normal for her to give a running commentary on everything she saw or talk about anything that popped into her head.

"Bridget, there's a goat in Mr. Beans's stall," said Rowan as she spotted the smaller animal on the other side of the donkey. The goat stuck his head under Mr. Beans's neck to peer up at her. He had floppy brown ears and little horns that curved backward.

"It's okay. That's Ralph," said Bridget. "The other donkeys weren't very fond of Mr. Beans and constantly nipped and kicked at him. When I moved him out of their pasture, Ralph immediately decided the donkey was his best friend and hasn't left his side since. I don't think Mr. Beans feels as strongly about Ralph, but he tolerates him."

"He can't see," little Molly informed Rowan in a serious tone, her gaze earnest. "Ralph tells him where to go."

"I'm glad they're friends," Rowan told her, matching her tone and expression.

She's adorable.

"I'd like to take Zack outside for a few minutes," said Evan. "Can you run interference with Charlotte?" he asked Bridget.

"Yes. Although she won't be happy to lose her assistant. She's enjoyed telling him what to do. Theodore doesn't put up with that." Bridget pointed at a door beyond where the two kids worked. "Take him out there. It'll be quiet."

Evan headed toward the kids but stopped and looked back at Rowan with a small frown. "Do you mind coming?"

"Not at all," she answered, surprised. "What for?"

"I want a second pair of eyes and ears." He grimaced. "And you'll be a softer presence than me. I'm worried I'll be too stiff."

"No, you won't." She walked down the wide aisle beside him, Thor at her heels. "He trusts you."

"Hey, Zack," said Evan as they reached the stall where the boy was scrubbing out a waterer as Charlotte supervised. "Can I talk with you for a bit?"

Zack had immediately straightened and searched Evan's eyes, clearly looking for good news. He didn't see it, and his face fell. "You haven't found her?"

"Not yet." Evan motioned the boy out of the stall. "We'll be back," he told Charlotte.

For once the young girl was silent. She'd seen Zack's hopeful expression too.

Evan, Rowan, and Zack stepped outside into the sunshine and found themselves near a small, fenced pasture. Two donkeys lifted their heads, studied the trio, and went back to eating. But a small sheep approached. It stopped at the fence and butted its head against a board. Zack squatted and reached between the rails to scratch its head. Thor sniffed at the sheep and then glanced at Rowan, his gaze eager.

/play/

"Sit," she told him.

He sat and stared forlornly at the sheep.

Evan leaned against the fence, looking out at the donkeys. "What do you think of the ranch, Zack?"

"It's nice. I like being around the animals—especially the dogs. There's a lot to do, though." He made a face. "And everything poops." As if on cue, the sheep dropped several tiny balls into a pile. Zack sighed.

"True," said Evan. "Bridget said you played video games with Theodore."

Zack's face lightened. "Yeah. I'm a lot better than he is because he only got his first PlayStation two months ago."

Evan turned toward Zack. "I want to ask some questions about your mom. That okay? I know they can be uncomfortable, but I need to know everything. You never know when some small detail that doesn't seem important could turn out to be very relevant later on."

Zack nodded and stood, looking Evan in the eye.

Good. He's ready.

"What can you tell me about your mom from the past week or two?" Evan asked. "Was she happier than normal? More sad? Maybe stressed?"

Zack looked back at the sheep and lifted one shoulder. "I don't know. Normal, I guess."

"Did she ever mention she was worried about money?"

Confusion crossed Zack's face. "Not exactly. But she always complains about the price of gas and doctor bills. Is that what you mean?"

"That's a good answer," said Evan. "This is a hard question for me to ask, but do you know if she was scared of anyone? Maybe had a bad argument? Say with a neighbor or at work?"

"I've thought a lot about that," said Zack. "And I don't remember anything like that." His eyes grew wet. "But I doubt she told me everything."

"That's her job as a mom," said Rowan. "Moms want their kids' lives to be happy. Parents shouldn't share their adult problems with young kids."

"That's true," agreed Evan. "Do you know if she was concerned about your grandpa recently?"

The boy wrinkled his nose as he thought. "No. She says he eats too much red meat and drinks too much beer, but she says that all the time."

Rowan watched Zack for any more hints of distress. He'd wiped his eyes and pushed through. She was proud of him.

"Do you know when she saw him last?" asked Evan.

"Last Sunday, probably. We always eat dinner there on Sundays. Sometimes he comes to our house, but we've mostly been going there. I don't know if she saw him since then."

"I've done a few Sunday dinners there," said Evan. "It's been a while, though."

"Yeah, sometimes his other friends or a neighbor is there, but usually it's just us."

"What about last Sunday?"

Zack thought. "One of his old police friends was there. I think his name's Brian? He's missing two fingers. He always tells a story about how he lost them in a fight with a suspect."

"Dean O'Brien," said Evan. "Everyone just calls him O'Brien." He gave a half smile. "He likes to tell the fight story, but he actually lost the fingers in an accident with a saw."

Evan met Rowan's eyes and silently mouthed, "Saw and tequila."

"Ian was at dinner too," added Zack.

"I don't think I know Ian," said Evan.

"Mom's boyfriend."

Rowan blinked.

I didn't know there was a boyfriend.

According to the shock on Evan's face, he hadn't known either.

13

Evan asked Rowan to look up Tara Tilson's number in his phone as he drove her and Thor back home. His astonishment at Zack's announcement had waned, and now he was angry that he'd missed such an important detail.

Why did no one tell me about a boyfriend?

He'd struggled to hide his surprise in front of Zack, not wanting the boy to realize he'd been clueless. A few more questions revealed that Zack didn't know Ian's last name or what he did for work and didn't know how long Sophia had been dating him.

Zack had stared at him as understanding dawned. "You haven't talked to Ian?"

"No one told me about him."

The boy had blinked several times, and horror filled his gaze. *"Do you think he has Mom?"*

"Nothing has made us suspect that, Zack. But I'd like to talk to him." He didn't want the boy's imagination running wild.

When asked for a description, Zack had said, "He reminds me of Iron Man. Not that he's a genius, but his eyes and his beard thing look like the actor's. His hair's a lot longer, though."

Looks a bit like Robert Downey Jr.

That was all Evan had to go on.

He made a mental note to check in with the lab that was attempting to get into Sophia's phone and laptop. He suspected she'd have pictures of a man who resembled the actor. No doubt her cell phone records would show calls to his number.

Could he be the burner phone she called on Friday?

Running down the list of people Evan and Noelle had interviewed, he realized none of them had been close enough to Sophia to know she was seeing someone. Except for one person: her business partner, Tara.

"Why hasn't this Ian contacted us?" Evan muttered for the third time. "His girlfriend is missing."

"It makes him look guilty, doesn't it?" said Rowan. "Although it's only been thirty-six hours. Maybe they don't talk that often."

Is Ian our suspect?

"I've got Tara's number. You ready?" Rowan asked.

"Yes, put her on speaker."

Tara answered on the second ring.

"Tara, it's Evan Bolton. I have a quick follow-up question."

"Whatever you need, Detective."

"Why didn't you tell me Sophia was dating someone?"

Silence filled the line.

"I didn't know she was," Tara finally said. "Are you sure?"

"Her son says she was dating a man named Ian. Has a goatee. Sound familiar?"

"No. Not at all. Could Zack be mistaken?"

Evan didn't think so. "Sophia would have told you if she was seeing someone, right? You two talk about that stuff?"

"Only to an extent," said Tara. "In the past, she didn't tell me about anyone until she believed it could go somewhere. I got the impression she'd dated a few guys, but it didn't last beyond a second date or so."

"She took Ian to dinner at her father's."

"Oh. That sounds like they were serious, doesn't it?" Tara sounded a little wounded that Sophia hadn't confided in her.

"Could she have met him at the shop? Maybe he's a client."

"I'll check names of our customers," said Tara. "And ask employees if Sophia told one of them that she was dating. I'm at the store, so I can get right on this."

Evan thanked her and ended the call. He pulled into their driveway a minute later to drop off Rowan and kissed her goodbye.

Rowan sighed. "I'd ask when you'll be home, but—"

"I have no idea."

"Exactly." She kissed him again, and her brown gaze held his. "It's okay. I want you to find her as much as you do." She hopped out of the SUV and let Thor out of the back seat. "And eat something. You haven't had lunch."

Evan looked at the time. "Shit. I'll grab something on my way in." He shifted into reverse and headed back to work.

Twenty minutes later, a bagel sandwich in his stomach and a large coffee in hand, he entered the conference room. It was quiet. It felt as if no one were paying attention to the case, but he knew Noelle, Maxine, and Detective Shults were all on the job. No one would have a day off until every lead had been exhausted.

Tara had called back and said none of the employees had known Sophia was seeing someone, and Tara knew the only Ian in their database; he was in his seventies and married. Dead end. Evan set down his coffee, looked up a phone number, and called the other person who had been at dinner with Rod and Sophia.

Dean O'Brien had been a patrol lieutenant when he retired from Deschutes County a year before Rod McLeod did. A longtime member of Rod's circle of friends, O'Brien had never been Evan's favorite person. He seemed like a decent guy, but he always laughed a little too loud, drank a little too much, and told too many bullshit stories—like the one he'd told Zack about his missing fingers. Evan had always brushed aside his dislike of the man since the guy *had* lost some fingers and was a good cop.

Evan's call went to voicemail. "O'Brien, it's Evan Bolton. Call me back as soon as you can."

His phone rang within thirty seconds. He'd suspected correctly that O'Brien wouldn't answer a call from a number he didn't recognize.

"Evan!" O'Brien said. "Is this about Rod and Sophia?"

"It is."

"I almost called you yesterday to check in, but I didn't have anything important to tell you. I knew you had enough on your plate, and you'd get to me when you were ready."

"I appreciate that," said Evan. "It's been crazy. When did you last talk to Rod or Sophia?"

"Both of them at dinner last Sunday at his place," O'Brien replied promptly.

"Tell me about Ian, the guy Sophia brought."

O'Brien paused for a long second. "The new guy. I knew she hadn't introduced anyone to her father in a long time, so I figured she liked this one. Seemed all right. Rod was polite, but I don't think he was very impressed. I left before they did, so I didn't get to hear Rod's opinion."

"Did you get a last name?"

O'Brien sucked in a breath. "Wait. You don't know who *he is*?"

Evan grimaced, stung by the highlight of the gaping hole in his investigation. "No. I didn't even know she was dating until Zack said something today. Sophia's business partner, Tara, didn't know either. What can you tell me about him?"

"That means he hasn't contacted you about her disappearance. Shit. I don't remember a last name," O'Brien said slowly. "Not even certain it was spoken. He did tell me he was an accountant for some place. When I said I wasn't familiar with the company, he told me they're based in Boston. He had a subtle Boston accent but said he moved here a few years ago and works remotely. We mainly talked about skiing, which was one of the reasons he moved here."

"Nothing else to help me track him down?" Evan didn't like it. "Any chance he mentioned he was going out of town? Maybe a work trip to Boston?"

"I'm thinking. Hang on. Memory turns to shit as you age. Your turn will come."

Evan checked his email while O'Brien thought and spotted a message from the public information officer, asking Evan to approve a press release. He opened it and Sophia stared back at him. It was a good photo. The press release stated she was missing and also included photos of vehicles like hers and her father's, asking the public to notify the sheriff's department if they were spotted. There was no mention of Rod's murder or the horrific scene in Sophia's home. Evan scanned the copy, didn't see any errors, and sent his approval. It would be posted on the department's social media and sent to all local news outlets.

"Sorry, Evan," said O'Brien. "I can't think of anything he said that was helpful. Seemed like a good enough guy. Can't say I saw any sparks between him and Sophia, though. You know how it is when a relationship is new and you're always smiling at each other? These two acted more like acquaintances, not boyfriend-girlfriend."

"But you were told they were?"

"Well . . . I guess I jumped to conclusions there. Don't know why else she would have brought him to dinner if they weren't involved. He got along real well with Zack. But damn . . . you know as well as I do that you need to quickly rule out the boyfriend."

"Need to figure out who the fuck he is first." Frustrated, Evan changed gears. "Did Rod have issues with anyone recently?"

"I would have called you immediately if I knew the answer to that, Evan. Haven't heard him grouch about anyone for a while. He was in a good mood Sunday. Relaxed. But didn't mention plans he had coming up for the week, so I don't know what he's been up to recently."

Evan pressed his lips together, debating whether he should mention Rod's private files.

Might as well.

"Have you ever been in Rod's office upstairs?"

"Yeah. Looks exactly like his desk setup at work, doesn't it? I gave him crap about it."

"I noticed that too. Did you know that Rod kept some photocopies of old cases?"

Two seconds of quiet filled the call. "No . . . I've never seen any, and he never talked about them. That definitely crosses a professional line, but I've heard of other detectives doing that when they retire. They can't let go of an unsolved case."

"These were all solved cases."

Silence.

"Huh. Maybe he kept them as mementos? Work he was proud of?" Uncertainty filled his tone.

"He wasn't involved in all of them."

"How many cases are we talking about?"

Evan hesitated. He'd already revealed more about the evidence than he should. "A lot."

"Weird. I don't know what to make of that." O'Brien sounded as confused as Evan felt.

"Me neither." Evan was not going to tell him that some case files were missing. Disappointment rushed through him. He'd hoped O'Brien had an explanation for Rod's collection. "Who else should I talk to? You knew him best, and honestly, I hadn't seen him much for the last year or so. We'd text a few times a month."

"You know Rod thought of you like a son." O'Brien sounded hesitant, clearly uncomfortable speaking about feelings. "And don't feel guilty that you didn't stay in constant contact. The phone works both ways, you know. Anyway, he told me several times that he was proud of you, but I think he took more credit than he should for your skills as a detective." O'Brien snorted.

A lump formed in Evan's throat. "He was the best."

"He always hoped you and Sophia would give it another go."

Evan smiled. "Yeah, he told me that a few dozen times. Neither of us were on board."

"Oh! Wait a second." Excitement filled the line. "That asshole ex of Sophia's. Rod said he was getting out of prison early. He never trusted that guy."

"No one did," said Evan. "And with good reason, but I've already talked to Charlie Graham. He's got a pretty good alibi that we're checking out." He'd sent Detective Shults to Graham's group home to examine video of his comings and goings.

"Rod was watching him after he got out. Said he wanted to know if the guy ever came within a hundred yards of Sophia."

"Are you saying that Rod had Graham followed?"

This is new.

"He was doing it himself. Of course he couldn't do it twenty-four seven, but he put some substantial time into it. I know he followed Graham to some bars and restaurants. Watched him go out with a woman a few times. Rod didn't like that and tried to stick close in case Graham got violent with her. He said it only lasted three dates."

"Sounds like Rod was keeping busy." Evan didn't like it. The actions were creepy and obsessive.

Look at his filing system. He had obsessive quirks.

"I told him to knock it off. If Graham ever spotted him, who knows what the guy would do."

"When was Rod doing this?"

"Let's see. I think he did it for about two weeks but stopped right around St. Patrick's Day. I had a bunch of guys getting together to celebrate, and Rod was going to pass it up so that he could tail the asshole.

That's when I confronted him about it. I laid into him about being out of line and acting like a freak."

"Are you sure he stopped?" St. Patrick's Day was about a month ago.

"He told me he did, and he showed up at my party. *Shit.* Think he kept following Graham?"

"Don't know. But he was a stubborn man. You know how he was when he was focused on something."

"It's what made him a good cop. He called you stubborn too."

One side of Evan's mouth lifted. "A few people have told me that." He always took it as a compliment. "Anything else you can tell me?"

"I've been racking my brain since I heard. Sophia's ex is all I've got, and I forgot about that guy until just a minute ago. You'll keep me informed, right?"

"I'll see what I can do," Evan said, understanding the man's need for information but not planning to share additional elements of the investigation. Clearly O'Brien was still connected to law enforcement gossip. Anything Evan told him could spread and grow contorted as it traveled along the grapevine.

Evan ended the call and stared at one of the whiteboards in the conference room. Charlie Graham's name was prominent. He'd been treated for his gunshot wound and released from the hospital the same day.

Rod followed him.

Did he get too close?

Graham warranted another look. He checked the time. Lori Shults would still be at Graham's halfway house, and he knew she'd call immediately if she found something. He tried to focus on the work in front of him, but his mind kept wandering to one thing: Rod's autopsy was in a few hours.

This will be my toughest viewing ever.

14

An hour later, Noelle strode into the conference room with Detective Lori Shults behind her.

Evan had picked up his phone to call forensics to ask why he hadn't received any preliminary reports yet, but the annoyed look on Noelle's face caught his interest, and he set down the phone. "What happened?" he asked.

Noelle pointed at Lori. "She'll tell you."

Lori snorted. "Noelle heard my story in the hallway." The detective was a petite woman, and standing next to Noelle, who was wearing her usual high heels, made Lori appear very tiny. She was in her early thirties, but in the face looked no older than a senior in high school. She'd had to work hard to prove herself as a cop, always battling people's perceptions, and Evan admired that she had become a detective.

"I just got back from Charlie Graham's . . . halfway house . . . living situation . . . whatever you want to call it," Lori said. "It's an older house, but it does have an impressive security system. The owner is a private citizen contracted with the state, and he takes his job very seriously." She snorted. "I don't want to call him a warden, but I think that's how he sees his role. He clearly enjoys being in charge of the five men living there. Runs a tight ship. Anyway, he showed me video of Graham entering the home around six thirty p.m. on Friday, which would make sense if he got off work at six. The men also each have a key card that they scan anytime to go in or out one of the exits. Graham's card didn't show an exit until eight thirty a.m. on Saturday. I also have a record of his comings and goings for several days before that. If we can figure out when Sophia disappeared, we can compare them then.

"I talked separately to two residents who said Graham had eaten dinner and watched TV with them that evening until late and then went to bed." She raised a brow. "Of course Graham could have told them to cover for him, but one of the men said, and I quote, 'Graham is a dick.' I sensed a lot of genuine dislike from him, so I don't think he'd cover for him if Graham asked. So the alibi is strong. Not one hundred percent, but I'd say maybe ninety-five percent. We all know there are ways to get around security systems. The question is: Would Graham bother?"

Evan wondered too. "Graham seemed legitimately surprised when we asked him about Rod and Sophia, so what you found falls in line with that," he said. "But why are you annoyed, Noelle?"

"She's annoyed because I told her how Graham was running his mouth while I was there," said Lori. "His arm was in a sling, and he gave me some shit for checking up on his comings and goings. Then he said the department should pay him for missed work time, since it's our fault he was shot."

Noelle rolled her eyes.

"He's still pointing the finger at us for that?" asked Evan.

"Yep. Says he's talking to a lawyer about suing the department, which I'm sure is a bunch of bull. When I pointed out that Detective Bolton had nearly been shot, too, he got pissed and said, 'Yeah. They missed him. How *convenient*.'"

Noelle's expression was thunderous.

Again Evan abruptly recalled the sound and sensation of the bullet passing within inches of his head, and he fought back a shudder. "Graham may be walking the straight and narrow these days, but his mouth sure isn't."

"It'll get him in trouble," agreed Noelle. "We've mostly cleared Graham's alibi for placing Rod's body in the junkyard, but as far as making progress on the shooting yesterday, they couldn't find either of the bullets."

"There was a lot of equipment in the shop for them to disappear into." Evan was disappointed but not surprised.

"And the explorers turned up nothing in the area where we think the shots came from. Some random bits of debris, but I don't think any of it shows promise." Noelle brightened. "On the other hand, I went through the cell phone records I finally got from Sophia's provider, and there is a number registered to an Ian Martin."

Evan sat up in his chair. "You should have told me that before Graham's update. Did you call?"

"I haven't called yet. I thought you'd like to be in on that conversation."

"Thanks for thinking of me," said Evan. She was right.

Noelle opened her laptop and pulled up a report.

"I'd love to stay for this," said Lori, "but it's back to my desk to dig into the people from Rod's case files."

"Anything yet?" Evan asked, keeping his hopes in check.

"If there's a common link, I haven't found it yet," said Lori. "Deputy Coates, Maxine, and I are determined to find something."

"I skimmed them and didn't see anything obvious," said Evan. "I don't envy you. Is Coates's back surviving through all that sitting?" Sometimes light duty for which a person sat all day was worse than the regular job.

Lori grinned. "Yes. He gets up and moves around and has three pillows lining his chair. I think he's enjoying the break from patrol. Keeps mumbling about how nice it is not to deal with stupid people doing stupid things every day."

"He'll get bored reading files eventually," said Evan to Lori as she stood up. "One thing about patrol, it's different every day."

"I remember very well." Lori left and closed the door.

"Here's Ian Martin's number," said Noelle. She turned her laptop screen to Evan.

"Where's that area code located?"

"Boston."

"What else did you find on him?"

"Owns a home in southwest Bend. A few previous addresses in Massachusetts."

"When was the last call or text between them?"

"Monday. It was a phone call. She called him."

Evan let that sink in. "Seems a long time to go without speaking if they were a couple."

"Maybe he saw her in person for a few days last week." Noelle frowned at the call log.

"But no texts to set up those meetings?"

"Should we visit him in person instead of calling?" She held his gaze.

"I don't think we'll reveal our hand with a phone call," Evan finally said. "If he's guilty, he knows the police would want to talk to the boyfriend, and he's had plenty of time to run." He put the number into his work cell and left it on speaker. "Probably will go to voicemail."

"Hello?" a man answered.

Noelle looked as startled as Evan felt at the fast answer.

"This is Detective Evan Bolton of the Deschutes County Police Department. Is this Ian Martin?"

There was a long pause. "Are you calling to tell me there's a warrant for my arrest, and I need to pay five hundred bucks immediately with Apple gift cards?" asked the man, disdain in his tone.

Evan snorted. He'd heard about the widespread phone call scam dozens of times. "That would be a no," he said. "I have some questions related to an investigation. If you'd like, you can phone the department and ask for me."

"I'll do that." The man abruptly ended the call.

"Well, he's not stupid," said Noelle. "And I assume that's Ian Martin. I heard a faint accent. Think he'll actually call back?"

"I think he will." If Ian was guilty, he would call because he didn't want to look guilty. If Ian had nothing to do with it, he'd call out of curiosity.

As they waited, Noelle went to the whiteboard that showed a list of elements in their investigations. "Neither Sophia's or Rod's vehicle have turned up," she said, tapping those entries with a finger. "And we're still waiting on forensics for both of their homes. Is forensics backed up? We should have had some preliminary reports by now."

"They're always backed up," said Evan. He opened his email to check for the forensics reports for the tenth time that day. "Not yet." Scanning his new email, he saw nothing that appeared relevant to the investigations, and then he deleted two spam emails. One pretended to be from Craigslist, asking "Is this still available?" and another was supposedly from a British lawyer with awkward grammar about a distant relative who'd left Evan a fortune.

Only two pieces of spam meant it was a good day.

The phone on the conference table rang. Both Evan and Noelle had set calls to forward from their desk phones.

Evan raised a brow at her as he pressed the speaker button. "Detective Bolton."

"Okay, you're legit," said Ian. "What can I do for you?"

Evan was tempted to ask for Apple gift cards. "What can you tell me about Sophia McLeod?" he asked, keeping his question vague and open ended.

"Sophia?" Ian hesitated. "What do you need to know?" Curiosity filled his tone.

"How do you know her?"

"Sophia and I dated for a while. She's a good person. Her dad was also a police detective—he was with Deschutes County, I believe. Retired a while back. Why?"

Evan noticed the past tense of *dated*. "Yes, he worked here. You and Sophia are friends?" He ignored Ian's question.

"We were," said Ian. "We broke up recently and agreed staying friends wouldn't work for us. It was a full break."

"When did you last see or speak with her?"

"What's going on? Is she okay?"

He sounds genuinely concerned.

Which meant nothing to Evan now. "Can you answer my question first?"

"I last saw her on Sunday," said Ian. "We had dinner at her dad's house. And I last talked to her the next day, when we agreed this wasn't working."

A good explanation for why he hasn't contacted the police or called Sophia's phone.

"What's going on?" Ian asked.

"Sophia McLeod is missing," said Evan. "She hasn't been seen for several days." He wouldn't share details. "Do you know of anywhere she could have gone? Did she mention plans?"

"She's missing? What about Zack? Is he missing too?" Shock filled his voice. "Have you talked with her dad? Rod—"

"We've questioned the people closest to her, and Zack is staying at a friend's," said Evan. "What can you tell us about Sophia?"

"Am I a suspect?" Ian asked cautiously. "I know you guys always look at the husband or boyfriend first. Do I need a lawyer?"

"Only if you have something to hide," lied Evan. "Do you *not* want to tell us where she could be?"

"I honestly don't know," said Ian. "She loves her job and went to her dad's house a lot. She didn't mention any upcoming trips. I guess she could have left town because of our breakup, but I believe she'd tell her dad where she was going. And since she broke up with me, I don't think she'd need to go out of town to get over that." A sour tone lightly touched his voice.

"She dumped you," Evan stated. Noelle met his gaze, a question in her eyes.

Did he get angry?

"It wasn't like that," Ian said quickly. "It was rather amicable. If a woman breaks up with me, I take that at face value. I have no interest in pursuing someone who's not interested."

Evan wondered how true that was. "You haven't texted her since the breakup?"

"No."

At least we know that is true.

A soft knock sounded at the conference room door, and Evan turned to see Rowan peek through its small window. He held up a finger, and she nodded.

Evan looked at Noelle and gestured at the phone.

Any more questions?

She scribbled on a piece of paper. *His location?*

"Are you in Bend right now?" Evan asked.

"No. I'm in Boston for a meeting tomorrow—my employer is based here. I flew out Saturday."

Noelle held up a hand, tipping it back and forth.

Convenient that he left on Saturday.

His travel would be easy enough to verify, but Evan hoped he could discover when the ticket had been purchased without having to subpoena the airline. "You fly back often for work?"

"Once every other month," said Ian. "Always for this particular meeting."

So he should have bought a ticket well in advance.

Or could have scheduled Sophia's disappearance to coincide with when he'd be out of town.

"Do you think she's all right?" Ian asked in a worried tone. "I'm confused that she didn't take Zack or tell him where she was going. She lives for that kid."

Evan wondered if her devotion to Zack was part of the reason Sophia had broken up with Ian. "We don't know what to think at the moment," said Evan. He asked Ian a few more open-ended questions, but it appeared the man had no other helpful information. Evan ended the call, promising to ask Sophia to contact Ian when she returned.

Evan took a deep breath and leaned back in his chair. "What do you think?" he asked Noelle.

"He sounded convincing, but we know that can mean nothing. He quickly asked about Zack, which I thought was a good sign, and he told you to contact Rod, which was logical." She threw up her hands. "But he could be the world's best bullshitter."

"I want to know when he bought his ticket to Boston."

Noelle nodded and turned to her laptop.

Evan reviewed his notes from the phone call and added *Boston ticket* with a big question mark. He also made a note to have a deputy go to Ian's home and verify that no one was there.

Rowan.

Evan pushed out of his chair, embarrassed he'd forgotten that she'd knocked minutes ago.

This job requires focus.

But he was determined to not let it affect his relationship. He'd seen too many law enforcement marriages go down in flames. He opened the door and spotted her standing near Detective Shults's office. Lori knelt on the floor in the hall as she scratched Thor's chin. The smell of Thai food reached him, and Evan's gaze locked on the large plastic bag in Rowan's hand.

Food.

He was suddenly starving.

Rowan saw him, excused herself to Lori, and patted her thigh for Thor to follow her before coming down the hall. She met his gaze and smiled.

His heart did a stuttering beat.

She takes my breath away.

Rowan wore faded jeans, an old black shirt with a Nine Inch Nails logo, and ratty tennis shoes she refused to part with. Long sections of hair had come loose from her braid.

Gorgeous.

"Hey," she said in greeting. Thor greeted Evan with a nose to his crotch.

Rowan kissed him, and Evan eyed the bag, the bagel he'd eaten long gone. "Is that Thai?"

"Yes. I texted Noelle to ask if this was a good time to drop in. I have food for her too." They walked back to the conference room, and she asked, "How are things going?"

"Shitty. No word on Sophia and no inroads on Rod's killer." It didn't matter how much work they had put in. The results were the only thing that mattered.

Being a smart woman who'd spent a lot of time around law enforcement, Rowan nodded instead of pointing out all the effort they'd already made. "I'm sorry."

In the conference room, she set the bag on the table and unpacked the big containers. Thor went to Noelle for attention, which was promptly bestowed. Evan gave Rowan a greatly abbreviated rundown of what they'd worked on, his gaze locked on the food. When Evan mentioned that O'Brien said Rod had been tailing Charlie Graham, Rowan frowned. "Does that sound like something Rod would do?" she asked.

"Yes." He didn't like admitting it, but how Rod would dig into that concerned him.

"What did the fingerprints report show?" Rowan asked.

"Don't have them yet," said Noelle with her mouth full of pad thai. "And we need the damned things from both homes."

Evan dished up a big serving of curry over white rice and paused. He had an autopsy to attend this evening. A spicy, big dinner might not be the best option.

But it smells amazing.

He took a bite.

And tastes amazing.

He decided eating was fine. He never had problems in the autopsy suite, unlike Noelle, who'd pay a lot of cash to avoid attending one. He noticed Rowan was still standing, no food on a plate. "Aren't you eating?"

"No. I just brought it for you guys. And there should be plenty to share with anyone else." She glanced out the open door as two deputies swiveled their heads, scenting food as they passed by. "I knew I'd be asleep when you got home tonight, so I wanted to see you."

"Awww," said Noelle. "You two are relationship goals."

Rowan turned a speculative eye on Noelle, causing Evan to swallow before he finished chewing. He and Rowan had discussed a few men for Noelle to date but had decided none were right. The detective was a force. Strong in body and will. Tall and always perfectly put together, not a platinum blonde hair out of place. She'd been married twice but never talked about it. Rowan had asked some leading questions in the past, but Noelle always changed the subject.

"Don't look at me like that," said Noelle, pointing her fork at Rowan. "You people in couples always think us singles would be happier if we had a person too. Not true."

Rowan pressed her lips together, again proving she was smart by not arguing with the detective. Instead, she turned to Evan. "I need to go." She gave him a kiss and then stopped him as he stood to walk her out. "I'm good. I'll see you when I see you," she said, holding his gaze and making him regret he had to work. She snapped Thor's leash on and left.

"That was a big sigh," said Noelle.

"What?" asked Evan.

"You watched her leave and then sighed as if you'd been told you couldn't play outside."

Evan paused with a bite of curry halfway to his mouth. "That's rather accurate."

She snorted. "New love. It'll change."

"Pessimistic much?"

Noelle turned away and focused on her laptop.

Yep, doesn't want to talk about her past relationships.

Evan felt a little sorry for her.

Rowan and I are in it for the long haul.

Another knock sounded and Evan turned, hoping to see Rowan again, but it was Crystal, one of the administrative assistants, in the window this time. He waved her in. Crystal was a quiet woman in her thirties who had worked in the department for about ten years. Evan knew she had young twins and an ex-husband who had moved out a month after they were born.

"Sorry to bother you, Detectives," she said, looking from Noelle to Evan. "I wanted to say how sorry I am about what happened to Rod. He always had bad jokes to tell me, and I didn't realize how much I looked forward to those until he retired."

Evan smiled. "They were lame, weren't they?" Five other employees had stopped Evan to make similar comments.

"He and his wife sent new clothes for the twins every few months before she died. She said she liked the excuse to buy little-girl outfits."

"That's adorable," said Noelle.

Evan wasn't surprised. Rod had said Ellen always wanted more grandkids.

Crystal looked down at her feet. "I felt a need to share that." She glanced up, a fierce light in her eyes that Evan had never seen before. "Please catch who did this," she said in a harsh voice. She turned and left, closing the door behind her.

"I'll be damned," said Noelle. "I've never seen—or heard—that sort of fire from her before."

"She's raising twins on her own," said Evan. "She has to have it." He turned back to his computer, oddly touched by the words that had clearly come from deep in Crystal's heart.

I will catch him. That's a promise.

15

"Bolton! Hang on a minute."

Evan had just shoved open the exit door of the sheriff's department on his way to Rod's autopsy, but he turned around and saw his lieutenant hustling to catch him. Louis Ogden had been with the department for at least two decades. Evan found him to be rather unimaginative when it came to investigative work, but he had a knack for supervision, delegation, and organization. He was a solid but dull boss.

Evan wasn't complaining. During investigations, Louis gave Evan everything he asked for—within reason. Louis always knew where to hunt down extra hands and was fair with expenses. He caught up to Evan, his face red from the sprint. Louis planned to retire the next year and had noticeably cut back on maintaining his physical health. And increased the doughnuts. On his dark tie was telltale white powder, the leavings from a doughnut.

"What can I do for you, Louis?"

"I got part of the forensics report from Rod McLeod's house." He frowned, looking around at the number of people close by. "Let's talk in my office."

Evan checked the time. He didn't need to be there for the whole autopsy. But it was important to him to attend at least some of it in person. He always tried to be present for the victims in his cases. It was a matter of respect. "I've been waiting on that report," said Evan as they walked down the hallway. "How come it went to you instead of me?"

"You'll see."

Louis was putting out antsy vibes. Not his usual relaxed-but-competent aura. Evan studied the man from the corner of his eye. "Anything helpful?"

"Not sure."

A small chill went up Evan's spine. Louis was rarely so close-mouthed, and Evan wondered what had shown up in the evidence. There hadn't been any obvious signs of violence in Rod's home. No blood. No destruction. But his computer tower was gone, the key had been left in the filing cabinet lock, and his files had clearly been tampered with. Someone had been there.

Maybe shit's hitting the fan because Rod had photocopies of those files.

Whatever it turned out to be, Evan was ready for some more leads. "Anything from RCFL?" The FBI computer forensics lab in Portland.

Louis gave him a look. "You just sent them the McLeod phone and computers yesterday."

"Just checking." He'd hoped that if Louis had gotten the forensics report first, maybe he'd heard from the computer forensics lab already. It occurred to Evan that the forensics report might have gone to Louis first simply because Rod had been one of them. Retired, but still one of them.

They entered his office and Louis shut the door.

That cold feeling crawled up his spine again. Louis rarely closed the door. Whatever Louis had to tell him, it was private and important. Evan took a seat and looked expectantly at his boss. "I was on my way to Rod's autopsy, so I don't have a lot of time."

"Shouldn't take long. Just a minute." Louis hit a button on his desk phone. "He's here?" he said into the receiver. "Yeah, tell him to come in." A second later there was a double rap at the door. It opened and Deputy Hartley stepped inside, his eyebrows going up at the sight of Evan. Louis gestured for Hartley to sit in the other chair, by Evan.

"Okay," Louis began. "Now that you're both here, I have some questions about what you found at Rod's. Evan, walk me through it from the moment the two of you went in the door."

"I already did this," said Hartley. "An hour ago."

"I know," said Louis. "But now it's Evan's turn."

Evan froze and his skin prickled.

Someone just debriefed Hartley about our time at Rod's home? And now it's my turn?

He suspected they had done something wrong in the house, and now the department wanted both their views. Evan thought hard, retracing their steps, unable to think of what they'd done incorrectly. He knew proper procedure. Hartley did too. The only odd thing had been the neighbor woman showing up with the casserole. There wasn't procedure for that.

We should have sent her away and not spoken with her.

Is that what this is about?

Evan cleared his throat and described how he and the deputy had cleared the home, working their way up to the second level and ending in Rod's office. He explained how they'd seen the persistent neighbor from the upstairs window, how he'd refused to let her in the home and then shown his ID. They'd accepted the casserole to make her leave, and then they'd returned to the office and noticed the missing tower and files.

"Were you gloved?" asked Louis.

"We gloved up before we touched anything in the office," said Evan. "After Hartley noticed the computer tower was gone, I opened the filing cabinet. Every other door or knob had been elbowed or bumped open while we cleared." He turned to Hartley and lifted a brow. The deputy nodded in agreement.

"The report said there was a key in the filing cabinet lock," said Louis.

"Yes," said Evan. "I knew Rod would never leave a key like that. It was one of the reasons I opened the drawers."

"But you didn't turn the key."

"I did with gloves on and discovered it was already in the unlocked position."

"I opened the fridge without gloves," said Hartley with an apologetic shrug. "I put the woman's casserole in there."

"Oh . . . I opened the front door without gloves to tell her to leave," said Evan. "Forgot that. Does it matter? Forensics already has our prints on file for elimination."

"Were you in each other's sight the entire time?" asked Louis.

Evan was liking the questions less and less.

"As I said before—" began Hartley.

"I'd like to hear from Evan." Louis looked at him.

I feel as if I'm walking into a trap.

"While clearing we stuck together. If we were apart, it was for a split second."

Hartley nodded.

"I left Hartley in Rod's office when I went to answer the door," continued Evan. "But he came down probably within fifteen to twenty seconds of when I opened it. I didn't follow him when he put the casserole away." Evan had to think for a second. "I went back to the office while he was still in the kitchen. I was going to take a closer look at Rod's gun safes. Hartley walked in seconds later and pointed out the tower was gone. Then we gloved up." Evan forced himself to not look to Hartley for confirmation.

"The only thing you touched barehanded was the inside doorknob of the front—" Louis started.

"And the outside handle," added Evan. "I unlocked it with a key from Sophia's."

Guilt swamped him from forgetting two small things.

Is that all I forgot?

"You didn't touch anything in the kitchen?" Louis asked Evan.

"No." He was positive on that. "As soon as I realized files were missing, we exited the home and waited for forensics."

"What about Rod's desk? Did you move things on his desk?"

"No," said Evan. "There was no need." He gave a half laugh. "And I think it was still engrained in me to never touch Rod's desk at work. He was particular about where he placed things."

Louis's smile was sad, memories in his gaze. "Wasn't that the truth." He adjusted his seat and cleared his expression. "The only time you were alone in his office was looking at the gun safes a few seconds before Deputy Hartley entered. Do you know the safe combinations?"

"Yes, that was the only time I was alone in his office, and no, I don't know Rod's combinations." Evan was ready for Louis to get to the point of this questioning. He was treating Evan like a suspect—questioning him exactly the same way Evan questioned his suspects. Repeat. Rephrase. Clarify.

Louis looked at Hartley. "You didn't see Detective Bolton in the kitchen or see him move things in the office?"

I just said that.

Slow-brewing anger replaced the chill in his spine.

"No, sir."

My prints turned up somewhere. And they don't like it.

"Louis, you know I've socially been in Rod's house tons of times over the years," said Evan, fighting to keep his tone even. "I've used the bathroom there, made food in the kitchen, opened the back sliding glass door and screen. I've used the big barbecue on his deck, and I've been in his garage. If my prints have turned up in a place I didn't mention just now, there's plenty of reasons why." He met Louis's gaze and waited.

"Deputy Hartley said earlier he had the impression you'd never been in McLeod's home office," said Louis.

"That's true," said Evan. "In fact, I'd never been upstairs in that house. The first time I saw the office was yesterday."

"And you touched only the filing cabinet."

Evan leaned forward, holding Louis's gaze, giving his best "Don't fuck with me" glare. "If you have something to tell me, get to it."

"Evan, forensics found your prints on the key in the filing cabinet, on top of the cabinet, and on the sides. They were also found on the dials of both the gun safes, and on several items on Rod's desk." Louis took a breath as Evan stared. "Several knives in Rod's butcher block have your prints . . . but nothing else did."

His vision tunneled until all Evan could see were Louis's glasses.

How . . . ?

"That's impossible." Evan struggled to speak. "Maybe they could be on the knives from a previous visit . . . I honestly don't recall. But I didn't touch the key without gloves. I'm positive." From the corner of his eye, he saw Hartley nodding emphatically.

At least one person backs me up.

Louis sighed. "It's possible there's a mistake somehow. Let's get your file fingerprints retaken."

"It has to be an error," said Evan, his mind whirling and feeling unbalanced. "I'd never been in his office. I knew about the gun safes, but I'd never seen them, let alone touched them."

It doesn't make sense.

He stared at Louis.

No wonder he questioned me like a suspect.

And that's why the report went to him first.

"Get new prints and then get back to work," said Louis, standing to show the meeting was over. Evan stood and followed Hartley out the door.

Several yards down the hall, the deputy turned to Evan, sympathy in his eyes. "Sorry about that. I had no idea that's where he was headed with those questions. That's a bunch of bullshit."

"Who questioned you earlier?" asked Evan.

"My lieutenant. Had me walk through our time there like you just did. I didn't think anything of it. I figured they were being extra careful to dot their i's and cross their t's since it was Rod's case."

"No more careful than with anyone else," said Evan, knowing that wasn't quite true. Rod's case was on every law enforcement member's mind. He clapped Hartley on the back with more enthusiasm than he felt. "See you later. I need to get printed."

Then I have an autopsy to get to.

Evan walked away.

This has to be a mistake.

16

Evan took a deep breath and opened the door to the autopsy suite. It was late in the day and already dark outside. The fingerprinting hadn't taken that long, but annoyance still simmered in his gut that he'd had to do it. He'd texted Rowan to check in, and she'd replied with a photo of Thor looking very sad and said it was because Evan was still at work. And then sent three red hearts.

He'd spent a few minutes in the parking lot arguing with himself. Duty, guilt, and fear had battled inside him. Fear had finally been overcome, and he'd entered the medical examiner's building.

Evan didn't know the exact source of the fear. Fear of seeing Rod's abused body again? Fear he might fall apart during the autopsy? Or fear of seeing something that he wouldn't forget for the rest of his life?

All of the above.

Evan still struggled with what he'd seen in the junkyard. Rod's body in the trunk had haunted his hours nonstop, the sight burned into his brain. He didn't want to add more memories. But there was no getting around it at an autopsy. He could recall visuals from each autopsy he'd ever attended.

A child with bruises covering 80 percent of his body.

A young woman with her head barely attached.

Usually these memories popped up when least expected. Like when he was out to dinner. Or trying to get to sleep. Or grocery shopping.

Inside the suite, Evan stopped to put on the provided protective equipment. The mask helped. It acted as a barricade, helping to hide his emotions. He wished he could pull it over his eyes.

Get yourself together.

His emotions boiled close to the surface. Just the wrong sight or word could make them spill. He didn't want Rod to see that.

I loved the guy. Why am I scared I'll fall apart at his autopsy?

Professionalism seemed to be his primary reason. Evan was proud of how he handled his job. He never wanted to be the man who embarrassed the department. He worked by a strict code of ethics and expected the same from his coworkers.

Doesn't mean I can't show emotions.

Dr. Natasha Lockhart stood on her little custom platform, which circled the autopsy table. Petite, she'd had to get creative to effectively access her patients. "Glad you could make it, Evan," she said as he moved closer. Soothing cello music filled the room. A detour from her usual rock songs of past decades, it cast a solemn atmosphere in the cold suite.

Then he realized it was an instrumental cover of a Metallica song.

In spite of his anxiety, he smiled behind the mask. "I needed to be here, Natasha."

She looked up, meeting his gaze. "I know."

He finally looked at the body before her. Rod's chest cavity was open, which meant she'd already done a full external exam. She handed an unidentifiable organ to her assistant to weigh.

"You said you'd tell me your history with Rod," Evan said, remembering her tears at the junkyard. He glanced at her assistant, wondering if the medical examiner would share in front of her.

"I did." Natasha set a blade on a stainless steel table next to a spread of forceps, scalpels, scissors, and knives of every size. "Marina already knows the story. I told her before we started today."

Her assistant nodded, sympathetic brown eyes flashing behind her shield.

"It was more than a decade ago. I'd just finished medical school and was about to start my residency when my mother was killed in a hit-and-run."

"I'm so sorry, Natasha." Evan had a hunch where her story was going.

"My grandmother lived with my mother and depended heavily on her. My grandfather had died twenty years before, and my father had remarried and moved away long ago." She looked at the body. "Rod handled the hit-and-run investigation and promised me over and over that he'd find who killed my mother. But now my grandmother was alone, and I realized I needed to leave school to care for her. She wouldn't go to an assisted living place; that was out of the question for her. And I agreed."

"Rod wouldn't hear of you leaving school." When Evan had considered getting his master's in public safety administration, Rod had been his biggest supporter, and had pushed hard for him to continue when he nearly quit. Evan could see him doing the same for Natasha.

"Correct. He found a network of good people to care for her in her home. His wife, Ellen, helped. She'd even visit my grandmother for tea and conversation several times a week. She understood the need for companionship, and my grandmother adored her. Because of them, I didn't feel like I'd abandoned her. They treated her like family. They helped for four years, and I grew close to both Rod and Ellen. It crushed me when Ellen died too."

"How did I not know this?" asked Evan. "I remember Ellen was helping the grandmother of an out-of-state medical student. I never knew it was you or that it had anything to do with one of Rod's cases."

"He was probably protecting my privacy. It was my story to share with people, not his."

"Rod found the driver?"

"He did. It took five long and agonizing months. But the man served time in prison for it."

"Do you have any family left?" Evan regretted the question the second he asked it.

"Family by blood, no. But I have the family I chose. Amazing friends who have always stood by me."

"The best kind. I'm glad to hear it." Evan felt more centered, no longer battling with himself. Hearing her story about Rod and Ellen had made his fears diminish. He turned his attention to the body on the table.

That's not Rod. This was just the carrier for his energy, his passions, his skills.

Rod is gone.

Evan slowly exhaled. "What have you found so far?" he asked.

Natasha's eyes saddened. "He had horrible coronary disease that I suspect he purposefully ignored. There's no way his doctor didn't know about it, and it would have caught up with him soon."

"Damn." Evan couldn't recall Rod ever mentioning a heart condition. What he did recall was Rod being out of breath as they climbed the stairs in a restaurant. He'd claimed he'd been sick recently and had some lingering effects.

Not true.

"His digestive system is completely empty. He hadn't eaten."

"They starved him," Evan said flatly, anger spreading through his veins.

"I wouldn't say *starved*. I've seen *starved* and this isn't it. But he would have been hungry." She pointed at his wrist. "Ligature marks. I found some tiny natural fibers in the wounds that I'm ninety percent certain are from basic rope. It chafed the skin raw in places."

"Tied up and hungry."

"Ankles had been tied up too. And as I pointed out at the junkyard, the lividity didn't match his position in the trunk. He died while on his back, not his side. There are some odd little shapes that blanched the skin of his back when he lay on something for a period of time after death. I don't know what would cause them."

"Show me."

Natasha gestured for Marina to help, and the women rolled Rod to his side. Evan studied the three little white shapes. He could only describe them as mushrooms—but not really. Each had a long stem with a small disconnected umbrella shape at the top.

"I don't know what those are either." Evan removed his gloves and snapped a picture with his phone. "Is that a tattoo?" Surprised, he leaned closer to study a pattern low on Rod's hip. It hadn't been noticeable at the junkyard because Rod had been lying on that side.

"Yes. It's a ship. Mean anything to you?"

"Not that I can think of. He used to tease Ellen that he wanted to live on a boat after they retired, and she had a very low opinion of that idea. I think he only said it to get a rise out of her."

"Look here." Natasha lowered Rod and turned back the skin tissue that had been folded open from his chest.

Evan couldn't keep from glancing in the chest. Clearly the lungs had been removed, but the remainder of the organs were unknown lumps to him. On the skin, Natasha indicated several small round marks; he recognized them immediately. "Cigarette burns. Not very old."

Charlie Graham had burned Sophia with cigarettes.

Evan made his mind stop racing ahead. "What else?"

"He's covered in bruises. Big ones. And dozens of recent cuts." She took a deep breath. "He might have been tortured. Not just randomly beaten."

"Tortured?" Shock raced through him. He studied the body. What he had thought were death changes of the skin he now recognized as bruising and cuts. They were easier to see with no flies crawling about. "What would they want from him? What makes you think torture?"

Her eyes turned miserable. "His tongue was removed. Before death."

Evan spun around and strode out the suite door, his vision tunneling, a loud ringing in his ears. Somehow he found his way to the building's exit, ignoring everyone he passed in the halls. As he pushed through the outside doors into the dark parking lot, he ripped the mask from his face and took deep breaths, Thai food churning in his stomach.

What the hell!

Images of torture assaulted his brain. Natasha hadn't shown him Rod's mouth, but his imagination supplied dozens of heinous possibilities.

He strode away from the doors, needing space between himself and the building, distance from its smell, its cold air, its horrors. He ripped off his paper gown, gloves, and booties and angrily shoved them and the mask in a garbage can at the edge of the parking lot.

Then he vomited into the can.

Fuck me.

He'd never gotten sick at an autopsy, an accomplishment that gave him license to tease those who did. Although technically it wasn't the autopsy that'd made him sick; it was his imagination. He made a beeline for a bench twenty feet away and collapsed onto it, thankful that lighting in the lot was poor and hoping no one had seen him. He ran a hand across his forehead, wiping away heavy sweat.

It's fifty degrees outside.

I need to go back.

But he wasn't ready. Going into that autopsy suite had been one of the hardest things he'd done in a long time. Going back a second time seemed impossible.

But duty weighed heavy on him. Rod had been his friend and deserved to have his killer caught. Collecting every bit of information possible was the key to finding that person.

Like the cigarette burns. They could indicate Charlie Graham.

But a lot of people smoke.

Is Graham capable of cutting out someone's tongue?

He was uncertain. Graham was a bully at heart. Bullies were insecure and lashed out to appear tough, often driven by their own fears. Whoever had mutilated Rod had no empathy and had a twisted need to inflict pain. Graham was definitely an asshole, but Evan didn't think he was a psychopath.

I could be wrong.

He took several more deep breaths, got to his feet, and headed to his SUV. Opening the back, he grabbed a bottle of Gatorade from his supplies. He rinsed and spit several times and then downed half the drink. More than anything, he wanted to get in the front seat and drive away. But he worried that if he left, he'd never attend another autopsy.

I need to know what else Natasha can tell me.

Evan could have her call him. Or just read her report. But that wasn't how he operated. He'd given respect to other homicide victims by being present for their autopsies. He wouldn't do less for Rod. He slammed down the SUV's rear door and strode back into the building.

In the autopsy suite, he put on more PPE, feeling wasteful that he'd trashed the first set. Natasha and Marina watched him approach, caution in their eyes.

"I'm sorry about that," he said, returning to his original position next to Natasha.

"No apologies needed," she said. "I had my own moment when I discovered what had happened."

"Was the . . . the tongue . . . with the body?" His mouth didn't want to form the words.

"No."

"What's next?" he asked, ready to focus on anything else.

"I'm almost done with the weights and samples from the organs," said Natasha. "Fluids have been pulled, and Marina is running a preliminary tox screen on his blood. The other fluids and samples will be sent to the lab for testing."

"Blood and urine?"

"And bile and vitreous humor."

From the eye.

Evan looked at the head, keeping his gaze on the entry wound in the forehead. Natasha hadn't opened the skull yet. "You've examined the bullet's point of entry?"

"I have. And it's two bullets, Evan."

"He was shot twice? Where is the second?"

"They fired twice in the same spot." She moved to the head. "Look here. You can see where they pressed the weapon against his forehead. The front sight left an indentation among the heavy stippling."

Evan saw a small notch jut up from the entry wound. Not every handgun's front sight was flush with the end of the barrel. It would help narrow down possible weapons. The stippling from the explosion of gunpowder looked like masses of tiny grains of black sand embedded in the skin, starring outward from the wound. He studied the entry. "I wouldn't have guessed they fired twice. The barrel must not have left the skin before the second shot."

"It wasn't until I found a lump at the base of the skull that I realized there had been two shots. One bullet is still under the skin at the base of his skull. The other exited behind his ear."

"We've got a bullet." Evan couldn't believe their luck.

The corners of Natasha's eyes crinkled behind her face shield. "We do."

I can match the bullet to a gun.

But first I must find the gun.

17

Rowan opened the glass freezer door at the 7-Eleven and grabbed a pint of Häagen-Dazs.

Sometimes nothing else will do.

She also grabbed a small bag of Doritos to share with Thor because he loved the Cool Ranch flavor. She'd left him home for her dash to fill up her gas tank and get ice cream. Guilt hovered around her head.

Not that he cares when I leave.

From where Thor lay on the sofa, he'd opened one eye when she picked up her keys and then promptly closed it, so she'd let him be.

"Hey, Rowan!"

She turned to see a gym acquaintance standing near the Slurpee machine. She struggled to recall his name as she cheerily greeted him and then felt embarrassed about the late-night sugar and fat in her hands. She'd often thought he resembled Evan a bit—if Evan were in his late twenties, lived at the gym, and had the lowest body fat percentage possible. The muscles in his arms rippled as he nabbed a Slurpee cup of the largest size.

Okay. Not a die-hard sugar hater.

They chatted for a long moment about nothing at all as he filled his cup with every flavor of the sweet, blended ice.

Rowan lowered her estimate of his age to early twenties.

He continued to talk as they both paid and went out the door. She tried to wrap up the conversation, but he continued, not picking up her gotta-go body language as she inched toward her SUV. He wasn't hitting on her; he simply wouldn't stop talking. She listened another minute and then said, "I need to go before my ice cream melts."

He respected the need to protect her ice cream, and they parted.

I still don't recall his name.

She sped home, exhaustion sinking in, and considered saving the ice cream for another day. A few minutes later, she turned onto her street and wound her way along the long road of old ranch-style homes. She steered around the last sharp bend and caught her breath, her heart racing.

That's my house!

Smoke poured from a broken living room window and another on the rolling garage door. Orange flames flickered inside, making the house glow in the dark.

Thor!

She slammed on her brakes and parked at the curb because three people with buckets were frantically running in her driveway. Her neighbors. She grabbed her phone as one man sprinted toward her. *"Where's your hose?"* he shouted.

"Did you call 911?" she yelled back, jumping out of the SUV.

"We all did!" It was Jason from across the street. His wife was in their driveway, filling buckets with their hose.

"My hose and spigot are in the garage!" She lunged back into her Tahoe and hit the garage door opener.

The fire is already getting oxygen through the window. Opening the door won't matter.

The door rolled up, and gigantic clouds of smoke spilled out. They were dark and heavy with small sparks of flame inside, indicating the smoke was incredibly hot.

"Get back! Don't go in there!" she yelled at a neighbor who tried to dash into the garage to grab the hose. "Did Thor get out?" she shouted at Jason.

He froze, his mouth falling open. "He's not with you?"

Sirens sounded in the distance.

Thor!

Her dog hated fire and smoke. As her heart attempted to pound out of her chest, she darted to the back of her SUV and opened the hatch. She grabbed a duffel, ripped it open, and dug out a handful of N95 respirator masks. She pulled off her sweatshirt, slipped on a mask, and shoved the others into Jason's hand. She plunged her sweatshirt into his bucket of water, soaking it through.

"You can't go in there!" he told her.

"My dog is fucking in there!" she shrieked, blocking mental images of Thor with burning fur.

"Maybe he got out!"

"He was locked inside when I left!" Regret that she hadn't taken Thor for the quick trip swamped her, making her weak in the knees. She put the sweatshirt on head, covering her hair, and tied the sleeves under her chin. She rummaged in the duffel for her heaviest gloves and then ran up the lawn to the front door.

Hang on, buddy!

He must be terrified.

"Rowan!" Jason screamed after her. "Don't go in there!"

There was no going through the garage: dense black smoke continued to roll out, completely filling the space from floor to ceiling. She approached the front door, arcing around more smoke pouring from the broken front window.

Who broke the window?

Heat baked her skin, and she tugged the wet sweatshirt forward to cover her cheeks.

"Fuck!" She ripped off her gloves to punch the code into the door lock. She hit two numbers and stopped to dig her burning fingers into the wet sweatshirt.

The fire is right behind the door.

Thor is in there.

She pressed the last two numbers of the code, slipped her glove back on, dropped as low as she could, and opened the door, shoving it inward. More black, heavy smoke poured out as she huddled on her knees, her hands instinctively protecting her covered head. "Thor!" she screamed into the house.

The fire roared in her ears, a crackling, rushing, thunderous sound. "Thor!" she screamed again, trying not to imagine her dog's terror.

She covered her eyes with her gloved hands, trying to peek between the fingers. Heat dried her eyeballs and pushed through her clothing. Through a brief break in the smoke, she saw a wall of fire just beyond the front door.

I can't go in.

She glanced back. A fire truck now blocked her driveway, and the firefighters were unloading their equipment. Jason grabbed one firefighter and pointed at Rowan. The firefighter did a double take at the sight of her kneeling in front of the open door and strode her way.

He'll make me leave.

"Thor!" She considered dashing through the flames to find her dog. But she was already too hot. Smoke rose from her gloves and jeans. She needed to get back from the fire.

Barking sounded from inside. Maybe.

"Thor!" she screeched into the house.

More barking. But it was faint.

He's in the basement. The door must be shut.

There was a door at the top of the stairs that led down to the basement. It was usually left open because Rowan's office was down there along with their workout equipment and the laundry room. Somehow it had closed.

He's got to be okay. Fire and smoke go up.

But she wasn't taking any chances. There could be flames in the basement too. She lunged away from the heat, stumbled to her feet, and ran toward the side of the home. At the back of the house, a slider on the main level opened to a deck that had a dozen stairs leading down to the yard. At the basement level, there were two wide but short windows, one in the laundry room and another in the bathroom. The windows were level with her shins, the basement rooms mostly below ground.

Rowan had never opened the windows in all the years she'd owned the house. There'd been no point; the basement always maintained a pleasant temperature.

But she'd check the window locks every six months or so. When Evan moved in, he'd added small posts that lay in the tracks, keeping the windows from opening more than two inches.

I'll break a window.

How will I get him out?

Thor weighed nearly eighty pounds. From inside the basement, the windows were six feet off the ground and only about eighteen inches high.

If that.

It would be a tight squeeze for Thor. Assuming she could lift him up to the window.

She tore around to the back of the house in the dark, her lungs straining to draw in deep breaths through the respirator. She threw herself to the ground and tried to peer through the basement's frosted glass window into the laundry room. She beat on the window. "Thor!"

More barking. But not near the window.

He's definitely louder down here.

She'd worried that he'd ended up in one of the main level's bedrooms instead of in the basement.

It was dark inside the home, so she wouldn't be able to see his black blur through the window, but the door to the laundry room was usually closed. At least there didn't appear to be flames in the basement. She rolled to her back, jacked up both legs, and thrust them at the glass with all her strength. Then again and again.

Come on!

Nothing happened. Panic chilled her bones.

I need a fireman's axe or a heavy tool.

Thor barked frantically. The smoke had started to flow out from under the roof's eaves on the home's back side, and she knew it could eventually start to stream into the basement through duct work and under the door at the top of the stairs. The fire was spreading inside from the front to the back of the house, and the continuous shriek from her smoke alarms made her sweat. The screeching of the sirens competed against the screaming fear inside her brain for her dog. Rowan leaped to her feet, squinting into the dark of the yard for a big rock or anything she could use to break the window.

The playhouse.

The little plastic house bordered her property. Ten-year-old Lily next door had outgrown the house, and her father had recently tried to pop the plastic walls and roof apart with a sledgehammer. But the joints were stuck tight. He hadn't wanted to break the walls; they were supposed to come apart. Supposed to. So he'd paused the task for a few days.

Rowan closed her eyes, picturing her yard. She'd looked out her kitchen window and seen the sledgehammer leaning against one of the little house's walls. But when had she looked? Yesterday? The day before?

Will it still be there?

The playhouse was much closer than the fire truck. She couldn't see the structure in the dark, but she knew where it was. Rowan jogged down the gentle slope of her yard.

Hang on, Thor.

The outline of the little house under the firs came into view. And there was something thin leaning against it. Rowan grabbed the sledgehammer and raced back to the basement window. She lifted the sledgehammer like a golf club and swung it against the window.

It shattered. Sharp pieces of glass fell onto the tile floor of the laundry room, and jagged pieces remained stuck in the frame. Rowan knocked the bigger ones out with taps of the hammer. The older window had regular glass, not tempered glass that would fall apart in little safety squares. The frequency and volume of Thor's barking increased at the noise, and she laid her sweatshirt across the bottom edge of the window and shimmied in backward, on her stomach. Tiny shards in the frame poked through the sweatshirt, and she tried to raise her torso over them as she scooted back into the laundry room.

Impossible.

She gave one last shove and dropped to the floor. Pain radiated from her stomach and chest; the glass had cut through the sweatshirt as she dragged her body across it.

Can I get Thor across that?

She hit the small room's light switch and hesitantly touched the doorknob. It was cool. She yanked open the laundry room door, and Thor plowed her over, knocking her onto her rear, frantically licking her face.

"Hi, buddy! Are you good? Are you okay? We'll get out of here." She hugged the squirming, furry dog, feeling him everywhere for any injury. He was okay. Just terrified from the smoke.

A layer of black smoke flowed into the laundry room, hovering at the ceiling, and Rowan was glad she had her mask. A loud crash sounded upstairs, and Rowan pictured the roof falling in. She pushed to her feet, slammed the door, and eyed the broken window and the shattered glass all over the floor.

I've got to cover that, or he'll have a million glass slivers.

Rowan opened the dryer and grabbed the load of bath towels. She covered the floor, her brain in fast-forward as she scrambled for ideas to get Thor out the small window. The six feet up to the window suddenly seemed twice as tall. He couldn't leap from the floor; he'd hit the top of the window frame.

The weight bench was impossible for her to move on her own. Her office chair was on wheels but not very tall. Her desk was at the other end of the basement and would never fit through the door.

The dryer.

Rowan leaned over the dryer to see behind it and yanked the cord out of the wall. She got a grip on the round door opening and pulled, putting all her weight into moving the heavy machine. It slid forward with a horrible screech, its feet dragging across the tile. Thor abruptly backed up, staring at the new monster.

That sound is better than the roar of flames upstairs.

Loud crashes continued above her. She didn't know if the firemen had entered the home or things were falling over. The overhead light flicked off, and the room went pitch black.

"Shit." No light came through the little window, but Rowan knew where everything was. She pulled and pushed and strained to move the dryer the ten feet to below the window. The vent hose made a scratchy hiss as it came out of the wall. Rowan looked around as if she could see in the dark room.

"Thor. You still here?"

A nose pressed against her thigh. "Good. Don't go anywhere. Sit." She knew there had to be glass she hadn't covered on the floor. He coughed several times, and she wished she had a mask for him. She shoved the dryer, getting low against it and pushing with her legs.

This is a beast. Would the washing machine have been lighter?

Small crackles sounded under her feet; the dryer had pushed the towels ahead, and she was stepping on glass.

Rowan gave the heavy machine all she had, and it crashed into the wall under the window.

Thank God.

She attempted to rearrange the towels to cover the glass shards again, thankful for her gloves, but it was hopeless.

Get him out.

"Okay, Thor." She went back to her dog and attempted to lift him. It was as impossible as she'd expected. She could lift eighty pounds, but that weight spread out over a wiggly, scared dog was different. He whined and coughed as the din grew louder above their heads. "I know," she soothed. "It's okay." The stinging of her eyes told her the smoke was growing thicker in the room. She led him across the room and patted the top of the dryer. "Up!"

His nails clacked and scratched on the metal as he jumped. Hearing his feet slide around on top, she told him, "Sit!" And was thankful the dryer top was flat.

Now the hard part.

Her sweatshirt was still in place on the window frame, but she knew his back would rake along the broken glass at the top of the window. A few cuts were better than being in a collapsing home. Standing beside the dryer, she lifted one of his paws to the lower window edge. "Up!"

Thor lifted his other paw, stood on his back legs, and then sat again. He whined.

They'd never practiced something quite like this. She had taken him under low obstacles, but not ones he had to jump up to and through.

"Rowan? Are you back here?" Shouts came from the yard, and boots pounded on the stairs up to the deck.

Rowan closed her eyes in relief.

Thank God.

She'd regretted not going back for help when she realized she'd have to hoist Thor out the window. "Down here!" she shouted. "I'm at the low window."

The boots tramped back down the stairs, and a moment later a flashlight beam zipped across her window and then abruptly returned, blinding her and Thor. "She's down here! And the dog! Let them know we've found both of them!" A fireman knelt at the window and set down his flashlight to illuminate the area. "Close your eyes for a sec." He knocked out more of the glass along the top of the window frame as she placed a gloved hand over Thor's eyes. "Will he let me pull him out?" he asked Rowan.

"I think so. I'll push." She lay a folded towel over Thor's back to try to avoid any cuts from the top of the window. Then she directed Thor to put up both paws again, and the fireman got a grip in Thor's armpit and on his scruff.

"Now!" He pulled, and Rowan got a shoulder under Thor's butt and shoved.

Thor yipped in pain but scrambled out, the towel falling back onto the dryer.

"Now you." The fireman held his hand through the window.

Rowan struggled to crawl on top of the dryer, her legs and arms shaking. The rush of adrenaline was gone, and her limbs wouldn't obey. She sucked in a deep breath through her mask and shakily got onto the dryer. She set the towel over the window's bottom edge and managed to climb out without the firefighter's help.

That was much easier than dropping inside.

"Good job," the man said, patting her shoulder as Thor came to her side. "Are you hurt?"

"No. But I think he scraped his back getting out and probably has glass in his paws."

"I don't think that's your dog's blood." He indicated her white T-shirt.

Rowan glanced down. Large bloodstains were visible in the weak moonlight. "It's from the glass when I went in. They're shallow cuts."

She grabbed Thor's collar, and the man led them around the house the same way she'd sprinted to find her dog, giving the burning home a wide berth. Beside her, Thor pulled against her grip on his collar, a loud whine in his throat. Her legs shook, and she stared in shock at the inferno that was her home.

My God.

It's completely destroyed.

"How'd it start?" the firefighter asked.

"I don't know. I wasn't home." Rowan paused, taking in the firefighters as they sprayed the home and staring at the scared faces of her neighbors who'd gathered across the street. Her home lit up the entire block. "When I got here, I saw two windows had been broken and smoke was pouring out. One in the garage door and one in the living room. But maybe my neighbors did it while they were trying to put out the fire."

"The neighbor who told me you'd run around the house said they were already broken when they noticed the fire," said the firefighter.

Rowan couldn't speak.

Did someone deliberately set my home on fire?

18

Wrapped in a blanket, Rowan sat with a group in Jason and Julie's driveway, numbly watching the fire. Julie had brought out blankets for her and Thor as Rowan inspected her dog for injuries and glass. She'd found blood on his back, but nothing was heavily bleeding. She'd removed a few pieces of glass from his fur, but no glass glittered in his pads.

Julie had fussed over Rowan's bloody shirt, making her lift it so she could inspect her stomach. There were several long, deep scratches. Two continued to ooze, and the woman covered them with large bandages. Tiny sharp pains told Rowan there were glass splinters embedded in her skin.

There has to be glass in Thor's feet.

She'd tackle that later, when she could see better. It'd grown darker, and Jason brought out a few bright camping lanterns, their road too rural for city streetlights. The orange of the flames was mostly gone, but smoke of all shades continued to pour out as firefighters sprayed water into the house.

It'd been her grandfather's home, an inheritance that Rowan had purchased from her sisters after his will had been read a few years ago. The house was brick and the roof made of asphalt, but there had been plenty inside to burn. The home still stood, her earlier fears of it collapsing unfounded. But the house would be a hollow shell.

There can't be anything left in there.

I need to call Evan.

Rowan had attended to her dog first. She patted her pants pockets. *Shit.*

"I lost my phone," she told Julie. She recalled grabbing it when she arrived at the fire but had no idea where it had ended up. Julie tapped in a password and pressed her phone into Rowan's hand.

Rowan stared at the keypad. She didn't have Evan's number memorized. A curse of modern technology. She searched for the sheriff's department's number, called it, and asked to be connected to Evan. She was politely told they'd pass on her name and number because Detective Bolton was out of the station.

"Please," said Rowan, her voice cracking. "There's been a fire and we live together and I lost my phone and I don't have his number memorized." Her words ran together as tears burned. The struggle to reach Evan felt like a tipping point into emotional chaos.

I'm still in shock.

Rowan handed the phone to Julie. "Talk to them." And then buried her face in Thor's fur. He had promptly moved into her lap when Rowan had sat on the ground, not caring—or unaware—that he was not lapdog size. Rowan had wrapped her arms and blanket around her dog and watched everything she owned be destroyed.

It barely registered that Julie was speaking fiercely to the sheriff's department, telling them that Detective Bolton needed to be contacted immediately because his home was burning to the ground.

Not the ground.

At the moment it was an important distinction to Rowan that the house still stood.

She didn't know if ten minutes or an hour had passed when Evan came sprinting up the street, having been forced by fire personnel to park away from the scene.

"Rowan!"

Thor leaped out of Rowan's lap, causing her to gasp, *"Oof."* She shakily pushed off the ground to stand.

Evan's arms were instantly around her, pulling her tight to him. "Oh my God," he said four times, running his hands over her hair and her back, stepping back to take a look at her face and then hugging her again. "What the hell happened?"

Rowan shook her head against his neck, her eyes closed. She didn't have an answer.

"We saw the flames," Julie told him. "Both your vehicles were gone, so we'd hoped you weren't home. There was no getting through the front door by then anyway."

"Rowan made it to the door," she heard Jason say. "Thought she was going to run inside the burning house to get Thor."

Evan stepped back, his hands on Rowan's upper arms, scanning her face. "Thor was inside?"

Miserable, she nodded, unable to look him in the eye. "I left him home to run an errand, and when I came back, I couldn't get in the house." Tears streamed.

"Fire lieutenant said she bashed in a back window and got him out," said Julie.

Evan was still studying her face. "The slider?" he asked, referring to the door on the deck.

"No. Laundry room."

He blinked several times. "Jesus. How did you get him out?"

Rowan pushed forward into his arms, unable to talk about it or meet his gaze, wondering where her mental and emotional strength had gone. It'd been there when she had to save her dog.

I used it up.

❖ ❖ ❖

It was obvious Rowan was drained.

Evan couldn't imagine her distress when she'd returned to find Thor trapped inside. His anxiety had exploded when the department switchboard had called and said it'd been reported that his house was on fire. He'd only stayed sane because he'd been told Rowan had made the call. Evan had called her phone a dozen times on the drive from the medical examiner's office, even though he'd been told she'd lost it.

"Which one is the lieutenant?" he asked Jason, who indicated a man speaking with two other firefighters. Evan tightened his arms around Rowan. "I need to talk to him," he told her. "I'll be right back."

She nodded. "I'm okay."

Evan wasn't so sure about that. He knew she would be but wasn't just yet. His emotions and mental stress were still all over the place, and he hadn't even been in the house. She had to be ten times worse. He tipped his head at Julie to take over.

As he strode toward the lieutenant, he accessed the camera views from his security system at the house. Understandably, all cameras were currently offline, but video had been backed up to a cloud. Evan stopped as he pulled up the camera view that had covered the street and watched as a black truck turned into his driveway and a man got out of the passenger side. The driver was impossible to see because of the glare of the home's outdoor lights on the windshield. The passenger lit a device in his hand and prepped like an MLB pitcher before he hurled it through the garage window. He got another from the truck cab and did the same with the living room window. He calmly got back in the vehicle, and they drove off.

It was deliberate.

Evan paused the video and zoomed in on the passenger. He was dressed in black with a black baseball cap that blocked the view of his face the entire time.

He knew where the camera was.

The truck's front license plate was covered, and the rear never came into view of the camera. Evan fast-forwarded until he saw Jason tear up his driveway. Several minutes had gone by, and smoke nearly hid Jason from view. It'd been too little, too late.

This was well planned.

He continued to fast-forward the video, watching various neighbors enter and exit the smoky camera angle. Then it abruptly stopped. The fire had been too much.

As Evan approached the lieutenant, the heat from the smoking house baked his face.

How did Rowan get near the front door?

Evan held out his ID for the lieutenant to see. "I live here too," he said grimly.

"That's your wife?" The man pointed at Rowan.

"Girlfriend." Evan didn't like the word. It didn't fully convey their relationship.

"I've seen people do dangerous things to get to their pets," said the lieutenant. "She was lucky that her dog was in a safer part of the house, but I don't know that she would have gotten him out if I hadn't given her a hand. They were in a tight spot."

"She would have made it happen somehow." Evan shuddered, fully aware Rowan would risk almost anything to save her dog. "What happened? I heard there were broken windows." He would show the lieutenant the video in a minute. He wanted to know what was being said about the fire first.

"That's what I was told too," the lieutenant said. "If the home cools down enough tomorrow, they'll start the investigation. Possibly the next day."

"Think something was thrown through the windows?" asked Evan. "Some sort of Molotov cocktail?"

"If that's the case, it won't be hard to confirm. Accelerants leave signs that the investigators can spot."

"I have video from the front camera," said Evan, pointing to where the camera was positioned under the eaves, now a useless black shell.

He showed the lieutenant the video, watching anger cross his face as the devices were thrown through the windows.

"Our fire investigator will want that footage," he said.

"Not a problem. I want them caught." Evan stared at the smoking home. Rowan loved the house, and his heart broke for her loss.

We've been very happy here.

They would be happy elsewhere too. Belongings were replaceable. Rowan and Thor were not.

Was the house targeted?

The thought made him uncomfortable. Yesterday he'd nearly been shot in the head, and today had been a close call for Rowan and Thor.

Did someone think I was home?

He couldn't comprehend why someone would target Rowan. All she did was help people. And love dogs.

Me . . . on the other hand.

He easily saw himself as a target. He'd pissed off plenty of people over the course of his career. Evan thought about how he'd been searching through Rod's files for an angry suspect who might have gone after the retired detective.

Is the same thing happening to me?

It felt like his life had been going to shit the last couple of days. Rod killed, Sophia missing, the near-miss gunshot, and now the fire. Two gunshots. If Charlie Graham hadn't made Evan step back, the first shot could have hit him.

And my fingerprints in Rod's office.

He was confident that would turn out to be an error; he hadn't touched anything in the office. But damn, Evan hadn't liked the look on Ogden's face as he questioned him. It'd made him feel guilty for something he hadn't done.

Or did someone place my prints in there?

Evan shook his head. He was being paranoid. The last two days had been stressful and long, making his thoughts run wild. He needed to sleep for a day or two.

But that won't be in our house.

Evan watched the video again, zooming in on the useless covered front plate. The truck was a dark-colored Ford—

"Shit."

Evan played with the video, backing up and forwarding through every image of the Ford truck. He was positive it was black.

Like Rod's missing truck.

Evan racked his brain, trying to recall if he'd previously noticed anything about Rod's truck that could indicate this was the same vehicle.

A hand slipped into his. Rowan had stepped next to him, Thor at her side. She held up her other hand to block some of the heat from her face. He saw an N95 had left a faint outline on her nose and cheeks. "I'm ready to leave," she told him, exhaustion in her eyes and voice.

"Where should we go? Iris or Ivy's house? Your parents'?"

Rowan shook her head. "Can you imagine the smothering we'd get from my sisters? I guess my parents' is a better option. But I really don't want to face anyone and answer a bunch of questions right now."

"A hotel, then."

She looked at their smoking home, her lips pressed together. "It's gone, isn't it?"

Yes.

"We'll see," said Evan. "We don't know what kind of damage has been done." He squeezed her hand. "I think a hotel is a good idea," he said, trying to redirect her thoughts. "Quiet. No one talking to us."

"I don't have any clean clothes," Rowan said slowly. "I can shower, but how will I get the smell of smoke out of these clothes?"

The problem was minuscule in light of what had just happened, but Evan suspected she was still in shock and that to her the issue seemed important at the moment. "I'll borrow some things from Jason and Julie. We can shower at the hotel."

"Okay." Some of the worry left her face.

One problem at a time.

He knew she'd be more like herself the next day.

"But maybe we should stop at the emergency room first," Rowan said. She let the blanket fall from her shoulders and lifted her shirt.

Evan was stunned by the sight of the blood-soaked bandages under her stained T-shirt. Long bleeding scratches raced down her torso.

"I thought it'd stopped bleeding. I guess not," Rowan said slowly, staring down at her belly. "I can feel glass in the cuts."

Evan turned the two of them in the direction of his vehicle. "Hospital first. Everything else can wait."

He would tell her about the video on the way to the hospital. It was going to be a long night.

But everyone is safe.

19

"You shouldn't be here," stated Noelle the morning after the fire, glaring at Evan from her chair in their case room.

"Me sitting around doesn't help anyone." He'd been restless for the last few hours.

"You should be with Rowan."

"I spent all night and all morning with her. We agreed it was important that I not let up on these cases, and she's doing fine. Her family is about to swoop in and take over. She won't need me for a while." Evan was exhausted. Even if he stayed in the hotel, he'd be thinking about the cases, so he'd gone to work.

Last night, while Rowan had been in the ER getting glass slivers picked out of her torso, Evan had made a sprint through Walmart just before it closed. He'd grabbed sweatpants, T-shirts, socks, underthings for both of them, and a few basic toiletries. For himself he'd also picked out a pair of jeans and a collared shirt to wear to work the next morning. And he'd remembered to get dog food for Thor.

Rowan had brought up dog food five times before he left for the store.

Priorities.

The two of them had nothing, and Evan was overwhelmed by the thought of replacing everything they used daily. After a fitful night's sleep with Rowan sleeping between him and Thor, they'd had a frank discussion this morning about their priorities.

He would return to work; she would replace the immediate necessities.

And she would call her family, who they knew would promptly help.

Evan had showered while she made the calls and then dressed in the black shirt and jeans he'd bought without trying on last night. The jeans desperately needed a belt, and he'd stared at the sagging pants in the mirror for a long moment, again overwhelmed by what they'd lost.

On his way to work, he'd stopped at Walmart for a belt.

Rowan had watched their camera's video in the ER waiting room, her face blank. She'd handed the phone back to Evan as he told her it looked like Rod's truck. She'd been silent a long moment and then said three words. "Why do that?"

Evan had no answer.

Rowan's family had reacted as expected. Highly emotional and jumping right in to take care of everything they needed. The twins were more than excited to shop for Rowan's clothes—she didn't feel up to it. She'd told them to start at a sporting goods store, and Ivy had loudly protested over the speakerphone.

"You know how I dress," Rowan had said pointedly. "I need clothing I can wear out in the field. You're wasting time with anything else. No dresses, no heels. That can come later. Much later."

In the office Evan sat down at the big conference table and opened his laptop. He smelled the smoke that clung to his shoes. He hadn't been near the fire that long, but it'd been enough to permeate everything he'd worn. After examining the video footage on his laptop's bigger screen, hoping to see more detail of the arsonists and the truck, he'd sent the video footage to the Oregon State Police Arson Unit detective who handled the Bend area.

Enlarging the video hadn't helped. He still had no leads.

Noelle's intense stare burned into the side of his head as he looked at his computer. "Do you need to rent a place to stay?" she finally asked.

"No. We agreed to stay with Rowan's parents for a few months until my renters' lease is up. Then we'll move into my place."

"A few months? Rowan's house will probably be rebuilt by then."

"She's not sure she wants to live there anymore." Rowan had been upset about it this morning, saying she couldn't go back without reliving her terror about losing Thor. But she also felt guilty that she'd have to sell her grandfather's home. They'd agreed not to make any fast decisions, but Evan suspected she'd hold firm to selling.

"That's too bad," said Noelle. "But understandable."

"She might change her mind."

"How is she doing?"

"She's doing well." Evan had watched her closely as he dressed for work and listened to her talk to her family. "Yesterday was traumatic, but she was clearheaded this morning. A little emotional. But she's tough. I don't think she'll be down for long. Her family won't let her."

"They're a force," said Noelle. "Good people to have on your side during a crisis."

"You don't know how true that is." Evan turned his attention to the whiteboard, ready to stop thinking about the fire. "Where are we at?"

"Same place as when you left yesterday," Noelle said. "It probably feels like several days have gone by."

She was right. Rod's autopsy seemed as if it had happened long ago instead of the previous evening.

Evan gave her a quick recap of autopsy results and enjoyed Noelle's reaction of delight when she heard they had a bullet.

"We're going to nail who did this," she said with relish. "And don't get mad at me that I didn't tell you first thing, but I just got the blood spatter results this morning. I'd thought you'd take the day off like a normal person. But forensics says that most of the blood at Sophia's home was Rod's."

"I'm sorry, what?" Evan's thought process froze.

"The majority of the blood is Rod's. There is another person's blood, too, but without that person here to give us a sample, we're not sure whose it is."

"Rod was attacked at Sophia's," Evan said slowly. He'd known it was a possibility, but he'd honestly thought it was Sophia's blood. He'd let himself fall into the deadly trap of making assumptions.

I know better.

"What does that mean?" he muttered to himself.

"Well, it raises *my* hopes that Sophia is alive." Noelle paused, then asked delicately, "Evan, is there any chance that Sophia could be our suspect in Rod's death?"

Evan was floored. The question went against everything he knew about Sophia and Rod's relationship. "Absolutely not."

Noelle eyed him.

"Absolutely not," he repeated as a sick feeling filled his gut.

I just told myself to not make assumptions.

Did I do it again?

"I *know* her," Evan said slowly. "Of course I can't say I'm one hundred percent certain, but I will say I'm ninety-nine."

"We have to consider everything," said Noelle, an apology in her tone.

"You're right," said Evan. "So looking at it from another angle, maybe Rod wasn't targeted. Maybe they wanted Sophia, and he got in the way. But the missing computer tower and files at his place push me to suspect he was the target. I feel if we knew which files were missing, we'd know who killed him."

"Or the missing files aren't related at all," said Noelle. "Maybe nothing is missing, and Rod was killed trying to protect his daughter."

"Thank God Zack wasn't there." Evan had repeated it a hundred times since the boy had turned up. He stood and walked over to the board, eyeing the list of eleven names of local people who'd gone to prison because of Rod's investigating and now were out. He'd visited only Archie Crook. "I've got to cross some people off this list."

"I've looked at those people," said Noelle. "I think you're relying too heavily on location. From what I've found online and in our files, none of them seem likely to be a killer."

Shit. I have the same gut feeling.

"You're right," Evan stated. "I went to Archie first because of his size. No one else had jumped out at me. But like we just said, this could all be moot because Sophia was the target."

Frustration roared through him. It suddenly felt as if they'd made no progress at all. He wanted this case *solved*. Now. "What else did they get from the blood spatter?"

"She said it's not as much as it looks like. To me, it looked like the person wouldn't have any blood left in their body."

"I thought so too."

"It was smeared around a lot. Covered more area. She said it looked like there was quite the struggle on the floor. Here are some of the photos from her examination." Noelle turned her computer for Evan to see. "See these wavy, skinny lines? That's from hair. Short hair, she said."

Evan stared at the photo, barely seeing what Noelle indicated. It was a small, faint imprint in blood on the tile floor. "I'm glad these experts know their job."

She showed him three more photos of impressions in blood on the floor. "Partial palm print. Shoe tread dragged sideways. These straight lines of ribbing are from a sweater."

"The partial palm print could help when we get a suspect."

"The specialist said when we have a suspect to request his glasses and belts. They often throw out clothing, but people keep their glasses. They might hand-wash their glasses, but they rarely get all the blood off—if they even think of it. Same with belt buckles. Shoes too. She also said that washing clothes isn't foolproof and that luminol can unmask flecks of dried blood that even a microscope can miss."

"There were blood drops outside. Were they Rod's?"

"No. Those are from our mystery bleeder."

"Either Sophia or our killer. I hope Rod did some damage to him." Evan thought for a second. "Can't they test the blood to see if the person is related to Rod? Some sort of DNA-typing technology?"

"They could. That takes time, though. And if it was confirmed that it's Sophia, I don't think that will change our investigation tactics at all."

"True."

"I followed up on Ian Martin's plane ticket to Boston," said Noelle. "It was purchased Friday afternoon."

"He bought the ticket the day before the flight?" Evan didn't like it.

"Maybe that's normal for him. That's something we can confirm with his boss today." She frowned, looking at their whiteboard. "I keep coming back to Charlie Graham. Even though Lori checked his alibi, I still feel he has the personality and motivation."

The man hadn't left Evan's mind either. He sifted through his email, remembering that O'Brien had said that Rod was tailing Graham. "I think I saw a 35-millimeter camera on Rod's desk, and I'm checking to see if it was collected as evidence. I'd like to know if Rod took any pictures and which might show us where Charlie has been hanging out." He scanned the list of items from Rod's office, and his gaze locked on a line. "Got the camera!" He immediately sent an email, requesting all the camera's photos and video taken within a few weeks before and after St. Patrick's Day.

"Do we need to talk to Graham again?" asked Noelle.

"I think he's said all he's going to say unless we show up with some evidence in hand."

Someone knocked at the door, and Detective Maxine Nelson stepped inside. "Evan? What are you doing here?" Shock filled her tone. "I thought . . ." She let the statement hang.

"I already questioned him about the fire," said Noelle. "He wants to work."

Maxine stared at him for a long second. "Okay . . . I understand that. It's a distraction from what happened. Is Rowan all right?"

Evan reassured her that Rowan was fine and in good hands with her family.

Maxine didn't look convinced. "I've got a decent-sounding tip on a Sophia sighting."

"What is it?"

"This morning I went to the construction area behind Sophia's home, hoping to catch some of the workers to question."

"The area where Thor lost the scent?" asked Noelle.

"Yes. Anyway, one of the men said he had come back on Friday night after work because he'd left his sunglasses—he thought it was close to ten p.m. He said there was a sedan parked in the cul-de-sac with someone behind the wheel—he couldn't tell if it was male or female. And they were wearing a ball cap. He'd thought it was odd and figured someone was drinking or smoking pot. He parked up the street and got his glasses. When he'd returned to his truck and was about to leave, he noticed a woman walk up to the car and get in. He said she had dark hair."

"He didn't worry that someone was messing around at the site? There's some heavy machinery there."

"He said all the big equipment was where they'd left it earlier in the day. And he knew there was nothing smaller that could be stolen. After seeing the woman, he assumed it was some sort of romantic meetup."

"Did he see them leave?"

"Sort of. He noticed it appeared they were leaving when he stopped to turn onto the main road."

"Did he give any details on the woman or car?"

"Not really. He thought the sedan might have been silver or a light color. Said it was a small four-door. Couldn't tell make."

Evan met Noelle's gaze and could tell she'd had the same thought. Archie Crook's obnoxious mother had a small silver Corolla in her garage. Noelle's forehead furrowed. "That doesn't make sense," she said to Evan. "We asked about Archie's whereabouts on Friday night to see if he had anything to do with Rod at the junkyard. What would the Crooks have to do with Sophia?"

"Crooks?" asked Maxine, looking confused.

"Archie Crook and his mother," said Noelle. "He was an old case of Rod's that went to prison and now is out." She looked at Evan again. "But neither of us felt them for it."

"No." Evan wondered if he'd made a mistake. "Any chance the construction worker felt the driver was a large person?" he asked Maxine. "Both Archie and his mother are . . . larger than average."

"He didn't." Maxine thought for a moment. "He said he was unsure if the driver was male or female. I'd think he'd automatically wonder if it was female because of the driver's size? Meaning women are generally smaller, so he thought a woman was possible. Am I making sense?"

"Yes," said Evan. "But also making assumptions about his impression of the driver."

"True. Want me to go back out there and see if I can get something more?"

"Yes," said Evan. "Make sure not to lead his responses."

"Got it." She turned to leave.

"Hang on, Maxine," said Evan. The mention of Archie Crook had reminded him that he wanted to revisit the cases in Rod's filing cabinet. Maxine had been the investigator on one of them. "Did you review the Sorelli case from eight years ago?"

"I did." Maxine frowned. "Tony Sorelli did some time for armed robbery. He's out now. I read everything thoroughly, and I can't see why Rod would have a copy of the case. He had absolutely no involvement."

"Tony in town?" asked Noelle.

"No. He's in Idaho."

"Not that far," said Evan. "But we're looking for someone focused on Rod."

"I didn't see anything that would point Tony at Rod." Maxine lifted her hands in a "Who knows?" gesture. "I'll let you know what I find out from the construction worker." She left the office.

"I want to ask Sam Durette about his investigation in Rod's filing cabinet too," said Evan. He went to add the task to his list. "Shit. It's already on there. This is the reason I write things down." He rubbed his forehead and wondered how many important things he'd forgotten.

"I immediately write things down," said Noelle. "I have little faith in my memory these days."

Evan's cell phone rang. "Bolton."

It was a dispatcher.

Sophia's car had been found.

20

"Thor! To me!"

A hundred yards away, in the green space near her parents' home, the dog turned on a dime and raced toward her.

As he ran, Rowan watched Thor's GoPro feed on her phone and snorted. The image leaped and jerked and zipped from side to side as she caught occasional glimpses of herself. A blurry pink flash would enter the view for the fastest moment—his flappy tongue. Thor didn't mind the camera mounted on the chest of his harness, and Rowan enjoyed watching the world through her dog's eyes, pleased that the camera had been safe in her SUV instead of the house. Watching Thor's point of view brought instant happiness. Something she needed today.

And that gets my mind off last night.

Her family had been great. They'd looked at the list of things she and Evan needed and then divided up the items between them and headed to different stores. Her sisters had been calling or texting every fifteen minutes with questions about clothes and shoes and sending pictures of things they thought she'd like. They'd tried to follow her rules, and Rowan had said yes to everything except the pink camo jacket.

She still wasn't certain if Iris had sent that as a joke.

Now she and Thor were soaking in the fresh air as she told herself that the world had not tipped on its axis, that life still followed its routine.

My brain will eventually return to normal.

Anxiety would ripple through her at the smallest provocation. Her mother had dropped a mug in the stainless steel sink, and Rowan had almost fallen off her barstool. Which had caused Thor to leap to his feet, looking around for whatever evil had startled her. She'd reassured her dog and then taken him for a walk, needing fresh air and to be out of the house.

I've only been there a couple hours.

But she'd found herself sniffing the air in the home, listening for crackles, checking electrical plugs. Her fight-or-flight reaction was highly tuned to flight, and she wondered how long that would last. It was exhausting. Last night it had been fight. She'd fought for her dog and wouldn't change a thing she had done during the fire.

She'd encouraged him to trot through the small field at first, letting him roam on his own for a bit, watching through the camera to see what caught his interest. He'd paused to view a butterfly and sniffed dozens of rocks, dirt clods, and plants. There'd been a glimpse of something small, brown, and furry, but he'd stopped and looked back at Rowan to see if she'd tell him to ignore it.

Such a good boy.

She wished she could mount the camera on top of his head to accurately see what he turned his head to look at, but she knew he'd never tolerate it. He ended his dash back to her a few feet away, his dark eyes excited and his ears at attention for her next command. Instead, she went down on a knee and held out her arms, and he rushed in, licking her cheek and neck as she hugged him and thumped his chest. He'd had a bath that morning and smelled like dog shampoo, but she still picked up faint hints of smoke.

I don't know if I'll ever get the scent of smoke out of my nose.

After a long moment of loving, she detached the camera. "What did you think of that?" she asked, scratching his head. He sniffed the camera and met her gaze.

/treats/

"Of course. You were a good boy to put up with that thing on your chest." She dug out the ever-present kibble from her pants pocket. "But it was a lot of fun for me. I needed that." Some search dogs wore them all the time, but Rowan hadn't found it necessary. In the past when they'd tried, she'd found watching jolting video for too long nauseated her.

She was thankful that so much of her and Thor's equipment had been in her vehicle. Rowan stored it there so she could leave on a moment's notice if called on a search—she was even prepared to camp overnight for several nights. It'd taken years to assemble exactly what was needed, and she knew where each item was in her backpack. It would have been a pain to replace.

Her phone rang and Thor perked up, his focus on the noisy thing in her hand.

"It's Evan," she told him. She swore her dog brightened at the name. She answered and gave Thor an extra treat.

"How are you doing?" Evan asked, clearly in his vehicle.

"Good," she answered honestly. "Thor and I had to get out of the house, so we're down at the green space playing around with the GoPro. It's exactly what I needed."

"Your family is being helpful?"

"Yes. Driving me a little crazy with questions, but they mean well. Where are you going?"

"Sophia's car has been found at the Todd Lake trailhead."

Rowan straightened. "Any sign of her?"

"No. A ranger just called it in. He looked around and yelled her name for a bit but didn't find her. I've got two deputies on the way to cordon off the scene and requested some explorers to start a search."

"Do you want Thor to come check?"

"It's not necessary."

His tone told her he wanted Thor to help but was reluctant to ask.

160

Rowan pictured the popular location. It was the start of a short hike to the lake and led to other, longer hikes. "Thor and I can be there in twenty minutes. I'd appreciate the distraction. I don't want to shop, but I'm restless sitting around the house."

"Are you sure? I don't want you to feel obligated. We're both tired."

"I want to do this," she said. "Is there snow?" Rowan strode back toward her parents' home. A search was just what she needed. A distraction and an opportunity to help.

"A little. The ranger said the snow is heavier up the trails, but not bad."

"That could be helpful for footprints."

"Well, sounds like dozens of people went hiking there over the weekend," he said.

"Not surprised. Maybe the vehicle was simply dumped."

"I'm not jumping to conclusions," said Evan. "Do you need another scent article?"

"That would be best."

"The one Thor used Saturday was turned in with the evidence. I already signed it out. I didn't want to make assumptions, but I wanted to be prepared in case you said yes."

"You couldn't keep me away," said Rowan. "See you in a bit."

Almost a half hour later, Rowan pulled into the trailhead parking area. The graveled forest road had been a potholed and rutted mess, and she'd apologized several times to Thor as he lurched around in the back seat. She spotted Evan speaking with a deputy next to a dark-green Subaru Forester, and he waved at her. Caution tape cordoned off most of the parking lot and the beginning of the trail. There were a few civilian cars present. Probably belonging to people still out on the trails.

The trailhead was at about six thousand feet in the Deschutes National Forest. She zipped up her jacket and tugged on a knit hat, her hair in a single braid down her back. The temperature was brisk, but the sky was a lovely blue. Patches of old, crusty snow dotted the lot, and she was glad she had her warmest hiking boots. She eyed the position of the sun. There was plenty of daylight left.

She let Thor out of the back and attached his leash. He saw Evan and pulled in his direction. "Hey," she told her dog. "You know better than that."

Thor looked over his shoulder with a guilty expression.

/friend/

"I know you love him," Rowan said. "He's the best." She shaded her eyes against the bright sun. From fifty feet away, Evan appeared tense. He gripped a plastic bag in one hand, which Rowan recognized as containing the scent articles from the search at Sophia's house.

This has been so hard on him.

She guided Thor across the muddy gravel lot.

"Hi, good boy!" Evan squatted and gave Thor some love. The dog's tail energetically wagged, and the deputy stepped out of its strike zone. Evan looked up at Rowan. "Hi to you too."

Rowan met the deputy's gaze. "I'm always second," she said with a grin, noting his last name was Hartley.

"Look at all that thick black fur. He's gorgeous," said Deputy Hartley.

Rowan thought so too as she watched her dog nuzzle Evan's armpit.

Both of them.

"Ready?" asked Evan as he stood, giving Thor a final scratch on the chin.

"Yes. Did you find anything with the car?" she asked.

"It's locked. I don't see any blood inside and can't see anything else of interest through the windows. I had a clear view of all the space." He winced. "No trunk."

"Will you break in?"

"At some point. Depends what we find here."

Hartley stepped away to intercept a pair of hikers coming off the trail.

Rowan stepped closer. "Are you okay?" she asked softly, studying his eyes. There were shadows there, and she didn't think they were solely from the stress of the fire.

"Yesterday was rough." Evan looked away, focusing on the deputy and hikers. "Between Rod's autopsy and the fire, it was a pretty shitty day. I'm feeling drained, and I can't get what I saw at the autopsy out of my head. I don't ever want to do that again for someone I know."

"I'm sorry."

He met her eyes, determination in his gaze. "I didn't tell you yet because we've had other things going on. But a bullet was found during the autopsy, and it was in good shape. If I can find the gun, I've got strong evidence."

"Good!" She tried to be upbeat because the shadow in his eyes had been growing darker by the second. She could almost feel his anger and sorrow.

He dropped his gaze and fondled Thor's ears.

There's more.

"The ME thinks he may have been tortured," Evan said slowly, speaking toward the dog. "He was covered in bruises and cuts." He pressed his lips together as if to keep from saying more.

"That's horrible," said Rowan, shock flooding her, understanding why he hadn't brought it up. "Do you think they wanted something from him?"

He glanced up. "I don't know." Evan sighed and stretched his back, exhaustion on his face. "Is Thor ready to search?"

He's deliberately keeping something to himself. It must be awful.

"Yes." She removed Thor's leash, took the bag, and opened it near his face. He plunged in his nose, eager to start work. "Find it!" Thor darted to the right, immediately starting his usual sweep pattern, but quickly stopped and turned to the car. He trotted over and circled it. Rowan held her breath as he paused near the back of the car. There was nothing—and no one—in the back of the car, but that didn't mean that there hadn't been something there at one time.

Thor continued around the car. He stopped at the driver's door and sat, looking at Rowan. It was logical; it was Sophia's car. He made a chattering sound.

/here here here/

She praised him and then led the dog a short distance from the car, indicating she wanted him to search the parking lot. "Find more." He searched, jogging back and forth, sweeping the lot. "He's still checking, but the lot doesn't seem to have anything," she said to Evan after a few minutes.

"Take him up the trail."

Rowan nodded. She let Thor finish the lot. He got a treat and praise. He'd done what she asked even though he hadn't found anything. She led him to the trailhead and asked him to search again. He circled around the big wood sign at the starting point several times, leaving paw prints in the shallow snow as he sniffed the sign and nearby pines. She indicated for him to go up the trail, and he did.

He's got nothing.

She followed him at least forty yards up the reddish dirt trail, Evan trailing behind. Thor searched as she asked, darting back and forth and occasionally trotting several yards off the path. Rowan watched carefully for that pause and sudden head lift that signaled he'd found something.

"I don't think she came this way," Rowan said over her shoulder to Evan.

Thor suddenly stopped, his head lifted and ears forward. Rowan studied him. It wasn't the right sign for a scent. She couldn't describe the subtle differences in his posture; she simply recognized them. After working for years with her dog, she knew what every pause and small movement meant. Right now something had distracted him. She gave him a few seconds to get back on task before she gave an order.

He looked back at her.

Something's up.

Voices reached her. "Someone's coming," she told Evan. She called Thor back, and he bounded down the trail. She pulled out a toy and started a tug-of-war with him. Evan's focus was up the trail, waiting for the people to appear. He appeared calm, but she knew he was mentally preparing to deal with the worst.

It'd taken Rowan a while to become accustomed to Evan's always-on state of mind. He constantly scanned the people around him, their movements, their hands, and what held their focus. When they went out to eat, she'd learned to let him have the seat that gave the best view of the doors and room. It made her a little sad to think he rarely lowered his shields, but it also made her feel safe. Currently they were both armed. He with a gun—maybe two—and she with bear spray in an outside pocket of her backpack.

If she'd been alone, it would have been in hand.

Two hikers appeared around a bend in the trail, jogging slowly, women Rowan estimated to be in their early twenties. She immediately classified them as experienced hikers; they had the appropriate gear from hat to boots, and it was well used. Not fresh off the shelf from REI. She attached Thor's leash.

"Do you have a phone?" one asked as they drew closer. "We can't get a signal."

The other woman wore a red cap and looked sick to her stomach. Rowan wondered if she needed medical help.

"You're almost to the trailhead," Evan told them. "You can probably get a signal on the road."

Rowan noted he hadn't answered their question.

"Don't go up there!" moaned the ill-looking woman.

Evan grew more alert. Rowan had been looking at him and noticed the change. It reminded her of Thor when he caught a scent. She started to smile at the mental comparison, but the woman in the red hat spoke again.

"There's a dead body back there! She's been shot!"

The woman burst into tears.

Rowan froze, sympathy flooding her, as the crying woman stepped to the side of the path and started to dry-heave, pressing her hands against her stomach. Her friend set a hand on her back and pushed the woman's hair out of her face. She spoke in low tones, trying to calm her down and reassure her that everything was all right. The friend shot a distressed look at Rowan. "It was horrible to come across."

"I can understand that," said Rowan. She'd stumbled across a few shocking things in the woods that she wished she hadn't seen.

When the heaving stopped, Evan showed his ID to the women. "If you'll tell me where the body is, I'll take over from here," he said grimly. "And get the right people up here to handle it." He glanced at his phone. "I've got a bar of service. Hang on." He stepped away to make a call, and Rowan kept her eye on the sick woman and listened to him talk to Deputy Hartley.

"Tell Sawden to call and get a medical examiner, a forensics team, and a few more deputies up here," Evan said into his phone. "I'd like you to come walk these women back and get statements while I take a look at the scene." He was silent for a few moments, listening to the deputy.

"What're your names?" Rowan asked, trying to distract the two women. "I'm Rowan and this is Thor." Thor whined softly, picking up on the anguish, and Rowan stroked his head.

"Charity," said the calm woman. "She's Kerrie." The sick woman had tentatively stood straight, and Charity put her arm around Kerrie's shoulders. "I can't fucking believe this happened. That poor woman," said Charity. Kerrie started a fresh round of tears.

Evan ended the call, turning back to the three women with a somber expression. "Tell me how you found her."

Charity took a deep breath. "We were headed back to the car. We'd come up for a quick hike around the lake and to see how much snow was left." She gestured up the trail. "It's probably back a hundred yards where—"

"I heard a cat," Kerrie interjected. "Well . . . I thought I heard a cat. I know people dump pets up here sometimes, so I went off trail. Charity stayed, and I planned not to go out of shouting distance." She wiped her eyes. "I didn't hear anything else in the trees and was turning around to go back when I caught a glimpse of her shoe, so I went closer." Kerrie's face crumpled.

"She came tearing out of the woods," added Charity. "Told me there was a dead woman. I asked if she was positive, and Kerrie told me she was blue and had a hole in her forehead."

Rowan glanced at Evan. A muscle flexed at his jaw.

Just like Rod.

"I insisted on taking a look," said Charity, giving an apologetic look to Kerrie. "I wasn't going to call the police until I saw it for myself." She swallowed hard, blinking rapidly. "I followed Kerrie's footprints in the snow. The woman was on her side, facing away. It was so hard to walk all the way around her body to get a look." Charity shuddered. "Her lips were blue and there was a hole. I touched her neck, checking for a pulse *just in case*, but there was nothing."

"Charity came back and neither of us had a signal for our phones," said Kerrie, appearing calmer, but leaning into Charity. "We marked where we went off trail and were headed out to call the police when we ran into you guys."

"What was she wearing? Age? Hair color?" asked Evan. His face was expressionless.

Rowan ached for him.

But Thor didn't pick up Sophia's scent.

167

"Ummm. Jeans. Navy coat. Maybe late thirties or in her forties," said Charity. "Brown hair."

Rowan saw Evan's jaw twitch again. Sophia was a brunette.

Sophia is younger, but age can be hard to guess. "Detective Bolton?" Deputy Hartley was walking up the path. "The ME and a forensics team are going to take some time. There's been a few calls today."

"Would you take these women back to the lot?" Evan asked Hartley. "I'm going to check the scene." He looked at Charity. "How did you mark the trail?"

"I dragged a three-foot-long deep groove in the dirt with my heel. It's on the trail's right edge and parallel to the path, but you want to turn to the path's left instead. I didn't want it to look too obvious to any other hikers. Once you step off the path a few steps, look up and you'll see I wrapped a blue scrunchie around a branch. Walk straight out for less than a minute from there. I took a picture of where I marked it." She pulled out her phone and showed several pictures of the trail, groove, and hair tie.

"AirDrop those to me," Evan said.

"I don't know if I can without a signal." Charity frowned at her phone.

"It'll work," said Rowan. "If you're near, the phones can connect without anything." She'd done it dozens of times out in the wild.

Seconds later, Evan nodded and saved the photos. "Perfect. About a hundred yards up the trail, you said?"

"I don't know," said Charity, looking down and pressing a palm against one eye. "I don't know how far back it is . . . we didn't walk that long." Their situation had sunk in, and anxiety filled her voice. She wiped away a tear.

It can affect the strongest people.

"We'll find it," said Evan. "Hold up a foot so I can see your boot treads," he directed. "That way I can identify which tracks are yours." He snapped a few views of their boots and a full-body shot of each woman and then looked at Rowan. "I want you to come with me while Hartley gets their statements."

Rowan nodded. Not thrilled. She'd seen her share of dead bodies and really didn't care to see more. But she wanted to be there for Evan. This could be the body of his friend. "I can keep Thor out of the way."

"Good."

The two women headed toward the trailhead with the deputy, and Rowan and Evan continued deeper into the national forest.

"Thor didn't pick up Sophia's scent," she said quietly.

"Maybe it's not her." His tone said he thought it was.

Thor doesn't make mistakes.

"What if we meet more hikers?" Rowan asked.

"We'll smile, nod, and keep walking. Hartley or Sawden will stop them at the trailhead and get statements. If we're discreet, Kerrie and Charity will be the only civilians who saw anything."

They continued up the trail in silence. Rowan took his hand, giving it a little squeeze, and he turned to her with a sad smile. "I needed that."

She stopped and pulled him to her for a long second, lightly touching her forehead to his, simply breathing. His eyes closed, and she hated that he carried so much weight on his shoulders. After a long moment she pulled back, and he opened his eyes.

So much stress there.

"What aren't you telling me?" she asked, wondering if he'd found out something about how the fire had started. "Have you heard anything on the fire investigation?"

His face cleared a fraction. "No, it's too soon."

"Then what is bothering you?"

He looked away. "I don't want to talk about it right now. We have work to do."

"I get it." She did. But it still stung that he couldn't confide in her. *Did something happen at Rod's autopsy?*

They moved up the path for several more minutes, not meeting any other hikers. Around them, snow covered more of the ground. The trail had little elevation gain, but the trees were closer together and blocked the sun from melting the snow. They walked on the dirt, trying to avoid the snow and not leave shoe prints, but plenty of other prints dotted the path. The trail had been busy over the weekend. The dirt was packed and dry, not muddy like the parking lot, and Rowan noticed their boots barely left an impression.

"There." Evan pointed to the right of the trail. The groove where Charity had dragged her heel was readily visible—but only if you were looking for it. He moved to the left and started scanning the tree branches.

"She said you had to walk in a bit." Rowan scanned the ground and spotted coming and going boot prints in patches of snow. "Let me see the photos of the women's treads." He held out his phone. She nodded. "Both sets of women's tracks are easy to see." Rowan stepped carefully, giving the tracks a wide berth, making sure Thor was right behind her.

His tracks won't be confused with anyone's.

But she wouldn't take a chance of his disturbing other evidence.

Evan moved past her into the woods, watching his steps and taking pictures of the women's prints. "There it is." He'd spotted the scrunchie. A blue indicator that humans had been in the pristine forest. He photographed that too.

They moved in as straight a line as possible. They'd walked for less than a minute when Evan stopped, and Rowan saw his shoulders rise in a deep breath.

He sees her.

She looked past him and saw a glimpse of boot and denim.

Evan continued with his photos, taking pictures in every direction and then moving in closer. It was quiet except for the clicks from his phone and Thor's quiet panting. Needing to center herself, Rowan looked up, spotting glimpses of blue sky among the pines.

It's not a bad place to die. Peaceful. Beautiful.

They drew closer, and Rowan ordered Thor to sit and then stay. She knew he'd sit in one place for thirty minutes. He'd probably sit longer if needed. She let Evan move farther ahead. From where she stood by Thor, she could see the lower half of the woman's body and her black Muck boots. Rowan studied the treads, packed with dark-red dirt. If there'd been snow in the treads, it'd melted.

How long has she been here?

Evan circled the body, shooting more pictures. Rowan watched his face, his emotions hidden behind his blank shield. He knew how to compartmentalize. It was part of his job.

That didn't mean she had to like it.

Evan stopped his slow circle and lowered his camera, staring at something on the body. His shield dropped and wonder entered his eyes. He looked up and met Rowan's gaze. "It's not Sophia."

21

"It's Tara Tilson."

Evan lowered himself to a squat; his gaze locked on the face of Sophia's business partner.

It'd taken him a moment to recognize her. It'd been several years since they'd last met, but Noelle had pulled up the woman's driver's license photo as he'd talked with Tara on the phone.

I spoke with her yesterday.

He struggled to wrap his brain around the fact that the woman he'd talked with was now dead. Relief had swamped him that it wasn't Sophia but then had been instantly replaced with heavy guilt about feeling relieved. A woman was dead; it didn't matter who it was.

But why Tara?

Rowan spoke from behind him. "I don't understand. Tara's involved somehow? Was it because of the ten thousand dollars?"

Evan said nothing. He had no answers. Looking at his phone, he saw he also had no bars. "I need to call Noelle. Maybe she'll have an idea how Tara is involved in this." His brain was spinning rapidly. "Did Tara drive Sophia's car here? If not, where is her car?"

"Her killer took it," Rowan suggested. "Maybe he drove Sophia's car to the trailhead and left in Tara's."

"Could be. Would make sense if he set up a meeting with Tara— but I don't know why they would have a meeting. We'll get fingerprints from Sophia's car. If it wasn't wiped down, maybe we can at least confirm if it was Tara."

"I suspect the car was left on purpose and whoever did it knew the police would examine it," said Rowan. "I'll be surprised if prints were left behind. And even if you do find Tara's fingerprints in it, it's possible Sophia loaned her the car for some reason in the past."

"Correct." Possibilities were evaporating as quickly as he could think of them. "If Tara did drive Sophia's car up here, then she knew what Sophia has been doing." A wave of anger went through him. "And she lied to me on the phone yesterday."

Rowan touched his arm. "From what I understand, these women were close. Maybe Tara thought she was protecting Sophia."

"It doesn't make sense," Evan said, hating that he was stating the obvious. He studied the body and then carefully used a pen to check Tara's pockets. They were empty. "No identification."

"Most likely in a purse," said Rowan.

Evan stood and twisted to study the ground. Where Tara lay, there was dirt for a few yards in every direction. "Do you see any tracks besides Charity's and Kerrie's?" He didn't want to take any more steps than he had to.

"I've been looking for a while. I haven't seen any," said Rowan. "There have to be some."

"Unless our killer ran a branch of pine needles over them as they left, but I'd think that would be obvious too."

"It's hard to tell in the dirt in this light. I don't think that would work if they tried it in the snow. It's too crusty to be changed with the sweep of a branch," said Rowan. "It's practically packed ice. Can you tell if Tara was killed here? I'd think someone walking with a body over their shoulder would be noticed. But a gunshot would be heard too."

Evan had already noticed the pinkish purpling on the side of Tara's face closest to the ground. After her heart stopped pumping, the blood had succumbed to gravity. "She died here. Livor mortis is light, but I can see it."

"Then she hasn't been here that long. I think it starts to appear around an hour after death. Although the cold temperatures might slow it down."

"I need to head back to the trailhead," said Evan. "I'll send a couple of deputies up here to cordon off the scene and keep people out. Then I'll start making my phone calls."

"I don't mind staying until the deputies arrive," said Rowan. "Thor and I can wait on the path and show them where she is."

Evan nodded. But his feet wouldn't move. Part of him didn't want to leave the dead woman. She seemed vulnerable and abandoned in the quiet and cold woods.

I'll get help for her.

"Go. I'll stick around," said Rowan, as if she picked up on his reason for hesitating.

He finally moved and Rowan followed. When they reached the path, Evan gave her a long hug. "It's Rod that's bothering me," he finally said quietly next to her ear. "I told you the medical examiner believes he was tortured."

Rowan pulled back and studied him. "There's more?"

"They cut out his tongue." Bile burned in his throat.

Horror and sympathy filled Rowan's eyes. "I'm so sorry, Evan."

"Yesterday was a spectacularly shitty day. I couldn't bring myself to talk about it this morning. We had enough going on with the fire and getting settled."

"Yes, it was a lot. I'm glad you did tell me."

"I do feel better," he admitted. "Not sure why I feel I have to shoulder certain things alone."

"You'll get better," she said, a sad smile on her lips. "We both will."

Should I tell her about the mess-up with my fingerprints?

Not until it's confirmed. She doesn't need more on her plate right now.

Evan looked at her as if seeing her for the first time. Dark eyes that reflected her moods, a light scattering of freckles across her nose, and long, blonde hair that her sisters fussed over more than she did. It was a fact that she was a lovely woman, but the most beautiful thing to him was the empathy and kindness that radiated from her.

How did I get so lucky?

He'd always felt as if a piece of himself were missing. For fifteen long years, he'd attributed it to the loss of his sister, Bridget. But now that Bridget was back and he'd met Rowan, he realized that Rowan filled the rest of the void.

He'd met a rare woman.

Thor huffed, and Evan glanced down to find the dog studying him, his tongue hanging out, his eyes cheerful. "I swear sometimes your dog can read minds," he said.

"Definitely," said Rowan. "Well . . . maybe not minds, but he certainly reads the slightest change in body language. What were you thinking?"

Evan smiled. "That I'm fortunate to have you in my life. Thor was letting me know that he was lucky too." He gave her a kiss on the forehead. "I'll be back in a bit." He reluctantly left her and headed down the path, his mind shifting back into work mode.

It took several hours for the forensics team and a medical examiner to arrive at the trail to investigate and document Tara Tilson's scene. They'd just begun their work when Evan received a call about a truck found in a lake that matched the description of Rod's. Rowan and Thor had already left, and Tara's site was crawling with law enforcement. He struggled for a long moment, mentally pulled in two directions, but then admitted to himself that the team would have Tara's examination and removal well under control. They didn't need him peering over their shoulders.

But as he drove away, he still felt as if he'd abandoned Tara.

Now Evan stood on the boat ramp watching two divers investigate the truck in a lake several miles outside of Bend. His stomach churned. He'd already dealt with one dead body today and didn't know if he could handle another.

Could Sophia be in the truck's cab?

His gut told him it was Rod's truck. The roof barely showed above the water, but he didn't think that many black trucks of this specific make and model had gone missing recently.

"This is insane," said Noelle at his side. "I'm glad things are happening and moving forward with our cases, but now it's going so fast I can't keep up."

"I feel the same," said Evan. The discovery of Tara Tilson's murder had expanded two cases that were already complicated. Once the truck was removed from the lake, they'd have Sophia's Subaru *and* the truck to search for evidence. "I don't know what sort of information we'll get from Rod's truck. Being underwater could really screw things up."

One of the divers made his way up the boat ramp, moving his mouthpiece so he could speak. "There's no one in the truck," he said to Evan and Noelle. "Ready to haul it out?"

Relief flowed through Evan.

Sophia's not in there.

"Yes, let's get it out," said Noelle. She gestured at the tow truck driver, who'd already backed his rig down the boat ramp. The diver conferred with him on how to attach the cables and chains to pull the truck out of the water.

Evan had already spoken to the fisherman who'd called it in. When the man had fished at the lake the day before, there'd been no truck.

"Why ditch the truck now?" asked Noelle. "Are they worried we're getting close?"

"They clearly knew about the camera at the fire last night. They made certain their identities couldn't be seen on video but knew we'd suspect it was Rod's truck," said Evan. "So they decided to try to destroy any physical evidence by dumping the truck in the lake—we'll see if that worked. Although I can't decide if it was cocky or stupid to use Rod's truck to start the fire."

"We don't know that it was his truck for certain," said Noelle in a tone that clearly indicated she believed it was.

Evan did too.

The truck slowly emerged from the water, its tailgate coming into view.

Evan cursed. "They removed the plates." He had Rod's plate number handy for an immediate identification. "We can use the VIN."

"The missing plates will only slow us down for a minute," said Noelle.

Water gushed from the truck as the rear wheels came into view. Evan crouched to look at the wheels and pulled up a screenshot he'd taken of the truck's wheels in the fire video.

Same.

He'd already verified that the wheels shown in the fire video weren't from Ford; they were custom.

Evan moved to the corner of the windshield the second it was accessible. He motioned for the tow truck driver to pause as he snapped a picture of the VIN.

He followed a sheriff's deputy to her patrol vehicle and watched as she popped it into the vehicle's computer. "Rodney McLeod," Evan stated as the name showed on the screen.

I knew it.

"At least we've got both missing vehicles now," said Noelle as she peered at the screen over Evan's shoulder. "Between the two of them, there has to be some evidence to lead us to Sophia or to find Rod's killer."

Evan made a noncommittal noise. Even with all the blood evidence left behind in Sophia's home, they were at a standstill. But they had the blood of a mystery person, and they had a bullet from the autopsy. When they found their suspect, they'd be able to build a case, but for the moment they needed more evidence.

Evan's brain wandered down a tangent where he wondered if it had been intended for the police to find those two pieces of evidence. They'd practically been gifted to the investigation.

Is someone trying to mislead us?

A suspect could try to alter evidence in a home, but Evan doubted anyone had the skill to purposefully leave a bullet under a scalp.

His phone rang. Maxine.

"Bolton."

"I've found something interesting in Rod's location history from his cellular provider," Maxine said in greeting.

"What is it?"

"He made a trip to Deer Ridge ten days ago."

The state prison just north of Bend.

Where Sophia's ex served his time.

"Did you contact the prison?" asked Evan.

"I did. I knew it'd be the first thing you asked. Rod visited an inmate by the name of Damian Collinson—who I believe you're familiar with. Or you're at least familiar with his case."

Collinson's file had been in Rod's filing cabinet.

"Armed robbery from about fifteen years ago," said Evan. "It was Sam Durette's case."

"Correct."

Evan tried to recall the details. Collinson had been linked to a string of jewelry store armed robberies. From what Evan had read, it'd been a cut-and-dried case. Plenty of evidence and even a confession from his partner. Collinson should have been out by now but was still in prison because he'd stabbed a guard and attempted to stab another inmate.

I need to read that case file again.

"I'll call—" Evan started.

"I got you an appointment at the prison tonight," said Maxine. "I explained who Rod was and what had happened, and they said they'll get you in to talk to Collinson. They're bending a lot of rules for you."

"Bless you, Maxine." He was serious. She'd paved the way, making his job easier.

Only hearing Evan's side of the conversation, Noelle raised an eyebrow, curiosity in her eyes, but she waited patiently for him to end the call.

"When is the appointment?" asked Evan.

"Eight p.m."

Evan checked the time and saw he had an hour. It was doable. "I'll leave right now," he told Maxine. "And thank you again." He ended the call.

"Want to take a drive to Deer Ridge?" he asked Noelle. "I need to review a case, and it would help if someone drove while I looked at the file."

She lifted one shoulder. "How can I refuse a vague offer like that?"

"Rod visited Damian Collinson at Deer Ridge ten days ago."

Her eyes lit up. "One of Rod's purloined case copies."

"It was Sam Durette's investigation."

"Sam is a legend," said Noelle. She and Evan had met the retired detective last summer on a consult for an old case. The three of them had become fast friends and met for coffee once a month along with Rowan.

"I need to be there by eight." Evan studied the black truck, which was now fully out of the water. The tow truck driver was about to pull it onto the flatbed of his truck, but it appeared he was waiting for the lake water to stop running from every cranny. "Is there anything else we need to do here?" he asked Noelle.

"Looks good to me. Let's go for a drive." She headed toward her SUV.

Evan sent a text to Rowan to update her on his whereabouts and another to Deputy Coates, the deputy on light duty who'd been meticulously going through the files from Rod's office, asking him to email a copy of the Collinson file. "I'll grab my laptop and be right there," Evan told Noelle.

He jogged to his vehicle and noticed his pulse was racing.

This feels like a good lead.

22

Damian Collinson didn't look like a person who would stab someone.

The prisoner was a small, wiry man in his fifties with a wide, cheerful smile and perfect white teeth. Instead of hair, several uneven tattoos covered his bare skull, and from where Evan sat, he spotted two tattooed cat faces with names and dates.

Evan fought back an urge to stand and examine the rest of the tattoos.

He and Noelle sat across from Collinson in a small interview room. A grumpy guard had brought in the prisoner, attached his cuffs to the bar on the table with a chain, and then left the room after glaring at Evan and Noelle and pointedly stating they had twenty minutes.

But Collinson was definitely happy to be there and looked from Evan to Noelle with an eager smile. "What's up? After-hours visits are unheard of here. I'm the talk of the block tonight." Pride filled his voice.

"Sam Durette sends his regards," said Evan. During the drive to the prison, he'd spoken with the retired detective, who'd originally investigated Collinson. Durette had had two of the cases that had turned up in Rod's filing cabinet, and he couldn't think of a reason why Rod McLeod would have copies of either one.

"Durette? That old coot is still alive?" The prisoner's eyes lit up in a happy way.

Almost sounds like he cares about the guy who put him here.

"Sam is doing well," said Noelle. "Retired, of course."

"Usually sends me a Christmas card. I didn't get one this past year and was concerned."

"He sends cards?" Evan blurted in surprise.

"Yep. Told me he sends them to everyone he put in prison until they get out. I think it's more of a big fuck-you than a Season's Greetings, but I looked forward to them."

"Huh." Noelle seemed as dumbfounded as Evan felt.

I can think of a few people I'd like to send fuck-you cards.

"You're very striking for a cop," Collinson told Noelle, intently studying her face. "You look like one of those Greek goddess statues. You know . . . the tall and elegant but strong ones that look as if they could kick your butt and smile while happily doing it," he said in a hopeful voice.

"Grow the fuck up," snapped Noelle. Then she gave a cold imitation of the smile he'd described, making Evan suspect she would kick Collinson's butt if given the opportunity.

"Wow." Collinson continued to stare, admiration in his eyes.

"Hey!" Evan waved his hand in front of Collinson's face, pulling his attention. "Week before last, you had a visit from Rod McLeod," he said, trying to get the interview on track. The clock was ticking.

"Yep." Collinson flashed his white teeth.

"What did he want to discuss?" asked Noelle.

"Why do you ask?" The prisoner's face was open, genuinely curious.

"Did you know McLeod before he visited?" asked Evan, ignoring the question.

"Nope. Never heard of him; never met him. He told me he was retired Deschutes County. Was he lying to me?"

"No," said Evan. "What'd the two of you talk about?"

A sly smile appeared, and Collinson narrowed his eyes. "What's in it for me?"

"Nothing," stated Noelle at the same moment Evan said, "Twenty-five bucks in your prison account." She glared at Evan.

"Make it fifty."

"Deal."

Collinson leaned back in his chair, his chain clanking on the table, his expression open and happy again.

"Fifty bucks is all it takes?" asked Noelle, suspicion in her voice. "I figured you'd want your case reopened or something ridiculous."

"Nah. I'm guilty. That'd be a waste of time." The smile returned.

"Well . . . that's refreshing," said Noelle, sounding a bit stunned.

Collinson shrugged. "I tell it like it is . . . like I first did with you," he said, admiring her again, making her groan. "What was the question?"

"Your talk with McLeod," said Evan, trying to remember if he had fifty dollars in his wallet.

"He wanted to go over details from the Golden Goose job."

"Not the other two robberies?" All three cases had been grouped together in Rod's filing cabinet, but all the case details were present for the Golden Goose, while the other two files were summaries. The Goose had been Collinson's third robbery.

"Nope. The dude had drawn a detailed floor map of the jewelry store and wanted me to trace our paths and tell him step-by-step everything that had happened inside."

"Isn't that all on camera?" asked Noelle.

"There's a few short periods of time where I stepped out of view, but most of it's on video. My partner, Doug, was on video the whole time."

"What did you do during those seconds?" asked Evan.

"Nothing different than was on the rest of the video. I continued to smash and grab while Doug kept the employees out of trouble."

Translation: Doug held them at gunpoint.

According to the case file, the evidence found at the Golden Goose had confirmed what was visible on video.

"You didn't ask McLeod why he wanted to know?" asked Noelle.

"Sure I did. Several times. He said he was just trying to get it straight in his head." The prisoner leaned forward and lowered his voice. "But that was all bullshit. He knew exactly what I was going to say each time before I said it. It was like he was just looking for me to make a mistake or claim something else happened while I was off camera."

Evan sat still for several heartbeats.

Rod came here to confirm something he already knew?

He thought back to the stills in the file that had been pulled from the robbery video. Both men had worn full face masks and were unrecognizable on video. But Collinson had sliced his arm on one of the glass cases he'd broken, leaving substantial blood behind. Then he had stupidly gone to an urgent care center an hour away because it wouldn't stop bleeding. An alert nurse had called the police. DNA had connected him to the Golden Goose and then to the other two robberies.

"If you hadn't cut yourself, you probably wouldn't have been caught," Evan stated.

"Tell me something I don't know." Collinson shrugged.

Something hovered just outside Evan's thoughts. He felt as if there was a connection right in front of him, but he couldn't see it.

But Damian Collinson's case was clean. He'd been found guilty and hadn't tried to fight the facts.

Why did Rod keep this case?

Evan met Noelle's gaze and saw his question reflected there. She didn't appear to have the answer either.

"We talked about fishing too," Collinson said. He looked from one to the other, an "I'm trying to be helpful" expression on his face. "And his grandson. Don't recall the name, but Rod said he's smart as a whip."

Evan said nothing, slightly annoyed that a prisoner knew that Zack existed.

"Did McLeod bring up any other past cases he was looking at?" asked Noelle.

Collinson scratched his neck. "No. He asked if I knew Charlie Graham but didn't say nothin' about his case. Told him I knew who Graham was but had never spoken to him. I'd heard he'd gotten out."

"*Never* spoken?" asked Evan.

"Nah. Different block. Saw him around a few times. Heard he was an ass."

Accurate.

Evan wondered if Rod's goal had been to get information on Graham. "Did McLeod say why he asked about Graham?"

"Didn't say and don't know." Collinson gave a one-shouldered shrug. "Seemed random. Didn't ask about anyone else."

Evan raised a brow at Noelle, who shook her head.

No more questions.

A few minutes later they'd collected their weapons and were headed through the cool night air to her SUV. "Think Rod was here to ask questions about Graham?" Noelle asked as she tugged her jacket tighter.

"That crossed my mind. But I don't see a link as to why Rod quizzed him on those robbery cases and then asked about Graham."

"Rod only asked about the Golden Goose robbery case," Noelle stated.

"Another connection I don't understand. Obviously that robbery broke open the other robbery cases, but other than that, why is the Golden Goose important to Rod?"

"Don't know. All I can come up with is that it was an excuse to ask about Graham."

"Then why didn't he talk to someone from the right cell block? And Rod took the time to draw a detailed map of the jewelry store. If the robbery was a reason to get info on Graham, it would have been easier to simply ask questions. And it sounded like he was specifically curious about the times that Collinson stepped out of camera view. I think he was there looking for information on the robbery. Or a confirmation about something he believed."

They climbed into Noelle's SUV as Evan continued to think out loud. "It *had* to be about the Golden Goose robbery; he kept a copy of the case file. Graham could have been an afterthought. Maybe Rod was hoping for a little prison gossip."

Noelle started her vehicle. "I hope we didn't waste a few hours by coming here."

Evan thought for a long moment, examining how he felt about the conversation with Collinson. "I don't think we did," he said slowly. "My gut tells me we're onto something that leads to why Rod was killed, but I can't see the full picture yet. I know we've identified who Rod has called over the last couple weeks, and none of the names on the phone lines matched the convicted suspects from his files, but maybe he made calls to their families or known associates to get in touch with them."

"Or he used a burner for some reason to make those particular calls," said Noelle. "There's no record of him calling the prison, but clearly he made an appointment to meet with Collinson somehow."

"Why a burner?" muttered Evan.

"Because he was trying to keep things hidden from someone," said Noelle. "But that person—or people—caught up with him anyway."

"Shit. Is it just me or did this trip create more questions?"

"More questions," agreed Noelle. "But like you said, it feels like we're onto something with Collinson and the Golden Goose. We just don't know what it is."

Evan opened the Golden Goose case file again. "What are we not seeing?"

I better figure it out soon.

23

In the early morning's light, Evan trudged toward the sheriff's department employee entrance. The night before, it'd been difficult to fall asleep after the prison visit. His mind had traveled down too many tangents, looking for answers. At 3:00 a.m., he still hadn't figured out why Rod had visited Damian Collinson in prison. Rowan had complained about the bags under her eyes that morning and then instantly apologized. "I've got no right to whine," she'd told him. "We still have each other, and I'm thankful for that."

Inside the department, he greeted a few people as he strode down the stark hall. One officer stopped him. Govier had been around forever. A cop's cop. But Evan had never seen his eyes as sad as they were today.

Here come more condolences.

"Detective," said Govier. "I'm so sorry about McLeod. He was one of the good ones. We went back a long way."

"He spoke highly of you," said Evan.

"Thanks." The older cop was restless, his hands moving from item to item on his belt. "I just talked to him a few weeks ago. Bumped into him at Ed's Tavern."

Over the past few days, Evan had heard several stories about Rod that started this way. He tried to lighten the situation. "Would have been odd if you hadn't seen him there."

Govier gave a half grin. "True. We both like to shoot the shit. Bitch about suspects and everyone else." He frowned. "Never dreamed that'd be the last time I talked to him. We saw a lot of crap together over the years."

Evan clapped the cop on the shoulder, giving a firm squeeze. "I bet. We'll all miss him."

Somehow it's become my role to comfort people.

"He was proud of you," Govier said, meeting Evan's gaze. "Said you were a good detective. I know you'll figure this shit out and get the guy."

Evan's heart twinged. He'd now heard that several times. Each time it stabbed a little deeper.

He took a breath and mentally searched the files he'd recently read, trying to recall if Govier's name had popped up.

Collinson.

"Say, did Rod ever talk to you about the Golden Goose case?"

"The jewelry robberies? Funny you say that. We talked about it the last time I saw him."

A mild electric current went through Evan's extremities. "Yeah? What did he say?"

Govier rubbed his chin as he thought. "I was one of the first responders to the Goose. He knew that fact, which I thought was odd because he never worked on the case. It was Durette's."

Evan nodded, impatient for the cop to keep speaking.

"We talked about a half dozen cases that night," said Govier. "Don't really remember what we discussed specifically on that one."

"Do you recall which other cases?"

"Aw, shit. You would ask me that. There was a lot of beer involved, you know."

"Could be important," said Evan. Tension tightened in his neck.

Govier's brows shot up. "Oh yeah?" He frowned, clearly thinking hard. "Let's see. Ummm . . . the shooting at Home Depot. Two dead—that was an old one."

And one of the cases in Rod's filing cabinet.

"We talked about the Livingston assault down in the Old Mill area. Dude nearly killed his wife. Man, that was an ugly scene. I was one of the first there. I don't know how she lived."

Not in the filing cabinet.

Evan made a mental note to review the Livingston case. Possibly it was one of the missing ones. He recalled the woman had been in a coma for weeks.

"And we talked about the love triangle case," continued Govier. "Guy shot and killed the husband when he was caught with his wife. It was self-defense 'cause the husband pulled a gun. He got off."

"The Meyers case," said Evan. It wasn't in Rod's filing cabinet, but Evan knew it very well because he'd teamed with Rod on the investigation. But Rod had only photocopied cases that had ended in a successful prosecution.

I'm interested in bitter people getting out of prison.

"I was on the scene for that one," said Govier with a shudder. "Brains everywhere."

"I remember all too clearly," said Evan.

Govier was still thinking. "Not sure what other ones we talked about." He looked sharply at Evan. "You think it was someone from an old case of his?"

"Looking at all the possibilities," said Evan, keeping it vague.

Govier snorted. "Guess I had that coming. I'll let you know if I remember any others." He raised a hand at Evan and continued on his way.

Evan headed down the hall to the "war room," as he now thought of their conference room for the cases. He turned the knob on the war room's door and nearly banged his nose on the door as it stayed locked in place.

He could tell a light inside was on, so he'd assumed it was unlocked. He knocked and then dug in his pocket for the key.

"Bolton!"

He looked up to see his lieutenant, Louis Ogden, speed walking down the hall, trying not to spill anything from the WORLD'S GREATEST BOSS mug in his hand. "In my office." Louis jerked his head and turned around.

What is it this time?

Evan had assumed the collection of his fingerprints had checked out fine since he'd heard nothing the day before, so he hoped that Louis had something helpful for their investigations and not a lecture. He caught up to his lieutenant. "What's up, Lou?"

Louis shot him a look. Some of the detectives called him Lou-Lou, as in "Lieutenant Louis." He didn't like it and clearly had expected Evan to say it.

He knows I don't call him that.

Unease settled in Evan's chest. Louis was antsy again, like he'd been the other day when he told Evan his prints had shown up in Rod's home. He followed Louis into his office and kept his face neutral, but something told him bad news was coming.

"Sit."

Evan sat.

His lieutenant dropped into his chair on the opposite side of the desk. He hadn't looked Evan in the eye since they'd entered the room. Not a good sign.

Evan waited.

Louis sighed, wrapped both hands around his coffee mug, and finally looked at Evan. "There wasn't a mess-up with your prints. They came back the same as before. What's new is that your prints also turned up in Sophia McLeod's home."

The floor seemed to drop away under Evan's feet, and he was thankful he was sitting. "That can't be right." His voice didn't sound like him. "Sophia's home had been determined to be a crime scene before I got there. I touched nothing in the home. And I'd never visited her at that house. She hasn't lived there very long."

"They've got your prints on the broken glass from the back door and on the counter in the bathroom."

"I touched neither one." A loud ringing started inside Evan's head, and sweat broke out on his upper lip.

This isn't happening.

"This is bullshit! Is this some sort of joke?" Evan asked.

"No joke." Louis looked him dead in the eye. "I need your badge, weapon, and keys. You're on suspension until this gets straightened out."

"You're suspending me?" Fury made Evan see red. "You *know* this isn't right!" He took a deep breath and thought back to walking through Sophia's bloody house. "Wait. At the scene, Noelle told me there were no prints on the back door's knob—we'd discussed that it was premeditated since the person must have brought gloves. You're saying my prints are on the glass but not on the doorknob? What kind of stupid criminal does that?"

"I can't explain anything, Evan. I just know what information is in front of me." Louis cleared his throat. "And you need to turn over Rod's computer tower."

Evan blinked. "What . . . what are you talking about?"

"The missing tower. The one you have for sale on Craigslist."

Sweat spread to other parts of his body. "I don't have anything for sale on Craigslist. I've never used that site."

Louis sighed. "We found an old receipt for the tower in Rod's office, so we know what kind it is. It's normal to scour resale sites for stolen items—"

"Don't tell me how to do my job," Evan snapped. "I knew about the receipt and had Coates checking the sites."

"When it turned up, we subpoenaed the site for the email associated with the seller. It's a Gmail with your first and last name in the address."

I didn't hear about a subpoena.

Someone on the investigation had gone to Louis behind his back.

Who?

"I don't have a Gmail with my name in the address," Evan said, trying to keep his voice steady. "But I got a spam Craigslist email the other day . . ." He thought hard. "Possibly it wasn't spam. It had asked if some item was still available, and I deleted it. But how would that end up in my actual email if the posting was set up under a fake email?" He held Louis's gaze. "Do you think I'm stupid enough to put a stolen item on Craigslist within days of it going missing?"

"All I know is the information that I have in front of me," Louis repeated, breaking their eye contact. "Yes, a lot of this seems unlike you—"

"*All of it is unlike me.* This is my fucking job, Louis. I take a lot of pride in what I do. I'm not a dishonest person, and I put everything I have into doing the best investigation possible."

"I've known you a long time, Evan. This doesn't make sense to me either. But until I get to the bottom of it, I can't have you on the job."

Evan got to his feet and paced the small office. "You know this isn't right. I don't know what the fuck is going on—but it feels like I've got a target on my back." He stopped and looked at Louis. "You know I was almost shot the other day. Twice. And someone burned down Rowan's house! *Where we live together!*"

His mind sped in circles. He'd written off the idea that it seemed like shitty things were purposefully happening to him—because that didn't happen in real life.

I was right. Someone wants me out of the way.

Who?

"You *can't* take me off Rod's case," Evan stated forcefully. "We both know I'm our best chance to find out what happened."

"Detectives Marshall, Shults, and Nelson have got things under control." Louis snorted. "An all-female team. We'll have to call them Charlie's—no, Louis's Angels." A grin filled his face.

Evan just stared. "You're making jokes—fucking distasteful jokes—when I'm about to lose my job."

Louis's expression immediately went serious. "You're not losing your job," he said in a condescending tone. "It's just temporary until we figure out what's going on."

"You think I stole a computer tower from Rod McLeod," Evan said through gritted teeth as he stopped to glare at Louis. "And you think I left my prints all over two crime scenes. So what I'm hearing is that you think I'm an idiot who hasn't even watched a damned episode of *CSI*. Not a detective who's solved cases for over a decade. *Are you kidding me?*"

"All I know—"

"Do *not* say that to me *again*." Evan removed his gun and carefully set it on his lieutenant's desk. He did the same with his identification, badge, and keys and then added his work cell phone, ignoring a childish urge to slam it down. Without another word, he opened the office door and then closed it loudly behind him. A few faces glanced his way. From the corner of his eye, he saw a deputy do a double take. If his face reflected a fraction of the anger he had inside, he must look ready to strangle someone.

He heard the lieutenant's door open behind him. "Can someone give you a ride home?" Louis asked.

He wants my vehicle.

"As soon as I get my shit out of it." Evan kept walking.

"Laptop too."

Evan stopped and turned around. "Anything else?"

Louis's cheeks were flushed. "Not that I can think of." He glanced at the employees who'd stopped what they were doing to watch.

Evan nodded and continued his trek toward the exit.

I'll Uber. It'll give me a chance to cool down before I talk to Rowan.

"Evan?" Noelle was coming down another hallway, her jacket still on and a to-go carrier with two cups in her hand. "Where are you going?" She held out the tray, and he automatically took the cup with "USA" written on it. Noelle always bought him an Americano. The chai was hers.

"I'm going home."

Her forehead furrowed. "You don't look great. Are you sick?"

"You could say that."

Someone on the investigation went behind my back.

He had a hard time believing it could be Noelle. "I'm suspended. My prints were confirmed at Rod's scene and also at Sophia's."

Her coffee carrier dipped dangerously, and his hand shot out to steady it.

"*What?*" Noelle's mouth opened and closed several times. "They suspended you? There's clearly an error with the prints. Ogden is a blind ass if he can't see that."

Evan stepped close to her and lowered his voice. "Do you trust me, Noelle?" He searched her eyes as he continued to hold one edge of the coffee tray.

She stared back for a long moment. Confusion and then clarity flitted in her gaze. "With my life," she whispered.

"I'm being targeted," Evan said. "I don't know why, and I don't know who, but whoever it is has access to our investigation and can communicate up the chain."

I said it out loud.

It felt right. It was the only thing that made sense. It was someone in the department.

Noelle straightened, pulling back the slightest bit and tugging on the tray. Evan let go and held her gaze. "Do you know what you're saying?" she hissed in a whisper.

"I know exactly what I'm saying. I've been shot at, Rowan's house burned down, and my prints are places I never touched. I've also been accused of stealing evidence and trying to sell it online."

Are they mad? Shock filled her eyes. "What is going on?"

Evan was grim as the events of the last few days suddenly sank in. "I don't know. But . . ." He stopped as a new thought occurred to him. "Maybe Rod had discovered something that . . . someone here didn't want him to know."

Unease filled her face. "And now they don't want you finding the same. But what about me? We're on the same cases and nothing has happened to me . . . yet."

"It feels personal," admitted Evan.

"I need you on these cases," urged Noelle. "Maxine and Lori are great, but you're our team leader. You *know* these victims."

"It's out of my hands." He'd never felt so untethered. In a matter of seconds, Louis Ogden had yanked away Evan's identity and a huge piece of his self-worth. He was in law enforcement to help others. The need to help people was part of his DNA. He hadn't joined Deschutes County for an ego boost and guns. He'd wanted his life to have purpose.

Now it'd all been ripped away.

And he felt empty.

"They have my phone, so you'll have to use my personal number," Evan said numbly.

She said nothing and just looked at him.

Noelle can't call me about a case I'm no longer on.

"Shit." He would have to shake his investigation mindset. "Please keep me in the loop," he said in a quiet voice. "Sophia and Rod are my friends."

"I know." She looked about to cry. "I can't believe how wrong this is. I'll figure out who did this to you."

"No. Concentrate on finding Sophia."

Evan would investigate his own mess.

No one can stop me from doing that.

He gave her a one-armed hug, holding the cup of coffee she'd kindly bought him and avoiding the off-balanced carrier in her hand. "It'll be okay," he said lamely. "Good luck."

He hated the weak phrases. His mind was full of forceful words, but none were appropriate at the moment.

The look in Noelle's eyes said she understood. "I'll call you."

Evan nodded and blindly turned away, heading for the exit again.

How will I explain this to Rowan?

24

Iris pressed a mimosa into Rowan's hand a minute after she sat in Ivy's chair.

"I don't want this." Rowan tried to hand it back. She had no interest in alcohol that morning. She was tired enough. Between the house fire two nights ago and Evan's constant tossing and turning last night, she felt like a zombie.

"It's orange juice," said Iris as Ivy expertly draped her salon cape over Rowan, avoiding the drink. "You need the vitamin C and energy." Ivy patted the seat of the next salon chair, and Thor immediately hopped up and sat, his ears forward. "Good boy," Ivy said, scratching his chest. For some odd reason he liked to sit in the salon's chairs, stare at himself in the mirror, and watch the people around him.

"I didn't sleep well," Rowan admitted, and took a cautious sip. Iris hadn't lied; it was orange juice. Rowan shifted in the chair, trying to lean back a bit so there was less pressure on the skin of her torso. She was 99 percent certain all the glass splinters had been removed in the ER, but the healing scratches were tight and annoying.

My sisters must think I'm a hot mess.

The twins had asked Rowan to meet them at their salon to pick up the items they'd purchased the day before for her and Evan. And then refused to let her go until they trimmed her hair. Rowan didn't see the point of a trim, but at least they hadn't wanted to do her color. That took hours. A trim should only take a few minutes.

The twins loved to use their beauty skills to make people feel good about themselves. It was also their way to give comfort and support, as people made casseroles or baked to show their compassion. Rowan knew that when the twins worked on her hair, they were showing their love.

The twins owned Dye Hard in downtown Bend. It was stylish with elegant lines and black-and-white decor. Huge mirrors covered the walls, and intricate chandeliers hung from the high ceilings. The only color in the salon was the rich greenery of the long plant wall. And Ivy's always-present red lipstick.

Ivy's hair was in an elegant bun on top of her head, her makeup minimal apart from the lipstick. Iris had opted for a Wednesday Addams look, her own long, black hair in braids. Rowan eyed the fun black-and-white-striped stockings, jealous that Iris could pull off the look while Rowan knew she'd look ridiculous in them.

"I'm really sorry about the fire," said Ivy for the tenth time that day.

Rowan nodded, tired of thinking about it. The twins had bought tons of clothing and necessities and then loaded up the back of Rowan's SUV that morning. Rowan had stared at the pile of shopping bags and nearly burst into tears. It'd been a heavy weight knowing that she and Evan had so much to replace.

More of her family's love and support expressed in their second-favorite way: shopping for others.

Rowan's phone rang. She awkwardly slipped it out of a pocket and brought it out from under the cape. It was Evan's sister, Bridget. She glanced at Ivy, who was snipping at her ends.

"Go ahead," said Ivy.

Evan had spoken briefly to his sister about the fire, but Rowan hadn't talked to her yet. She took a deep breath and prepared herself for a dozen questions. "Hi, Bridget," Rowan said in greeting.

"Rowan, is Evan with you?" Bridget's voice was full of panic.

Rowan looked around as if she expected to see him in the salon. "No, he's working today."

"Zack is missing," Bridget said, her words running together. "I'm so sorry, but I don't know what happened. Charlotte was with him at the barn and thought he'd come back to the house, but we can't find him."

Rowan sat up straight and set her juice on the counter, as if emptying her hands would help her hear better. "He's gone? Are you sure?"

"We've been searching for ten minutes. My husband and the kids are still looking," said Bridget. "I've left messages for Evan several times and also called the police." She started to cry. "We promised to keep Zack safe. He trusted us. *Evan trusted us.*"

"Evan must be tied up with something at work," said Rowan, her brain spinning.

Did the person who grabbed Sophia locate Zack?

Rowan eyed Thor, who watched her with eager eyes and ears. "I'm headed your way. I've got Thor with me. He'll find Zack." She ended the call and glanced at Ivy, who was already removing the salon cape from her shoulders. She pulled Rowan's hair back into a high ponytail, deftly creating a more polished look than Rowan ever could.

"What happened to Zack?" asked Iris. Her look of concern matched her twin's.

"Don't know," said Rowan, gathering her bag. "He was at the Kerrs' ranch one minute and then gone the next."

"A wild animal?" asked Ivy.

Rowan cringed. She hadn't considered that. But if he'd been near Charlotte, surely she would have heard something. "I doubt it. He probably wandered off and got lost. It's what usually happens." She'd found dozens of kids—and adults—who'd intended to step off a trail for a quick moment only to find themselves utterly lost.

Please let that be the situation.

She hit Evan's contact on her phone and signaled for Thor to hop down. Evan's phone promptly went to voicemail. She didn't bother with a message and shot him a text to call her.

He's probably in a meeting or doing an interview.

She gave her sisters quick hugs. "Thank you for everything you've done for us. It means so much." The twins reluctantly said goodbye, worry in their expressions.

Rowan strode to the door, Thor at her side.

What happened?

Zack seemed like a smart kid. Him getting lost didn't feel right in Rowan's gut. But she'd seen the most intelligent people get lost. It happened.

Evan was worried about Zack's safety.

Rowan hated to think that someone had grabbed the boy. They'd thought no one could connect Zack to the Kerrs' ranch. It'd been a perfect place to hide him.

Did someone follow us there on Sunday?

She opened her SUV door so Thor could leap in, then slammed the door and got in on the driver's side. The drive to the Kerrs' would take about forty-five minutes.

I'll hear from Evan by then. And most likely Zack will have turned up.

But she pressed heavily on the gas, a sense of dread bubbling under her skin.

Everything will be fine.

◆　◆　◆

Everything wasn't fine.

Rowan approached the Kerr home and spotted two sheriff's patrol units parked at the house. She noted neither was a K9 unit, which made sense. The county K9s were primarily trained as tracking and apprehension dogs, not search and rescue dogs. Their purpose was to find and stop suspects—usually with their teeth. In the department they were sometimes called "bitey dogs" and were trained to appear aggressive. Not a great skill when a child was missing. Thor knew to sit and wait for Rowan when he found his quarry. He never barked but often did his soft little "found it" chatter. The last thing a search team wanted to do was scare a missing child.

Or an adult. A few times Rowan had been on a case in which an adult had become confused and then hidden when they heard searchers' calls. One time Thor had found a missing senior woman with dementia within a hundred yards of the searchers' starting point. She'd crawled deep inside a fallen, rotted tree trunk, thinking the people calling her name wanted to harm her.

Would Zack believe he needs to hide?

Bridget approached as Rowan changed Thor's harness to his work one. He knew that when it went on, work was coming. Excitement radiated from him, his tail wagging a rapid beat. He met her gaze.

/go go go/

"Soon," she told him.

"No luck yet?" Rowan asked, knowing the answer by Bridget's tears and the stress in her eyes. She noted the woman carried a plastic grocery bag of clothing.

Scent articles for Thor.

"No. The deputies are looking," said Bridget. "And so are Victor and Theodore. I made Charlotte stay in the house, and she's not happy about it at all." She looked at Thor with hopeful eyes. "I'm so glad you two are here."

Rowan grabbed her backpack out of the rear of her SUV. On a job she always carried supplies for a few unexpected nights in the wild because shit happened. She also had bear spray, a gun, a medical kit, and her GPS. "We'll find him. Has Zack acted okay since he's been here? Anything weird?" she asked as she walked with Bridget toward the barn.

"As normal as can be, considering the boy's mother is still missing," said Bridget. "He's eating well. Seems to enjoy being around the other kids and the animals. I know he's texted Evan a few times asking questions about the investigation."

Rowan nodded. Evan had mentioned he'd heard from Zack. It had been difficult for him to be honest yet not crush or raise the boy's hopes. "Where are the deputies?"

"They split up. One went with Theodore into the woods and the other with Victor—he has Molly with him—on our ATVs. But first they insisted on searching the house and all the outbuildings, even though I told them I didn't believe Zack would hide from us."

"Standard procedure," said Rowan. "Missing kids often end up in a hidey-hole close to home if not in the home." She scanned the ranch. A large part of it was flat open fields that extended far to the east, but to the west it was densely wooded. Far off in a field, she saw two ATVs appear as they came up a gentle rise and then slowly vanish.

Not so flat after all. Easy to hide.

"Here comes Theodore and the deputy," said Bridget, turning to the woods.

By the slump in the boy's shoulders, Rowan knew they hadn't found anything. She recognized the Deschutes County deputy from the Todd Lake trailhead, where Sophia's car had been found the day before.

Along with Tara Tilson.

Deputy Hartley raised a hand to Rowan and greeted Thor. "No sign of the boy. No tracks of any kind." He looked at Theodore and raised a brow. "Right?"

Theodore shook his head, meeting Rowan's gaze. "Nothing."

She knew Evan's nephew was an excellent tracker and could find his way anywhere in the local woods. "Okay. Where was Zack last seen?"

"Charlotte said he was taking a load to the poop piles," said Theodore. "His wheelbarrow and shovel are still over there."

"The what?" asked Rowan.

"Manure piles," clarified Bridget. "We compost it and use it as fertilizer."

"The wheelbarrow is on its side by one pile," said Deputy Hartley. "Still some manure in it."

"Zack knows better than to leave it like that," added Theodore.

Would he run away?

Rowan didn't know. If he was frustrated that his mom was still missing, he might take off, believing he could help somehow.

"I didn't find anything around the manure pile," said Hartley. "We looked for tracks, but nothing was obvious."

"Let's start there," said Rowan. She pointed at the bag in Bridget's hand. "That's for Thor?"

"Yes. Some things from his dirty-clothes hamper."

"Moooom!"

Everyone looked toward the house. Charlotte stood in the doorway, hands on her hips, her little dog, Oreo, at her feet.

"Can I come out now?"

Bridget glanced at the deputy, who looked at Rowan.

"She won't interfere with our work," said Rowan, knowing the strong-willed girl liked to be a part of everything. "Keep her with you."

Bridget gestured for her to join them. "Leave Oreo inside." Charlotte shooed the dog into the house and sprinted across the gravel.

The five of them made their way past the barn and a second out-building before reaching several long, narrow manure piles near the edge of the woods. The wheelbarrow lay on its side by the third pile.

"The manure scents won't confuse Thor?" asked Bridget.

"No, a dog's sense of smell is pretty amazing. Once he knows what he's looking for, he can sift through all other smells and ignore them."

"Dogs are smart," said Charlotte. "Oreo knows when I'm upset. He's like glue, following me everywhere and jumping on my lap until I feel better."

"Shush," muttered Theodore.

"Don't shush me," Charlotte snapped.

"Kids!" Bridget gave *a look*, and both went quiet.

"I'll have you guys wait here for now," said Rowan when they were about ten yards from the wheelbarrow. She took the bag from Bridget and walked Thor over to the pile. She unhooked his leash and held out the bag. Thor plunged in his nose. "Find it!" The dog spun around and trotted closer to the pile. He did a slow sweep on the south side of the pile, and within seconds his ears quirked and his head jerked. His sign.

That was fast.

He sped up, continuing his gentle sweeps but moving due west, toward the forested part of the property. Thor circled some small pines and then plunged into the woods.

"What's in this direction?" Rowan asked over her shoulder. She'd followed a few yards behind her dog, giving him space to work. The others did the same but stayed farther back.

"Just more woods. There's a dirt-and-gravel forest service road about a mile from here in that direction," said Bridget.

"Did Zack know that?" asked Rowan, stopping to let the others catch up a bit.

Bridget glanced at her kids.

"Zack and I never talked about that," said Charlotte, wrinkling her nose. "Why would we discuss something as boring as roads?"

"No," said her brother.

Rowan suspected Theodore's answer was deliberately short to contrast with his sister's.

They followed Thor deeper into the woods. A woman spoke on Hartley's radio, informing him that she and Bridget's husband, Victor, had not found anything while out on the ATVs and were now back at the house.

"We're following the search and rescue dog west into the woods," said Hartley into his mic. "He appears to have scented the boy." He jogged to catch up with Rowan. "Let me know if you think we need to escalate this," he said in a low voice.

"Let's see what Thor finds first," said Rowan, her GPS in hand, aware of the crisscrossing and circling trails a missing person could create. The subtext of Hartley's statement had been about whether to notify the FBI. Missing children were a priority for the bureau. "Theodore, have you noticed any tracks?" she asked, her gaze locked on her dog. Thor's head and tail were up as he moved deliberately; he still had the scent.

"Not yet."

There should be something.

Zack had clearly come this way. She didn't think he had any motivation to deliberately try to hide his tracks. They continued to follow Thor, and Rowan checked her phone. No service. "Does anyone have cell service?"

"No," said Deputy Hartley.

"You won't get service out here," said Bridget.

"Wait!" Theodore shouted.

Rowan turned around. The boy had moved to the north of the group to look for tracks or any sign of Zack. Theodore carefully pointed with his foot at something on the ground.

"Thor!" Her dog stopped and looked over his shoulder. "Sit!"

He sat.

Rowan and Hartley joined Theodore. She immediately spotted the footprint.

Could be an old print.

"It's fresh," said Theodore, as if hearing her thought. "See how the dirt is darker on the sides of the depression? It's still damp. Hasn't dried out yet." He held his foot above it. "The shoe size is smaller than mine."

Not an adult.

Rowan pressed her lips together and scanned more of the ground. There was only one print. Theodore and the deputy stepped away, their gazes focused downward.

"I've got another," said Hartley when he was about ten feet from the first print. "It's smaller, like that first one." Theodore joined him and squatted to study the ground from a smaller angle.

"There's a second," said Theodore, pointing at a nearby depression. The boy swallowed hard. "It's a lot bigger than the other," he said quietly.

Rowan crouched down next to Theodore, her gaze following his finger.

He's right.

She didn't need Theodore to point out the darker damp dirt at the edge of the print this time. This print was recent, and it appeared the two people had been walking together.

Or Zack was being followed.

"Thor should keep going," said Rowan as she stood. "These tracks suggest he's definitely following Zack."

And Zack is with an adult.

Hartley met her gaze. "You armed?" he asked quietly.

"Yes."

He thinks this could turn ugly.

She didn't disagree.

Hartley turned to Bridget. "Take the kids back to the house," he said. "Lock the door and stay inside."

Charlotte started to protest, but Bridget firmly placed her hand on her daughter's shoulder, and Charlotte went silent. The mother had paled. She understood what could be ahead.

"I can help," said Theodore with a stubborn tilt to his chin. "I know these woods."

"I'm sure you do, son," said Hartley. "But the dog will find the boy." He gestured at Bridget to get moving. She took Theodore's upper arm as he shot a sulky glance at Rowan and the deputy, and then she led both kids away.

Rowan checked her phone again. Still no service.

Texts from Evan will probably pop up once I'm in range.

Hartley touched his mic and asked the other deputy to drive around to the service road that Bridget had mentioned, and then he called for more backup. He looked at Rowan. "Time to escalate?"

She nodded. There was an unknown adult with Zack. "Have them contact the FBI." She looked over at Thor, who was still patiently sitting. "I don't know what we'll find. But I suspect we'll discover Zack—and possibly someone else—was picked up at that road."

Is it the same person who has his mother?

25

Rowan watched Noelle stride up the gravel road to where she and Thor had waited for almost an hour.

She's not happy.

Which was understandable, considering that the frustrating cases Noelle and Evan had been handling had now grown darker with the possible abduction of Zack. Beside Noelle were two more deputies and a forensics tech to collect the footprints and tire tracks Rowan and Deputy Hartley had found on the side of the gravel road.

Earlier, Thor had trotted up and down the road when Rowan and the deputy finally reached it, doing wide sweeps, trying to find Zack's scent again. Rowan had a gut feeling the boy was gone. She tried to pinpoint where Thor had lost the scent, and she spotted a set of tire tracks that crossed over all other tracks where a vehicle appeared to have turned around.

Evan kept swirling around in her mind, but she hadn't asked Deputy Hartley to request that someone contact Evan. Zack was missing; nothing else mattered.

"Doesn't look good?" Noelle asked instead of greeting Rowan. She did give Thor a head rub.

"No," said Rowan. "We tracked him more than a mile from the Kerr farm. Thor had his scent until we reached the road."

"Hartley told me about the larger shoe prints," Noelle said grimly. "We'll need to see those too." She included the forensics tech with a gesture.

Rowan recognized the woman as the tech who'd also worked the scene at Sophia's home. She stretched her memory to recall her name. "Thanks for coming, Cynthia." Rowan had met the competent woman on scenes a few times over the years.

Cynthia nodded. "If you don't mind, Detective, I'll get started on the road." She had a 35-millimeter camera in hand. At Noelle's nod, she started photographing the area.

"Say, Noelle." Rowan hesitated, knowing this was the wrong time but unable to stop herself. "I haven't been able to reach Evan for hours—I've been out of range, but even before that he was quiet. Have you talked to him recently?"

A strange look crossed Noelle's face. "You talked to him this morning, right?"

"Only at my parents' before he left for work."

Noelle looked away, and her expression blanked. "Shit."

Unease stirred in Rowan's stomach. "You haven't heard from him?"

"I saw him when I got to work this morning," Noelle said slowly, avoiding Rowan's eyes. "I really think he should be the one to talk to you—"

Rowan grabbed her arm. "What happened? Was he injured?" Her heart was in her throat.

"No! He's fine—well, he's not injured." Discomfort filled Noelle's gaze. "This really isn't my place—"

"Tell me what happened." Rowan had relaxed only a fraction when Noelle said he wasn't injured.

Something is up.

"I'm sure he's tried to contact you and just couldn't get through," Noelle said. "I texted him a few times around lunch and didn't hear back, but that was understandable."

"Understandable *how*?" Rowan tightened her grip on Noelle's arm, and the detective pointedly looked at it, making Rowan abruptly let go.

"Shit," Noelle said again. "Rowan, he really should talk to you. I'm not sure how this happened exactly, but Evan was suspended this morning. He was leaving when I arrived and said they'd taken his work phone, so I assume they took his gun—"

"What? He was suspended?" That hadn't been on Rowan's list of fears. "What happened?"

Noelle looked around. Anywhere but at Rowan. "I assume you heard they found his prints in places they shouldn't have been in Rod's home, so they had him give new prints?"

"No. He didn't tell me that."

Why didn't he tell me?

"Well, the prints came back the same. And his prints were at Sophia's—where I didn't see him touch anything ungloved—and he told me he'd been accused of stealing evidence."

Rowan struggled to speak. "Don't they know *anything* about Evan? He'd never do that!"

This can't be true.

"You're preaching to the choir," said Noelle. "He said—" She pressed her lips together and looked at the ground.

Something she doesn't want to tell me.

"What did he say?" Rowan whispered. Her mind was spinning.

Is this why Evan didn't return my texts earlier?

Frustration filled Noelle's face. "He said he felt targeted. The auto body shooting. The fire. The fingerprints and now the suspension. He said it felt personal."

Rowan froze. "What are you implying?"

The woman turned away and walked in a small circle before returning, stepping close to Rowan and speaking in a low voice. "He thinks someone with access to the investigation is targeting him. And he wondered if Rod had been targeted for the same thing." Noelle's gaze was distraught. "I know how ridiculous this sounds."

Rowan stared at her, Noelle's words circling in her head as she tried to make sense of what she'd been told.

Evan thinks someone in law enforcement burned our house down. And shot at him.

"That can't be right," she whispered.

"I know. It's crazy." Noelle glanced around at the deputies. "Evan was pretty emotional when I saw him, so he might've been talking out of his ass. But like I said, he didn't return my texts, and it sounds like he didn't return yours either. Would he go radio silent until he was ready to talk about what happened?"

Rowan thought. "I don't know. My first impulse is to say definitely not. But this is huge, so I'm not sure what he would do. His sister said she couldn't reach him either when Zack disappeared."

"Probably by the time you get in range, your phone will blow up with texts from him," said Noelle.

Rowan eyed her, positive the detective didn't believe a word she'd just said.

The sound of tires on gravel made the women look over their shoulders. A black SUV parked and two people got out.

"That's Mercy," said Rowan at the same time that Noelle said, "The FBI are here."

FBI special agents Mercy Kilpatrick and Eddie Peterson approached. Rowan had first met Mercy more than a year ago, when the agent had vanished while working undercover. The agent and her husband had been friends with Evan before that and since then had met several times with Evan and Rowan socially.

After a quick debrief with the agents, it was decided Rowan would go with Agents Kilpatrick and Peterson back to the Kerr home, and Noelle would stay at the scene. Rowan and the two agents climbed into the FBI vehicle, and Mercy casually asked, "How's Evan holding up through all this?"

Rowan sucked in a breath and poured out her fears to the agents.

◆ ◆ ◆

Several minutes later they drove down the twisting drive to the Kerr home.

"Any texts yet?" Agent Peterson asked Rowan. The two agents had been stunned by her recap of the last few days.

"No." She now had cell service. Rowan hit REDIAL and her call went to voicemail. Again. "Fuck! This isn't like him."

"We'll make some calls," Mercy said. "See if we can locate his vehicle or find out where he last used his phone."

"Thank you," said Rowan, relief rushing over her.

Has he vanished like Sophia and Zack?

"You don't track each other's phones?" asked Mercy.

"Lord, no. Do you?"

"Yep." Mercy stared straight ahead, and Rowan recalled how distraught her husband, Truman, had been when the agent vanished and nearly died at the hands of a local militia. From the passenger seat, Eddie reached out and gently squeezed Mercy's shoulder as she drove. He'd witnessed Truman's anguish too.

I guess tracking is understandable for them.

"After this, I'm tempted to add tracking," said Rowan. "It doesn't feel right that he'd go silent to lick his wounds."

"Evan doesn't seem like that type of person," agreed Mercy. "I'd think he'd jump in and get his hands dirty instead of keeping his head down for a bit."

"That sounds like him," said Rowan. The agent parked, and the three of them stepped out. "But getting suspended has to hurt. Evan's job is a large part of his identity. To hear that his department didn't find him trustworthy—I don't know what that would do to his psyche."

"I can't imagine," said Mercy.

"Evan bleeds blue," said Eddie. "He's a cop through and through."

"Do you think he's been taken?" Rowan steadied her voice. "Like Sophia and Zack? Am I jumping to conclusions?"

Mercy exchanged a look with Eddie. "Evan just experienced something crushing. Maybe it's affected him more than we believe it would, and he's keeping quiet for a bit. But it doesn't hurt for us to put some things in motion."

"I'll make some calls and be right in," said Eddie, pulling out his phone. "We'll find him," he said, meeting Rowan's gaze.

She and Mercy approached the Kerrs' front door, and it was abruptly thrown open by Charlotte, Oreo under one arm. "Did you find Zack?" Her eyes were wide.

"Not yet," said Rowan, her heart breaking at the concern in the girl's face.

"Are you here to help, Agent Kilpatrick?" Charlotte asked. Rowan knew she'd worked with the agent last summer.

"Yes," said Mercy, holding out her hand for Oreo to sniff. "Don't worry. We'll find him."

Bridget appeared, her face hopeful when she saw the agent. "Mercy! I'm so glad you're here." Her face fell a bit as she took in their expressions.

"They haven't found Zack," Charlotte announced. "Yet."

"Please come in. Both of you."

"Have you heard from Evan?" Rowan asked as they entered the home.

"No," said Bridget. "But I left him another message, that Thor had followed Zack's scent and that you'd found tracks." Her smile faded. "What's going on?"

"Not sure," said Rowan, trying to stay calm. "I'll be right back." She stepped back out of the home and called her mother. And then called both of her sisters. No one had heard from Evan, but his truck was no longer at her parents'.

Sweat beaded on the back of Rowan's neck as she stared at his contact photo on her phone. She kept imagining Evan dead in a vehicle trunk. "Where the fuck are you?" she whispered.

His phone at his ear, Agent Peterson was pacing near the SUV. One hand gestured emphatically as he spoke.

Thank God they can help.

"Zack," she said out loud, reminding herself of the true issue at hand. She pulled herself together and went back into the house to find Mercy speaking with the kids, Bridget, and her husband, Victor.

"I'm going to talk to Bridget out back," said Mercy. "When Eddie comes in, he'll talk to you, Victor."

"What about us?" demanded Charlotte. "Theodore and I spent the most time with Zack. Don't you want to interview us?"

"You're next," promised Mercy. "Does anyone have a picture of Zack?"

Bridget looked at Victor and they shook their heads.

"I do," stated Charlotte. She set down the dog and then slid a cell phone from her jeans pocket. She showed them a photo of Zack glaring at the camera and holding a shovel of manure. "He didn't want me to take his picture right then," she said. "But I thought it was funny. He kept saying how bad it smelled. I thought he was going to gag at first."

"Perfect," said Mercy. "Thank you, Charlotte. Can you text it to me?"

Pleased, Charlotte cut a smug glance at her brother, who rolled his eyes.

Mercy motioned for Rowan to follow her and Bridget out the back door. Outside there was a wood picnic table in the sun, and the three of them took a seat.

"Why are you separating Victor and me?" asked Bridget.

"This allows each of you to give your perspective without the influence of the other person," said Mercy. "Different people remember things different ways. We want to hear it all. First I'd like to know how someone found Zack here. I know how off the grid your family is, Bridget. Did Zack call someone? A friend, maybe?"

"We took away his phone," said Bridget. "Evan had asked us to hold it in case his mother tried to call. We let Zack use it each evening for a little bit under close supervision. I know he called Evan, and he also called his mother's cell a number of times."

"Sophia's phone is in custody," said Rowan.

"He knows," said Bridget with a sad smile. "I think he couldn't help himself."

That poor kid.

"Maybe Evan or I was followed here," said Rowan, hating the thought that they had led a possible killer to the boy. "I drove Zack here the first time, and then Evan and I came out again the next day."

"I hate to say it, but that seems the most likely scenario," said Bridget. "We haven't left the ranch or had any visitors since Zack came."

Mercy made a note. "Bridget, can you walk me through what Zack did today?"

"Do you really need me for this?" The question burst out of Rowan. She hated to be rude, but she was unable to sit still and wanted to find Evan. "I told you all of Thor's findings, and Noelle knows a lot more than I do about Zack and his mother."

Mercy pressed her lips together. "You're right. I'll check in with you later." There was assurance in Mercy's gaze that she hadn't forgotten about Evan. But it did little to calm the churning in Rowan's stomach.

She said her goodbyes and nearly sprinted for her vehicle, Thor at her side.

Where can I look for Evan?

26

Rowan slowly drove through the parking lot of her and Evan's favorite restaurant, feeling like a stalker. It was nearly 6:00 p.m., and the lot was full. But there was no sign of Evan's silver truck.

Just as there'd been no silver truck at their shell of a burned-out home, their regular Starbucks, his gym, the trailhead of their favorite hike, the top of Pilot Butte, or two other lookouts they liked.

Where are you?

She couldn't get the thought out of her head that he'd been abducted. Like Rod and then Sophia and Zack. As each hour passed, her hands grew tighter on the steering wheel, and the painful knot in her gut grew larger. She'd called every acquaintance she could think of, but no one had spoken with Evan recently.

Deflecting their curious questions hadn't been easy. Rowan had finally come up with a story about Evan's phone not working. Lame, but people seemed to believe it.

Special Agent Peterson had called her an hour ago and said that Evan's phone appeared to have been shut off around eight that morning, because there'd been no cell tower connections since then. According to Noelle, she'd run into Evan at about 7:30 a.m., as he was leaving the sheriff's department.

He vanished within a half hour of leaving.

Special Agent Peterson had put out a BOLO for Evan's truck and then asked Rowan another dozen questions about Evan's routines. He'd said that since Evan was a law enforcement officer investigating the murder of another, the situation definitely warranted attention from the FBI.

"But what about Zack?" Rowan had asked. "You should be looking for him."

"We have plenty of resources to do both," he'd assured her.

Twice she'd left messages for Evan's lieutenant, Louis Ogden, but he'd never called back.

"Asshole," she stated loudly in her vehicle. "Avoiding me because he probably thinks I'm pissed about Evan's suspension."

She *was* pissed about the suspension.

Noelle had contacted several officers and other detectives to see if they'd heard from Evan but come up empty. She had called Rowan a few minutes ago, saying that a general unease was spreading through the department about Evan's disappearance.

"Unease?" Rowan had snapped. "It's getting dark, and I'm going out of my head with worry. If he was recovering from the shock of being suspended, he'd have contacted me by now. *This isn't normal.* Something has happened to him!"

Noelle had agreed and asked Rowan to meet her at the department at six thirty.

Rowan arrived fifteen minutes early, parked in the visitors' lot, and looked at the black, furry face in her rearview mirror. "Ready, Thor?"

A moot question.

She let him out and attached his leash. Together they headed toward the public entrance.

"Hey. Aren't you the search and rescue dog lady?" asked a young guy slouching near the front doors.

Rowan shortened Thor's leash and scanned the man. He wore a backpack and appeared to be in his late twenties. Occasionally she and

Thor were recognized by someone who'd been involved in a previous search or read about them in the media. "Yes, that's me."

"Cool. I've heard about you two. Figured the big black dog strolling into the sheriff's department could only be Thor. Can I get a picture of him?" He pointed a large camera at Thor. Rowan hadn't initially noticed the 35-millimeter hanging around his neck.

She stopped, accustomed to requests to pet Thor or take his picture. He was a striking animal; she understood people's fascination. He looked like a dog who should have his own TV show.

The camera clicked a few times. "You're the girlfriend of the detective that got suspended this morning, right?"

Rowan suddenly noticed the camera had moved to point at her, not Thor.

How can he know Evan was suspended?

He's a reporter.

Angry, she directed Thor toward the doors a few steps away.

"Hey! I heard he was selling stolen evidence. Is that true?"

He moved a step closer, but Rowan yanked open the door and guided her dog inside.

"He's going to be canned, right? This is going to open up a shitstorm of queries into the integrity of—"

The door closed behind her, cutting off his voice.

What. The. Fuck.

Fury raged through her, and she welcomed it. The sensation was much better than the constant fear that had settled in her bones.

Who leaked his suspension?

She mentally rolled her eyes at her question. Law enforcement was notorious for gossip. It would be more unusual if no one knew about the suspension. Rowan stopped at the desk to check in. The deputy at the desk immediately recognized her—and Thor—and gave Thor a dog treat.

Thor knew full well he'd get a little snack every time they came in. One time a new employee had forgotten, and Thor had planted his butt and stared at him, refusing to move until Rowan requested the treat.

"You've got a reporter hovering out front," she told the deputy. "He took my picture as I came in."

"I know," said the deputy. "I kicked him out of the waiting area, but there's not a lot I can do about him out front unless he's causing bigger problems." She informed Rowan that Noelle hadn't returned to the department yet and told her to have a seat.

An idea struck. "Is Lieutenant Ogden still here?" Rowan asked.

The deputy checked her computer screen. "Yep."

Rowan took Thor through the metal detector and moved deliberately toward the locked inner door. "Can you tell him I'd like to talk for a minute?" She paused at the door, and the deputy remotely unlocked it.

"You bet."

"Thanks!" A flicker of guilt went through her that she'd taken advantage of the young woman's familiarity. But Rowan had a bone to pick with the lieutenant. She and Thor worked their way toward Louis Ogden's office, occasionally pausing as various people greeted her and her dog. As they passed by, Detective Maxine Nelson stepped out of the conference room where Evan and Noelle had set up their investigations.

"Rowan!" Pleasure and then guilt flickered in her eyes. "I'm sorry to hear about Evan."

"Just what have you heard?" Rowan's voice was sharp.

"Ahhh . . . that he was suspended." Maxine took a half step back, making Rowan wonder how angry she appeared.

"What else?" When Maxine hesitated, Rowan said, "I'm headed to talk to Louis. This is bullshit. Everyone knows that."

"I spoke to Louis," said Maxine. "Until some evidence clears Evan, he really had no choice."

"Guilty until proven innocent? Fuck that." Rowan continued down the hall, her vision tunneling.

Will no one stand up for him?

The lieutenant's office door was open, and he was putting some items in a messenger bag, clearly getting ready to go home for the day. He glanced up as she entered. "Rowan! And Thor, of course. What can I do for you?" The cheer in his voice sounded fake.

"Have you heard from Evan since he left this morning?"

"Uh . . . no, I haven't."

"He's missing," Rowan said flatly. "No one has talked to him since you suspended him. His phone has been turned off since eight a.m."

"Well . . . give him some time. I'm sure it was a shock—*I* was shocked." He raised his eyebrows as if he truly were surprised by what he'd had to do.

"He's missing!" Rowan snapped. "I've gone to every place he could be and spoken to his friends. And the fact that it happened while he's investigating a cop killer case along with other missing people is highly unnerving. Did you know that Sophia's son, Zack, was possibly abducted today?"

Louis stopped nervously packing his bag and looked her in the eye. "I know. And the FBI has taken the lead on Zack McLeod."

"The FBI is also stepping up because a law enforcement officer has vanished. Unlike this sheriff's department, who sits around twiddling their thumbs!" Her words were unfair. But only a tiny bit. "Evan told me he felt someone was targeting him. First the auto body shooting. The fire. And then the false evidence and *now this*!" She couldn't stop. "What are you waiting for? His body in a trunk?"

The mental image terrified her.

Annoyance shone in Louis's eyes. "Procedure dictates—"

"*You know him, Louis.* You've worked with Evan for years. He would never do this!" Thor circled Rowan and then pressed his ribs against her leg, reacting to her emotions.

"Maybe he needed some time—"

I don't believe that.

"Who has opportunities to fuck with evidence, Louis? To me that points at someone in *your* department. Why? Why would someone try to get Evan in trouble and kicked off a case?" She couldn't stop talking, her panicked brain in fast-forward. "Who *could* do that? And if making him look bad wasn't enough, who could make him vanish into thin air?"

All emotion left the lieutenant's face. "I put up with your rant because I like you, Rowan, and you've done good work for us. But you've crossed a line. I'm done talking." He picked up his bag. "I'll walk you out."

I can't let him end this.

"No thanks. I've already dealt with a fucking reporter out front who knows all about Evan's suspension." Rowan paused as an idea occurred. "Actually, I bet that reporter *doesn't* know everything. I can fill him in on how Evan was suspended due to false evidence and that he was working on a cop killer case." She sucked in a breath, not caring how hard she pushed him. "And now he's vanished, and *his employer doesn't seem to care!*"

Louis leaned toward her. "I care!" he said in a loud whisper. "My hands are tied at the moment. He's a fucking adult who can come and go as he pleases. And there's no evidence of an abduction."

"Have you looked for evidence?"

"Like what? Unless someone reports to us that they saw something, I'm not sure what you want me to do."

Stunned, Rowan couldn't speak for a long moment. "You're the head of the detectives department and you don't *know what to do*? Are you joking?"

"*Fine.* I'll assign someone." He pointed at his office door. "After you."

Relieved, Rowan turned and led Thor out the door.

Why don't I feel pleased?

"Start in your own parking lot," said Rowan. "I don't know how he got to my parents' to pick up his truck, but someone from here drove him—or he Ubered. He didn't go in the house or speak to anyone at home."

"Cameras?" Louis asked as they walked down the hall.

"Evan's truck wasn't parked in camera view. He had parked on the street."

"So you don't know that it was Evan that picked up his truck," stated Louis.

Rowan blinked. The lieutenant was right. "No."

"Maybe you should leave the investigation to us," he said sourly.

She halted and spun toward him. "The only reason you're even going to look is because I just made a scene."

He held her gaze. "You implied a lot of things about my department that were out of line. You're lucky I didn't kick you out of the building."

Rowan searched his eyes and spotted concern lurking behind his annoyance.

I've made him worry too.

"Thank you." She forced out the words. "Evan's often said you were someone he could rely on."

Please let me rely on you now.

His expression softened. "We'll find him."

Her knees suddenly seemed weak, and her muscles unreliable. She'd been running on adrenaline, and it'd suddenly exited her body.

I hope so.

I don't know what I'll do if they don't.

27

Five days.

Five agonizing days had crawled by since Evan vanished. And Zack too.

Rowan sat on the sofa in her parents' home, staring out the window at the backyard, half hoping to see Evan stroll across the grass.

It seemed as possible as anything else.

How many hours over the last two days have I sat here?

The first few days, Rowan hadn't stopped moving. She'd searched high and low for Evan's truck, constantly driving through town and then expanding to the more rural areas, figuring that even if someone else had taken the truck, it was the biggest and best clue to his disappearance. She'd hounded Detective Shults and Special Agent Kilpatrick until even-tempered Mercy had told her she needed to let them work.

She'd been surprised that Lieutenant Ogden had assigned Lori Shults to lead Evan's case, but Louis had told her that since Evan's disappearance could be tied to the McLeod cases, it seemed logical. He'd given the team working the cases an additional two deputies to help with legwork.

But suddenly the investigations dried up.

Leads were followed up on and dismissed.

Evidence from the crime scenes led nowhere.

And Evan seemed to have evaporated into the night along with Sophia and Zack.

But in the media, the story exploded about the detective who'd suddenly vanished. Now everyone had an opinion and wanted everyone else to hear it.

The opinions weren't kind.

The reporter who'd taken the picture of Rowan outside the sheriff's department had started the rumors with an article for a news website. He didn't say much about Rowan, but he twisted the story of Evan's disappearance and implied that he'd run off when the department discovered he'd been tampering with evidence. Suddenly people Evan had investigated in the past came forward in droves, stating they wanted their cases looked at again since they'd dealt with a detective with a history of altering evidence.

Rowan had read the articles with her jaw hanging open.

Charlie Graham was one of the most vocal, and the reporters kept returning to him for more soundbites. He threatened to sue the Deschutes County Sheriff's Department and Evan—if he ever turned up. Claimed they'd ruined his life and then brought up how someone had suspiciously shot him after Detective Bolton had made him stand outside his work building, where he could be clearly seen.

"Bolton was dirty. He was trying to clean up his mistakes. Now that people are onto him, the coward ran off," Graham had said. "Ask anyone I work with—they were all there when I got shot. He made me a target."

Noelle had been furious after reading that article.

"That little piece of shit," she'd said, glaring at the story on her laptop. "We risked our lives to get him out of the line of fire, and then he mouths off that Evan was dirty and tried to get him killed."

He's not dirty. Not Evan.

Rowan knew it in her heart. But the story continued to grow. Some cops had been anonymously quoted as saying that they'd always thought there was something fishy about Detective Bolton.

The reporters are lying. Trying to create clickbait articles.

But still, no one knew where Evan was.

Wherever he was, Rowan hoped he didn't have access to media. The lies and half truths about the job he loved would rip him apart.

Tips had come in. Sightings of Evan from out of state. He was seen buying an energy drink in a Texas 7-Eleven and going through the drive-through at a coffee kiosk in Arizona, the reports fueling the lie that he might be headed to Mexico. Locally there'd been several reports of silver trucks like his, but none had panned out.

Sophia's disappearance had also made the news. More conspiracy stories swirled around her and Evan and her father. The most talked-about rumor was that Evan had done something to Sophia because she'd discovered he'd been involved in her father's murder.

The stories were growing like healthy weeds.

Sophia sightings had come in on the tip line. One had led to a dark-haired woman who was locked in a shed. She and her husband had rented the property, and he'd trapped her in there after a fight. Neighbor kids had heard her yell and peeked in a window. One had told their mother, who'd called the police.

A fortunate end for the woman, but not the lead the detectives had hoped for.

The only positive step in the investigations that Rowan knew about was the discovery that the bullet that killed Tara Tilson had been fired from the same gun that shot Rod McLeod, definitively linking those cases. If they could find the gun, they would find their killer.

Of course, an article had suggested that Evan had taken the weapon with him when he ran.

Speculation was rampant that Evan had burned down Rowan's home to hide more evidence. Somehow the video from their home's camera had been leaked and heavily studied by armchair investigators who were positive that Evan was either driving the truck or throwing the Molotov cocktail.

The official fire investigation supported what was shown on the video. Accelerants had been found in the home along with broken glass from the two containers thrown through the windows. Rowan had avoided several calls from her insurance company about the fire. She couldn't deal with its questions at the moment.

I'm so tired.

The sofa cushion shifted, and Rowan noticed her mother had sat beside her. And then she realized her mother had asked a question. An echo of the question hovered just out of reach as Rowan tried to grasp what she'd asked. "I'm sorry. What did you say?"

Her mother's smile was sad. "I asked if you'd like some lunch. I've got leftover pizza or stew."

"Pizza." She wasn't hungry, but Rowan knew her mother would pester her until she made a choice.

What did I eat for breakfast?

Rowan couldn't remember.

"I picked up your mail. Do you want to look through it now?" her mother asked.

"No."

What do I do with his mail?

Two nights ago, she'd fallen apart. The nightmares of Evan being tortured in the same way as Rod McLeod had caught up with her, and she'd leaped out of bed in the middle of a full-blown panic attack. She'd stridden to the back door and gone out on the deck, feeling as if she were suffocating inside the house. And then her brain had shut down, unable to figure out what she should be doing. Her brother, Malcolm, had heard her step outside and cautiously approached, softly saying her name. She'd fallen into his hug, unable to stop crying. Since that night, she hadn't left the house.

She still wasn't back to herself yet.

Focusing on tasks was difficult. Not that she had anything to do. Her family had taken charge, getting Thor out for walks, making her meals, even answering her phone. They'd probably give her a bath if she let them.

Then Malcolm spoke. He'd taken her mother's place on the sofa with his dog, Zeke, beside him. She turned, studying Malcolm's mouth as if she could read his lips.

"I said you'll get through this," he told her. "I know it's shit at the moment, but you're stronger than you know."

Tears formed in her eyes. "You're the strong one. Look at what you went through. My problems don't compare. In fact I'm embarrassed that this has flattened me."

He put his arms around her and pulled her close. She buried her face in his shoulder and tried to catch her breath. "The man you love has disappeared," said Malcolm. "The fact that you're still upright is amazing. You can't compare my apples to your oranges."

A wistful smile tugged at her lips, and she hugged him back, observing that she could no longer feel his ribs. He'd worked hard to gain weight and build strength. Under her cheek, she could feel the definition of his shoulder muscles. Doctors had been concerned that years of malnutrition would have a permanent effect on his bones and organs, but Malcolm was determined to prove them wrong. "You lost so much," she whispered to him.

"But I found it all again. You will too."

He can't promise that. No one can.

"You'll figure out how to keep moving," he said, his voice low and soothing. "At first you'll have to pretend. But then it will become habit, and you'll start to see good in the world again."

"How could you possibly see good?" she whispered. He'd been a captive in hell.

"I found it. Small moments. Animals that I could tempt to come close. A book I hadn't read before. A cool-looking rock."

A cool-looking rock.

She dissolved into sobs. Crying for her brother who'd suffered so much and for the torture Evan could be going through.

"What happened?" her mother asked.

Malcolm patted Rowan's back. "She's okay. She needs the release," he told her. "Once she hits the bottom of the pit, she'll see her way out."

Rowan hated how certain he sounded.

He knows because he's been in that pit. Probably hundreds of times.

She sighed and leaned back slightly to wipe her cheeks, and Malcolm didn't let go. She pulled back a little more until she could see his face, drinking in the sight she'd believed she'd never see again. "I love you, big brother."

"And I love you, little annoying sister."

Rowan snorted and noticed she felt better. A very tiny bit better. She met her mother's concerned gaze from the kitchen.

Look who I've got in my life.

The most caring support system anyone could wish for.

In the kitchen, Rowan's phone rang, and her mother picked it up to look at the screen. "Detective Marshall," she said.

Rowan recoiled, and Malcolm gripped her tighter. "It's okay," he said.

I can't talk to her.

She shook her head, fearing Noelle would share the news that filled her nightmares: Evan was dead.

Her mother answered the phone, and Rowan blocked her voice. The first few days after Evan's disappearance, she couldn't hear enough from Noelle. Now she avoided the detective, feeling as if upsetting information wouldn't exist if Rowan didn't speak to her.

A raised inflection in her mother's tone caught Rowan's attention. "I think you should talk to Rowan."

Meeting her mother's gaze, Rowan violently shook her head.

I don't want to know what she has to say.

"It's okay, Rowan," her mother said with a light in her eyes.

Rowan's heart sped up and eagerness flooded her.

It's good news.

The phone still at her ear, her mother held up her hand in a signal to stop. "Rowan. *No.* It's not that."

They didn't find him.

Her heart sank through the floor, and she could barely lift her arm as her mother handed her the phone. "Noelle?" she asked.

"Rowan! We found Sophia! She's all right."

28

Rowan was thrilled to hear about Sophia, but then guilt washed over her when she became upset that it wasn't Evan who'd been found. Noelle offered to drive her to visit Sophia in the hospital but warned Rowan that the woman was badly hurt and seemed confused. She'd been found very dehydrated and covered with injuries.

"Where did they find her?" Rowan asked as they drove to the hospital.

"A couple of hikers came across her in the woods a few hours north of here," Noelle said.

"A few hours . . . how close to the Columbia River?"

"Maybe a couple miles away," Noelle said. "The hikers had tracked their route with an app and said they knew where they came across her, but I haven't had a chance to review it. The Wasco County sheriff has sent deputies to scour the route, and I know the FBI is headed up there."

"Thor—"

"Could he work a route backwards?" Noelle asked as she steered into the parking lot. "If he starts where she was found, could he lead us to where she'd been?"

"We've never tried," Rowan said slowly. "He's trained to follow the most recent and strongest scent, which would lead in the opposite direction. I know others have been trained to do it, but Thor hasn't."

Should we try?

She didn't want to pass up any opportunity to find Evan. But this would be asking Thor to do something he'd never done. In her gut, she knew it wouldn't work.

There has to be another way.

"You said Sophia couldn't answer *any* questions?" Rowan asked.

"She gave her name. That was it."

Rowan was bursting with things to ask, and she could tell Noelle was too. The detective's voice was louder than usual, and expectations shone in her eyes.

Please let this lead to Evan.

A few minutes later, the two women strode down the hall toward Sophia's room. A deputy stood outside the door, and Noelle and Rowan signed his log. Other than hospital staff, Rowan noticed that only Detective Maxine Nelson and two other deputies had been inside the hospital room.

Rowan sucked in a breath at the sight of Sophia's beaten and swollen face. Beside her, Maxine sat in a chair, holding the woman's hand. "She's asleep," Maxine whispered to them.

"Holy shit," Noelle muttered under her breath.

Rowan agreed. Sophia had heavy bruising around both eyes, which colored the skin in shades of ugly yellow and purple. Her lips had been split several times. Some gashes appeared almost healed; others looked fresh. Someone had cleaned her face, but crusted blood was still visible in both nostrils. Her arms were a mess of cuts and bruises and her hair stringy.

"Beat up like Rod," Rowan mumbled. Evan had told her about the battered state of the man's body. "She *must* have been with the same people. Did they let her go?"

Maxine shook her head. "We don't know yet." She nodded at an IV drip bag. "They've given her something for the pain, so she hasn't said anything new. She's getting lots of fluids and electrolytes too." She took a deep breath and looked at Sophia's face. "She's lucky to be alive."

"The hikers said she was sitting up when they found her, but she was delirious," said Noelle. "They gave her some water and wrapped her in an emergency blanket. One stayed while the other hiked out for help. They hadn't heard about a missing woman, so they had no idea who they'd found."

"It's been well over a week," said Rowan to Noelle. "Do you think she was starved all that time?"

"Yes," said a quiet voice.

Rowan gasped as she looked to the hospital bed. Sophia's eyes were open, and she was studying her. Then Sophia's confused gaze went to Maxine and finally Noelle. Clarity filled her eyes as she spotted Noelle's badge on her belt.

"Thank God," Sophia muttered, her lids drifting closed. "It's not a dream. I got away."

"How do you feel?" Rowan asked.

Stupid question.

"Like shit." Her eyes opened, and her gaze landed on Rowan again. "I think I know you, but I can't place you."

"That's because we've never met. I'm Rowan Wolff. Evan is—"

"You're Evan's girlfriend. I've heard a lot about you. Seen some pictures too."

Rowan caught her breath at Evan's name, desperate to ask Sophia if she knew where he was. But when Sophia had said his name, she'd shown no sign that she believed he could be in peril.

But she just started talking. Her brain needs to catch up.

Sophia looked at Noelle and raised a brow.

"Detective Noelle Marshall, and sitting next to you is Detective Maxine Nelson," Noelle said. "We've been looking for you."

"I know both your names," Sophia said. "My dad—" Her words cut off as her face went white under her bruises. *"My dad,"* she whispered. Tears ran from her eyes.

Rowan moved to sit on the foot of her bed. "You know about your dad?" she asked in a kind voice.

"Were they lying? Is he really dead?"

"I'm sorry, Sophia, but he is." Rowan's heart broke at the pain in her face. The strong reaction when Sophia spoke of her father made Rowan more certain that she knew nothing about Evan's situation. She wanted to ask about him but didn't want to throw too many questions at the woman.

"That's what they told me, but I didn't know if I could believe them. I saw the blood and knew it had to be bad." More tears ran and her lips quivered. Her eyes widened. "Zack! Is Zack all right? Where is he?" Her gaze scanned the room, and she struggled to sit up.

Maxine gently urged her to lie back down as Noelle asked, "When did you last see Zack?"

"He . . . he was at a friend's. I called the mom and asked if he could stay longer." Her wide gaze shot among the three of them.

"Zack came back on Saturday," said Noelle, in a flat voice. "But we couldn't find you."

Rowan cringed. Noelle hadn't told the complete truth, but Rowan understood why.

Sophia sank deeper into her pillow, relief on her face. "I didn't know whether to believe them. They claimed they had Zack. Showed me a video. Must have been fake. I'm so glad I got out of there."

Shit. They do have him.

The detectives exchanged a long look. Rowan could almost hear their thoughts about whether to tell Sophia her son was missing.

"Where is he?" Sophia asked, getting worked up again. "I need to see him."

"Sophia, *who* showed you a video of Zack and told you your father was dead?" asked Noelle, avoiding the woman's question.

The woman blinked as she moved her gaze to Noelle. "I don't know. Two of them. But their faces were always covered."

Sophia spoke more clearly, and her eyes were less confused. The fluids and painkillers doing their job. Dehydration was serious. It could kill, but if it was reversed quickly enough, people could perk right up.

"Are these the people who beat you?" Noelle asked.

Fear flickered in her eyes. "Yes."

"Why did they do that?"

"I'm not sure," Sophia answered in a weak voice as her brows came together. She appeared to be thinking hard.

Rowan watched Noelle exchange a look with Maxine.

She doesn't want to push too much.

"A minute ago you said you saw blood," said Maxine, redirecting the topic. "Where was that?"

"My house. It was everywhere. He told me to leave, but I had to come back and check." She lifted the hand with the IV to wipe her eyes but instead stared at it for a long moment, her gaze perplexed. She slowly set her arm back down and then used the other.

She's still confused.

Rowan glanced at Noelle. The detective's attention was locked on Sophia, a small frown on her lips.

She sees the disorientation too.

Noelle sat on the other side of Sophia's bed, opposite Maxine and Rowan. "Sophia . . . do you know what happened in your home? What caused all the blood?"

"They came for him. Just like he said they would," she whispered. Her gaze was inward as she remembered. "He'd warned me. Wanted me to be prepared." She closed her eyes.

"Who warned you? Was it Evan?" Rowan couldn't resist slipping his name into the conversation again, hoping to trigger something in Sophia's brain to indicate that she knew where he was. Rowan felt Noelle's gaze on her, the detective displeased with what she'd done.

"No, my dad. He said I couldn't tell anyone . . . not even Evan." Fear filled her face again, and her gaze took in all three women. She blinked rapidly and moved up the bed as if to get away from them.

"Sophia," Noelle said firmly. "What's wrong? We're here to help you."

"No." The woman shook her head. "I can't . . . I shouldn't . . ."

Rowan remembered how Evan had implied that someone in law enforcement with ties to his investigation wasn't to be trusted. He'd been hurt that Rod hadn't confided in him . . . just like Rod had told Sophia not to do. "Sophia," Rowan started slowly. "Did Rod tell you not to trust anyone in law enforcement? Because Evan . . ." She swallowed hard. "Evan has been dealing with some things and wondered the same."

Sophia held her gaze and gave the smallest nod.

"Shit," Noelle muttered under her breath.

"I don't understand," said Maxine, looking from Noelle to Rowan.

"Sophia, we want to find the men who did this to you," said Noelle, focusing on the woman. "It's extremely important that we do. I know you might be scared to say anything to us, but you have to agree that these men need to be found."

Sophia gave a short nod.

"We know it was your dad's blood in your home. Can you tell us what happened?"

Sophia closed her eyes. Her lips twitched, and the fingers of her right hand started to tap the sheets.

She's reliving something.

"Can you give me a few minutes alone first?" she asked softly, her eyes still closed.

"Sure. We'll move outside for a bit," said Noelle. She stood and waited for Maxine and Rowan to do the same. The three women stepped out of the room and closed the door, all their expressions grim.

"No one except hospital staff goes in," Noelle told the deputy standing guard. "And take a good look at their IDs."

"We've got to tell her about Zack," said Maxine in a low voice as they moved a few steps away and then stopped in a huddle.

"I know," said Noelle. She pressed a hand against her forehead. "I'm afraid she'll fall apart, and it'll delay us finding who did that to her."

"Or it will make her push harder," said Rowan. "Don't underestimate a mother."

"I can see her being tough like that," said Noelle, indecisiveness in her eyes. "We'll give her a few minutes to pull together. I need to find some coffee and then figure out how we'll approach her again. Agreed?"

Maxine and Rowan nodded.

"Where's the cafeteria?" asked Noelle, looking up and down the hall.

Rowan pointed at a directional sign near the ceiling. Silently the three women went to find caffeine. Every cell in Rowan's body pleaded with her to question Sophia more, not walk away.

Only Sophia knows who might have taken Evan and Zack.

We've got to speed up this investigation.

29

Evan had woken up in some sort of shed, one wrist chained to a huge eyebolt anchored in the concrete floor. And that's where he'd been kept for several days. He'd been given water but no food. A blanket, a thin, foul-smelling pad to lie on, and a bucket were all he had.

The concrete was cold, but no drafts came through the walls. The structure was very solid. Evan had gone over every inch he could reach from his chained position. And he'd worked and worked at the concrete around the eyebolt, trying to chip some away. He'd vomited a few times at first. His brain had been fuzzy, his right temple painful and swollen, and he suspected he had a concussion. He had no idea how long he'd been there.

And he had no idea who had given him the concussion—or why.

Someone had knocked Evan out with a blow to the head right in front of Rowan's parents' home. Evan had just arrived at their house after being suspended, his mind and emotions a wreck. He'd gotten out of an Uber and walked over to his truck, intending to go for a long drive to clear his head. As he'd reached for the truck handle, he'd heard someone behind him and turned to see a metal bar swinging at his head.

There'd been pain. Then nothing.

He'd suspected it was the same person who'd killed Rod and taken Sophia, but his and Noelle's investigation had kept hitting dead ends. They had no primary suspect, no name.

He ached for Rowan, knowing how upset she'd be that he'd vanished.

Will I end up like Rod?

And then the man finally showed his face.

Evan hadn't recognized him. His hair was long, and he'd grown a beard. Evan had simply looked at the strange man who stood in the doorway, waiting for an explanation. He hadn't seen the point of demanding answers; this man was currently in full control of Evan's life.

"You don't remember me," the man stated, anger in his tone.

"Sorry, I don't. Did you always have the beard?" Evan squinted at him. It was bright outside yet dark in the shed.

"You *ruined* my life. It's been seven years of hell, and *you have no idea who I am*!" The man paced in a small circle. "I knew it. You went on your merry way after leaving me to pick up the pieces of my life. You enjoyed your fancy job and got a hot girlfriend and now own *two* houses. I have *shit*."

"I wouldn't call my job fancy," muttered Evan.

The toe of the man's work boot caught Evan's cheekbone and whipped his head to the side.

He's nuts! Who is he?

"What did I do to you?" asked Evan, struggling to catch his breath. This time he saw the boot coming but was too slow to get out of the way. Pain radiated from his other cheek. He scrambled back as far as the chain would allow, creating as much space as possible between him and the angry man.

"You'd know me as Dale Forbes."

Evan stared as memories swamped him. He remembered everything about Dale Forbes's case seven years ago. But the main thing he recalled was that the man had walked away from a manslaughter charge—even though Evan and Rod had had their doubts.

How did that destroy his life?

"I remember now." Evan hoped his answer was safe enough that he wouldn't receive another kick to the face.

"So now you understand."

No, I don't.

"You got off," said Evan. "Didn't even have a trial."

"I was tried in the media!"

This was true. The story had the sensationalism the media loved. A jilted husband. A murderous affair.

It must have screwed up his life.

"Yes, you were," said Evan. "The media can be cruel."

"It was your fault! You and that asshole, McLeod!"

"Rod was kept in here, wasn't he?" Evan asked. The boot swung toward his face, and he jerked away but toppled to the ground.

"Dale—"

The boot found a new target in his ribs, and Evan gasped, trying to catch his breath and control the pain.

"I don't go by that name anymore. It's a cursed name. Dropped it years ago. But it didn't help. People still wouldn't hire me." The boot crashed into Evan's ribs again.

"Oooof." Evan writhed on the cold floor, remembering the bruised body of Rod McLeod.

Is this what happened to Rod?

"I lost my job after I was arrested, and it's your fault!"

"I was doing *my* job!" Evan managed to say and then realized his mistake as he was kicked in the thigh. He saw stars and wondered if his femur was cracked.

"Your life went on like normal! I lost my job, my house, and my fucking girlfriend too!"

Maybe you shouldn't have cheated on her.

Evan caught a glimpse of the man's eyes. Frenzied and angry.

Dale left and slammed the door.

Evan took shallow breaths, each one painfully expanding his ribs.

239

He's going to kill me. Just like Rod.

◆ ◆ ◆

Evan determined that Dale enjoyed talking and then kicking the shit out of him. He learned not to reply unless asked a direct question. And to think carefully before he answered. Dale did not like to hear the truth.

Still no food, and Evan didn't dare ask for some. The man brought water. Evan figured that if Dale wanted Evan to have food, he would have given him some, so there was no point in asking. His stomach eventually gave up and stopped aching.

Other parts of him ached nonstop.

Dale liked knives too. He'd cut off Evan's shirt, tossing it aside. He'd blown up after seeing the expensive brand of the shirt, which Rowan's sisters had just bought for him. After that, Dale had ranted on about money and the things he'd had to go without. Which of course was Evan's fault.

Evan didn't know how many days he'd been there before Dale showed him photos of Sophia. Her face was beat to hell. Evan looked away, knowing he'd failed her somehow.

"She was a fighter," said Dale, enjoying Evan's reaction. "Talked back too. Tough little bitch. Too bad she had to end up like her father."

He killed her.

Evan kept his expression calm.

"I know you found her father's body," said Dale, fury growing in his voice. "So you know what I did to her too. Don't give me that *calm cop face*." He dug his knife into Evan's thigh and twisted it, making him shriek. "That's better. That's what I like to see." Dale pulled out the knife, a grin on his face.

He gets off on my pain. "Why Sophia?" Evan choked out, hoping the oozing gash in his thigh and his screams had satisfied Dale enough to put him in a talkative mood instead of an abusive one.

"Because Rod died before revealing his evidence," said Dale. "Sophia seemed the most likely person he would have told. But she claimed she didn't know either."

"Evidence?" The cut in Evan's thigh was agonizing, making speech difficult.

If he doesn't kill me, infection from this filthy place will.

"Sophia said you knew where it was."

Evan jerked as if Dale had kicked him.

What did Sophia think I knew?

"Knew what?"

This time the kick hit him in the swollen temple. Blessed blackness enveloped him.

◆ ◆ ◆

Dale was gone when Evan woke.

He'd vomited on the concrete floor at some point. The sour stench was nauseating. He didn't know how he'd managed to throw up since he hadn't eaten in days. His head felt as if it were in a vise. Simply moving his eyeballs made lightning bolts of pain shoot through his head. He kept his eyes closed and lay as still as possible on the disgusting pad.

Sophia is dead.

He'd fought hard to find her and failed. And now he was next.

Evidence?

Evan had no idea what Dale had meant, but he inferred that Rod had found something that was bad news for Dale.

Why didn't Rod tell anybody?

Dale believes Rod told me.

Evan racked his brain, trying to recall his last conversations with Rod, but thinking was difficult. And painful. Instead, he let his mind wander, holding as still as possible and thinking of Rowan.

She has to know I'll meet the same fate as Rod and Sophia.

The thought hurt worse than any pain Dale had inflicted. Evan didn't care if he died—well, he cared, but he was more crushed by the pain Rowan and his family would experience when his battered body was discovered. Rod's death had devastated him.

It was always the worst for those left behind.

Although judging by Rod's remains, he had truly experienced the worst.

The cuts, the bruises, the missing tongue.

Tears leaked from Evan's eyes.

I'm scared.

30

"I want to speak to Rowan. *Only* Rowan for now."

In the ten minutes they'd been gone, Sophia had made a decision. The detectives looked at Rowan in surprise. They'd bought four cups of coffee in the hospital cafeteria and worked out their questions for Sophia.

As they'd stood in line to pay, Noelle had stated that she and Maxine would ask all the interview questions.

"Interview?" Rowan had asked, not liking the term. "Sophia's been through a brutal ordeal and just found out her father is dead. She needs support and to get her story out."

"Do you want to find Evan?" Noelle stared her down.

"Don't ask me a question like that," snapped Rowan, hurt. "You know I do. But clearly Sophia knows nothing about where he is. She didn't react at all when I said his name."

"That's also why Maxine and I will ask the questions from here on out," said Noelle pointedly. "You nearly crossed a line—I take that back. You *did* cross a line by deliberately throwing Evan's name into a question. You shouldn't even be in the room, let alone talking to her. I'll let you stay, but you need to be quiet. I agree with you that Sophia doesn't know where Evan is, but we're all pretty certain that it's the same men behind all of this—Rod, Sophia, Evan, and Zack. Our priority is to figure out where she's been." She held Rowan's gaze. "That will help us find Evan."

Before it's too late.

Rowan had reluctantly agreed to be quiet. Noelle had every right to send her home; Rowan was relieved the detectives hadn't shut her out.

But now Sophia had flipped the script.

Back in her hospital room, when Rowan had handed her a cup of coffee, the woman had made her announcement.

The room went quiet.

"But—" began Noelle.

"No buts," said Sophia. "I want to be alone with Rowan. For now." While they got coffee, the woman seemed to have gained more mental clarity and physical strength. Her eyes were sharp and her hand steady as she accepted the coffee.

"For now," firmly repeated Noelle. She and Maxine left the room without a look at Rowan.

"Sheesh." Sophia pointed at the chair where Maxine had originally sat. "I think the temperature dropped ten degrees in here."

Rowan took a seat. "They're the investigators. It's urgent that they figure out where you've been and find those men." She collected her thoughts. Once Noelle had told her she wasn't to ask any more questions, she'd tuned them out as they made their plan in the cafeteria. "First of all, why me?"

"Because you're not law enforcement," said Sophia. "Yes, you have a connection, but it's a connection to Evan, who my dad and I trust."

"Didn't sound like you trusted him," said Rowan.

"What you said about him suspecting something was going on in the department made up my mind. My dad was convinced that someone there was doing something they shouldn't."

"Be more specific."

Sophia sighed and looked toward the window, suddenly appearing exhausted again. "Dad found something that indicated evidence had been changed in one of his old cases. He didn't tell me which case, but the more he poked around, the more he feared that someone would retaliate. He feared that someone didn't want the truth to come to light and would stop at nothing to stop him. And that someone worked in law enforcement."

Sophia took a sip of her coffee and then set it on the nearby tray table.

"My dad had become very paranoid. He brought me several burner phones and told me to stop calling him from my cell and to only use a burner. He wanted me to hide them in different places in my home, at work, and in my car."

"That seems extreme." Rowan was alarmed.

But Rod was brutally murdered . . . so maybe not extreme.

"I thought so too. My dad talked about several cases, wondering if the outcomes weren't what they should have been. He talked a lot about justice being served, and that he needed to correct it, so I think he started poking around in these other ones too. Anyway, he cautioned me to keep my doors and windows locked—which I'd always done anyway. Daughter of a cop, you know. He started to follow me home after work, insisting on clearing the house before I went in."

"I take back when I said the multiple burner phones were extreme," said Rowan. "*That* behavior is extreme—except it appears his paranoia was justified. Why didn't you have a security system?"

"We were getting to it. He'd ordered some specific system that hadn't arrived yet."

"What about all the blood in your house?" Rowan asked quietly.

Sophia closed her eyes and leaned back into the pillow. "My dad spent the night on Thursday." She seemed to struggle to get the words out. "Said he didn't want to be in his house alone and didn't want me alone either. He'd talked about me and Zack moving in with him, but I'd put my foot down. I needed my independence, and I'd just bought that house. I didn't want to live with my father—even though I loved him dearly.

"On Thursday I woke up in the middle of the night to his shouts. I could hear a struggle going on. I opened my bedroom door and heard him fighting with someone in the living room and shouting for me to leave. Thankfully Zack was at a friend's. I ran to the garage, where I had spare keys, and then went out the side garage door. My car was in the driveway next to his truck. My garage was still too full of boxes of moving stuff to be used yet. I got in and left."

"You just left." Rowan was stunned.

"I know it sounds awful, but it was what he'd drilled in me to do. Especially in the weeks before that. Over and over. He'd ordered me to leave my cell phone behind if something ever happened. Claimed the burners were untraceable." Sophia studied the ceiling. "Part of me thought he was going nuts. But a larger part of me knew to listen."

"Noelle and Maxine should hear this," said Rowan. Guilt was growing in her that the detectives had been pushed out. What Sophia had said was crucial to their investigation.

Sophia picked at her blanket. "Maybe."

"Where did you go after you left that night?"

"Tara's."

Rowan was silent a long moment, realizing Sophia didn't know her friend had been murdered. She struggled to stay silent, knowing that news should come from the detectives. "Not a motel?" she blurted, her brain at war with her guilt.

"My dad had said I was to go to a hotel—he wouldn't let me tell him which one I would choose. But now I understand he didn't want to reveal the name under force."

Rowan wondered if he had been interrogated for the hotel name while being tortured.

"I panicked," continued Sophia. "I went to Tara's home, and she took me to a motel. I was freaking out. He'd warned me not to go pick up Zack, so that no one would follow me to him." She turned wide eyes to Rowan. "Did he think someone would hurt Zack's friends? Or that they'd get Zack to use against me?"

"Possibly either one," said Rowan. Rod had clearly thought through every possibility. "Wait a second. Did he warn you about Zack *that* night? Did he know something was going to happen on Thursday?"

Sophia rubbed her eyes. "He'd mentioned Zack that evening since he wasn't with us, but I don't think he knew that would be the night. He often reviewed stuff like that with me. His warnings depended on where we were and what we were doing. Even if we were in a restaurant, he'd ask me to spot the exits."

"He's always been like that?"

She considered. "It'd gotten worse recently. I wasn't sure whether to attribute it to this case he was studying or perhaps a retired-cop-with-too-much-time-to-think type of thing."

"Which case was it?" Rowan wondered if she should ask Sophia about the copies of cases in Rod's office.

"I don't know. He wouldn't be specific. I do know that it was one he worked with Evan because he kept wondering out loud if he should discuss it with Evan. I think he wanted more evidence before he took that step."

Rowan knew Evan hadn't worked on any of the cases found in Rod's filing cabinets.

It must be one of the missing cases.

"What happened after Tara took you to a motel?"

"She stayed the night with me. We sat up all night and talked about what to do."

Rowan wondered if Tara wouldn't have been murdered if she'd told Evan and Noelle the truth instead of lying that she hadn't heard from Sophia when they asked her.

"The next day—Friday—I got a text on one of the burners. It said that I had to drop off ten thousand dollars, otherwise they'd kill my father. They used his burner phone to contact mine."

"I really think the detectives should hear this, Sophia. I'm positive they're not part of whatever scheme your father was worried about." The truth weighed heavy on Rowan. She didn't know how long she could talk to Sophia without blurting out what had happened to Evan, Tara, and Zack.

"In a minute. I'm still thinking through what happened." Sophia frowned. "I don't want to make things worse."

Rowan resigned herself to waiting a bit longer. "The detectives watched video of you withdrawing the money at the bank. But you'd left your purse behind Thursday night. How did you do that without a driver's license?"

"I have a couple copies of my license." She shrugged. "My father suggested it. You just tell the DMV you lost yours."

So much caution from her father.

"Where did they want you to take the money?"

"They wanted me to drop it off at midnight Friday in a park."

A thought occurred to Rowan. "I took Thor to your home to search for you on Saturday. He followed your scent to a construction area behind your house and then lost it. The police thought the abductors had taken you there and then got in a vehicle."

"Tara drove me back to my house Friday night and dropped me off near that construction site so I could sneak back safely," said Sophia. "I had to see what had happened inside my home . . . part of me wondered if I'd find my father there." She looked away. "I was shocked at the amount of blood. And the bathroom door had been bashed in. He must have fought so hard." Tears ran down both cheeks.

Rowan took her hand. "I'm sorry you had to see that."

"But I was relieved that his body wasn't there. That meant there was a chance he was alive, and that confirmed my decision to drop off the money." Deep breath. "Then Tara drove me to the park. When I was stashing the bag of money near a bench, I heard someone behind me. I'm not sure what happened, but I think they hit me on the head." She gently touched the right side of her head. "I woke up in a horrible place with my head killing me."

"The money was a ploy to capture you," said Rowan. "Ten K is a cheap ransom these days."

"That occurred to me later," she said grimly.

"What I don't understand is why they grabbed you," said Rowan, thinking through the story Sophia had just told. "Did they believe your father had shared his concerns about that case with you? I'm assuming this is all about someone trying to cover up that some case evidence had been altered."

Sophia closed her eyes and didn't speak for a long time, making Rowan wonder if she'd fallen asleep. Her last few sentences had been slightly slurred. Possibly a fresh wave of side effects from the pain medication. "They wanted to know what my dad had told me about what he found." She flinched, jerking her head as if avoiding a punch.

Should I stop?

Rowan worried she was making things worse. She didn't know how to question someone. She wanted information, but she didn't want to harm Sophia mentally any more than the woman already had been.

"But that was only part of it," Sophia said quietly. "They wanted to know where I'd hidden some evidence. They beat me and beat me for that information. Threatened to kill Zack." Her eyes opened and reflected her pain. "I told them I never had any evidence or was told where my dad hid it, and they didn't believe me." Sophia flinched again and then gently touched her split lip.

Is she lying?

They threatened her son. She wouldn't lie to them.

"I'm so glad Zack is safe," she mumbled. "I need to see him."

Oh shit. Someone has got to tell her.

Sophia closed her eyes and turned her head away from Rowan. "It's hard to keep my eyes open. I'll rest for a bit and then talk to the detectives."

Guilt weighing heavy, Rowan squeezed her hand. "There's no rush."

Now I'm lying.

Evan and Zack can't wait.

31

Evan woke up to discover Dale staring at him from the shed door.

The hot fire in his thigh reminded him he'd been stabbed, and his stomach did a slow churn from either hunger or fear.

Probably both.

It was dark behind Dale. Night. Evan had no concept of what day or time it was. He had no means of keeping track, and he might have easily slept through a day or two.

"Where is the evidence?" asked Dale.

He's not going to like any answer I give.

"I understand Sophia said I had it," Evan said slowly. "But if I do, I'm not aware of what it is. I'd only texted with Rod over the last few months. I haven't seen him. He hasn't given me anything or mentioned evidence. I mean . . . maybe it's something I've had for quite a while and don't know it?" He braced himself for a boot.

Dale said nothing and continued to stare.

Evan took that as a good sign. "If you tell me what it is, maybe I'll recognize it."

"It's photos."

That's the first helpful thing he's said.

Now how to figure out which photos.

"You know that I work with a lot of photos in my job."

"But how many of them pertain to me?" asked Dale.

Evan's brain scrambled through the past few years. He hadn't thought about Dale Forbes in forever. "You're referring to photos that were part of the evidence back then?"

"No!"

Boot. Gut.

Evan couldn't breathe. He rolled into a ball, his vision tunneling. Terror swamping him. He heard Dale laughing as if from a distance.

He closed his eyes, waiting for his diaphragm to relax, and then he finally drew in a shuddering breath.

"I've got an assignment for you," said Dale, sounding as if he'd never lost his temper.

"Okay." The word squeaked out of Evan.

"You get to tell Zack his mother is dead. And that it was your fault."

Zack? Fuck. Did Dale find him?

"In a phone call?" Evan asked, still trying to breathe normally.

Dale laughed. "No." He stormed out of the shed, slammed the door, and locked it.

Evan melted into the floor in relief.

He's fucking with me. Enjoys making me suffer.

He lay there and focused on his breathing, willing his muscles to relax and the pain to ease. But nothing calmed the pain in his thigh. He gently touched the surrounding tissue. It was hot. Infection had started.

Who knows what was on his knife.

He cringed as he imagined the same knife had been used on Rod. Or Sophia.

The lock clinked and the door opened. Dale shoved someone inside. "Tell him." He shut the door and locked it again.

The room was completely dark.

"Zack?" Evan asked tentatively.

"Yeah." The fearful voice came from near the door.

Relief along with fear swept through Evan. The boy was here, but what were Dale's plans for him? "It's Evan Bolton. Are you all right?"

"Where's my mom?" Tears were in his voice. "He said he was bringing me to her."

"What happened?" asked Evan, avoiding the question. "How did you get here?"

The boy sniffed, but the sound was closer. "I was stupid."

Oh no.

Zack shared the tale of how he had been grabbed at the farm. "I don't know how long I've been locked in a bedroom. I know it was Tuesday when I got here."

"That's the same day I was locked up here," said Evan, not wanting to tell the boy about his injuries.

"Have you seen my mom?" Zack's voice cracked.

"No. Was the man who just brought you here the one at the farm?"

"It was another guy. Not as old," he said. "They must have put my mom in a different room. I yelled for her at first, but the older guy slapped me. Told me he'd burn me with his cigarettes if I didn't shut up."

"I'm sorry," said Evan.

"My dad burned my mom like that," Zack whispered. "I asked her about the scars. She said it hurt really bad. I'm glad my dad went to prison for it."

"I am too," said Evan. "I haven't seen a second man here. Can you describe him?" he asked, hoping to figure out who was helping Dale.

Zack's general description could have been that of any man.

"I'm really tired," said Zack, the tears back in his voice. "I can't sleep in that room. I think I've been awake for days."

"There's a pad on the floor here if you want to lie down. It's not great." Evan scooted most of the way off and felt the pad shift as the boy crept over. Zack lay down, his arm pressing against Evan's. He knew the boy needed a comforting touch and patted his hand.

What will Dale do to me if I don't tell Zack his mother is dead?

Evan decided to wait and find out. Any beating was better than breaking the boy's heart.

32

Rowan stepped out of Sophia's room and quietly closed the door behind her.

"You should know that Sophia is asking to see Zack," Rowan said to the waiting detectives. "And she told me that the men beat her because they believed her dad had shared some information and possibly given her some evidence and wanted to know where it was. But she knew nothing. It sounds like they didn't get what they wanted from Rod, so they went after Sophia."

"And then grabbed Zack to convince Sophia to talk?" Noelle asked.

"That's my guess," said Rowan. "She didn't want to talk in front of you because her dad was convinced someone in law enforcement didn't want the information he'd found to get out. I'm not sure, but she could have been lying when she said she didn't know any particulars about what he found. She's pretty paranoid—although not as paranoid as Rod was, I think." Rowan grimaced. "She doesn't know that Tara was murdered. Tara had helped her get to a hotel the night her father was attacked, and then Tara brought her back to the house Friday evening to see if her father was still there. That's when Sophia saw the blood, and that's when she made the trail that Thor and I followed. She was told to bring the ten K as a ransom payment to a park Friday at midnight, where she was grabbed."

"Okay." Noelle frowned as she processed the information. "What about how she got away? What kind of place was she kept in? What does she know about her kidnappers?"

"We didn't get to that," said Rowan weakly, realizing she hadn't asked some important questions. "But she did say she would be ready to talk to you after she rested."

"We need to tell her about Zack." Noelle closed her eyes for a long second. "I don't think telling her about Tara's death is necessary at the moment. One piece of shitty news at a time." She set her shoulders, put on a calm, professional expression, and then faced the door. "Let's go."

Inside, Sophia opened her eyes as they entered and tried to push up into a sitting position.

"Hang on," said Maxine. She found the remote and lifted the head of the bed until Sophia held up a hand for her to stop. The three women took their original positions, Noelle and Rowan perched on the sides of the bed and Maxine in the chair.

"Sophia, we need to know everything you can tell us about the place you were held and the people who were there," started Noelle.

I thought she'd start with Zack.

She must want as much information as possible before upsetting her.

Sophia blew out a breath. "It was bad. I was locked in a small room with a concrete floor, a blanket, and a fucking bucket to pee in. The room smelled horrible when I got there." She looked away. "I don't think I was their first guest." She paused for a moment. "I'll guess my father had been held there too," she said softly.

Noelle didn't ask if she saw her father while there. According to the ME, Rod had been killed before Sophia was kidnapped Friday night.

Is Evan in that room now?

Rowan didn't care if he was held in a room that stank. Anything was better than if he turned up in a car trunk.

"Was the room part of a house?" asked Noelle.

"No. Maybe it was part of a shop or outbuilding? It wasn't heated, and I occasionally smelled motor oil or rubber. The walls were old. Covered in ancient fake wood paneling like they used decades ago. It was cracked and parts were missing. I'd say the room was maybe ten by ten."

"Auto body shop?" Maxine murmured to Noelle.

"Don't think so. That building was pretty new, and there weren't any outbuildings on the property. Also too far away from where she was found. Unless they transported you somewhere before you escaped?" She looked back to Sophia.

"No. I was held the same room the whole time. I managed to escape by clawing off the fake paneling. Someone had installed it over a small old window in the room. I knew something was different behind the paneling because the wall was colder in one spot and sounded different when I rapped on it."

"They didn't notice the window from the outside?" asked Rowan.

"It was boarded up from the outside. Thin plywood had been nailed over all the siding on one outer wall of the building, but it was warped and rotten in places. I was able to kick through it once I broke through the window glass. The wood frame was too old and warped to open the window."

Rowan shuddered as she recalled breaking a window to save Thor.

"The bucket was an old metal one. I put it over my hand to break the glass," Sophia said quietly.

"Then what?" asked Maxine.

"I got out," she said simply. "The plywood and glass scratched me up pretty good, but I didn't give a shit. I wrapped up in the blanket and ran."

"Barefoot," stated Rowan. Under the hospital blanket, the lumps created by Sophia's feet were twice the size they should be due to the heavy bandages. Rowan couldn't imagine walking through woods without shoes.

Sophia gave a quick nod. "I used the dirt drive to the home to guide me away but tried to stay out of sight by moving through the trees along it. It was pitch black when I got out. Eventually I lost the dirt road and there were just trees. My feet grew numb, which actually helped—I couldn't feel the pain anymore. I just kept moving.

"At some point I stopped to rest and heard voices. I tried to hide but couldn't move. Turns out that was a good thing." She gave a weak smile.

"Why would you hide?" asked Noelle.

Sophia blinked a few times. "Because it could have been them looking for me."

"You said you followed the dirt road away from the house . . . It was a house where you were held?" asked Maxine.

"Yes. My room was a dozen yards from a house. I didn't realize that until I was outside." Her eyebrows came together as she thought. "I didn't tell my rescuers there was a house?"

"No," said Noelle as she tapped on her phone. Rowan assumed she was texting an update to someone searching the area where Sophia had been found. "You weren't making sense when they found you. What can you tell me about the house? One story? Two? Color?"

"One story. Not sure about color. Something dark. It only had one outdoor light, so it was hard to see."

"Maybe a manufactured home?" asked Maxine.

"Maybe," Sophia said hesitantly. She closed her eyes. "I recall seeing a front door and a small, covered porch before I dashed away. The building I'd broken out of was off to one side. My room"—she winced—"was attached to a larger outbuilding. There might have been other outbuildings . . . I feel like I recall large shapes on the other side of the house."

"Were you outdoors for only one night?" asked Noelle.

"I'm not sure. Things are a little fuzzy. What is today?"

"Sunday," said Rowan. "The ransom drop-off was the Friday night before last."

Sophia stared at her as the amount of time sank in. "Oh my God."

"What about the people who held you?" asked Noelle. "How many were there?"

"I only encountered two, and like I said, their faces were always covered."

"Were they about the same age?" asked Maxine.

"No." Sophia shook her head. "One was definitely older. He was heavier, his voice rougher, and seemed to be in charge. He would stand in the doorway and tell the younger one what to do—especially when it came to emptying my bucket." Her lips lifted on one side. Not a smile, but an acknowledgment of the pecking order. "But it was the older one who always asked the questions and hit me." She forced out the last two words.

"Were they Caucasian?" asked Noelle, making notes. "Heights?"

"I could see their hands. They were white men. Both were taller than me by maybe six inches . . . probably more than that. I'm five-three," she added. "No accents. I'd say they were blue collar. Clothes were jeans, work boots, heavy jackets. All the clothing was well worn." The detectives stayed quiet as Sophia thought for a long moment. "They didn't have refined speech, but it wasn't sloppy either. The older seemed intelligent to me. The younger was quiet. His job was to do what the other said."

"This is all excellent information." Noelle paused. "Sophia, is there any chance you heard Charlie Graham's voice?"

Sophia's jaw dropped open. *Charlie is involved in this?*

"We don't know that," Noelle said rapidly. "I'm asking you if that's possible. As you know, he's out of prison."

Sophia had shaken her head the whole time Noelle spoke. "Not Charlie. It can't be him. He wouldn't do this to me . . . or *that* to my father."

"You have old cigarette burns from him," stated Rowan, unable to stay quiet.

Sophia glared at her. "I'm well aware of my scars, thank you."

"Your father's body had them," said Noelle. "We questioned Charlie about your disappearance, and he denied any involvement. But we also found out that your father had been following him occasionally since he was released from prison."

"Jesus." Sophia's shoulders slumped. "That sounds like Dad. He never liked Charlie—for good reason. But I didn't see or hear anything that indicated Charlie was involved. These men were focused on something to do with my dad."

"Tell me more about what they wanted from you. What would they say?"

Sophia exhaled heavily, her gaze turning inward. "They wanted to know where I hid it. Where was the evidence my father gave me," she recited in a flat voice. "I kept telling them that I didn't know what they were talking about. I did describe my father's behaviors, saying he'd been worried and supercautious but that I didn't know why. They didn't care."

Rowan ached for the woman. Tears were rolling down her face, and her words were stilted.

"They mentioned evidence . . . but then they said a device."

"Device?" Maxine asked sharply.

"Like a thumb drive or some sort of other storage device. He asked about evidence but then would suggest it was on a device." Sophia raised one shoulder. "I got the impression they weren't sure what they were looking for."

"A computer tower was missing from your father's home," said Noelle. "And we think some physical files were taken too."

Sophia nodded slowly. "They mentioned a tower. It sounded like they couldn't get into it. I don't know if they took files."

"Sophia," said Noelle. "Did you get a sense of *why* these men wanted to know where the information was? I know you're worried about law enforcement being involved in what your father was investigating. Did these men confirm that fear?"

The woman frowned. "The older man seemed worried about something being found out. Both said 'If the cops find out' in a negative way. They definitely weren't in law enforcement. I grew up in that world; they weren't part of it. I guess they didn't actually say that cops had done something dirty."

"Your father was concerned about who in law enforcement could have been involved in covering something up," said Rowan. "But you heard these men say, 'If the cops find out.'"

Sophia nodded. "That feels accurate. Confusing but accurate."

Noelle looked up from her notepad. "I don't get it. Your father thought cops were already involved . . . but your abductors were worried that law enforcement would get involved. Which is it?"

None of the four women had an answer.

"My father did say at one point that Evan was his insurance policy," Sophia said slowly.

Rowan straightened. "What? What does that mean?"

"My dad knew he was digging into something dangerous," she said. "Why else would he be so paranoid? I didn't understand why he would involve Evan if he was trying to avoid other law enforcement." She shot a nervous glance at Maxine and Noelle.

"But you said your dad said not to go to Evan," Rowan choked out. Talking about him was painful. She ached to tell Sophia that he was missing but wouldn't until Noelle agreed.

"I know. I don't understand either." Confusion filled Sophia's gaze. "I think my dad wanted to confide in him . . . but maybe worried about the people around Evan? He must have had faith in Evan if he called him his insurance policy . . . but I didn't ask what he meant. Maybe ask Evan?" Shame filled her face. "I told them what my dad said about Evan being an insurance policy. The men who had me were convinced I knew *something* about the evidence they were looking for. When you're having your face beat in, you'll say anything," she finished quietly, picking at the thin hospital blanket.

Rowan's throat closed up. Sophia had given the men a reason to question Evan. She looked to Noelle and saw she was also struggling with what to say.

Rod was killed . . . so the insurance policy is in effect? Is that why Evan is still missing?

Sophia looked up. "When will Zack get here?" The first real smile filled her face.

Maxine and Noelle exchanged a look that made Rowan tense up.

Here it comes.

Noelle set down her notepad, took one of Sophia's hands, and in a soft voice said, "I need to talk to you about Zack."

The next few minutes turned into hell.

33

"We might have the place." Noelle strode into the hospital room the next morning, startling Rowan and Sophia. Thor's head swiveled her way, his ears and eyes locked on the detective.

Rowan had brought him to visit Sophia, knowing dogs made everything better. A couple of nurses had gushed over his black fur and then given a thumbs-up for Rowan to take him into the room. His presence had eased a bit of the bleakness in Sophia's eyes. But nothing would touch her despair. Knowing the two men who had beaten her now had her son—and Evan—was crushing her.

They'd had to hold Sophia down after telling her that her son was missing. She'd ripped out her IV and tried to leap out of bed, convinced she could find him. After she'd realized there was nothing she could do, for an hour Sophia had berated the detectives—and Rowan—alternating between fury and despair that Zack hadn't been protected.

She'd unsuccessfully begged nurses for stronger pain medication, wanting escape from her current reality. Crying jags were interspersed with long stretches of deep sleep or simply staring at the wall.

Rowan would have welcomed some drugs for escape too.

Noelle swung the little side eating tray over Sophia's lap, set a large tablet on it, and brought up some photos. Rowan stood to get a better look. On the screen were aerial shots of a home surrounded by woods and a few outbuildings. "We got these photos from the Wasco County sheriff moments ago. Could this be it?" she asked Sophia. Her voice was calm, but Rowan heard the urgency in her tone.

Rowan watched Sophia's face as she studied the photos. With shaking fingers, the woman scrolled through five photos that must have been taken by a drone. There appeared to be a main building, its perfect rectangular shape indicating it could be a manufactured home. It had a large outbuilding on its south side and then a smaller one on the north. Sophia stopped on one photo and zoomed in on the larger outbuilding.

"I think this is it," she said softly. She touched the far side of the building. "This is where I broke through the window, and then I must have gone in this direction, because I looked back and saw a door and porch light on the home." She dragged her finger southeast, following the drive, which was barely visible through the trees. She met Noelle's gaze. "It fits. I can't tell you for certain that this is it, but the buildings and dirt road are placed as I remember. Is it close to where I was found?"

"It's several miles," said Noelle. "You covered more ground than anyone would have guessed."

"I wanted to get away. I just went until I couldn't go anymore."

Not too surprised, Rowan studied the photos. Missing people wandered. Often going much farther than searchers expected.

"Are they there?" whispered Sophia, referring to Zack and Evan.

"We're about to find out," said Noelle. "We've had SWAT on standby since yesterday. I'm giving the go-ahead to head to this location."

Sophia leaned back into her pillows. "Oh my God. This could be it." She took several deep breaths as tears started to flow. "Please tell them to be careful. Zack . . ."

"I know," said Noelle, understanding in her gaze. "They'll do everything in their power to get him out safely."

Rowan said nothing, anticipation and fear setting her every nerve on edge.

Evan. Please be safe.

SWAT members were trained professionals. They drilled constantly for high-risk situations. Negotiators, snipers, entry teams. They knew what they were doing.

But shit happened.

Rowan stood up. "I'm going. I need to be there."

Noelle's gaze narrowed on her. "You know you can't. You'll be in the way."

"I'll stay behind the command center. I'll talk to no one. I just need to be there."

I have to know if Evan is alive.

Noelle studied her for a long moment. "I'll see what I can do."

"Thank you." Relief rushed through her veins, and she quickly sat as she grew dizzy.

I'll find out right away if he's alive.

"Who owns the property?" she asked, waiting for her lightheadedness to pass.

"Catherine Woods. Age seventy-eight. Clearly not one of our kidnappers, but we're looking into her family members. One of them might be using the property."

Rowan looked at Sophia. "Does the last name Woods mean anything to you?"

She shook her head. "I didn't hear my dad say it." She glanced at Noelle. "What if it's the wrong place? What if I've made a mistake?" Her voice rose.

Noelle patted her shoulder. "Then we'll keep looking."

Something crumpled inside Rowan.

How long will that take?

The dizziness returned, and Rowan wondered how much longer she could stay functional. She wanted to crawl into bed and pull the covers over her head until someone informed her that Evan was alive.

Four hours later, Rowan waited behind the SWAT command center's RV. The team had set up a half mile from the home. Two snipers had been in position for nearly an hour, hiding in the trees, watching the home through the scopes of their weapons. They'd reported there had been no visible movement in the home but confirmed that a window had been broken on the south side of the largest outbuilding.

Sophia's escape hatch.

Rowan was relieved to know that they were in the right spot.

Noelle and Rowan huddled together outside in the cold air, listening on Noelle's radio as the SWAT members communicated with each other. A discussion on how to get in touch with whoever was inside was underway. Negotiation was always the first step in hostage situations.

The light wind was icy, and Rowan adjusted her thick scarf, pulling it up to her ears.

"How did Sophia deal with these temperatures with just a blanket?" she muttered.

"When your life is at stake, you can do a lot of things you usually couldn't," answered Noelle, who eyed Rowan's scarf with envy as she tried to pull her coat collar together. Her jacket had left her neck exposed.

Noelle had a point. When Rowan was a small child with a broken leg, her brother—still a child himself—had carried her for miles to get her to safety. "True. Or when someone else's life is in danger."

The radio crackled, and they heard a woman speak. "This is the Deschutes County sheriff's office! We would like to speak to you!" The negotiator was in the RV, but her voice had been broadcast from a speaker close to the home.

Rowan had been inside a few mobile command centers. They had multiple screens showing different views of the target and three or four people monitoring them. There were at least two negotiators. One to speak and the other to help listen and advise. If necessary, the second would take over if the first grew exhausted or if it appeared the negotiator couldn't establish a rapport with the subject. Negotiation was a delicate process. It had to stay fluid and rapidly adapt to what worked or change course when things went south.

"No movement," reported a sniper through the radio.

"Same," said the second sniper.

The woman waited about thirty seconds, then repeated her request in a patient tone.

"This could be a long afternoon," said Noelle.

Rowan had packed water, protein bars, and dog food in anticipation of exactly that. "What'll they do next?" she asked the detective. Her skin crawled with tension. She wanted them to storm the buildings and get Evan out. Not sit around waiting for someone to reply.

If they don't enter soon, I'll crack.

"If the person inside doesn't offer a phone number for communication, they'll provide a phone," said Noelle.

"Throw it through a window?" asked Rowan.

"Yep. It's unlikely someone will open the door and expose themselves to pick up a phone on the step."

True.

After twenty minutes of silence from inside the home, a warning was given that a phone was coming through a window. A SWAT member crept close to the home, broke a window, and threw a phone inside.

Finally! Now we'll get somewhere.

The negotiators waited as they called the phone over and over.

"Usually people can't ignore a ringing phone," said Noelle. "I swear it's in our DNA."

Rowan agreed, thankful they couldn't hear the phone ringing through her radio.

For the next half hour, they listened to the team members discuss the next steps and agree to give the kidnappers a little more time to open up communication. Rowan wanted to scream.

They're waiting too long.

She wondered how the team stayed patient. The men were waiting in the BearCat, the county's armored vehicle, about fifty yards from the home. Rowan had glimpsed a few of them before they moved into position. Each wore tan camouflage and heavy armor with SHERIFF across the back, helmets, headphones, and a mic, and each carried multiple weapons. She spotted a several AR-15s, M4 carbines, a lot of handguns, and an orange-trimmed less-lethal weapon that probably shot beanbag rounds.

The commander stepped out of the RV to stretch his legs. He spotted Thor and his eyes lit up. He walked over and crouched down to scratch Thor's chest.

"We should add a dog to the team," he said. "Good for stress relief. It's fucking tense inside there." He looked up at Rowan, his gaze deadly serious. "We'll get Evan and Zack out," he promised.

Rowan nodded, unable to speak.

He can't guarantee that they'll get them out alive.

"Want to step inside for a few minutes?" he asked. "Coffee's hot."

Absolutely.

"For a bit," said Noelle. "We don't want to be in the way."

"There's room. Just be quiet." He tousled Thor's ears and stood. The women followed him around the RV, up the few steps, and inside. Noelle turned off her radio. The three people seated inside glanced up from the monitors. Their faces were lined with intensity but brightened as they spotted Thor.

Rowan pulled the scarf from her neck. It was almost too warm in the RV. The multiple screens and computer equipment were putting out heat. The commander opened a few windows and then held out his hand for Thor's leash. Rowan handed it off.

He walked Thor over to a woman who must have been the voice they'd heard requesting the kidnappers to communicate. She gently patted Thor's head and slowly exhaled. "I don't think they'll answer the phone. We've given enough time," she told the commander.

"Agreed." He raised a brow at the other two people inside, who nodded, their faces grim.

He lifted a phone and gave orders.

They're going in.

Rowan tensed; she'd been waiting hours for this moment. There were few more dangerous situations than breaching and entering a building into an unknown situation. The fatal funnel. None of the SWAT team knew what to expect behind that closed door, but it was their job to breach it and be prepared for anything.

Two of the monitor screens were divided into views from all the SWAT members' body cameras; currently those views were of other members as they waited in the BearCat. The views suddenly started to jerk more as the vehicle moved closer to the property. Three other monitors showed stationary views of the property, and after a few moments, part of the BearCat appeared on one. Rowan looked away from the dizzying body cams as the men streamed out of the vehicle. Three took off to the back of the property, and the others rapidly approached the front door, carrying shields.

They went up the small porch steps, and one produced a small but heavy battering ram. Two swings of the ram blew open the door, and the men streamed inside. It appeared to be a disorganized rush, but Rowan knew the movements were carefully choreographed; every man had a role.

Rowan's gaze moved from one jolting body camera view to another as the team rapidly cleared the house. Shouts of "Clear! Clear! Clear!" filled the RV. The snipers continued to report that no one was seen on the grounds. So many people were talking at once, she wondered how the commander could keep track of what was happening.

No one was in the home. Closets and cupboards were opened and cleared. The home had recently been in use. There were dishes in the sink and unmade beds and toiletries in the bathroom. Two members stayed inside while the rest went to check the outbuildings.

Rowan held her breath as she watched one of the still cam views as the men took positions to the sides of the largest outbuilding's door. One man tested the doorknob and then stepped back as another moved forward and swung the battering ram at the door. It thrust open on the first hit and the team rapidly moved inside with precision movements. Rowan watched the body cams. The team passed through what looked like a garage area. It was stacked with boxes—too small to hide in—and two walls were lined with several workbenches. The team followed the same technique to open a door at the back of the building. It led to a small room. Inside there was nothing to hide behind or in.

That was the extent of the outbuilding.

No Evan.

Where is he?

She wanted to cry.

It was almost like Schrödinger's cat. She wouldn't know if Evan was alive or dead until she saw him. Both scenarios existed simultaneously in her brain.

It was an exhausting emotional roller coaster.

A filthy twin mattress took up most of the floor, and one of the team members kicked over a metal bucket. Rowan spotted the broken window on one of the body cams, and she stared, imagining Sophia crawling out the small window.

"Fucking reeks of shit and piss in here," commented one member.

A chorus of agreement.

"Handcuffs," stated one. "Ropes. Cattle prod. Lighters." The items came into sight, tossed into a corner of the room.

Rowan closed her eyes for a long moment, assaulted by images of Evan being tortured.

Was he tortured like Rod?

Most of the team moved to the second outbuilding. Inside they found another mattress and more tools of torture. But no Evan or Zack.

"They were running a fucking torture hotel," muttered Noelle. "Sick pricks."

Rowan sat down, her legs shaking, and Thor immediately put a paw up on her lap, his gaze searching hers. "Good boy," she whispered, and then buried her hands and face in his fur. She inhaled his doggy smell as she tried to slow her pounding heart. The tension of the last few hours exited her body in a rush, leaving her empty and running on fumes.

Now what?

Noelle silently took a seat beside her and set a hand on her back. "I know," she said to Rowan. "We'll find him."

Rowan lifted her head. "What if we're too late?"

"I think we would have found him here if we were too late," Noelle said softly. "But we'll tear this place apart. Figure out where they went. They're too fucking sloppy to have left no trace behind."

"Noelle." Rowan lowered her voice to a whisper. "What if someone warned them SWAT was coming? There were dishes on the counter. It looks like they left in a hurry."

Noelle stared back at her, horror, then anger, filling her eyes. "Fuck."

Was Rod right not to trust law enforcement?

"Commander," came a voice over the speakers. "We've got a small sunken area in the ground back here behind the second outbuilding."

"How small?" asked the commander.

"Maybe three feet long. Foot and a half wide."

"Shit," muttered the commander.

The negotiator shook her head. "That takes time," she stated. "That's not one of our hostages."

Rowan looked from one to the other in confusion. "What did he find?"

"A grave," said Noelle. "A lazy one. I'm guessing they didn't bury the body very deep. The depression happens as the torso decays and the dirt above it sinks down. How much do you want to bet that's Catherine Woods? The seventy-eight-year-old property owner?"

Or a previous hostage.

Rowan took strength from the fact that the negotiator was right. It would take time for a depression to form where someone had buried a body. There was no way it could be Evan.

Where is he?

34

"Wake up! Get moving!"

Evan forced his eyes open as Dale came in the door, confused because there was no way Evan could move while chained to the floor.

Dale hauled a half-asleep Zack to his feet and zip-tied his hands behind his back.

Evan wondered how long Zack had been in the shed with him. One day? Two?

Dale had found a new way to please himself. It was making Evan suffer to protect Zack. Evan didn't know how many times the man had burst into the shed and held a knife to Zack's throat until Evan begged to be cut instead. Sometimes he'd cut the boy anyway.

And then do Evan.

This was how Evan and Zack had learned that the bigger and more emotional their reactions, the more satisfied Dale was. And then he would leave them alone for a few hours. The two of them had become good actors.

Dale dragged Zack out of the shed, and every cell in Evan's body tried to lunge after them, only to be stopped by the chain. He stared at the light coming in the shed door and realized a vehicle's headlights were causing it. He had no idea what time of night it was.

What is he doing to Zack?

Evan yanked on the chain for the millionth time, ignoring the grinding pain at his wrist. But it was hopeless. Dale knew Evan would do anything to protect the boy. He reveled in it. At one point he'd walked into the shed and offered to let Evan go. Zack had sat up eagerly, a hesitant smile on his face. Dale told Evan that they were currently in the middle of the woods, and it was unlikely he'd find his way out, but he'd give him the chance.

Evan had been skeptical, but his heart had still lifted. Then Dale had stated that Zack was to stay. The boy's face had fallen and then gone blank as he looked to Evan. The boy had been willing to let Evan leave without him. His heart crushed by the acceptance on Zack's face, Evan stated he'd only leave if he could take Zack with him. Dale had laughed like that was the funniest thing he'd ever heard and then left.

After that Zack had cried and begged Evan to leave without him. It'd taken a long time for the boy to believe it was just another game. Dale had had no intention of letting Evan go when he made the offer.

Dale seemed to have forgotten about making Evan tell Zack his mother was dead. Sophia hadn't been mentioned since he'd dumped Zack in the shed. Evan continued to keep the fact to himself. He didn't have the strength to tell the boy.

Evan had been getting weaker by the day from the lack of food. His motivation and mental strength had also been rapidly fading. But he tried to stay strong for Zack.

Dale stalked back in the shed, the headlights behind him creating a tall shadow on the wall beside Evan. He didn't have Zack. Evan started to ask about the boy and then stopped when the light reflected onto Dale's face. His expression was all business, but there was a hint of fear in his eyes.

Something is up.

Dale knelt and yanked Evan's hands behind his back, fastening his wrists with a zip tie. Then he released the chain that held Evan to the floor and jerked him to his feet. The blood rushed out of Evan's head, making him dizzy. The chain had kept him from standing up since he'd been there. Dale pulled Evan's upper arm and led him out of the shed as Evan struggled to stay upright.

Outside, he sucked in breaths of fresh air. He'd grown accustomed to the foul smells in the shed, and the air outside was crisp. Dale pushed him forward into the rear bench seat of a pickup's king cab and made him lie down, scrunched up on his side. Evan was relieved to see that Zack was already in the back but bound in the same position on the floor. Dale added zip ties to Evan's ankles and then used short bungee cords to strap Evan to the bars under the seat. The only thing he could do was lift his head a few inches. Dale did the same to Zack, securing him to the floor. Then he climbed in the driver's seat, showed them a gun, and said that if one of them caused problems, he'd shoot the other one.

The ride was long, and Evan grew more despondent by the minute, wondering why they were being moved. The only logical answer was Dale's fear of discovery. Either he felt someone was close to finding his hostages, or the mystery second man had threatened to expose him.

Evan wondered if that man was still alive; he had no doubts about Dale's willingness to kill anyone in his way.

But Zack and I are still alive. There's some reason he hasn't killed either one of us.

Dale had asked about the photos a few more times, which had earned Evan more cuts and painful ribs when he couldn't answer. Dale was desperate to find the evidence.

Is that the only reason I'm alive?

Will he increase Zack's torture to make me talk?

35

"I've got a distant male relative of Catherine Woods who lives in the area and could fit the age range we're looking for," said Detective Shults in an eager tone. "Take a look at his driver's license photo. His height and weight don't rule him out." She swung her monitor for Noelle to see.

Rowan sat silently in the conference room at the sheriff's department. She studied Lori's screen, seeing a dark-haired man. The detectives had done a half dozen internet searches on potential subjects who could have had access to the home that SWAT had invaded. With each one, Rowan had gotten her hopes up, only to have them crash as the person was ruled out.

"He's a step-grandnephew," said Lori. "Jeremiah Bradley Fry. Goes by JB. No current work history. He's twenty-seven and on medical disability, so we've got current records on his whereabouts. Address is an apartment on the east side of town."

"How severe of a disability?" asked Noelle.

Rowan listened, prepared to have JB crossed off the list.

"Not sure. But he's collected it for several years."

Noelle popped his name into a Google search. "I love it when names are a bit unusual," she said as she scanned the results. "Makes people easier to find. Hello, JB." She grinned at her computer, and Rowan saw she was scrolling through a Facebook page. "His page is public," said Noelle. "Idiot. Letting the world snoop through your stuff. But good for us." She clicked on a few photos. "He appears physically active. Recent photos show him skiing and hanging out at a pool. He appears to be the same shape and size as the man who threw the Molotov cocktails into Rowan's home. Shall we pay him a visit?"

"He won't be holding hostages in his apartment," said Rowan. Her limbs were heavy, and she ached to take a nap. The longer the search went on, the more it felt as if she were being sucked into the earth. Slowly. Deliberately. Soon she'd be unable to breathe.

"No, he won't," agreed Noelle, looking Rowan over from head to toe with a frown. "But he could be holding them somewhere else. We know there's a second man involved—perhaps he's the one with a location they're using." She paused. "You look like hell," she finished, staring at Rowan.

She tried to appear alert. "I'll feel better when we find Evan and Zack."

Find them alive.

Lori pulled up the same Facebook page. "I'll keep searching for the second guy. He could be in here somewhere . . . maybe he's a friend or in a photo. Have a deputy meet you at the Fry apartment. Has there been anything more from Maxine?"

Detective Nelson was currently at the home SWAT had entered that morning, searching for evidence of where the hostages could have been taken. She'd found a ripped shirt under the mattress in the second outbuilding that Rowan had identified as Evan's.

Proof he'd been there.

Rowan had stared at the blue shirt, recalling it on him as he'd left the house that morning. But without the rust-colored stains that now covered the front.

Proof he'd been injured.

The commander had let Thor do a property search. Her dog had kept returning to the driveway of the home, indicating that was where Evan had last been.

Where he'd been most likely put in a vehicle.

In the trunk?

That was when she'd started to sink. Again.

Noelle stood and grabbed her bag. "Nothing more from Maxine yet." As she headed toward the door, Rowan stood and followed, Thor at her side.

She focused on making her legs move appropriately, which took a high level of concentration. She was empty. Her lungs, her head, her heart. Everything felt hollow.

"Oh no you don't." Noelle had stopped at the conference room door and turned to find Rowan on her heels. "You're not coming with me."

Rowan froze. "Noelle . . . you've got to—"

"Don't tell me what I've got to do. You have no business going to check out a suspect. What if he doesn't want to talk and shoots instead? I don't need to worry about your safety. Not to mention if my lieutenant finds out you're shadowing me, I'll be working traffic."

She's right. I have no place in this.

But Noelle's gaze faltered, and she glanced away.

Rowan seized the detective's weak moment. "I'll stay in the car. I won't get out. I just can't sit in this conference room wondering what you've found."

"You could sit at home." She still wouldn't meet Rowan's gaze.

"With my hovering mother? You've met my sisters, right? Can you guess what it's like to be the center of their attention and pity?" Her sisters were at work and didn't live with her parents, but it sounded like a strong reason.

Noelle sighed. "Okay. But you *stay* in the vehicle."

"Of course."

Rowan got out of the vehicle.

"What did I say?" asked Noelle as she slammed her driver's door in the apartment building's parking lot. "I feel like I'm reprimanding a teenager."

"Thor's about to explode," said Rowan. She'd fully intended to stay in the vehicle, but he'd squirmed for the last five minutes of the ride. "It'll just take a second. Go do your thing." Rowan walked her dog to a grassy strip and watched Noelle and a deputy head down a sidewalk, searching for the right apartment.

Thor sniffed a bush. And then another. And then sniffed a big rock.

"Hey," said Rowan. "Hurry up. Noelle isn't happy with us."

Thor looked back at her.

/treats/

"No treats until you go."

Thor checked the rock again. He circled it and then lifted a leg.

Rowan politely looked away. And spotted a man sprinting toward her on the path Noelle and the deputy had just taken.

She recognized JB from his driver's license.

"Deschutes County sheriff! *Stop!*" the deputy yelled from fifty feet behind JB. He and Noelle tore after the subject.

JB didn't stop running. He locked eyes with Rowan.

"Thor, *ball!*" she whispered, and Thor immediately took several steps, ears forward, head up, making his leash tighten as he searched the area for the imaginary ball. "Deschutes County sheriff!" Rowan yelled at JB as he approached. "Stop or I'll send my dog after you!"

The man's gaze locked on Thor, who eagerly awaited him at the end of his leash, hoping he had a ball. JB slammed to a halt and lifted his hands.

"Don't move!" Rowan shouted at him. The sham had been a risk, but with Thor wearing a harness and Rowan in dark-brown pants and a beige jacket, similar to the color of the county uniform, it'd been enough to make JB think twice about running.

Rowan had seen it several times. Some suspects were terrified of being bitten by the apprehension dogs and would immediately give up when the dog appeared. Others ran and within minutes found themselves writhing on the ground with a dog toothily attached to one of their limbs.

Behind JB, the deputy gave orders for him to get on the ground. JB's gaze was still locked on Thor, and Rowan urged her dog to take a few steps in JB's direction. The man dropped to the ground and, before he was told, placed his hands on his head while keeping one eye on Thor.

Thor happily wagged his tail.

The deputy cuffed JB as Noelle approached Rowan.

Both women said nothing, but a silent exchange occurred within their gazes.

This is why I wanted you to stay in the vehicle.

You're welcome for stopping your suspect.

You got lucky.

"What happened?" asked Rowan.

"He must have seen us through a window," said Noelle. "We had just spotted the right apartment when he came tearing out the door." Noelle gave Thor some scratches. "Good boy!"

Rowan pulled a small floppy Frisbee from a pocket. She always had toys and kibble on her. Evan had quickly learned to empty all her pockets before doing laundry. She unhooked Thor and flung the Frisbee. It wasn't the promised ball, but Thor didn't care as he morphed into a black blur flying across the apartment grass.

The deputy helped JB to his feet. "What did I do?" JB asked with a grumpy frown.

"You ran when we told you to stop," said Noelle. "It's not complicated."

"I didn't know what you wanted."

"Most people *ask* that question instead of running like a zombie horde is after them," said Noelle.

"Actually zombies are slow," JB solemnly informed her.

"Then you haven't seen *World War Z*," said Noelle.

"Or *Dawn of the Dead*," said the deputy.

"*Zombieland*," added Rowan.

JB stared at them for a long moment, confusion lurking in his eyes. "What did I do?" he repeated. His jeans were wet at the knees from dropping to the damp grass, and he wore a faded Guns N' Roses T-shirt that had a large hole near the armpit. He was barefoot.

Nothing physically ruled him out as the man at the fire.

Not getting my hopes up.

"Let's go back to your apartment and have a little talk," said Noelle with a warm smile.

A few minutes later, JB was seated on his sofa with the deputy standing nearby. Noelle grabbed a chair from the dining area and sat on it directly in front of JB, recording audio on her phone. Rowan leaned against the wall near the door, Thor sitting beside her, his black eyes focused on JB, probably still wondering about the ball.

"Does your dog speak German?" asked JB. He'd kept a nervous gaze on Thor since being cuffed.

"He can only bark," said Rowan. "Or growl."

"You know what I mean."

"I give English commands. You're thinking of police dogs who are trained to apprehend suspects. Sometimes they work with German commands. Thor only does search and rescue." Rowan enjoyed the realization on JB's face as he understood that Thor hadn't been about to chase or bite him. At Thor's name, her dog glanced up at Rowan and wagged his tail, sweeping a fast arc on the linoleum.

/ball/

"Soon," she told him. He sighed and dropped to his belly.

"Now that we *all* know Thor won't bite you," began Noelle, "tell me how you know Catherine Woods."

Guilt flashed in JB's eyes. "I got nothing to do with that."

"With what?" asked Noelle.

JB went silent, clearly mulling over how to answer without admitting anything. "Why do you ask?"

"Not good enough, JB," said Noelle in a patient voice. "You know the reason we're here. Why don't you make it easy on yourself and cooperate? Lying or clamming up will make it worse. I can tell the DA you were hindering our investigation, or I can tell them you were helpful. It will benefit you in the long run if I say helpful."

JB's attention wandered as Noelle spoke, and he focused on Thor again.

"Does your dog speak German?" he asked.

Rowan tipped her head. JB appeared serious. She exchanged glances with Noelle and the deputy, who both seemed confused.

JB's shoulders sank as he looked at the floor. "I bet I already asked that, didn't I?"

"You did," said Rowan. "You don't remember?"

"I forget shit sometimes . . . well, a lot of the time."

"Convenient," Noelle said dryly.

His head popped up, and he glared daggers at her. "It's not convenient. It *sucks*. Do you know how hard it is to keep a job when you constantly forget what you're supposed to be doing?"

Is this his disability?

"How long have you been forgetting things?" asked Rowan.

JB screwed up his face in thought. "It's been a couple years. Cracked my skull in two places in a bar fight. For a while I could barely even talk. Was in the hospital several days." Confusion crossed his face. "Or was that from the car accident?"

He sounds sincere.

Rowan wasn't ready to trust him. And judging by the "You're bullshitting me" expression on Noelle's face, she wasn't either.

"I need to use the bathroom," JB announced.

Noelle's phone vibrated and she glanced at it. "I need to take this. Two-minute bathroom break," she said to the deputy. He grabbed JB's upper arm to help him off the sofa and walked him down the hall.

"Be right back." Noelle passed Rowan as she stepped out of the apartment, and Rowan spotted Maxine's name on the screen.

Her heartbeat sped up.

Bad news?

36

Noelle returned within thirty seconds, and the grim look on her face made Rowan's lungs seize. "What is it?" she asked the detective, feeling her heart sink.

"In the first outbuilding, Maxine found what may have caused the mystery white marks in the lividity on Rod's back. Did Evan tell you about those marks?"

"Yes. The odd shapes that were spotted during the autopsy. What did she find?"

Noelle opened a photo on her phone. Three large bolts lay on a stained concrete floor. "She thinks Rod happened to be lying on these when he died. The pressure would have kept lividity from forming, leaving sort of an unconnected T shape."

The dark stains on the flooring were more horrific to Rowan. A story of untold horrors that had happened in the room. She looked away, imagining the shapes on Evan's back.

The deputy and JB appeared, and he was returned to his original spot on the sofa.

"Okay, JB," began Noelle. "You were about to tell us what happened on Catherine Woods's property."

The man looked away.

"You're currently in deep shit," said Noelle. "Let's see if you can climb out and make things better for your situation." Her statements were vague, but the acquiescence on JB's face said they had hit home.

"I quit that," he said reluctantly. "Told him I was done and didn't care about the money."

"What money?" asked Noelle.

"He was going to pay me."

He? Man number two?

"Has he paid you anything?"

"No." A sullen frown filled his face.

"So he was screwing you over. Using you." Noelle skillfully drove a wedge between JB's relationship with the mystery man. "Has he done anything to help you? Compared to what you've done for him?"

"No." Anger flashed.

"Let's start at the beginning," said Noelle. "How did he get you involved?"

"Who get me involved?" A blank look in his eyes.

"The man who was to pay you." Patience in her tone.

"Oh, right. He needed a gun—but that was years ago. He wasn't going to shoot it; he just needed it."

Clear as mud.

"I'm not following," said Noelle. "How many years ago?"

JB thought hard. "Seven?"

"Seven years ago, this man who owes you money asked you for a gun."

"Well, not exactly. He asked my sister, and she asked me, so I gave it to her, and she took care of it."

Rowan didn't recall any mention of a sister when Detective Shults had come across JB.

"Okay," said Noelle, clearly just rolling with the story. "What happened next?"

"She got worried and told him an old cop was poking around."

Rowan's attention perked.

"She got worried seven years ago?" asked Noelle.

"No. A few weeks ago."

Is he confusing two stories?

"You jumped ahead seven years," said Noelle. "That's a big gap."

"Well, nothing happened during that time until recently." He shrugged. "She got worried and told him an old cop was poking around."

He's repeating again.

"The old cop was Rod McLeod?" asked Noelle, filling in a blank.

"Yeah." JB nodded emphatically.

"Who took the old cop to Catherine Woods's property?" she asked.

"Me and him."

"Let's give *him* a first name."

"Sid," he replied promptly.

Noelle sent a look to Rowan, who immediately texted Detective Shults to search for the name in relation to Rod McLeod's cases.

"I only did what Sid told me to do," said JB. "None of it was my idea."

"Good to know," said Noelle. "Who shot Rod McLeod?"

"Sid."

Will Sid be blamed for everything?

"Shooting a cop is pretty serious. That doesn't look good for Sid," said Noelle.

JB nodded. "I told him that. But Sid has a temper, and the old cop—Rod—said something that really made him lose it." His gaze was deadly serious, a hint of fear lurking behind the eyes.

Rowan's hands grew icy, and she shoved them in her pockets.

This is the type of man who has Evan and Zack?

"Wow," said Noelle, her voice slightly choked. "He must have said something awful."

"I didn't think so." Confusion crossed JB's face. "All he said was that someone—I don't remember the name—would figure it out. The old cop said he had left something behind . . . but I . . ." JB stopped speaking and stared at the ceiling, concentration in his gaze. "I don't remember what happened," he finally admitted.

"Did you help Sid capture Rod?" asked Noelle.

"Yeah, but I didn't make him bleed. That was Sid's knife. All I did was put him in a headlock, so that's not a big deal." He looked to Noelle for affirmation.

"Smart on your part. Did Sid make you help carry his body to the junkyard?"

"Yeah." He shuddered.

"Tell me more about Sid. What's his last name?"

JB's face closed off.

Noelle raised her brows. "You're protecting the man who used you? Who owes you money? Do you think he'll come back and pay you?"

JB stared at the wet knees of his jeans. "Nah, he doesn't have a job. But that's not his fault."

Rowan had the sense that JB was reciting something he'd heard.

"Whose fault is it that he doesn't have a job?" asked Noelle.

"No one will hire him. That's not his fault," he repeated. "I tried to help."

"That was nice of you," said Noelle. "What help did you give? I bet Sid was happy to get it."

"Found him a place to live for a while. Grandma Woods's place."

Aha.

"Catherine Woods? Sid lived in her home? She's not exactly your grandma, right?"

"We just called her that. She passed away a few years ago." JB concentrated. "I think it was a few years. Maybe it's been more." He shook his head in frustration. "I have trouble remembering things." He looked from Noelle to Rowan as if sharing that for the first time.

Rowan remembered the shallow grave found behind the house earlier that day.

"JB, where is your grandma buried?" asked Noelle, echoing Rowan's thoughts.

He looked away. "We buried her near the house. Otherwise it would have cost a lot of money. This way she was near the place she loved."

Again Rowan sensed he was reciting someone else's explanation.

"Who helped you bury her?"

"Sid." His face cleared. "I guess he has done something for me. I didn't know what to do when he found out she'd died."

Noelle subtly straightened in her chair. "Sid found her when she died? Was he living there at the time?"

"Yeah, not long after he'd moved in. She was old. It happens."

She would be seventy-eight now. Not old.

The deputy exchanged a knowing look with Rowan.

He thinks Sid was involved in her death too.

There'd been no record of Catherine Woods's death, so her Social Security was still being issued. From what Rowan knew about Sid, she assumed that he was collecting the funds. But he probably paid the home's property taxes to keep the government from taking a closer look.

"JB, you said earlier that you quit helping Sid," said Noelle. "Why did you make that decision?"

The man squirmed on the sofa, his hands still cuffed behind him. He looked everywhere but avoided all gazes.

"Remember," said Noelle. "We're trying to help you help yourself to make your situation better. It was a good decision to distance yourself from Sid after he did bad things."

JB nodded.

"Why did you quit?"

"He said he needed the woman because she knew what the old cop refused to tell him," JB said slowly. "It was important to find out what she knew."

The woman.

Rowan's nails bit into her palms as she squeezed her hands into fists, the pain a welcome distraction.

"Was the woman Sophia?" asked Noelle.

"Yeah." A struggle was reflected in his eyes. "It was important to find out what she knew," he repeated.

"What did she know?"

"Nothing. It made Sid mad that she was lying to him. He hurt her like he hurt the old cop."

Rowan closed her eyes, asking forgiveness for ever doubting pieces of Sophia's story.

Sid hurts everyone.

What did he do to Zack and Evan?

"You're doing great, JB," said Noelle. "What happened then?"

"Sid said we needed to find her son. He said that she'd stop lying if she thought Sid would hurt her son. He said he wasn't really going to hurt the boy," JB quickly added. "Just make her think he would. It would be okay as soon as she told the truth."

Sid's justifications are coming out of JB's mouth.

"Who found the boy? That would be Zack, right?"

"Yeah. Sid figured out where he was by following someone to a farm. But he sent me alone to get him. I showed the boy a fake message from his mother that instructed him to trust me and that she wanted him to go with me to meet her. I could tell he was nervous since I was a stranger, but I pointed out that only a few people knew he was at the farm. How would I know where to find him if she hadn't sent me? He was pretty willing after that. He said he knew his mother was hiding from people who'd hurt his grandfather." JB frowned. "But then he changed his mind. Said he needed to let the farm people know he was leaving. That's when I had to show him a gun."

"You threatened Zack with a gun to make him go with you?"

"Yeah." JB was quiet for a long moment. "I didn't like that. You shouldn't hurt kids, you know?"

"You hurt him?" Rowan blurted.

"No! Not me!" JB stiffened. "I scared him a bit to make him obey. Don't know if Sid has done anything to him since then. I told Sid I quit after I brought him the boy and left. I haven't gone back."

"So there were three people being held at your grandma's place?" asked Noelle.

Rowan held her breath. JB had yet to mention Evan.

But if Zack was there, Evan had to be too.

"The woman and the boy," said JB. "The old cop was gone by then. We got her right after we dumped him at the junkyard. She believed she was dropping off some money late one night, but Sid hit her with a bar."

"What about the other man being held at your grandma's?"

"What other man?"

"The other cop. Younger. He was a detective." Noelle's voice was tight.

Rowan leaned forward, watching for flickers in every muscle on JB's face.

I can't breathe.

"No other cop," he said, his eyebrows drawn together in confusion.

"Maybe you didn't know he was a cop. Who else was being held there?"

"The woman and her boy," JB said slowly. "I locked the boy in a bedroom in the house. She was in the garage. No one else."

The room was silent.

He never saw Evan? Thor smelled him there. His shirt was there.

Or someone planted it.

Rowan pressed her hands to her face, covering her eyes.

Where are you, Evan?

"JB," said Noelle. "How many days ago did you *quit* helping Sid?"

He thought. "A few days ago. I think. Doesn't seem very long."

"And when you quit, the woman and boy were there?"

"Yeah." He paused. "No one else," he added helpfully.

He doesn't know Sophia escaped.

"We were at your grandma's house today," said Noelle. "No one was there. Do you know where Sid would have taken them?"

Surprise flickered on JB's face. "Dunno. Sid liked that house."

"And you haven't heard from Sid since you quit?"

"Nope. And I *won't* go back even if he begs me. You don't do that to kids. I understood he needed help with the old cop and woman. They owed him. But when he made me lock that kid in a room, I was *done*." Righteousness filled his tone.

JB has standards.

"Have you heard the name Evan Bolton?" asked Noelle.

"Oh yeah." JB nodded several times. "Sid hates that guy. Says he ruined his life. Said it's his fault he didn't have a job or family now."

Rowan quickly texted Detective Shults, asking her to check Evan's cases for someone he'd put away named Sid. She looked up and met Noelle's gaze.

Already texted the request.

"But you've never seen him?" asked Noelle, turning back to JB.

"No. Sid talked to the old cop about him." He paused. "That's what made Sid so mad." He nodded to himself. "I remember now. The old cop said Evan would figure out what Sid did and put him in prison." He exhaled. "Never seen Sid so pissed. That's when he shot him. I hadn't expected that."

Noelle sat back for the first time, leaning against the back of the chair. Exhaustion hovered around her. Rowan admired the way she'd skillfully maneuvered information out of JB, but important pieces were still missing.

"I need Sid's last name," said Noelle, finality in her voice. "He's done horrible things. It's only fair that he be held accountable for them."

JB looked around the room, his gaze ending up on Thor, and curiosity shone in his eyes. "Does your dog speak German?"

He doesn't remember he asked that.

"Holy shit," muttered the deputy.

"JB! *Sid's last name.*" Noelle was out of patience.

His startled gaze flew to her, and he shook his head. "He'll be really mad at me. Don't want to be locked up in the garage. Said he'd use his cigarettes on me."

"He threatened to do that?"

"Yeah. Said I was a dead man if I told anyone what we'd done." His mouth hung open and horror grew in his eyes as the realization sank in that he'd told Noelle exactly what he was to keep secret.

Your faulty memory worked in our favor.

Noelle stood and gestured at the deputy to get JB up. "Let's see if putting you in a jail cell changes your mind about his last name."

As the deputy led him toward the door, JB froze. "Wait. I've got to feed my fish!" He pulled toward the kitchen, anxiety wrinkling his brow.

"Not now." Noelle was done.

"I'll do it," said Rowan. She'd never let an animal go hungry, and JB might be gone for quite a while. She walked into the kitchen, Thor at her heels. Two goldfish swam to the side of their bowl, clearly hoping for food. Rowan opened the container of flakes and sprinkled a few on the water's surface. Thor shoved his nose up near the bowl, his nostrils flaring at the flakes' stinky odor.

/treats/

"Not for—"

A loud crack made her drop to the ground and haul Thor close.

Gunfire!

"*Back, back, back!*" shouted Noelle, and a door slammed. Rowan crawled to the edge of the kitchen and took a quick glance into the living room. JB lay on his side on the floor as Noelle knelt next to him, her bloody hands trying to unlock his cuffs. The deputy was on his radio, shouting for backup and an ambulance as he reported a shooting.

Noelle's frantic gaze caught Rowan's. *"He's shot!"* The cuffs came off, and JB flopped onto his back. "Fuck me!" shouted Noelle as she ripped off her jacket and pressed it against the large entry wound in his forehead.

Blood rapidly oozed from under his head.

Rowan grabbed a kitchen towel and crawled into the living room. "What happened?" She tried to position the towel to stop some of the blood puddling on the carpet, knowing in her gut that the situation was hopeless. She'd seen a crater where the back of his head should be. Her towel was quickly soaked.

"We'd just stepped outside." Noelle's words rushed together. "His body jerked, and then I heard the shot. We dragged him back in and shut the door."

A spray of fine red mist coated one of Noelle's cheeks, bits of wet debris in her hair. She lifted her jacket, peeked at JB's forehead, and immediately pressed the jacket back down. "Oh my God." She closed her eyes, hanging her head as she knelt beside him.

Bile crept up Rowan's throat.

No one can survive this.

37

"JB had just said Sid would kill him if he talked," Noelle muttered again.

Rowan squeezed her shoulder in sympathy, but the detective didn't appear to notice. The women had driven back to the department's conference room after JB's body was taken away. The police response to the shooting had been immediate. Patrol cars with screaming sirens had streamed in, and a perimeter had been rapidly established as they combed the area for the shooter.

JB never took a breath. He'd died instantly.

Sid. He has to be the killer.

Rowan had finally stopped shaking, but Noelle continued to beat herself up for exposing JB.

"No one would have been prepared for that," Rowan had told her several times. "Why *wouldn't* you walk him to a patrol car?"

Her words had no effect. Noelle seemed determined to shoulder nearly as much responsibility for JB's death as the shooter.

Detective Shults entered the room. "I can't find a Sid mentioned anywhere in cases related to Rod or Evan. I've checked known aliases and am still coming up empty. It has to be a nickname that's unknown to us."

"Where's Maxine?" Noelle asked, her gaze on her laptop. She was looking up previous addresses for JB, hoping to find a connection to Sid.

Lori glanced at Rowan. They all knew Maxine was still investigating on-site at the Woods home. "She's at the Woods property."

"Maybe some of the other detectives who worked with Evan would remember a Sid," suggested Rowan. "Sounds like this man and Evan really butted heads. Evan might have talked to someone here about it."

"Good idea. I ran the name by Lieutenant Ogden, but I'll ask around some more." Lori paused. "Ogden says you're to meet with psych," she hesitantly told Noelle.

"Later." Noelle didn't look up.

Lori studied her for a long moment and then silently left the room.

"I don't have time for that right now," Noelle said tightly. "Ogden requested a local department to deliver JB's death notification to his parents in South Carolina. I've found someone who I assume is the sister JB mentioned during my interview. She's thirteen years older than him, but at one point they shared the same address." Determination filled her tone. "She might know who this Sid is. I'll notify her in person."

Rowan eyed the detective. Both of them had turned over their bloody clothes to the investigation team and then showered in the Deschutes County locker room. Rowan had put on the change of clothes she always kept in her SUV, and Noelle now wore yoga clothing from her gym bag. The detective's platinum hair was damp and hung straight, her face devoid of makeup.

Rowan had never seen Noelle not perfectly put together.

"It's almost six," said Noelle. "A good chance to catch the sister at home if she works normal hours." She pushed back her chair and stood but then steadied herself with a hand on the table.

"I'll go with you," said Rowan. "Let me drive. That'll give you a chance to think about what to say." It was a weak excuse, but Rowan didn't think Noelle should be driving at the moment. She was deep in self-blame. "Neither of us has eaten since breakfast. Food first."

"I don't think I can eat." Noelle's voice was soft, but she hadn't argued with Rowan's suggestion that she drive, so Rowan took that as a win. And a sign that Noelle's batteries were running low.

"Soup," said Rowan. "Something easy and warm. Maybe some fresh bread. I'll order ahead at Panera, and we can stop for a few minutes on the way."

Noelle reluctantly nodded.

"Do you have a jacket?" asked Rowan, taking in Noelle's pink yoga pants. "A department one?"

Noelle snorted. "Not very official looking, am I? Yes, I'll grab it." She sighed and finally met her gaze. "Thanks, Rowan. It's been several shitty days for you, yet you're holding it together for me."

Rowan appreciated the words but didn't consider herself to be holding it together. "I need to keep moving. Stay busy. Not sit for too long with my thoughts."

That was a lie. She briefly closed her eyes, taking deep breaths.

Evan is always on my mind.

She wished Thor were there; she needed to sink her hands into his fur, but she'd had Malcolm come get him, not knowing when she'd be home.

"We'll find Evan and Zack," Noelle said, and she gave Rowan a tight hug, resolve in her words. "I know we will." Then Noelle stepped back and looked her in the eye. "Let's go get some soup."

An hour later, they parked at the curb in front of a small house. An older black SUV was in the driveway. "Someone is home," said Rowan, turning off her vehicle.

She and Noelle felt better after getting some food in their bodies. During the drive, Noelle had rehearsed what she wanted to say to the sister, and they'd talked a bit about the shooting.

"The shooter today was very accurate," said Noelle. "It reminded me of when Charlie Graham was shot at the auto body shop. If he and Evan hadn't *just* moved that second, Evan would have caught the bullet—and that shot was fired from a good distance, like today's was."

"Sid must have extensive shooting experience or training," said Rowan. "I wonder if that could help you find him. Check local ranges to see if someone knows a Sid."

"I'll pass that on to Maxine to look into, but I'm hoping JB's sister knows where to find Sid," said Noelle, tipping her head at the house. "JB said Sid asked her for a gun."

"Seven years ago," added Rowan. "And that's a big maybe. JB's memory wasn't great."

Noelle didn't reply. Rowan glanced over and saw her expression had blanked.

Too fresh.

"What's the sister's name?" Rowan asked to redirect Noelle's thoughts.

"Lucinda Parnell."

"JB's last name was Fry, right?"

"Yes. Jeremiah Bradley Fry. Parnell is probably her married name."

Rowan sensed the detective had needed to say JB's full name out loud. A memorialization of the victim whose violent death she'd witnessed.

Noelle opened her door. Rowan did the same, and they headed up the crumbling walkway. The small home was from a previous decade. Simple design. One that didn't stand out or catch the eye. Probably built in the 1960s. The blue paint needed a touch-up, and the steps creaked as they moved onto the front porch. Noelle rang the doorbell, and she automatically stepped to the side. Suddenly feeling vulnerable, Rowan did the same and then felt slightly foolish.

This is a condolence call. Not a suspect visit.

A woman opened the door, and Rowan tried to place her familiar face.

"Cynthia?" Noelle asked in a confused voice.

Even in the poor light, Rowan saw her pale as she grabbed the doorframe.

"Detective Marshall," the woman answered, surprise in her voice. "What are you doing here?"

Rowan figured out where she'd seen the woman.

She's an evidence tech.

"Is your full name Lucinda Parnell?" Noelle asked.

"Yes. But I go by Cynthia." The woman blinked rapidly. "What's going on?"

"Is JB Fry your younger brother?"

Cynthia sucked in a breath and tightened her grip on the wood frame. "What happened? Is JB okay?"

Oh no. This poor woman.

Wait. Cynthia would have access to department information . . . Was she passing it on to JB? And he told Sid?

Rowan met Noelle's sharp gaze.

She's wondering the same.

"No, I'm sorry, he's not," said Noelle. "He passed away this afternoon. Can we come in for a few minutes?"

Cynthia froze for a long moment, blinking as Noelle's words took time to register. Then she silently took a step back, opening the door wider.

It occurred to Rowan how horrible it would have been for Cynthia if she had been assigned to process a crime scene and then discovered the victim was her brother.

Inside the home, Noelle took charge, leading a numb Cynthia to a table in the kitchen nook and encouraging her to sit down. "Is anyone else here?" Noelle asked as she and Rowan took seats at the table.

"No. My daughter is at a friend's."

Rowan noticed she didn't wear a wedding ring and assumed no one else lived there.

"What happened?" Cynthia asked, looking from Noelle to Rowan and back. Her face was still very pale.

Noelle touched Cynthia's wrist and held her gaze, sorrow in her eyes. "I'm really sorry, but he was shot at his apartment."

Cynthia shuddered and placed a hand over her eyes. Tears flowed down her cheeks. "Did he suffer for long?"

"There was no suffering," said Noelle. "It happened instantly. I'm confident in that fact because I was with him."

The woman looked up, bewilderment in her gaze. "Why were you there? Was this a police shooting?" she whispered, her expression changing to one of horror.

"No," Noelle said firmly. "Police were not involved. I was at his apartment to talk with JB about a case, and we'd just stepped out of his apartment when there was a single shot. I'm sorry, but we haven't caught the shooter yet. Police responded immediately but were unable to find him." She took Cynthia's hand. "We will find who did this."

Noelle is hiding her suspicions very well.

Suspicion that Cynthia was the department leaker didn't negate the fact that her brother had just been murdered.

Could she know where Evan is?

Cynthia pulled her hand away, dropped her head onto her arms on the table, and broke into full-blown sobs. Noelle placed her hand on Cynthia's shoulder and let her cry. Rowan had to look away, letting her gaze wander over their surroundings. She stopped on a framed photo collage of a young woman, the girl's looks implying she was Cynthia's daughter. Rowan wondered how close the daughter had been to her uncle.

Someone else to notify.

Cynthia started to wail, and Noelle shot Rowan a glance, her hand still on the woman's shoulder, patting gently.

The poor woman is a wreck. How will Noelle question her about leaking department information?

Cynthia lifted her head to briefly rub her eyes. "This is all my fault," she said amid tears. "It's all my fault. I didn't know."

"JB's death is not your fault," said Noelle, her voice low and sympathetic.

But Rowan saw the stricken look in Noelle's eyes. She still blamed herself.

"I'm gonna throw up." Cynthia started to dry-heave, and Rowan darted out of her chair to grab the garbage bin at the end of the kitchen counter. She slid it next to Cynthia.

"The only person at fault is the one that pulled the trigger," Rowan said to Cynthia, but she included Noelle with her gaze. "And the police will catch that person. He'll pay for this."

Cynthia continued to dry-heave over the garbage can. "JB struggles," she forced out between heaves. "He forgets. He doesn't understand what's going on sometimes."

"He told us that," said Noelle.

The heaves eased off, but her sobs continued. "I should have looked out for him better. This is all my fault."

"Rowan is right. The only person responsible was the one holding the gun." Noelle's gaze sharpened. "Cynthia," she said, slowing her words and speaking firmly. "JB told us he once loaned a gun to someone named Sid. Do you know who that is?"

"Oh my God. You know about Sid?" Cynthia's breaths turned heavy and wet as more tears ran.

She knows him.

What about Evan?

"Yes, he told us about Sid," said Noelle, controlled excitement building in her voice. "But that's not his real name, right? Do you know it?"

Instead of answering, Cynthia turned to Rowan, pleading in her eyes. "I'm so sorry about Evan. I know how upset you must be. It's just horrible." She wiped her nose, never breaking eye contact.

Rowan lost her breath.

She knows what happened to him.

Anger flooded her. "What's Sid's name?" Rowan forced out. "Tell us where to find him. *He has Evan and Zack, doesn't he?*"

Cynthia flinched, dropping her gaze. "This wasn't supposed to happen. None of it." A fresh round of sobs started.

"Cynthia! Sid's. Name. Now." Noelle's fingers dug into Cynthia's shoulder. Like Rowan's, her sympathy had rapidly evaporated.

"Dale Forbes!" she shrieked. "But he changed his first name to Sid! I didn't know he would do this!" She covered her eyes with her hands.

"Where is he?" Noelle turned her attention to her phone screen as she sent off multiple texts relaying the name.

"I don't know!"

"Where's he live? Where's he work?" Noelle shouted, looking from her screen to Cynthia and back.

"He doesn't work! He lives in that house from this morning! If he's not there, I don't know where to find him!"

"Is Evan alive? Is Zack?" Rowan spit out the questions, barely able to breathe. "What's he done to them?"

"I don't know! I don't know anything! I heard about the raid and assumed that would be the end. I was as shocked as anyone that no one was there. I don't know where they went!"

Noelle put her phone to her ear, pushed out of her chair, and strode from the kitchen. Rowan caught some of her instructions to someone to find everything they could on Dale or Sid Forbes. Friends, property, employment, prior arrests.

Cynthia's tear-filled gaze met Rowan's. "I'm truly sorry. I know how terrified you must be for him."

"You have no idea!" Cynthia's fears had made Rowan's escalate.

"He made us do it," Cynthia choked out between sobs. "He threatened my daughter. He threatened my job. I'm a single mom. I *need* my job!"

"Evan needs to live!" Rowan said in shock. "Sophia needs her son!"

"I said *I'm sorry!*"

"Shut. Up," ordered Noelle as she came back in the room. "Get a hold of yourself now. I need to know everything about Sid Forbes."

Cynthia sucked in several trembling breaths. It took three attempts to form words. "Years ago he dated my aunt. I didn't know much about him. He seemed decent enough."

Decent.

How wrong she was.

"I'd been divorced for about five years. Kinsey was ten, and I'd been working for the county for several years as an evidence tech. I loved my job," she said, her gaze pleading with the women to believe her.

"Get on with it," snapped Noelle. She stood at the table, feet planted apart, continuing to send off emails and texts as she occasionally shot Cynthia angry looks.

"Blackmail," Cynthia managed to say. "Sid blackmailed me. I don't know how he found out, but I'd screwed up some fingerprint evidence on a robbery case early in my career." She looked down at her clasped hands. "I moved some evidence around to cover it up, but I thought no one knew. I crossed a line."

Rowan couldn't speak.

She threw all her integrity out the window.

"But it was okay!" Cynthia turned desperate eyes to Rowan. "The guy was guilty. Everyone knew it. What I did supported that!"

"Jesus Christ." Noelle was floored. "You should have been fired! Every case you've worked on over the years is now suspect. What a fucking mess!"

"I know!" Cynthia shouted back. "*I know!* But I needed that job!"

"Why did Sid blackmail you? What did he want?" asked Rowan, trying to keep focused on Sid and not Cynthia's massive breach of integrity.

Cynthia seemed to shrink into her chair as she kept her gaze down. "Sid got arrested and immediately contacted JB. JB caught me just as I was arriving to start a scene investigation and gave me a gun. Sid wanted it planted at that scene."

"Dale Forbes was arrested for manslaughter charges seven years ago, but the case was thrown out," Noelle read from her phone. She stared at Cynthia. "Is that the case you're talking about?"

Cynthia nodded. "Sid was screwing around with a married woman. The husband came home and caught them. Sid shot him right there in the bedroom, claiming the husband had pulled a gun and was about to shoot him with it."

"Let me guess," said Noelle. "The husband's gun wasn't immediately found at the scene. You put it there and miraculously found it under something while collecting evidence."

Cynthia stared down at the table. "And later added the husband's prints to it."

"I'm fucking *stunned*." Her phone rang, and Noelle strode out of the room again.

"He threatened my daughter," Cynthia said quietly to Rowan. "He said he'd make her disappear and no one would find the body." Her hysterics seemed to have passed, but tears still streamed. She gazed at the photo collage on the wall, her eyes softening. "She's my everything. All I do is for her." She gave a shuddering breath. "Sid said the shooting was truly an accident," Cynthia continued. "He said he only meant to scare the husband with a shot, but the man stepped into the bullet."

"I think Sid fed you a line of bullshit," said Rowan. "Trying to make you feel better about what he asked you to do."

"I felt horrible," she whispered.

Noelle returned, fury still burning in her eyes. "Rod and Evan were the detectives on Sid's manslaughter case," she announced to Rowan.

Rowan hadn't seen that coming. "But Sid got off. Why would he come after Evan and Rod years later? What happened with Rod?" she snapped at Cynthia.

"I liked Rod." Her eyes welled. "I worked with him several times. He always had a bad joke ready to tell me. I missed him when he retired."

"Get to the fucking point." Noelle was steaming.

"Rod started asking questions a few weeks ago," said Cynthia. "Two other techs mentioned they'd run into him somewhere, and he'd brought up a few old cases. I saw him at Ed's Tavern, and he worked a few questions about Sid's case into our conversation."

"Sid's case wasn't in Rod's filing cabinet," Noelle told Rowan. "Probably one of the missing ones. And it never came on our radar because Sid wasn't convicted. We were focused on reviewing cases where the suspect ended up in prison. We assumed"—Noelle winced—"that someone was focused on payback for prison time."

"I heard about the filing cabinet from Sid," said Cynthia. "He broke in and grabbed his file. Said he took a few others, so his missing one wouldn't seem obvious."

"None of this explains why he killed Rod." Rowan's brain was trying to keep up.

"Sid believed that Rod figured out I planted the gun," said Cynthia. "Sid was convinced he'd end up in prison if the case was reopened. The victim's wife swore her husband didn't own a gun, and there was no record of him purchasing one. The detectives were skeptical the husband pulled a gun until one showed up."

"But Rod was talking to people about other cases too. Not just Sid's," said Noelle. "Evan and I visited Damian Collinson in prison to find out why Rod recently visited him."

"Collinson," muttered Cynthia, looking at the ceiling in thought. "Jewelry store robberies?"

"Yes. Damian admitted he'd done the robberies, but did you mess with the evidence anyway?"

"I worked only one of those robberies. It was straightforward. Collinson's blood was at the scene, and it was seen on camera when he accidentally cut himself. I never tampered with evidence in any other cases after Sid's," she said emphatically. "I wasn't about to get black-mailed again. Plus I had to live with the guilt."

Rowan turned to Noelle. "Could Cynthia be the common factor in Rod's filing cabinet cases? Was Rod looking for proof that she might have tampered with other cases? Making it more likely that she would plant a gun on Sid's manslaughter case?"

"I didn't mess with evidence on other cases!"

"I don't think you have the right to be indignant about anything at the moment," Noelle stated. "Your abuse of evidence is what started this."

Cynthia slumped in her chair.

Noelle set down her phone and removed zip cuffs from her jacket. "Stand up and turn around, Cynthia. You're under arrest."

38

The drive with Cynthia back to the sheriff's department was a tense one. As Rowan drove, Noelle continued to work her phone, relaying information to her investigative team as Cynthia gave it, trying to figure out where Sid would take his hostages. Cynthia would speak only when asked a question; she volunteered no extra information. She had texted her daughter to suggest she spend the night at her friend's because she was going to the sheriff's department.

She didn't tell her daughter why, letting her assume she was going to work.

"Where'd the gun you planted at the scene come from?" asked Rowan, keeping her eyes on the road. It was dark, and she cringed as she thought about Evan and Zack spending another night under Sid's thumb.

Assuming they're still alive.

"JB stole it when he was a teenager," said Cynthia in a flat voice. "It'd been customized for the original owner. Engraved and had a fancy grip. But since the owner had reported it stolen, I knew it would work as the husband's gun. Stolen property ends up in weird places. And the husband Sid shot was dead." She shrugged. "The victim wouldn't be able to answer any questions about where he got it."

Cold. Calculating. Where is the hysterical woman we saw in the kitchen?

Noelle focused on her phone.

"Anything?" Rowan asked the detective.

"No property listed under Dale or Sid Forbes. So they're still searching for a likely place he would use to hide Evan and Zack."

Not what I wanted to hear.

"Rod must have told Sid he had evidence the gun had been planted," Rowan speculated. "Is that what Sid wanted from Sophia?" She glanced at Cynthia in the rearview mirror. The woman was staring out a side window into the dark. "Sid wanted the proof? In a file or on a thumb drive? But Sophia had no idea what Sid was talking about, did she?"

"She swore she knew nothing—" Cynthia stopped. Her face closed off; her tears had dried.

Rowan caught her breath. "You were there! You saw him torture Sophia! You probably saw what he did to Rod too!"

Noelle whirled around in her seat. "Is that true?" Cynthia stayed silent. "You're in a lot deeper trouble than just moving evidence. You're an accomplice. You were there. You knew what Sid was doing!"

"He threatened my daughter!" Cynthia shrieked. "Do you not understand what that means? Of course you don't! Neither of you have kids. You have no understanding." She shook her head and looked out the window again. "This guy is terrifying. It's like he has no soul. All he cares about is wreaking havoc on people he thinks wronged him. His brain doesn't work right."

"Then you should have gone to the police," stated Noelle. "Your brain clearly wasn't working right either. It was focused on covering your ass."

"And protecting my daughter!"

Noelle said nothing and returned to her texts.

"You honestly have no idea where Sid could have taken Zack and Evan?" Rowan asked, fully aware Cynthia had already answered.

"No. I've been trying to think of where he would go. But he essentially has nowhere. That's why he ended up at our grandma's."

The inside of the vehicle was silent for a long moment.

"Sid said he made a mistake with Rod," Cynthia said, breaking the silence.

"A mistake?" Rowan clenched the wheel. "His injuries sounded very deliberate."

"He said he made a mistake in that the torture was over too soon. He admitted his temper got the best of him when he killed Rod. And he wouldn't make that mistake again. I saw joy and anticipation when he spoke about getting revenge on Evan. He wanted to draw it out and make it hurt." She met Rowan's gaze in the mirror. "*Now* do you understand what kind of man he is?"

Rowan pressed her lips together as a shiver shot up her spine.

"He knew about you, Rowan. He knew you and Evan had a happy relationship and a nice home. He'd seen articles about Evan, singing his praises for solving investigations. He wanted to *tear him down*. Destroy every happy and successful piece of his life."

"That doesn't make sense," said Rowan. "Sid walked free. Rod and Evan essentially did nothing to him."

Cynthia scoffed. "Not in Sid's mind. Before he was cleared of any wrongdoing, he lost his job, he lost his girlfriend, and became deep in debt. He'd been tried and convicted in the media. No one would hire him after. Guess who he blamed for turning his life to shit?"

"Sid Forbes deserves all the blame," said Noelle. "He shot an innocent man. That's who's to blame for turning his life to shit. Himself."

"You're preaching to the choir," said Cynthia. "I'm just telling you how he thinks. Evan Bolton has everything Sid used to have, and he has assigned Evan full blame for losing it. It makes him furious. Destroying Evan had been in his sights for a while. He'll want to draw it out, make it last."

Rowan tried to focus on driving, but her stomach churned with acid and her hands had turned to ice.

So much hate. And Evan had no idea.

"Wait!" Rowan accidentally jerked the wheel, then straightened the SUV. "He's behind the shit going on at Evan's job! He altered the finger—*no, you altered the fingerprints!* You had access to Evan's prints on file and planted them wherever the fuck you wanted! You were full of shit when you told us you hadn't altered any other evidence!" She took a deep breath. "Do you know what that did to him? Evan got suspended! And was horrified that people at work believed he'd lied about his investigations. That crushed him!"

Cynthia was silent.

Which was Sid's goal.

"I suppose you'll say he threatened your daughter and made you do it." Rowan was bitter, tired of the woman's excuses. "He and JB burned down my house. That was my grandfather's house! You have no idea of the memories that fire destroyed. And Thor could have *died!*"

Rowan wiped tears from her eyes. "I assume you were behind the Craigslist post? And figured out how to link Evan's email to it?" She snorted. "As if Evan would try to sell something he'd just stolen."

But she made Evan's boss believe it.

"You've been involved in every aspect of Sid's plan," said Rowan. "You can't lay all the blame at his feet. I can't believe you can work for the sheriff's department and would do something like that over and over."

Noelle looked over the seat. "You've had me doubting every person I work with. Those are good people! You made me trust *no one!*" She turned around and slammed her back against her seat. "Don't fuck with things like that!"

"But—" began Cynthia.

"*Don't say another word!* I want silence until I can get a camera on you and record all the shit you say."

Rowan gripped the wheel and pressed the accelerator.

What else is Cynthia lying about?

◆ ◆ ◆

Thirty minutes later, Cynthia had been placed in an interview room and left to stew.

"I need to cool down before I talk to her," Noelle muttered, watching the woman on her computer's camera feed. Cynthia had refused a drink and then laid her head on the table and not moved. She ignored any questions.

"What if she's lying about Evan and Zack?" asked Rowan, watching the motionless woman. She couldn't shake the fear that Cynthia's stalling was risking two lives.

"Even more reason for me to question her carefully," said Noelle. "She hasn't given us any information about them. Either she really doesn't know or she doesn't plan to share. I can't barge in there and yell at her, demanding answers. I've done enough of that with her today."

Noelle took in the people in the conference room. Both Maxine and Lori were present, along with the deputies Ogden had assigned her team. "We've got no leads on where Sid could have moved the hostages," Noelle announced to the group. "It appears the man had no friends—except for JB and Cynthia. He's a loner. We need to figure out where a loner would hide two people." She moved to the huge wall map of Deschutes and the surrounding counties. A dozen red push-pins marked Sid's previous home addresses and employment locations on record. "The ideal location would be an empty, isolated building or something with a basement or a lower level where sounds can't be heard."

The thought of Evan screaming while being tortured filled Rowan's mind. She shoved it away.

"Most likely locations are *not* near a neighborhood or businesses where people are always out and about," Noelle said. "I know I'm stating the obvious, but I want to hear any possible ideas from everyone. It might trigger an idea for someone else." She frowned. "I'm a California transplant. I don't know this area like the people who grew up here. Let's round up any longtime locals that are still in the building tonight. We've got Sid's previous addresses for home and work, so if we start at those locations and study what's nearby, we might come across an ideal site. He's going to take them somewhere he is comfortable with and knows very well. He's got two people to hide and keep quiet. He's not going to take a risk in a location he doesn't know.

"And it's the locals who know these places." She pointed to a marker in a rural spot on the map. "This is a previous home address for Sid. Look at all the empty country around it. I want to know if any homes in the area have been condemned or abandoned within a mile or two . . . or if there're empty sheds no one has used in a decade, or even fucking caves. Maybe an isolated and no-longer-used gravel pit. I don't care how odd the suggestions are that you have in mind. I want to hear them all."

Everyone stared at her.

That's searching for a needle in a haystack. They don't have the manpower to check every empty building in three counties.

But Noelle had nothing else to work with. No leads. No tips.

All she had was a woman who refused to speak.

"Go!" Noelle shouted. "I want every longtime local who's still in the building in this room in the next five minutes."

It's late. Most employees will have gone home.

But the detectives and deputies scattered.

Noelle looked at Rowan. "I don't know where else to start," she said quietly. "We've got a BOLO out on his truck, and his driver's license photo has been sent to all media outlets. Until tips start coming in, we've exhausted the few leads we had." She turned back to the map and touched a red pin. "Our speculation about Sid having weapons training appears to be accurate. He worked at this gun range for nearly three years before he was arrested. It lends credence to my theory that he is the shooter from today and the auto body shop." Her gaze went from pin to pin. "A diverse work history. A car dealership. Three restaurants. Two construction companies—"

"A construction company could have put him working in all sorts of locations," said Rowan.

Noelle looked drained, ready to collapse. But her eyes were determined. "I know. I'm trying to get a list of their projects from the last five years."

Rowan gestured at the view of Cynthia on the computer. "She's your best lead right now. Are you up for that yet?"

"Another minute." Noelle studied the screen. Cynthia hadn't lifted her head.

Maxine burst in the door, hauling an apprehensive older woman. "Carla's lived just outside Bend all her life." She took the woman to the map of markers. "Are you familiar with any of the areas around these red pins?"

Rowan noticed the woman's shirt back had the name of a local janitorial company and guessed she'd been working in the building with a cleaning crew.

We need all the help we can get.

Carla indicated one pin, and she and Maxine quietly discussed, pointing at places near the marker. A second later, Deputy Coates returned with two other deputies. Both carried energy drink cans and half-eaten sub sandwiches. They joined Maxine and Carla while Coates left to find more people.

Rowan met Noelle's gaze and saw a flicker of hope.

This isn't the worst idea.

"You've lived here all your life, right?" Noelle asked Rowan. "Get in there."

"I have, but I don't know anything of the marked areas. Sorry." Rowan felt useless. She knew the ins and outs of several neighborhoods, parks, and trails, but none of them were near where Sid had lived or worked.

One of the deputies stepped away, his expression apologetic. "Sorry. I grew up more south of here."

"Thanks for looking," said Noelle. "Send in anyone else you come across."

After he stepped out the door, Lieutenant Ogden entered with Lori right behind him. He frowned slightly as he noted Rowan's presence and then turned to Noelle. "I hear you're doing a mass questioning."

"I don't care what it's called," she said. "Unless you've got some good leads in your pocket, this is all I've got."

"He's lived here forty years," said Lori. She met Ogden's gaze and pointed at the map.

"True." He moved to look over Maxine's shoulder. She tapped a spot with her finger as Carla nodded emphatically.

"Hey, Noelle," said Maxine. "This is a condemned house on the outskirts of town not far from a restaurant where Sid worked. Carla said it's been sitting empty for years. Junkies used it for a while, but the city cleared them out and boarded it up. Worth a look."

"I'll send a patrol by," said Noelle. "Thank you, Carla. Check with your family and friends, please. See if anyone else has other ideas." The woman nodded and darted out the door.

Noelle took a deep breath. "I guess I'll see if Cynthia is ready to talk." She left the room and a minute later appeared on the computer screen in the interview room. Rowan watched with Ogden and Lori as Cynthia refused to even look at the detective. After ten minutes of Cynthia repeating that she didn't know anything, Noelle cuffed her again and moved her to a holding cell. She returned to the room, frustration in her gaze. "Maybe that will stimulate her memory," she said grimly.

I think Cynthia believes Sid can still hurt her daughter.

Over the next two hours, a small trickle of people filed into the conference room. Noelle asked patrols to investigate four locations, but all turned up nothing. No Sid or his truck.

No Evan or Zack.

It was past 10:00 p.m., and Rowan couldn't stop yawning.

"Go home," ordered Noelle, and then gave a jaw-cracking yawn.

"We all need sleep," Rowan said with a pointed look at the detective. Rowan didn't want to close her eyes. She suspected the minute she lay down, her mind would race, and then she'd lie there for hours, worrying, stressing, and imagining the worst.

Twenty minutes later, her brother, Malcolm, knocked at the conference room's open door, and Rowan stared at him in sleepy confusion. "Is Thor okay?"

"Yes." He pointed at Noelle. "She texted me. Told me what you've all been up to and to get you home for some sleep."

"Traitor." Rowan tried to glare at Noelle but was too tired.

"Tomorrow," said Noelle. "We'll have a fresh start tomorrow." The detective showed no indication that she was headed home.

I can't tell her what to do.

Rowan pushed herself out of the comfy conference chair as Malcolm stepped close to the map, studying the pins. Rowan waited, a pang of sorrow touching her as he looked. Malcolm had spent a lot of time exploring the county, trying to make up for decades of confinement. Places she took for granted were new and wondrous to him. He'd rapidly filled several memory cards with photos and videos, needing to preserve every new sight.

He touched the pin at the gun range where Sid had worked and then moved his finger a half inch away. "There's an old hydroelectric plant here. It's been abandoned since the forties or fifties, I believe. It's a small brick structure." He shrugged. "Kids covered it in graffiti at one point, but when I discovered it, the dirt road was hard to spot, and the old equipment inside was covered in undisturbed dust. Felt like no one had been there in years."

"That's the kind of tip I want to hear," said Noelle. "I'll send a unit to drive by. Thanks, Malcolm."

"It's not the kind of place you can drive by," said Malcolm. "The road is horrible, and the last bit is completely overgrown. They'll have to walk about a hundred yards in the dark, and it's downhill. It sits in a valley next to the creek."

"Crap." Noelle sighed. "I guess it can wait until morning, then."

"I know the way," said Malcolm. "I've probably been there a half dozen times. I can easily find it with a flashlight."

"That's not necessary," said Noelle. Her words didn't match her hopeful tone.

"You just need to know if his vehicle is there, right?" asked Malcolm. "It's on my way home. There's no way anyone could drive the last hundred yards unless they were in a Humvee, so if he's there, his vehicle will be easy enough for me to find without getting that close to the building."

"It can't hurt," said Rowan, eyeing Noelle. "I'll go with him. It'll take us a few minutes, and then we'll go on home. Then you can focus on other sites." She couldn't pass up an opportunity to do *something* that could help find Evan and Zack.

Indecision flashed in Noelle's eyes.

"Well . . . then have a good night, Noelle." Rowan met Malcolm's gaze. *We're stopping by.*

She headed toward the door as he followed.

"Hang on," said Noelle. "You're going whether or not I say yes, aren't you?"

"Yes," answered Rowan and Malcolm in unison.

"Jesus." Noelle sighed. "Okay. I expect a call either way in thirty minutes."

"You got it," said Rowan. "And then you should nap. Let Maxine or Lori take over for a while." Noelle's eyes were bloodshot, and she'd yawned as much as Rowan.

"Uh-huh." Noelle busied herself on the computer.

Stubborn.

"Let's go," Rowan said to her brother. Her exhaustion lifted, her mind pleased that she was doing something . . . anything . . . to help.

We've got to find Evan and Zack.

39

"You've got to be kidding me," said Rowan as she stepped out of Malcolm's Jeep and shined her flashlight on the brush ahead. The dirt road was more than overgrown. It was a dense forest. Driving in had been rough, the road severely rutted and full of rocks.

"I understand why you know about this place," Rowan had said as she hung on in the Jeep with both hands. Since he'd returned, Malcolm had searched out every nearby location to challenge himself and his Jeep. He'd joined a local Jeeping group that loved to spend weekends testing the limits of their vehicles.

A passion second only to baking.

"Let's look over this way," said Malcolm, pointing his flashlight to the left. "Are you armed?"

"No. I've got nothing with me except a flashlight." She frowned at him, noticing he carried a handgun. "Which is *all* we'll need to find out if Sid's vehicle is nearby."

"I can tell you right now that something has driven through here recently," Malcolm said. "See?" His flashlight scanned over crushed grass and broken branches. "They won't have gotten far, though. What's he drive?"

"A Ford F-150."

"I guess it could break a trail like this," Malcolm muttered as he started to follow the tracks. "Ground is hard enough. No rocks in this direction, but his paint job will be a wreck from branches. I don't know how he plans to get out."

"Maybe he's not planning to leave," Rowan said quietly, earning an alarmed glance from Malcolm.

"Suicide?"

Murder/suicide?

"I don't know," said Rowan. "But if he's here, he's put himself into a situation without a lot of options."

Would he kill Evan? And Zack?

She started to ask what type of person would kill a child and then shut her mouth just in time. Malcolm's kidnapper had been exactly that person. Her brother had experienced and seen things she couldn't imagine. She followed him, keeping her light on the ground as they carefully picked their way through the brush. The path gently angled down, and Rowan heard the quiet splashing of a creek far below.

Twenty yards later Malcolm said, "There it is." His flashlight shone on the back of a Ford pickup.

We found them!

Dumbfounded, Rowan stared at the truck, expecting it to evaporate before her eyes. She'd hoped to find it but had fully expected not to.

Its front end was wedged against a tree at a downward angle, a back wheel in the air. Sid would never be able to get it out without a tow truck.

"Call Noelle," said Malcolm.

"Let's check the inside first," said Rowan. Anxiety crawled under her skin.

Could someone be in it?

"I'll do that. Stay back." He drew his gun and slowly approached the truck. He pointed his light inside, checking the back and front seats. He glanced at her, shook his head, and then made his way back. "The floor is littered with soda bottles and crap. There's some ropes and short bungee cords in the back seat. He probably strapped them down for the drive."

Rowan exhaled. Hopefully, that meant Evan and Zack were still alive. She pulled out her phone to call Noelle and wasn't surprised to see she didn't have service. They'd moved partway down into a gully. She'd have to go back to the top, where they'd parked.

Distant screams filled the air, and Rowan nearly dropped her phone.

"That's a child," gasped Malcolm.

Rowan couldn't move. The child sounded as if he were being tortured. She looked at her brother in the dim light. He was frozen, his eyes wide.

He's remembering horrible things.

She grabbed Malcolm's arm and shook him out of his trance. "I don't have service! We need to go back up to call!"

"We can't leave him!"

"It'll just take a minute! And then the police will get here quick." She pulled on his arm. He wouldn't move. "Malcolm! We can't go in there!"

"He's hurting him!"

"*I know!*" Her vision blurred at the pain in Malcolm's voice. "We can't help until we call the police! That man is dangerous!" The screams made the hair on her neck stand up. She yanked on her brother, and he finally stumbled after her as they scrambled up the slope.

"*Fucking leave him alone!*"

At the far-off shout, Rowan and Malcolm halted.

That's Evan!

40

"He's alive!" Rowan grabbed Malcolm's arm. "That's Evan's voice!"

"Go call Noelle," Malcolm ordered.

"You're not going down there," said Rowan, realizing Malcolm wouldn't go back up with her. "That man is a killer! And he's a fucking good shot. We wait for the police!"

We've already had this argument.

She spun to go find cell coverage, hauling Malcolm behind her. They crashed through the brush at a run.

Am I leaving Evan and Zack to die?

She checked her phone. No bars. She pushed on, the distance feeling much longer than when they'd come. Malcolm had stopped resisting and moved on his own. They reached Sid's truck and suddenly Rowan had two bars of service. She stopped, panting hard as she dialed.

"Rowan?" Noelle answered.

"He's here!" Rowan forced out. "His truck is here, and we heard a child screaming and Evan shouting down at the powerhouse! You've got to get someone out here *now*! He's torturing Zack!" Rowan caught her breath and heard Noelle speak to someone in the background.

"We're on our way," Noelle said into the phone. "Do not go near the building! Someone will be there as soon as possible. Wait and show them how to find it." She ended the call.

The screams started again, fainter this time.

"Fuck." Malcolm looked back the way they had come. "I can't just stand here."

"We've got to wait!" Rowan's heart was at war with her words.

"You wait," said Malcolm. He took off at a run.

"Malcolm!" Rowan stared after him until his light vanished into the dark trees. "Shit." She turned in circles, searching as if she'd find an answer to her dilemma. She darted to Sid's truck and yanked on the handle. It was unlocked. She turned on its headlights, which shone in the direction in which Malcolm had disappeared. Then she ran back to Malcolm's Jeep and turned on those headlights.

The sheriff's office can't miss either vehicle.

She would follow her brother.

But damn, she felt vulnerable.

Rowan opened the back of the Jeep and lifted the mats to expose the storage space. Inside was a long black plastic box and a smaller one, just as she'd seen in the compartment weeks ago. "Shit." The boxes were locked. She stared at the keypad on the small one for a long moment and then punched in four digits. The locking mechanism clicked.

Bless you, Malcolm.

She'd used the date Malcolm had reunited with his family. He referred to it as his other birthday because his life had started anew.

She took out the handgun; the magazine was full. She shoved the second magazine into a pocket next to Thor's snacks.

And then ran after her brother.

Evan was exhausted, his voice almost gone. Ever since they'd arrived at the small brick building, Dale had alternated between threatening Zack and threatening Evan.

The building was one small room, and Evan figured his and Zack's proximity drove Dale to harass them nonstop. The building was a wreck. Plaster had fallen from the walls, exposing the brick. An inch of dust and debris covered the flooring. At one time there'd been a second level, but the flooring had rotted away, leaving gaping holes where Evan could see the slats and framing of the roof.

The windows were broken, but metal grates covered several of them. At one time someone had tried to board up the windows from the inside, but most of the plywood had been pulled off. Now pieces of water-swollen, rotting boards lay beneath the windows. The only light came from a portable unit Dale had grabbed from his truck. It cast odd shadows that made Evan constantly see things in his peripheral vision and check the corners of the room. The walls were covered with graffiti. Band names, initials in hearts, swear words, and drawings that ranged from a giant penis to a rainbow-striped rabbit.

In the center of the room, several pipes led to a huge piece of rounded machinery. It looked like a metal-encased wheel and took up a third of the building's interior. Evan had heard water flowing nearby and figured they were in an old place built for hydroelectric power that had long been abandoned. The machinery looked as if it hadn't operated in decades, and even the rock band names on the walls were dated.

Why did Dale bring us here?

The man was running on fumes. Evan hadn't seen Dale sleep much since they'd left the first place a day or two ago, and he was easily triggered into rants of rage. Evan and Zack had decided to cooperate as much as possible, keeping Dale satisfied with their reactions. Their pain and suffering seemed to be the only things that pleased him. Now Dale was spending more and more time sitting in a corner, his legs pulled up to his body as he stared at Evan and Zack.

He's deciding how to end this.

Evan watched Dale advance on Zack again while keeping an eye on Evan, hungry for Evan's emotional reaction.

I'm getting too weak to keep shouting.

But he had no choice. There was no food in the brick building, and the few bottles of water that Dale had brought had been emptied hours ago.

Dale can't go for more food unless he hitchhikes.

The Ford truck wasn't drivable.

Evan sensed their situation was coming to a head. They couldn't go on like this much longer.

Dale suddenly froze in front of Zack and cocked his head. "What was that?"

He dropped to the ground and slowly inched toward the door.

"Malcolm!" Rowan whispered loudly, and then stood motionless in the dark woods to listen.

The sound of the creek was all she heard. The screams and shouts had stopped. She turned her flashlight back on, trying to follow bent grasses and scuffs in the dirt as she worked her way down the hill. She hadn't found the building but knew that if she kept going downward, she should find it somewhere along the water.

"Noelle's going to strangle me," she muttered, imagining the detective's fury when she arrived and found no one waiting up top. Rowan didn't know what would happen next. Her only plan was to stop Malcolm before he did something he'd regret. Abused kids were a hot point for him. The thought of Zack being tortured had pushed all rational thoughts out of Malcolm's head, and Rowan worried about what he might do.

The police could arrive too late, so she understood why Malcolm had rushed to help Evan and Zack, but now she was frightened for the lives of three people.

Malcolm was her brother. She wasn't leaving him alone. He'd been alone for too much of his life.

She continued to sidestep down the hill, her fingers covering the lens of her flashlight, keeping the light dim. It was less noticeable but could still be used to spot her location. Shouting continued. Then abruptly stopped.

Silence.

"Damn." Rowan kept up her slow pace, trying to move as silently as possible, which was not very quiet with the crunching grasses and cracking twigs. Suddenly the ground leveled out and she crouched. A faint glow came from her right, and she turned off her flashlight. She moved closer and finally saw the outline of the building Malcolm had described. It was small, built into the slope. Soft light shone from all the windows and even through holes in the roof.

Shadows moved near the building, and she squinted in the dim light, spotting the tall shape of her brother. Relieved, she quickened her steps.

Then something else shifted in the blackness.

Two loud cracks of gunfire filled the air, and Rowan dropped, rocks and roots grinding into her stomach.

Malcolm shrieked in pain. And then went silent.

He's shot!

He'd fallen to the ground twenty yards away. Rowan fought to hold still and stay silent, wanting to leap to her feet and dash to her brother. Convinced the shooter would hear her heart pounding and her deep breaths, she dug her face into the dirt, tasting damp soil. A moment later she glanced up and saw the second shadow approach her brother. The man shined a flashlight in Malcolm's face and leaned over to pick something up.

Malcolm's gun.

Rowan pressed into the dirt again, terrified his light would catch her and he'd shoot her next.

"Who are *you*?" the man asked her brother.

Silence.

He killed him.

Every cell in her body started to silently scream in sorrow.

"Well, you're obviously not police." The man laughed. "Look at all that blood. You're gonna be dead in two minutes." He laughed again, his voice fainter.

He's not dead. Yet.

Rowan sensed that the man had walked away and lifted her head the tiniest bit just in time to see him enter the building.

Heavy, wet breathing sounded from her brother.

Rowan scrambled to him on hands and knees. Malcolm was on the ground two yards from the building. His breaths were forced and slowing.

"Where did he shoot you?" she whispered. She set down her gun and ran her hands over his head and chest, searching for blood.

"Leg."

He said the word just as she planted a hand in a warm puddle on the ground. A rhythmic spray of blood hit her forearm.

He's bleeding out. Femoral artery.

Not stopping to think, Rowan whipped off her belt and twice wrapped it high around his leg, then pulled it tight. It was just short of buckling on the last hole. Malcolm moaned.

"Shhh."

She pulled again and barely managed to get it buckled.

"You're not going to die," Rowan said firmly. The spray from his leg had stopped, but she knew it would still slowly seep. He couldn't have the tourniquet in place for longer than two hours or he could have permanent damage to his leg. She checked her phone. No service.

How do I get him out?

She wanted to cry.

Something crunched behind her, and a powerful kick to her back hurled her across her brother. She lunged for her gun, but it was too late. The kicker had grabbed it.

A man pointed his light in her eyes, and she lifted a hand to block it, spotting a gun in his other hand. Underneath her, Malcolm groaned. She'd landed on his thigh.

"Look who we have here," said the man. "The detective's little whore."

Sid.

Rowan's heart tried to pound out of her chest.

"The guy under you isn't dead yet? Won't be much longer."

Rowan kept her leg over the tourniquet, hoping Sid didn't notice it.

"He's no cop. Neither are you." Sid scanned his flashlight around them, lighting up the trees and creek. "No police. No SWAT. No hostage negotiators." He looked back at Rowan. "That means you came on your own hoping to rescue your man, didn't you? Pretty stupid, I'd say. Who's the dying guy?"

"My brother," she whispered.

"Your brother? I read about his kidnapping," said Sid. "He managed to get his happy little life back, didn't he?" Anger infused his tone. "Get up."

Rowan awkwardly stood, placing herself between Sid and Malcolm. Sid stepped to Malcolm's head and kicked hard. Malcolm was silent.

"Not much longer now." He waved his gun at her. "Inside. This is going to be fun."

Even in the poor light, Rowan saw how pale her brother was. His eyes stayed closed.

I'm sorry, Malcolm.

Sid shoved her. "Inside!"

She stumbled forward and walked away, feeling as if she'd left her heart to bleed out in the dirt.

41

Evan strained to hear what had happened outside. There'd been two shots, and a man had shouted in pain.

The police?

But then he heard Dale calmly talking. He couldn't make out the words, but clearly Dale wasn't injured or scared. And there'd been no more shots. It hadn't been a police response.

Then who?

Probably an innocent guy checking out the light at the powerhouse. Another victim for Dale.

Evan's bound wrists had been handcuffed to a pipe. Currently he lay with his cheek on the cold floor, watching Zack, who was cuffed in a similar position across the room. The boy sat upright, his face dirty from dust and tears. Evan hated the despair in his gaze.

I probably look the same.

He was so tired. Evan closed his eyes. He'd let Zack down. Dale was going to kill them. Here he was . . . a veteran law enforcement officer defeated by an asshole. He was incapable of even saving a child.

I'm sorry, Rowan.

He pictured her face as she'd grinned at him while petting Thor. At least Thor would take care of her, comfort her when Evan was gone. Their strong love had been cemented for years.

It eased Evan's worry.

The door scraped the floor, and Evan forced his lids open. Rowan stood at the door.

He lurched up to a sitting position, staring across the room. "Rowan?" He blinked several times to clear the instant moisture that'd flooded his eyes.

"Oh, thank God," she said, her gaze locked with his. She abruptly stumbled forward. Dale had shoved her in the back and now stood with his gun at her head. Her hands were behind her back, already bound with a zip tie.

I'll never be able to look at another zip tie.

"Sit," commanded Dale as he pushed her into a corner.

Her back against the wall, Rowan slid down to the floor, her gaze never leaving Evan's.

"Isn't this great?" Dale asked Evan. "The love of your life showed up. All alone—well, not alone. Her brother is dead in a bloody puddle outside."

Malcolm.

The agony on Rowan's face confirmed Dale's words. She finally looked around the room, her face brightening as she spotted Zack, but then her mouth opened in shock.

Evan understood. The boy was dirty, bloody, and very thin.

"Are you okay, Zack?" she asked. He nodded.

Her gaze came back to Evan's, and he tried to communicate through his eyes.

I couldn't keep him safe, Rowan.

It's not your fault, Evan.

It was as if her voice spoke in his head.

"Now we can really get a party started," said Dale. "Your girlfriend will liven things up."

Evan stiffened, images of what Dale could do to Rowan flashing in his head.

But fury filled Rowan's face. "The police know everything that has happened, Sid," she said. "Sophia talked. Cynthia talked. Even JB talked. There're no secrets anymore."

Why did she call him Sid?

Dale didn't correct her.

That must be the name he uses now, since the media hounded him after he killed his lover's husband.

"Funny," said Dale (Sid?), clearly enjoying her anger. "I don't see the all-knowing police here. Just you."

Rowan looked at her feet.

Why would she come without the police?

"I should have never relied on that family," said Dale. "Useless. Both of them. Especially JB. He couldn't do anything right, that idiot. Had to show off and make trouble. Deserved what he got. Those two never thought before they did anything. This is all their fault."

Evan bit back a retort.

It's always someone else's fault. Never Dale's.

"Pretty sure this is *your* fault," snapped Rowan. "I know you shot—"

Dale backhanded her across the face, and her lip started to bleed. Horror filled her gaze as she slowly turned back to him. She seemed to shrink into her corner.

"You need to learn how things are done here," Dale told her. "Your lover boy has learned. Even the kid understands the rules. First of all, don't talk back. Let's make that don't talk *at all*. Perhaps a little pain will help you remember rule number one." He hit her again.

Evan strained against his cuffs. Sudden liquid warmth on one hand indicated he'd sliced his wrist. Again.

Rowan's head hit the floor. She lay motionless for a long moment, her terrified gaze finding Evan.

Anger shot through his veins.

For days he'd been mentally prepared to kill Dale if given the opportunity. He'd hoped to get the man's gun. But now Evan knew he could strangle the man with his bare hands and have no regrets.

"Now," said Dale. "Let's play a little game."

Oh, fuck.

Dale grabbed one of Rowan's feet and dragged her across the room to Evan, leaving her just out of his reach.

"Please stop." Zack was crying. *"Don't hurt her!"*

"Well, isn't he brave?" Dale said to Evan with a wide grin. "He's more concerned about her than you are."

Evan forced tears to appear and hung his head. "She's all I've got. I love her more than life itself. Let her go and I'll do anything for you."

Feed his ego.

"Evan!" Rowan exclaimed.

She doesn't understand the game.

"Hmmm. You're making my job harder, Bolton." Dale tapped his chin with his gun as he acted deep in thought. "I thought I'd worked out a schedule for creating the most enjoyment. But now I'm not sure."

He's relishing this. Rowan's presence has pumped up his pleasure.

"First I'd planned to kill the boy and make you watch." His eyes glittered in the dim light. "And then second, I'd do the same to your girlfriend as you watched . . . lengthening your pain before I finally turned my gun on you." He pretended to contemplate. "But maybe I should keep you alive for another twenty-four hours so you could relive it again and again."

Evan held his breath, his gaze locked with Rowan's.

Is this it?

"But I find I'm struggling to outright kill a kid." Dale shrugged. "I guess that means I've still got some heart left. But that leaves only one solution." He crouched and ground his gun barrel into the back of Rowan's head. "Tell Bolton how much you love him and will miss him." He turned to Evan, genuine pleasure and anticipation on his face.

He's going to do it.

Terror filled Rowan's gaze. Then acceptance.

And he felt her love flow to him.

"No!" he shouted. Adrenaline raced through his veins; fear flooded his brain. "Rowan! Don't—"

A red mist exploded, showering Evan in warm fluid, forcing his eyes shut.

Zack's screams filled the building, and Evan's lids flew open, sticky with goo and debris.

Dale was on the ground. The left side of his head completely gone.

Rowan stared up at Evan, shock in her eyes, blood spray and gray matter covering her hair. She blinked several times, and he realized none of the blood was hers.

Dale didn't fire.

Evan's gaze went to a window. Noelle stood outside, her weapon still aimed through the metal grate.

He closed his eyes in relief.

It's over.

Rowan looked behind her at Sid's body and what was left of his face.

Oh my God.

Then she awkwardly lunged into Evan's lap, pressing her filthy cheek against his, both of them with their hands still secured behind their backs. She had to touch and feel with all her body that he was real.

He whispered that he loved her, and she cried as she said she loved him too.

"Are you two hurt?" asked Noelle from directly behind her.

"No. Not really," said Evan.

Rowan could only shake her head. *I was a split second from dying.*

"Hang on," said Noelle. "I'm cutting your zip ties."

Rowan's arms were released, and she flung them around Evan.

He's okay. Everything is okay now.

"You need to scoot over, Rowan, so I can reach Evan's hands," Noelle said gently.

Rowan shifted, but her arms stayed locked around Evan's neck.

He's alive. We're alive. I'm never letting go.

Suddenly he squeezed her back, and she nestled into him as closely as possible, taking several shuddering breaths.

Malcolm.

Her head shot up. "Malcolm!" She whirled around to Noelle. "He's outside. His leg—"

"We found him," said Noelle. "He told us you placed that tourniquet."

"He's alive?" she squeaked.

"Oh God. You thought he was dead?" Sympathy filled Noelle's face. "EMS is on the way. I sent two deputies back up top to grab a stretcher to get him out of here. I think he'll be okay."

Rowan turned to Evan. "I've got to go see him."

How can I walk away from Evan right now?

"Go. I'll be right here," he said with a half smile.

She took a good look at him. His face was so thin. "He needs EMS too," she told Noelle. She looked past the detective and saw two deputies talking to Zack. His hands had been released and he was rubbing his eyes.

Thank God he's okay.

"Poor kid," whispered Evan. "I don't know how he'll recover from this. I haven't been able to tell him his mother was murdered."

"Sophia's not dead," Noelle and Rowan said together.

Evan stared at them, stunned. "But Dale told me . . . oh. That asshole!" He ran a hand through his hair. "Thank God I didn't say anything to Zack."

"He goes by Sid now," said Rowan. "We found out that he was one of your cases—"

"But he got off," finished Evan.

Rowan blew out a breath. "I'll be right back." As she headed to check on Zack, she heard Evan ask Noelle if she had anything to eat.

"Hey." Rowan knelt by Zack and set a hand on his shoulder. "You okay?" The deputies backed away.

There was no expression in his eyes. "Yes. Did he hurt you?"

"No. I'm fine."

Just some blows to my face.

"You're going to be fine too," she said. "We'll get you to see your mom right away."

"She's back?" Tears streamed. "You found her?"

The deputies didn't tell him yet?

"Yes. She's at the hospital . . . resting. She's fine too."

Zack pressed his fists against his eyes. "I thought she was gone forever."

Rowan gave him a long hug, and a deputy brought over two emergency blankets, wrapping one around her and the other around Zack.

I can't wait for their reunion. They've been through so much.

"I'll be back in a minute, Zack," she said, pushing to her feet. She caught the deputy's eye and tipped her head at Zack. The man immediately knelt in her place.

Several portable lights had been set up outside, and she spotted her brother surrounded by police. They'd moved him to a stretcher and were about to take him up the hill.

I didn't think I'd see him again.

Being forced to walk away while Malcolm lay on the ground had ripped her up inside.

I'll never forget that feeling.

"Wait!" She pushed through the group, grabbed her brother's hand, and touched his face, needing to feel under her fingertips that he was still present.

"Hey, sis." He was very pale. "They said everyone survived?"

"Yes. Both Zack and Evan are okay. Thin and battered but okay."

"Good." Malcolm closed his eyes. "Thin and battered can be fixed."

He would know.

"His leg?" she asked a deputy.

"Bleeding's stopped, but he lost a lot. We need to get a move on."

She squeezed Malcolm's hand. "I love you."

"Love you too, sis."

She watched the men start up the hill with her brother between them.

This could have ended so much worse.

"I told you to wait for police," Noelle said behind her.

Rowan whirled around, ready to defend her actions, but stopped at the sorrow in Noelle's gaze.

"You did good, Rowan," said Noelle. "In your place, I probably would have done the same."

"Thank you for saying that. I knew I shouldn't have left . . . but I couldn't stop myself. And thank you for saving my life. I'm sorry you had to . . . stop Sid."

If I had listened to her, she wouldn't have been forced to shoot someone.

Noelle nodded. She looked broken.

Guilt flooded Rowan. Evan had shot a man the previous summer. His emotional and mental recovery was still ongoing.

Because of what Rowan had done, Noelle's life would never be the same.

My fault.

"I'm sorry," Rowan said again, feeling it in every cell of her being. "I'm so sorry." Too many emotions swamped her, and she started to cry. Noelle enveloped her in a hug, and Rowan felt the detective's tears.

"I'm sorry too," Noelle whispered.

42

One week later

Evan sat at a table on the back patio of the Wolffs' home watching Rowan throw a Frisbee for Thor in the yard. The dog's rapid acceleration turned him into a black blur against the green grass. It was unusually warm for spring, and the sky was as blue as always.

Almost as if nothing has happened.

As if their lives hadn't been flipped upside down.

He eyed the pile of mail Rowan's mother had set next to him.

"Rowan wouldn't go through it while . . . while you were gone," she'd said.

Evan had nodded in understanding. He didn't know what he would have done with Rowan's mail if she were missing.

We're very lucky.

He started tossing the junk mail into a separate pile.

The last week had been one of rest. He'd been given time off work and had been told to let the department know when he wanted to return.

Today I'm not sure I want to.

But he knew he would. The job was part of his identity, and deep down he loved it and knew he made a difference. He just needed more time.

Two days ago they'd attended Rod's memorial service. A wave of blue in the seats. Sophia and Zack had stuck close to one another. Both had a haunted look in their eyes but were thankful they still had each other. For Evan at first it'd felt odd not to have Zack within reach anymore. His protectiveness toward the boy was stronger than ever. They hadn't been flung together all that long, but it was as if they'd experienced a lifetime of pain and uncertainty.

Evan had asked Sophia about the "evidence" that Dale a.k.a. Sid had claimed one of them had. She'd said she didn't know what he'd meant. She'd told him that Rod had believed Evan would figure it out if anything happened to him.

"But he deliberately kept things from me," Evan had told her.

"I know. He did the same to me. I can't help but wonder if he'd still be here if he'd immediately told us of his suspicions." Her eyes had welled with tears, and Evan had hugged her, haunted by the same question.

Thor slid to a stop before Evan, the Frisbee in his mouth, his ears and eyes in an eager question.

/play/

Evan threw the Frisbee, and the dog rocketed away.

Rowan sat down in the next chair, fanning her face. "I'm done. It's your turn. He'll never stop."

"This yard isn't big enough for him. The Frisbee runs are too short."

"I know," Rowan agreed. "He misses our huge yard."

Evan watched her from the corner of his eye. She'd refused any discussion of their home and the fire. This was the first time she'd alluded to it. He'd been thinking about what to do, but it was her house. He didn't want to influence her decision.

"I miss it too," he said, still watching her.

"I've been thinking about it." She turned to face him. "What do you want to do? Sell the property? Rebuild it?"

"It's not my house," he said.

Annoyance flashed. "Yes, it is. It belongs to both of us now."

Evan turned his attention to Thor, who'd returned with the Frisbee but simply dropped it without begging and watched the two of them talk as if he knew this wasn't a good time to play.

"I loved that house," he said slowly. "But it was yours first. I know it's not what you intended, but I sort of felt like a guest. Not in a bad way," he quickly added as her face fell. "I don't know how to explain it."

"I think I understand. It's how I've felt staying at my parents'. I know I'm welcome here, and I have my own space, but it's not the same as *mine*."

"I want a space that's *ours*," he said as he added three credit card offers to the junk pile.

"So sell?" she asked.

Evan scanned the fenced backyard of her parents' home. "Your lot and location are perfect. Big, lots of room for Thor to run. It will always have the huge fields behind it."

She took his hand and squeezed, a smile filling her face. "Let's rebuild. Let's find a house plan we both love and make it happen. Make it *ours*."

"Is that what you want?"

"I do."

Evan grinned. "I do too. The idea has been stuck in my head for days."

She leaned over and kissed him. "It's decided, then."

"Lucky me." He leaned back in his chair, feeling the best he'd felt in weeks. His cuts and bruises were nearly all healed. A round of antibiotics had taken care of infection. And food had never tasted so good.

He picked up a small envelope, and a wave of nausea rolled through him.

"Rowan." He held the envelope out to her.

She studied it and frowned. "What is it?"

"Don't know. But that's Rod's address in the corner. It's postmarked three days before we found him." He slid the envelope through his fingers. "Something thin and rigid in the corner." His heartbeat had sped up at the sight of the address.

Do I need to treat this as evidence?

JB was dead. Sid was dead. Cynthia had admitted she'd planted the gun for Sid. Sid had told Evan he'd killed Rod.

The case is closed.

Evan carefully opened it and pulled out two sheets of paper. He tipped the envelope up, and a tiny memory card came out.

"That's got to be the evidence that Sid wanted," breathed Rowan. "He couldn't find it because Rod mailed it to you."

Evan looked at the first page. It was a high-quality photocopy showing three photos of JB.

"See how the photos have dates and comments on the side? Rod must have copied them from Facebook," said Rowan. She pulled out her phone and started to search for something.

In each photo, JB posed with several guns. Showing them off, holding them out tipped down like he was a wannabe gangster. Evan's gaze locked on one of the weapons, its distinctive engraving clear in the photo.

That's the gun Cynthia planted at Sid's crime scene.

"JB's profile no longer has these photos," said Rowan. "And according to the dates on them, they were posted months before Sid was arrested."

"Rod must have done a deep background dive into Cynthia and her brother," said Evan. "When he spotted these photos, he knew he had proof that the gun could be linked to Cynthia, who had the opportunity to plant it."

"Which made Rod look at other cases she'd worked on, wondering if she tipped evidence one way or the other. He also must have worried it involved more people than Cynthia, which is why he kept it to himself," added Rowan. "When she told Sid that Rod was asking questions, I bet one of them thought to go through JB's social media, spotted the photos, and made him take them down."

"But Sid rightfully worried Rod had already found them," added Evan. "Kicking off Sid's relentless search."

"Cynthia swears she didn't change evidence on other cases—except this one and that previous one, which gave Sid the opportunity to blackmail her," said Rowan. "But she's out of a job. And I heard lawyers are demanding the cases she worked on to be reopened or thrown out."

"It's a mess," Evan agreed.

He looked at the next page. It was a brief note from Rod. His lungs seized at the familiar printing. Perfect letters, perfect lines. Just how he'd always filled out his paperwork.

> Evan,
> Sending this because you'll figure out what it means.
>
> If you get this letter and I'm fine, we'll celebrate that our original gut instincts about this case were right. If you get this and I'm gone, know that you're the one person I trusted. You were always the best detective I ever worked with—you must have had an amazing mentor.
>
> Always hoped you and Sophia would work it out . . . but Rowan is the right woman for you.
> Rod

"Rod," Evan said quietly. "He suspected Sid would get to him. This was his insurance."

"That's so sad," said Rowan. "How awful that he felt he couldn't tell anyone."

"He could have told me," Evan said.

"He was protecting you."

I know.

Evan folded the papers, tucked them back in the envelope, and added the tiny memory card—which must have the photo originals. He set it on the table and took Rowan's hand.

He would never be the same; he'd seen and experienced things no human should. But it was okay. Rowan was beside him, and the future had rolled out a path for them.

Together they sat quietly, simply holding hands and looking at the trees against the blue sky.

"So peaceful." Evan would never take his life for granted.

Good job. Good health. And Rowan.

He met her warm gaze, and they both smiled.

She appreciates it too.

A second chance.

Thor shoved his cold, wet nose into their hands, startling Evan. Rowan laughed as she stroked his ears with her other hand. "Good boy, Thor."

Shining black eyes gazed at them.

/love/

ACKNOWLEDGMENTS

I enjoyed developing more of Rowan and Evan's story. They originally came together in *The First Death*, and I had numerous requests for more about their relationship and their families. Evan has been a regular secondary character since *A Merciful Secret*, and Rowan first appeared in *A Merciful Promise*. I know I keep promising to write Detective Noelle Marshall's story, and I'm currently (finally!) working on it. If all goes to plan, her book will be published summer 2025.

For *The Next Grave*, I spent too many hours watching quirky auto salvage and junkyard owners on YouTube, fascinated by the little treasures they discover left behind in vehicles. If you have time to burn, I recommend falling down this rabbit hole. The pump house in the book was inspired by an abandoned one within walking distance of a home I visited in Utah. The real one is quite creepy and battered, a sad relic of a past era.

As always, I'm grateful to my publishing team at Montlake, which promotes my work, gives me great leeway to write what I want, and has stood behind every book since 2012. Thank you to my editors, Anh and Charlotte, who've been with me for a very long time; I can't imagine creating books with anyone else. Thank you to my agent, Meg Ruley, who still holds the title of head cheerleader. The biggest thank-you goes to my readers. I love hearing that my books have provided hours of enjoyment and escape.

ABOUT THE AUTHOR

Photo © 2016 Rebekah Jule Photography

Kendra Elliot has landed on the *Wall Street Journal* bestseller list multiple times and is the award-winning author of the Bone Secrets and Callahan & McLane series, the Mercy Kilpatrick novels, and the Columbia River novels. She's a three-time winner of the Daphne du Maurier Award, an International Thriller Writers Award finalist, and an RT Award finalist. She was born and raised in the rainy Pacific Northwest but now lives in flip-flops. Visit her at www.kendraelliot.com.